THE GOLDEN KHAN

A. H. WANG

DISCLAIMER

The Golden Khan is the second book of the Georgia Lee series. While this book can be read on its own, it is intended as the sequel to The Imperial Alchemist, and hence contains some major spoilers.

The books in this series, in order:

The Imperial Alchemist
The Golden Khan

For Mum and Dad,
who made everything possible.

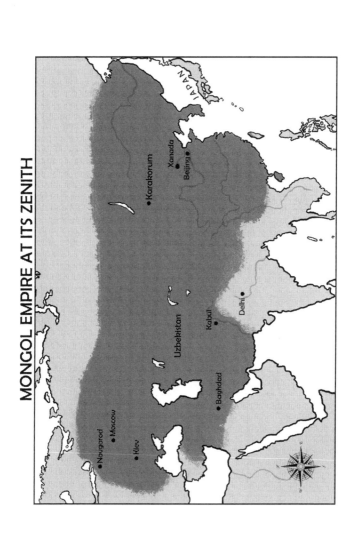

MONGOL EMPIRE AT ITS ZENITH

Novgorod
Moscow
Kiev
Baghdad
Uzbekistan
Kabul
Delhi
Karakorum
Xanadu
Beijing
JAPAN

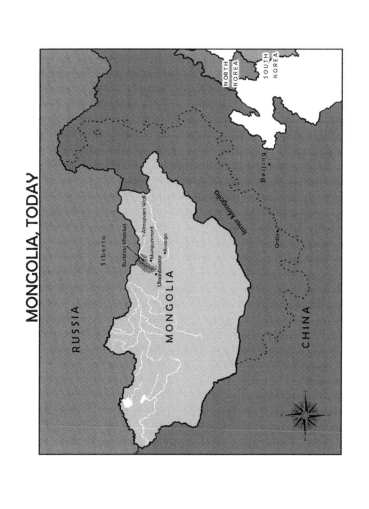

MONGOLIA, TODAY

RUSSIA

Siberia

Buriatian Khubkuri

Almighven Wall

Burtelan Khubkuri

Mungummorit

Avarga

Ulaanbaatar

MONGOLIA

Inner Mongolia

Ordus

Beijing

NORTH KOREA

SOUTH KOREA

CHINA

Truth is stranger than fiction.

- Mark Twain

PROLOGUE

1937, Shankh Monastery, Mongolia

M*AJOR* D*MITRY* P*ETROV* *stood before the row of kneeling monks, his teeth bared in a snarl of disgust. He needed one of them to talk, and he needed it to happen an hour ago. There was nothing he hated more than being deep in the land of Mongol filth, hunting down some obscure book that probably didn't even exist. But he was a soldier, and a soldier always obeyed his orders. And this time, the orders had come directly from Comrade Stalin. He knew full well that if he did not deliver what was asked of him, then his life would be forfeit, as would be the lives of his pregnant wife and son in Russia. Comrade Stalin himself had assured Dmitry of that.*

At the rear wall of the temple, two soldiers looted the library, dumping volumes of religious texts on the earthen floor. Others toppled over statues from the shrine, pissing on the heads and hacking the wooden sculptures to pieces. They swept offerings off the table, sending bowls of food and the censer clattering to the ground. The ashes of innumerable years of burnt incense bloomed into a nebula of dust.

I

They'd been in the monastery for over two hours, and they'd come up with nothing. Dmitry was certain that if the book he sought existed, then it was right here, in this dank little hut of a temple. All the clues he'd uncovered and all the Mongols he'd interrogated had pointed to this place.

The Shankh Monastery was the key.

That was what they'd all said, before Dmitry put a bullet in their skulls.

He paced up and down between the four monks on the floor in front of him, assessing them with growing irritation. Their eyes were downcast, and they all seemed to be praying. Even with the cacophony echoing through the temple, they were unusually calm. Dmitry detected not a tremble in any of them.

He needed to change that.

He picked the first man in the row and belted him across the head with his pistol.

His victim fell without a sound. Turning to monk number two, Dmitry began kicking him mercilessly until he rolled into a tight ball on the ground. Number three and four gasped, watching helplessly as their companion moaned in agony.

Eventually, the third monk spoke, uttering a protest Dmitry could not understand. The major turned to his Russian comrade, who translated: "He's begging you to stop. He says he's the head monk, and you should punish him instead."

"Where's the book?" Dmitry demanded. When the Mongol didn't reply to the translation, Dmitry squatted down to get close to his face. "Tell me where it is, or I will kick him until he shits his own guts out. And then I'll do the same to every one of your friends until I get what I want."

The head monk's eyes strayed back to the floor and fluttered closed. His body became still. Not a flicker of emotion passed over his leathery features.

Dmitry stood up, spat on the man's bald head, and resumed kicking the other on the floor.

"Major Petrov." Lieutenant Boris Baretski approached.

Monk number two shrieked as a hard blow landed on his back, possibly rupturing the kidneys. Dmitry straightened, the corners of his lips tipping up despite himself. Keeping his eyes on the man quivering at his feet, the major addressed his comrade.

"What?" he barked. His men knew perfectly well that he did not like interruptions during an interrogation.

"Sir. I think you'll want to see this—"

Dmitry swivelled around and stared at the soldier. "You found it?"

The young man shook his head, looking unsure. "Er—no, sir. This is something else. Something else you had on the list."

Dmitry emitted a frustrated sigh, gave Baretski a curt nod, and followed the lieutenant to the back of the shrine. Stepping over discarded books strewn all over the floor, the junior officer led him to the far corner of the building, stopping in front of a blank wall.

"Well?" Dmitry demanded, his patience wearing thin.

"It's an optical illusion, sir. Look at it from this angle," Baretski said, showing his superior by moving to the side and pointing at the corner of the wall.

Dmitry stalked to where the young man stood, and saw the line of the perpendicular walls shift, separating into three distinct segments.

"I'll be damned."

He reached out, expecting to touch the rammed-earth surface, but his hand moved through where the wall should have been. He took a tentative step forward and found himself walking into a hidden passage.

He paused, allowing his eyes to adjust to the darkness. Turning to his right, he moved cautiously towards the dim glow at the end of the hallway, with Baretski following closely at his heels. They must be behind the wall lined with bookshelves, a secret passageway that only the monks knew about.

In front of him, the corridor opened into a chamber lit by oil lamps. On the far side was another smaller shrine with an assortment of Buddhist deities. A square table covered with offerings of food and drinks stood in front of the statues. The smell of incense that Dmitry so detested filled his nostrils.

But the object that captured his attention was the Spirit Banner that stood erect at the very centre of the room.

He walked a slow circle around it, appraising the artefact. It was a trident with a long wooden pole. Tufts of black horsehair hung just below the spearhead, decorated with strips of tattered silk that had once been golden.

Dmitry released a breath he had not known he was holding onto. This was the key the Mongols had talked about. All along, he'd been looking for the wrong thing.

He grinned and grabbed the Spirit Banner with both hands, lifting it from the stand. It was lighter than he expected, and smaller than he'd imagined.

It wasn't much to look at, but what Dmitry held in his hands was said to contain vital clues to locating Stalin's ultimate prize.

Without taking his eyes off the relic, he spoke to his subordinate: "Well done, comrade. Well done indeed."

Then he pivoted and strode out of the room, heading straight for the main entrance so he could study the Spirit Banner in the light.

"Major," Baretski piped up as he followed Dmitry outside. "What about the book? Should we keep searching?"

"No." The major waved his hand. "It's not here. They would never keep it in the same place as the Spirit Banner."

"But Comrade Stalin—"

4

"Comrade Stalin will be pleased with this finding alone. Trust me. Let's move out. I'm sick of this place."

"Yes, Major. What about the monastery, sir?"

Dmitry took one look at the building behind him, his eyes travelling over the rammed-earth walls, the green-tiled roof juxtaposed with muddy-red columns. Goats and horses wandered around, grazing on grass. The faint odour of manure made him wrinkle his nose.

Repugnance filled his chest. He turned and marched towards the truck, ordering, "Burn it to the ground."

Four years later, Mausoleum of Timur Khan (Tamerlane), Uzbekistan

A HISS RESOUNDED through the gloomy burial chamber as the sarcophagus was cracked open.

Colonel Dmitry Petrov recoiled inwardly as an asphyxiating sweet smell mixed with musk filled the air. Bile rose in his throat, and he quickly swallowed it back down. A few men coughed, some gagged, and unease spread through the team as beams of torchlight swung wildly around the dark, cavernous room.

"It's okay." The archaeologist leading the team, Dr. Mikhail Gerasimov, reassured the soldiers. "Just the perfume of what they used to preserve the body."

Gerasimov instructed the soldiers to remove the nephrite gravestone. The men, eight in all, grunted and heaved, depositing the slab to the side with a resonant thud against the marble floor.

Dmitry adjusted the rifle slung over his shoulder and edged closer to the coffin. The foul scent intensified as he hovered over the large stone box. Averting his eyes from the decrepit, black-

ened wooden casket that lay inside, he focused on the foreign text on the gravestone instead.

"Baretski," he called. "What does this say?"

Captain Boris Baretski left the men to join the colonel and studied the script etched into the stone surface. Fluent in several languages, the captain was a useful member of the team as they hunted down the list of relics coveted by Stalin over the past several years. Especially now, as the war raged on in Europe with no end in sight, Comrade Stalin had stressed the vital importance of their latest mission. How he believed exhuming the body of a fourteenth-century conqueror would help them gain military advantage, however, Dmitry would never know.

Baretski looked up from the tombstone and with a quaver in his voice, he said, "It reads, 'When I rise from the dead, the world shall tremble.'"

Dmitry frowned.

"And this?" He pointed to some more text inside the stone coffin.

Baretski craned his neck to read the words. When he turned to address the colonel, his face had blanched. His voice lowered, he said in Russian: "'Whosoever opens my tomb shall unleash an invader more terrible than I.'"

A chill rose up the colonel's spine. But he quickly disguised it with an exaggerated roll of his eyes. It would not do to cause panic among the men now. Rumours of a curse had floated around the team as they got closer to the tomb. It had not been good for their morale.

On closer inspection, Dmitry could see that there were etchings covering the interior of the sarcophagus. "Document everything you see in there. I want it all translated into Russian."

"Yes, sir."

Dmitry turned to address Gerasimov. "Let's move along,

6

doctor. It's getting late. Comrade Stalin wanted Timur's body last week."

The young scientist nodded. "We're almost there. Please," Gerasimov urged the men as they lifted the casket out of the sarcophagus, "be very careful."

Dmitry was anxious to get the whole thing over with. Tombs always gave him the creeps, especially on an inky, moonless night like this. Under different circumstances, he could have appreciated the immense, elaborate architecture around him. The huge hall was adorned with mosaics over the walls and high ceilings, glistening gold and blue in the torchlight. The marble floor beneath his booted feet was polished to a shiny finish. Dmitry admitted that it was a beautiful construction. Even if it was built by Muslims.

But the fact that they were exhuming something — someone — long dead, greatly perturbed him.

What lies buried should stay buried, he thought.

Half an hour passed, then one of his soldiers on guard outside rushed into the room and whispered urgently in his ear.

Dmitry tensed at the news, his grip tightening on the rifle. He called out to Gerasimov as the men placed the coffin onto a wheeled platform.

"Doctor, we've got company. Let's go."

Dmitry ushered the team out of the mausoleum and into the dark, chilly night. They were only half-way through loading the coffin into the lorry when the first bullets flew past his head.

"Get down! Get down!" he yelled, diving around the side of the truck.

His men fell to the ground. Some crawled for cover, a couple shouted in pain from their wounds, and one lay deadly still, his arm twisted under his body. Dr. Gerasimov landed hard on the ground beside Dmitry, grimacing as he held onto his injured shoulder.

7

Dmitry swore. It was too dark. From his position, he could not tell where the local hostiles were situated, or how many there were. He glanced behind him. The coffin was still half hanging out the rear of the truck.

The deafening sound of shots continued as more of his men fell. The mission was turning out to be a complete disaster.

Dmitry could not return to Russia empty-handed. Comrade Stalin never tolerated failures.

He yelled at the two men beside him. "Kuzmin, get Gerasimov into the cab. Baretski, come with me."

Firing a few volleys into the dark, Dmitry rounded the back of the vehicle with Baretski. They pushed the casket fully into the truck and jumped in.

"Drive!" He screamed at Kuzmin in the cab as the concealed enemy unleashed another round of shots, tearing through the canvas over the tonneau. One of the bullets caught Baretski in the side.

"Go!" Dmitry roared again, and the lorry jolted forward.

He turned to see his men out the back, rising to their feet to return fire as the truck screeched out of the compound. Their rifles illuminated the darkness, the bursts of light growing small as the lorry gained distance from the colossal gates.

After several minutes, the thundering of gunfire faded into the distance, replaced by the humming of the truck engine.

"How bad is it, comrade?" Dmitry asked Baretski as he moaned in pain.

"I don't know, Colonel." Baretski struggled to sit up. "It's too dark. I can't see."

"Don't move," Dmitry commanded.

Rummaging through the bag next to him, Dmitry found a spare shirt and pressed it to Baretski's side. He could feel warm, sticky fluid soaking through the fabric within seconds. The young officer was not going to make it.

As if understanding his own situation, Baretski drew a notebook from his pocket. "The writing inside the coffin, sir. I wrote it all down, as you ordered. And there's a letter in there for my mother. Please give it to her for me."

With a grim nod, Dmitry took the small volume from Baretski's bloody hands, and sat by the soldier as he closed his eyes.

Long after, as the lorry drove into the night, Dmitry took out his torch and read the contents of the notepad. What he found in there shocked him to the core. Finally, he understood why Stalin had sent him on this ceaseless chase throughout Asia for the past four years. Stalin's endgame was much grander than Dmitry had ever dreamed of.

1

Present day, Sydney, Australia

"THIS IS FUCKED UP, GEORGIA," Sarah Wu declares as she paces back and forth over the small span of their shared, windowless office. The fifty-eight-year-old Chinese-Australian woman is enraged, and she rattles off more expletives in accented English before exclaiming, "We gotta do some damage control here."

"Yeah." Professor Georgia Lee nods at her assistant and falls quiet again. She sits at her desk, staring into space with stunned silence.

Her mind is reeling. Her body is numb.

Paul Flannigan, the head of faculty, left only minutes ago after delivering the devastating news that Georgia and her team have been removed from their excavation project in China. The 200 BCE tomb they uncovered earlier this year was a remarkable breakthrough, and it still has scientists scratching their heads over the puzzling artefacts that have emerged from the chambers. But soon after opening the underground burial site, Georgia became occupied with another quest instigated by the late Mark Lambert, the notorious billionaire. The trip took almost five months and nearly cost Georgia her life.

Peking University was their joint venture partner in the Chinese project, which was headed by Professor Chang. And Chang has used his time well during Georgia's prolonged absence. Knowing that he had at hand one of the most extraordinary archaeological discoveries of the decade, the man rallied the support of his university and the Chinese government to close the site off from all foreign involvement.

It is Georgia's first day back at work after many months of being away, and losing her project is a shocking blow.

But that is not the reason she cannot bring herself to focus on what her assistant is saying as the woman wears a track into the linoleum floor. Sarah is gesticulating wildly as she continues her angry tirade, the silver in her short-cropped hair glinting in the morning light as she runs her hand over her scalp in frustration.

And Georgia isn't listening at all.

Her mind keeps returning to the events three days ago when she visited Ethan Sommers in Melbourne, her childhood friend with whom she shares a complex history. Her intention was to apologise, to beg for his forgiveness for not returning his calls. But she came away from his house with something else entirely.

A startling realisation. A shocking discovery that has her gut churning every time she thinks about it.

Pins and needles prickle over her skin. She swallows thickly and closes her eyes.

"Hey," Sarah demands, stopping in front of Georgia's desk with fists planted on her hips. Despite her average build and height, the woman with the reputation of a foul-mouthed tiger mum can be intimidating when she chooses to. "Are you even listening to me? Do you understand the effect this is gonna have on your career? If it wasn't for the massive funding you got from Mark Lambert for the job in Taiwan, we'd probably be sitting in Paul's office discussing our severance package . . ."

Sarah's voice fades into the background as Georgia's thoughts overwhelm her once again. The image of her in Ethan's kitchen comes hurtling back: dropping the knife when she cut her finger, the wound healed right in front of her eyes.

And that was the moment she realised . . .

I'm immortal, she mouths the words as if to practise saying them. Then she shakes her head, dismissing the idea with disbelief for the umpteenth time.

"What did you say?" Sarah asks, frowning down at her.

Snapping her head up, Georgia stutters, "I . . ." She thinks quickly. "I said that this is the Chinese *government* we're up against. They're the ones who kicked us off the excavation project. There's nothing we can do."

Sarah opens her mouth to argue, but closes it again before saying anything further. She leans down, places both her palms on Georgia's desk and narrows her eyes, scrutinising Georgia from head to toe.

Georgia cringes inwardly, half expecting her assistant to read her mind. God knows the woman has an annoying knack for it.

A long silent moment passes.

Sarah straightens her spine. She crosses her arms over her chest and says decidedly, "You look like shit."

Georgia lets out a dry laugh. She rolls her eyes and reaches for her mug of coffee. "Thanks a lot."

"Alright. Spill the beans." Sarah pulls her office chair over to get into Georgia's personal space. "What's going on?"

Georgia leans as far away from her assistant as she can. She waves her hand with a flutter, thinking up an excuse. "It's just all this . . . academia stuff. I've worked so hard, and for so long. And I've had a decent career even before this China dig. My work in archaeology is about so much more than this one project. What do I need to do, and how much do I have to prove for the department to take me seriously? Just because we got *manoeuvred* off a project shouldn't mean my position at this university is in jeopardy."

"That's because you're a woman, and women have to work twice as hard to get anywhere in this world," Sarah explains as a matter of fact. She holds up her hand before Georgia argues. "But that's not what's bothering you."

Georgia furrows her brows. "What do you mean, th—"

"C'mon, out with it. You still haven't 'fessed up to what happened with Ethan when you went to see him in Melbourne. Did you two kiss and make up?"

"Ugh." Georgia makes a face and returns to her coffee. "I really don't want to talk about it."

"*Bingo*," Sarah says, flicking a finger in Georgia's direction as if she has pinpointed the problem. She's the only person Georgia knows who ever uses that word.

Saying nothing further, her assistant keeps her penetrating, expectant gaze on Georgia until she squirms.

After a drawn-out, awkward minute, Georgia finally protests, "Are you just going to sit there and stare at me all day?"

"Did you tell him?"

"Tell him what?" Georgia feigns ignorance.

Sarah lets out a dramatic sigh, looking unsurprised. "Did you tell Ethan why you couldn't return his calls? About what happened to you over the last five months? About how that billionaire Mark Lambert sent you on a hunt for the elixir of life, and how you met Charlie?" Her pitch escalates as she rants on, "And all that shit that happened in the mountains of Taiwan? And how you almost died when the cave collapsed—"

"No. Okay?" Georgia raises her voice. "No, I didn't tell Ethan."

"Why not?" Sarah demands. "We talked about this, Georgia. Ethan deserves the truth. After everything you two have been through, you need to come clean and tell him why you abandoned him in Taipei after you finally got together again. This is your second chance at life—at *love*—and you don't just throw it away. You need to let Ethan know how you feel."

"Yeah, but that was before I realised . . ."

"What? Before you realised *what*?"

Faltering, Georgia chews on her lower lip.

"Hey." Sarah softens her tone when she sees Georgia's expression. "I know it's scary to start over again, after everything that happened with Jacqui and Lucas. But you have to at least try—"

Georgia flinches at the mention of her daughter and ex-husband. She has just finalised her divorce with Lucas after two years of separation, something which has been a long time coming after the death of their daughter, Jacqui.

Annoyances rises. She shakes her head. "It doesn't matter. Ethan won't ever want to talk to me again."

"You don't know that—"

At that moment, Georgia's phone rings loudly, vibrating on the desk. Sarah cranes her neck to peek at the caller ID. She smirks triumphantly.

"See?" the older woman gloats.

"It's Ethan," Georgia says, incredulous.

"Pick up."

"No."

Sarah reaches over and presses the green dot on the screen, putting the call on speakerphone. Georgia's mouth drops open in silent outrage, and she snatches up the device, frantically stabbing at the phone and bringing it to her ear.

"Hello? Ethan?" Georgia's voice hitches as her cheeks flame with colour.

"Hey." His familiar sound sends tingles through her body.

Sarah scoots closer, pressing her ear to the other side of phone so she can listen in on the conversation. Georgia bats her assistant away and rises from her chair, walking out of the office to get some privacy.

But her conversation with Ethan isn't meant to be a long one.

"Look," he says, sounding panicked. "I know this is awkward after what happened between us in Melbourne. Sorry. But I need your help. I'm in Sydney now. Hiroshi has gone missing."

2

As GEORGIA DRIVES through the suburban neighbourhood where she grew up with Ethan, she is overcome by her childhood memories as well as an enormous sense of guilt. Ethan has been her closest friend since their sandpit days, but as Sarah said, she's shut him out yet again with no explanation.

After she left his Melbourne home three days ago, she headed straight for the airport, taking the next flight back to Sydney. Her mind racing in a confused fog over every detail of what happened in that cave in Taiwan, there was no way she could have had a conversation with Ethan about their relationship. Or lack thereof.

She had intended to call him again, of course, once she'd sorted herself out. In fact, she's been incessantly arguing with herself, debating over just how much to tell him, or even Sarah, about this new . . . *condition* she has. She doesn't even know how to begin. The idea is as insane as it sounds.

All week, she's been struggling to wrap her head around the new ways her body works: the speed at which it heals, the efficiency with which it moves, the strength in her muscles that she never possessed before. Georgia is not known for her athletic abilities, and has never been graceful or fast, but it appears the elixir has now fixed that too. Yesterday during her run, she clocked almost twice her normal distance within the same amount of time, and she wasn't even tired afterwards. In fact, she needs very little sleep or food these days, and she has to keep reminding herself to slow her movements so as to not attract attention. Already Sarah must suspect something, judging by the way she was staring at her this morning.

And all the while, as Georgia grapples with the idea of eternal life, the same question keeps circling around her mind.

Is humanity ready? Is this a gift she can share with the world, or is it a curse that should always be protected as a secret?

Georgia wishes Charlie were here. Charlie was over two thousand years old when they met, and he was the wisest person she's ever known. If he were alive, he could tell her exactly how to deal with this. Yet at the same time, she knows he'd most likely ask her to keep the knowledge to herself, warning of the dangers if word got out.

She grips the steering wheel as she pulls into the driveway of Ethan's parents' home. After all these years, Dale and Susan Sommers have remained in the same house they married and raised a family in, and looking around, Georgia sees that not much has changed. Her gaze sweeps over the familiar, well-kempt rose bushes that Ethan's mother loves, and the perfectly manicured lawn leading up to the two-storey red-brick house. She knows Ethan's childhood home as if it's her own. As a kid, she probably spent as much time here as at her parents' place.

Georgia remembers munching on sandwiches at the Sommers' kitchen table after school and coming here for Christmas Day lunch every year with her family. She remembers riding over on hot summer days and running through the connecting garden gate to jump into Ethan's grandparents' pool next door. And she remembers how she and Ethan used to sneak out of his bedroom window and climb onto the roof to spy on the neighbours. It was on this very roof that they tried their first cigarette together.

But for the first time in her life, as Georgia sits in her car looking at the house, she feels reluctant to go inside.

Then she mentally gives herself a slap on the back of the head, remembering what Sarah said. *It's high time you pull up your big-girl pants.* Besides, Ethan said on the phone that he wasn't calling about their relationship. This is about Hiroshi.

Hiroshi Akiyama. She hasn't heard that name in years. Her mind travels back to their school days, when Ethan spent two months in Japan over the summer holidays with a host family, immersed in their culture and language. Ethan became instant friends with his host brother, Hiroshi. The following year, Hiroshi also came to Sydney on an exchange programme, with Ethan's family acting as his host. Georgia remembers a scrawny boy of average height, with thick glasses and a quiet, thoughtful demeanour. Hiroshi never said much, but when he did speak, his words always carried much more weight than the other more chatty teenagers around him.

That summer, Georgia, Ethan, and Hiroshi were insep-arable. Ethan had just gotten his driver's licence and the three of them drove up the east coast of Australia, camping at pristine, remote beaches. Georgia would suck on icy-poles that dripped sticky juice down her hand while watching Ethan and Hiroshi out in the water, boogie boarding in the foaming sea. It was probably one of the most memorable summer holidays she's had, not only because of the stunning landscape that surrounded her, or the blanket of stars she slept under every night, but because of the long days and nights she spent with her friends. It was the first time she'd ever felt a sense of belonging.

It's been so many years since those carefree days. She's surprised Ethan and Hiroshi are still in contact. But then again, she and Ethan have hardly spoken over the past six years, so there is plenty she doesn't know about her own best friend's life.

With a fortifying breath, Georgia finally exits the car and walks up to the house. She presses on the doorbell, hearing it ding in the hallway. The floorboards creak as someone moves to the other side of the door.

"Ethan?" she calls with a nervous smile on her face. "It's Georgia."

The door finally opens, and Georgia's smile fades as she sees him. Ethan looks like he hasn't slept or eaten in days. He needs a shower and a shave. Shadows mark the undersides of his sky-blue eyes, and the pallor of his skin has Georgia frowning with worry. He's wearing an old, ripped t-shirt with the iconic picture of Salvador Dali's face and his ridiculous moustache, its long tips curled into a 'U' that reaches up to the Spaniard's eyebrows.

The sharp pang of guilt in Georgia's chest amplifies. She wonders how much of his appearance has to do with Hiroshi, and how much of it is actually her fault.

"George," Ethan says with relief, calling her by the name he has used since primary school. He gives her a quick embrace. She doesn't miss his darting, nervous glances around the yard before he pulls her inside. "Thanks for coming."

"What's going on?" Looking around and seeing the disarray of the house, she asks, "Are your parents here?"

"They're out of town. Gone camping somewhere with the neighbours."

Ethan leads her through the hallway and into the lounge room, sinking down in the middle of the sofa. Unsure of where to place herself, Georgia sits in the lounge chair across from him.

Ethan rakes his long fingers through his sandy blond hair and rubs his face twice before he blinks as if seeing her for the first time. He exhales a deep sigh.

"I'm sorry. I flew in from Melbourne yesterday. To meet with Hiroshi. I'm here, in Sydney, and then when . . . I just needed to talk to someone before um . . . You're the only person I thought of—" he rambles on, making no sense.

Alarmed, Georgia moves next to him on the sofa and reaches for his hand. She has never seen Ethan this way. Ever since they were kids, he has always been the cheerful larrikin who made jokes about any situation he was in. But that immutable mirth is now gone.

"It's okay. Hey," she says, placing her palm on his cheek. "Just tell me what happened. Start from the beginning."

Nodding, Ethan closes his eyes and takes a deep breath. Then he says, "Hiroshi called me a few days ago. We kept in contact over the years. Whenever I was in Tokyo or he was in Sydney on business, we would always try to catch up. But when he called this time, he sounded . . . different. Distracted. Scared, maybe. He told me he was coming to Sydney and asked if I could get myself here to meet with him. I tried to make excuses. I didn't want to come here when—" Ethan breaks off when he catches Georgia's eyes. He averts his gaze, and Georgia knows what he isn't saying.

She is the reason he didn't want to come to Sydney.

"Anyway," Ethan continues, shaking his head. "I wasn't ready for that. But Hiroshi insisted. He said he had to meet me in person. He also asked for you, but I said no. I told him you were out of the country."

Georgia shifts uncomfortably in her seat. She remains silent, waiting for him to go on.

"We met at his hotel yesterday. He told me this long, crazy story about his dad, who turned out to be a spy for the Japanese government—"

"Wait. What?"

"Yeah, I know, it's nuts. To think of all those months I spent with the family, and I never found out. Hiroshi's family didn't realise either, 'til the very end. It was all top-secret stuff. We always assumed that he just worked some menial desk job at the government . . . Anyway, Mr. Akiyama's last assignment was to steal something from the Russians. Apparently the Japanese and the Russians have been fighting over it for decades. He spent a long time tracking it down, and he finally had the chance to grab it. Of course, the Russians came after him."

He scratches the stubbles on his chin, then continues: "I don't know all the details of what happened, but Mr. Akiyama was killed. Before he died, he hid the object somewhere safe. He hid it so well that when the Japanese government came searching in the Akiyama home, they found nothing. Weeks later, when Hiroshi went to their lawyer's office for the announcement of the will, he was handed a letter from his dad. Following the instructions inside, he managed to find the hidden package."

"I hope you're going to tell me he returned it to the Japanese government," Georgia says, dreading the direction of the story.

"Yeah . . . no, he didn't. In the letter, Hiroshi's dad told him not to trust anyone. He said it was important to not get any authorities involved. He sounded paranoid as hell and made it seem like his murder was an inside job. He told Hiroshi that he must find Dr. Ken Fujimoto. Fujimoto would know what to do with the artefact."

"Fujimoto," Georgia repeats the name.

"You know him?"

She shakes her head. "Only by name. He's a Japanese archaeologist, known for his work in Mongolia. He's led a few excavations there."

Ethan acknowledges this with a nod. "Hiroshi hasn't been able to contact the guy. Then someone broke into his house and ransacked the whole place. They tore through every piece of furniture, slashed up his mattress and couch. He was pretty spooked. So he jumped on a plane—"

"—and came to Sydney," Georgia mutters, finishing Ethan's sentence.

"Exactly," Ethan says. "You know Hiroshi, he's a proactive guy. He never just stands around waiting for whatever comes next. He wants to find out what this relic is, and why his dad died for it. He wants to know why there are people coming after him. And he figured that the only person he trusted who might be able to tell him that was me."

Georgia nods as understanding dawns. Ethan has recently been appointed the head curator of the Asian art collection at the National Gallery of Victoria in Melbourne. His knowledge in the field is extensive.

As if reading her thoughts, Ethan says, "But this . . . is out of my league. It's not something I'm familiar with. I knew we needed you there, but I was . . . I was still hurting and stubborn about not calling you. So I told Hiroshi I had to do some research. He was fine with that. He thought it was best if I took the artefact with me, though. He just couldn't have it at the hotel. It was too risky."

Ethan splays his hands out on his thighs, his chest rising and falling twice before he speaks again. "So I brought it home and studied the damned thing all night, before I began to have an inkling of what we were dealing with. And then I went to see him this morning. But he was . . . gone. The door to his suite was left ajar, and the entire place was torn apart. Someone had been in there, searching. I tried calling him, but he'd left his phone behind. I have no idea where he is and what's happened to him."

He turns and stares at her with haunted eyes. "I found *blood*, George."

"Blood?"

"Yeah. Not a lot. But it was there, staining the carpet."

"Jesus, Ethan. We have to call the police." She pulls her phone out of her back pocket.

"I already did." Ethan places his trembling hand over hers. "Even though Hiroshi made me promise not to get any authorities involved, I did. They came, and they brought the Australian Federal Police. The AFP asked me a bunch of questions. I didn't tell them that Hiroshi gave me the artefact, though. I didn't bring it with me to the hotel anyway, and I figured if Hiroshi's still alive, then this is my only bargaining chip to get him back. I can't risk the police confiscating it. But I need to be sure of what it is first."

"Okay." Georgia realises this is where she comes in. "Do you want to show it to me?"

Ethan stands and heads for the narrow closet under the staircase. He pulls out a black, hard plastic case as tall as Georgia and places it on top of the coffee table. Clicking open the latches on the side, he lifts the lid slowly. The interior is lined with protective cut-out foam and covered with a soft, dark cloth.

Georgia gazes at the large object nestled in the case for a few moments, her mind searching for connections. Then all her knowledge of Asian history falls into place as Hiroshi's story finally starts to make sense.

Her breath leaves her.

"You tell me, G," Ethan is saying, his voice fading into the background. "Is this what I think it is?"

3

UNABLE TO BELIEVE what she's seeing, Georgia kneels on the floorboards to get closer to the object, examining the entire length of it carefully.

It's an ancient spear. The wooden pole, about four feet in length, is painted black. There are clumps of long dark hair and strips of tattered silk hanging below the trident spearhead.

She wants to pick it up, to feel the weight of it in her palms, but without her conservators' gloves, she reluctantly keeps her hands to herself.

"It's a Spirit Banner, isn't it?" Ethan asks when Georgia remains silent. "*The* Spirit Banner. Of Genghis Khan."

"*Chinggis* Khan," Georgia corrects softly, keeping her eyes on the artefact. "'Genghis' was the Persian spelling that was adopted by the West. But his name is actually pronounced 'Chinggis'."

"Chinggis Khan," Ethan repeats the words. Then he drags a hand over his face. "I'm no expert on Mongolian history. But from what I read last night, this was stolen from some monastery and has been missing since the thirties?"

"If this *is* the one that belonged to Chinggis Khan, then yes." She tears her eyes away from the Spirit Banner and straightens to look at Ethan. "How much do you know about it?"

"Next to nothing. Like I said, Mongolian history is not my area."

Georgia rises from the floor to sit beside him. "A Spirit Banner, or a *sulde*, was an important symbol for the Mongols. It was made with the mane of a warrior's best horse, the hair tied in a circle below the spear," she says, pointing to the black hairs of the Spirit Banner. "The *sulde* was both a man's guardian as well as his identity. The Mongols were shamanists, which meant that they considered all aspects of nature sacred, with one overarching deity: The Eternal Blue Sky. They believed that when the Spirit Banner was flown in the open plains of the steppes, it captured the energy of the surrounding landscape and channelled it to the warrior, giving him the power to fulfil his destiny. The connection between the *sulde* and the man was so strong, that when the warrior died, his spirit was believed to forever remain in the *sulde*.

"It's said," she continues, "that Chinggis Khan had two *suldes* made from his best stallions: one white, for times of peace, and one black, to guide the Mongols in war. The *suldes* were seen as divine signs from the Eternal Blue Sky and united the scattered people across the steppe into one. Unfortunately, only the black banner survived, and it was considered to be the resting place of Chinggis' soul. This was the *sulde* that had led the Mongol army into countless battles across Eurasia—battles that they almost never lost —and it was the ultimate symbol of Mongol military prowess. It was kept and worshipped in a specially built monastery by his descendants."

"So what you're telling me, is that this . . . is the *soul* of Chinggis Khan?"

"To the Mongols, yes. It is the very embodiment of their nation's founding father, and it was a central part of the Mongolian identity. Some thought to possess it would be to attain the powers of the greatest strategist and military genius the world has ever known. But it also had profound significance to many of the people the Mongol Empire had conquered. To them, it conjured up memories of the devastation the Khan had caused when his army swept through their lands. The *sulde* was considered an especially dangerous object by the Soviets."

"The Soviets?"

"Yeah. The Mongol Empire conquered a decent chunk of what is now Russia. In the early twentieth century, though, Mongolia was effectively under Soviet control. To the communists, Chinggis Khan was a reactionary symbol, a threat that could summon nationalist ideals. In the thirties, Stalin's Great Purge became the Great Repression in Mongolia. During this time, the Soviets launched a series of persecutions against scholars, political dissidents, historians, and teachers, executing tens of thousands of people. They raided monasteries, murdered monks, and incinerated their libraries. It was during this purge that Chinggis Khan's *sulde* was stolen from the Shankh Monastery and was never seen again."

"Until now," Ethan says.

Georgia nods, chewing on her bottom lip.

"And the Japanese?" Ethan asks. "How are they involved in this? They were never conquered by the Mongols, were they?"

"No, they weren't. That's another long story—"

Ethan interrupts her, abruptly placing his hand on her knee. His entire body turns rigid as he stares at the narrow window facing the front yard.

"Did you see that?"

"See what?" She follows his gaze, looking through the sheer white curtains to the garden outside.

She frowns. She sees nothing.

Then a man's figure flashes by. Then another.

At that moment, the doorbell rings.

Her pulse kicks into overdrive.

"Shit." Ethan stands quickly and shuts the case. Lifting it from the coffee table with one hand and pulling her with the other, he ushers her towards the laundry at the rear of the house.

He's about to open the tinted sliding door to the garden when they see a man dressed in black, darting down the lawn with an automatic weapon. Georgia's heart jumps to her throat.

"Oh, fuck." Ethan's grip on her hand tightens. "C'mon."

But they have nowhere to go. There are only two exits: the front and the rear door. Out of options, Ethan leads her back to the lounge and makes a sharp left, heading silently up the stairs. They sneak into Ethan's old bedroom at the end of the hall, now converted into a gym for his parents. He shuts the door quietly and flips the lock, then grabs his phone from his pocket and dials the emergency service.

Georgia paces the room as Ethan speaks urgently, giving the operator his address and warning that the intruders are armed. She creeps towards the bedroom window and peers through the thin voile out to the back-yard. The man they saw in the garden is still there, apparently keeping a lookout. When he rounds the corner of the house, she opens the sliding pane and removes the fly screen carefully. Before she fully registers what she's doing, she climbs through the opening. Her feet teeter on the narrow ledge only one-brick deep, and she feels the familiar sense of vertigo rush at her. It's been many years since she's been on this ledge, sneaking up to the roof with Ethan, but she knows its every dip and groove like it was yesterday.

"What're you doing?!" Ethan exclaims in a whisper.

"The police won't make it in time. We should get on the roof and hide up there until they arrive."

He thinks briefly on this, then hands her the black case without another word. He's about to climb through the window when a rattle, followed by a loud bang, explodes through the bedroom door.

Two armed men stream into the room. They shout incomprehensible words as Ethan turns and launches himself at them.

"Go, George!" Ethan yells. "GO!"

Frightened, shocked, unsure of what to do, she swings around on the ledge, momentarily forgetting the extra weight of the case in her hand. It throws her off balance and sends her veering from the side of the house, plunging into space. Her first instinct is to protect the artefact, and she grasps it with both arms as she plummets to the ground, landing on her side with a violent slam. The impact knocks the air out of her lungs with a sickening, hollow crunch. She screams as pain erupts from her neck down to her arm.

She breaks out in a cold sweat. Her stomach roils. She takes several seconds to recover from her fall. With no small effort she struggles up to a standing position. She reaches for the case, but cries out again in pain, her right arm hanging uselessly by her side.

She fights off nausea, realising that she must have broken her collarbone. She snatches the *sulde* with her left hand instead and bolts around the corner, only to run straight into a man headed in her direction. The collision sends her hurtling to the ground, and he falls heavily upon her, wrestling for the case.

Georgia scuffles with her assailant and brings her knee up, kicking him in the crotch with all her might. He howls and slides off her, both hands groping between his legs. As she scrambles to get away he grabs her hair, jerking her head back as he yanks hard. She drops the case, her left arm flailing as she struggles to break free, and she somehow smacks him across the jaw, surprised at her own strength. The man lets out a startled grunt and momentarily loosens his clutch.

Recovering her stance, she grabs the *sulde*, leaps away from the man and rounds the side of the house, heading for the first exit she can think of: the garden gate connecting to the front yard. But before opening it, she sees through the gaps of the fence a woman standing on the lawn. She has a pistol in her hand and her gaze is fixed on the house, waiting for her team to finish their mission. Georgia pauses, then makes a sharp right towards another gate, the one that connects to the neighbouring yard and what used to be Ethan's grandparents' home. She's surprised to find it unlocked, but then remembers that Ethan's parents have always been friendly with their neighbours.

She runs past the pool to reach the French doors that open to the back garden, tapping on the glass pane and hoping that the owners of the house are home. When no one comes to the door, she skirts past the house to the other side. She hides in the narrow strip between the fence and the brick wall, catching her breath and wondering what to do.

Ethan. She needs to go back for him. She has to do something.

Her right side has gone completely numb and lugging the heavy case around is throwing her off balance. Without thinking, she stashes it in the shrubbery lining the fence. She hurries along the side of the dwelling towards the front, and just as she's about to climb over the tall, wooden fence, she hears the shriek of sirens in the distance.

Police. Finally.

Georgia cannot see Ethan's front garden from this angle, but she hears yelling and commotion, and the dull *thud-thud-thud* of car doors being closed. Tyres screech as the vehicle zooms off.

Georgia bolts back through the backyard and the connecting garden gate, throwing open the laundry door to Ethan's home. She runs through the house, searching every room and screaming for him. She races up the stairs and into his old room. The entire place is in disarray: gym equipment toppled over, pictures knocked off the wall, shattered glass covering the floor. The sheer curtain billows into a white cloud as a breeze comes through the open window.

The sound of sirens grows to a shrilling squall as Georgia drops to her knees, losing the last battle to retain the contents of her stomach.

Ethan's gone.

4

THE OVERWHELMING REEK of ammonia assaults his nostrils, jolting him awake. Ethan Sommers opens his eyes with shock, grunting and puffing through his nose to dispel the sharp, irritating stench. Tears well in his right eye, and he registers that the left one has swollen shut. He scrunches up his face and shakes his head vigorously, desperate to get that burn out of his sinuses. The sensation is so offensive that it feels like a nosebleed. He reaches to check if he's indeed bleeding, only to find that his hands are tied behind him. His ankles are bound to the legs of the chair, too.

"Ah, good. He's awake," a woman's voice says, thick with a foreign accent. "The smelling salt works." She chuckles.

Ethan looks up, finding himself in an unfamiliar setting. Bare concrete walls and floor, the room is grey and cold. There's a window to his left, revealing the darkening sky. The chill of the draught raises goosebumps over his exposed arms. A single bulb dangles from the ceiling, throwing shadows in the unlit corners of the large space.

In front of him stands a tall woman. Two men are present in the room, both sporting military crew cuts and wearing black cargo pants and polished boots. Ethan remembers a third man in the car with them, the one who drove, but he's nowhere in sight.

The woman strides up to him, the echo of her high-heeled boots ricocheting around the room. She stands so close that he has to crane his neck to peer up at her. Dressed stylishly in tight black jeans, silk cream blouse, and a leather jacket, she's a striking woman in her forties. He would have thought her attractive, except for the glacial look in her pale hazel eyes. The woman smiles at him, and an icy tingle of fear travels down the back of his neck. She reaches behind her to remove the pin in her hair, letting her silky auburn locks fall around her shoulders.

Ethan stills as he eyes the long, sharp apparatus in her hand. He's seen other women use similar traditional Chinese hairpins, but this is not one of them. Silver and with an elaborate pattern covering the surface, it looks more like a dagger than an accessory.

Before he can react, the woman straddles him and sits on his lap, interlocking her hands behind his neck.

"Hello, Ethan. My name is Anya," she purrs.

He sucks in a breath, pulling back to stare at her with his good eye. He's trying to figure out her accent and decides after a few seconds that it's Russian. Wavy curls frame Anya's face like flames, her bright red lipstick a stark contrast to her porcelain complexion. She traces a finger along his jaw, the scarlet nail raking over his skin.

He recoils.

"My, you are a handsome one." Her smile broadens as her gaze travels over him. "Sorry about the eye. Lev is about as subtle as a bulldozer, I'm afraid."

34

Behind her, one of the guys shifts his stance, crossing his arms defensively. He's at least two metres tall, a solid wall of muscles glowering at him.

Ethan's gaze darts back to Anya. "How do you know my name?"

"Hiroshi told me."

His heart pounds in his chest. "What did you d—"

Anya silences him with a finger over his mouth, clicking her tongue with amusement. "I really wouldn't worry about Hiroshi right now. You've got more important things to think about. Your girlfriend took something of mine, and I'd like to have it back." She places her hands around his neck again. "You're going to call her for me."

Georgia. Relief floods Ethan's chest. She's escaped. But the initial elation quickly fades as he realises the danger she's now in. Guilt crushes him, knowing that he's the one who got her involved.

Anya cocks her head. "You know, you'll make it a lot easier for everyone if you convince her to give it back. After all, Hiroshi's father stole it from us. Now, that wasn't nice at all, was it? An upstanding citizen like yourself should really do the right thing and return it to the rightful owner."

"It belongs to the Mongolian people," Ethan retorts.

Anya's smile fades. She stares at him for a few moments, as if deciding how she can hurt him the most. She seems to think better of it, though, because she shifts in his lap to move even closer, pressing her blood-red lips to his ear. Ethan can feel the warm crush of her soft breasts against his chest.

"C'mon, Ethan. I'll make it worth your while," she drawls.

Anya takes a light nibble on his ear, then licks the spot

35

where her teeth have been. As the stench of ammonia dissipates from Ethan's nose, it is replaced by the scent of her floral perfume. She presses closer still, making gentle movements of her pelvis over his crotch as she feathers her tongue over his ear. Dusting her lips down the side of his neck, her breath leaves a warm trail in its wake.

After a few moments, Anya draws back and looks down between them. With a smirk, she meets his gaze and lifts a mischievous, perfectly manicured eyebrow.

"I know at least *this* part of you wants to," she says in a sultry voice.

Disgusted, ashamed, Ethan struggles violently, bucking in his chair to throw her off. Anya jumps to her feet, her shrill laugh bouncing off the naked walls.

"Now, now. Calm down," she playfully scolds. "I was just giving you the easier option. I'm always much more pleasant to deal with than Lev. He won't be so gentle on you, you know."

The silver hairpin reappears, and with its sharp tip she taps the hollow at the base of his throat. Ethan freezes, knowing that a push of her hand could very well end his life.

"One way or another, I'll get my *sulde* back," she says, amusement in her eyes.

"I don't get what the fuss is," he counters. "It's a bloody spear with horsehair tied around the end."

"Ah, the *sulde* is much more than that, Ethan." Anya gives him a condescending smile. "It's going to lead me to the tomb of Chinggis Khan."

Ethan blinks, suddenly realising Anya's objective. His knowledge of Mongolian history may be limited, but this is something he is familiar with.

The forbidden tomb of Chinggis Khan has been the

holy grail for grave hunters since the thirteenth century. Over the past eight hundred years, many have searched and failed. Despite his fame, the Great Khan's final resting place remains one of the most elusive archaeological puzzles of the last millennium.

The legend has been told countless times. When the Khan died, his body was secretly transported back to the Mongol homeland by his army, who murdered every living person and creature they came across during the cortege. After a private funeral in an undisclosed location, hundreds of horsemen trampled over the grave to conceal it. These warriors were then executed by a group of soldiers, who were in turn killed by others, so that the location would be completely concealed. Mongol officials then sealed off the entire area for hundreds of square kilo- metres until the forest grew over the Khan's secret grave and was forever lost to the world.

Many say that Chinggis Khan's burial site must contain unimaginable riches, with spoils from his countless conquests across Eurasia. All his years as an infamous conqueror, and strangely, none of the items of his plunders have made it into museums or private collections. The foregone conclusion is that whoever finds the tomb would uncover the 'treasures of the world', and even the wealth of Tutankhamun would seem measly next to that of the Great Khan. The magnitude of his fortunes has captured the imagination of explorers and scholars alike, evoking images of boundless, brightly coloured silk, robes embroi- dered with silver and golden threads, fine jewellery and ornaments of ivory and precious metals, gems, pearls, rubies, and emeralds.

And gold. Lots and lots of gold.

The Russians are nothing more than tomb raiders after buried fortunes.

Anya reaches into her back pocket and retrieves a phone. She raises an eyebrow at him. "Tell me your girlfriend's name and number."

"Fuck off," he spits out.

"Your choice." The Russian woman shrugs. "Lev," Anya barks as she turns to the big man on the left, her voice suddenly switching to a deep, commanding tone. She issues stern instructions in Russian, then pivots and stalks out the door with the other man following behind her.

Lev steps forward. He's young, probably no more than twenty-five, and he looks like he should cut back on the steroids.

"She would not have done it anyway," Lev says, his accented voice a low rumble as he rolls up his sleeves.

Ethan frowns. "Done what?"

"Fucked you," Lev explains as he stares down at Ethan. "Anya is . . . uh . . . how do you Americans say this? A cocktease. That is what she is. She likes to screw with your head, but she never fucks you."

"O-kay," Ethan says, his frown deepening. He's not entirely sure how he comes across as American to the big guy. They're in Australia, for God's sake. Lev is apparently not too bright.

Ethan narrows his good eye and squints up at Lev. Before he can stop himself, he says, "Are you . . . *jealous?*"

The blow to his cheek sends him toppling to the ground, the chair still bound to him. He hears a crack and groans, knowing that his jaw is probably broken. Rolling the coppery taste of blood around in his mouth, he spits, horrified when a tooth lands in the splatter of red on the dusty concrete floor.

The dim light is blocked out as the Russian stands over him.

"I am going to enjoy this," Lev says.

5

GEORGIA SNEAKS INTO THE LABORATORY, grateful that classes have ended for the day and the research students have taken off. She shuts the door behind her and flips the switch on the wall. The overhead fluorescent tubes flicker on, bathing the room in cool white light.

Walking over to the workbench, she places the large black case on the tabletop and sits down on the stool, blinking back tears. She takes a few deep, stuttering breaths to calm herself.

The police grilled her for hours, asking about every detail of the attack. Georgia told them the truth, with the exception of the *sulde*. Spinning a quick lie, she said that the kidnappers had taken it with them. Many hours later, with the authorities gone, she retrieved the black case from the neighbour's yard. Then she drove straight to the university. After what happened at Ethan's house, she wasn't sure where to go. She was afraid to go back home, so she came to the place where she has always felt the most safe and comfortable. At least there are still a few people on campus, and after-hours security patrolling the grounds.

Her fingers trace over her right collarbone—which she broke when she fell down the side of Ethan's house—and she notes that the initial lump has disappeared. Georgia exhales with wonder. It took less than five minutes to heal, so by the time the police found her in Ethan's room, it was as if she hadn't been injured at all.

This is something to get used to.

It's the first time she's seriously hurt herself since discovering her healing abilities, and she's still not sure how it all works. She remembers Charlie telling her that minor injuries heal within seconds, while others take longer, depending on how bad they are. But some cannot be healed at all.

Like what happened to Charlie and Wang Jian, when that cave collapsed on them.

And Naaya, when Wang Jian murdered her by decapitation.

She shakes her head, willing the memories away. She must focus. She needs to find Ethan. Even though the police are out there now looking for him, she has to do something to help her friend. And that means learning everything she can about the *sulde*.

Her gaze falls on the case in front of her, and she reaches to open its latches. The *sulde* is what the kidnappers want, so it is the key to getting Ethan back. If she can find something to give her an advantage, it could ensure that Ethan gets out of this situation unharmed.

Georgia puts on some conservators' gloves and a magnifying headset, then opens the case and carefully lifts out the Spirit Banner. She begins her examination from the spearhead, working her way down the tufts of horsehair and along the surface of the black pole. Then she turns it over, travelling back up the length of the spear, finding nothing out of the ordinary on first inspection. She scrutinises the artefact again, this time in a slower, more meticulous fashion, sorting through the delicate threads of hair, and noting every bump and groove of the painted wood.

She finds something hidden behind the strands, directly under the spearhead. Some patches of the dark paint have cracked and peeled, revealing inconsistencies in the wooden surface underneath. Her heart leaps into her throat and she hurries to the other end of the lab and returns with a set of conservation tools, selecting a few that will serve her purpose. Gently, she picks and peels away the concealing black paint. It takes her a little while. When she's finally done, she sits back to assess the result.

There are two vertical lines of Mongolian script etched into the wood. To conceal it, someone has filled the grooves with some kind of clay, then painted over the surface.

Unable to read the Mongolian writing, Georgia takes a few photos and is about to send the pictures to a fellow professor in the Asian Studies department when her phone rings.

A blocked ID.

Her pulse quickening, she picks up on the second ring. "Hello?"

"Professor Georgia Lee." A woman's voice, silky and deep, travels down the line. She has a strong Russian accent.

"Yes," Georgia says. "Who is this?"

The woman ignores her question. "You have something of mine, and I have something of yours. How about we trade?"

"Yes," Georgia whispers, nodding.

"Good," the Russian says, an audible smile in her voice. She rattles off an address and Georgia commits it to memory.

"One hour. Alone," the woman instructs. "Don't even think about calling the police."

"But that's all the way on the other side of Sydney—"

"One hour, Professor, if you wish to see your friend alive again."

Georgia swallows past the lump in her throat. "Okay."

"Oh, and Professor Lee?"

"Yes?"

"Here's a little incentive to help you get here sooner."

Georgia grips the phone as Ethan's tortured voice comes on the line. "George, I'm sorry. I didn't want to tell them . . . but they gave . . . they gave me something . . . I . . . shouldn't have gotten you involved . . ." Ethan slurs his words, mingled with an unintelligible garble of sounds.

"I'm coming, Ethan." Tears stream down her face as her chest clenches to the point of pain. "I'm coming to get you, okay? It's going to be—"

"It's going to be okay?" The woman is back, mirth in her deep voice. "You'd better get here soon if you want to keep that promise."

With that, the Russian hangs up. Georgia bursts into tears.

After a few seconds, she reins it in, sobs still jerking her torso as she sniffs and wipes at her face.

Keep it together, Georgia.

Quickly snapping the case shut, she grabs her car keys and runs for the door.

6

FINISHING up her paperwork for the night, Sarah shuts her laptop and rises from her seat, stretching out her weary bones. For months, she has been working overtime while her boss was away, covering both of their workloads. And now that their involvement in the Chinese excavation project has been cancelled, things are going to get a little quiet in the office.

She tries to ring Georgia on her phone, but the call gets rejected and goes to voicemail.

"Hi, this is Georgia," her voice says on the line. "Please leave me a message . . ."

Sarah grins, knowing that her boss almost never ignores her calls. She is hopeful this means Georgia is currently getting *busy* with Ethan.

The poor girl deserves a break in her life for once.

Sarah has known Georgia since she was just a young woman in her twenties, socially awkward but bright as hell. And in the fifteen years she has worked for Georgia, she has come to think of herself as her boss' surrogate mother. Weird as that may sound to some, it seems only natural because of their age difference. Plus, Georgia has few friends to speak of, and barely any contact with her own parents. It got even worse six years ago, after Georgia's two-year-old daughter, Jacqui, died. And worse still, after her recent divorce with Lucas.

Suffice it to say, Sarah's the only person on Earth that has Georgia's back. And her grandmother, of course, but she's halfway around the globe in Taiwan.

Sarah has always prided herself on being able to read Georgia's mind, but now, she doesn't know what's going on with her at all.

She thinks back to their conversation this morning, and how absent-minded Georgia was through it all. Granted, it was her first day back at work after many months of absence. And yes, she went through hell during her time in Taiwan. But she was seriously off her game, and Sarah has never seen the woman in such a state.

All the trouble started when Georgia was commissioned by the billionaire Mark Lambert five months ago to find out what happened to the imperial alchemist, Hsu Fu, whom Emperor Qin sent to find the elixir of life over two thousand years ago. Lambert was convinced that Hsu Fu had succeeded and remained alive after two millennia, but Georgia has always been a sceptic at heart, so she never expected to find Hsu Fu. At least, not alive.

But he was.

Known to Georgia as Charlie, the man then asked her to help him find the original source of the elixir. They finally ended up in a cave in Taiwan, where they were ambushed by Wang Jian.

Wang Jian was Emperor Qin's general, who'd been ordered to track down the defected alchemist. The man had harboured a grudge against Charlie over two millennia and pursued him across continents and oceans. He ended up getting his revenge by murdering Charlie in that cave. And Georgia was almost killed, too.

Maybe Georgia is still recovering from what happened, and maybe she's also distracted because of everything that's going on with Ethan.

But Sarah's razor-sharp instinct tells her differently.

Something is off.

She can't quite put her finger on it, but the woman that she works for is somehow different.

And before the week is over, she intends to find out exactly what it is.

7

WHEN ETHAN WAKES AGAIN, he's only vaguely aware of the fact that his hands and feet are still bound to the chair. In the fog of his drug-induced state, he lifts his head, then groans as a sharp, stabbing pain pierces his skull.

He is utterly exhausted. Barely able to keep his eyes open, he blinks a few times to clear his vision with limited success. His head lolls to the side as he tries to make out his blurry surroundings, noting with relief that Lev and Anya are both gone. There's only one man with him now, the one who drove the car when he was taken from his house. This guy is shorter than Lev, probably not on steroids, but still menacing enough. He sits at the other side of the room, watching Ethan silently.

Ethan coughs, swallowing the taste of blood down his throat and immediately regretting it. He distantly remembers talking to Georgia on the phone but can't remember what he said to her. Her face swims into his mind, and he wants to kick himself for getting her into this mess. Why did he even call her in the first place? This is the last thing she needs so soon after returning from Taiwan.

He still doesn't know what happened to Georgia after their one night tryst in Taipei. All he knows is that she claimed to be on the cusp of some great discovery, then vanished for weeks until she was found unconscious, deep in the mountains of Taiwan. Many weeks later, she showed up at his doorstep in Melbourne, ready to talk, but something spooked her so much she bolted out of his house like she'd seen a ghost.

He really should have gone after her that day. He should have done everything he could to support her with whatever she was dealing with. But he was just too proud to follow her through that door. He was so mad, and so hurt that she walked out on him yet again. After everything they'd been through, after all they'd been to each other, she still didn't trust him enough to confide in him when she was in trouble. He'd waited his entire life for her to come to him, instead of the other way around.

But she did, you idiot, Ethan finally realises with a start. She *did* come to him in Melbourne. And what did he do? He said a bunch of dumb shit that drove her away again.

Ethan grits his teeth, shaking his head with disgust. He groans at the pain the movement induces.

None of it matters now, he decides. If they ever get out of this nightmare alive, he's moving his arse up to Sydney and staying until he sorts things out with Georgia. He's officially having a do-over. He's done waiting. Being kidnapped and beaten half to death helps you get your priorities straight, and he realises with remorse that he's had it wrong all along. Georgia is the only one that has ever mattered in his life.

You're deluding yourself, his mind sneers at him as his heart screams for it to shut the hell up. Georgia has never told him how she feels. Even after he confessed his love for

48

her, she was her usual silent self. Hell, the last time they tried to talk, she practically ran away from him.

A sudden wave of nausea hits him, and before he can stop himself, he's vomiting all over the front of his shirt. His body convulses from the effort, bringing up what little there is left in his stomach.

The man on the other side of the room rushes towards him, and Ethan braces himself for another round of assault, but it doesn't come. He feels the press of something cold to his lips instead.

"Here, drink," the stranger whispers.

Too tired to fight, Ethan obeys, relieved as cool water washes down his throat. After a few gulps, he drops his head back down, resting his chin on his chest.

"You hold on now, buddy," the guy says softly, and Ethan frowns as he detects the Southern American twang in his voice. He's pretty sure the men in the car were all Russians. "Help is comin'."

Ethan tries to look up again. He has questions for the Russian-turned-American. But no matter how much he struggles, the dark void pulls at his consciousness. Try as he might, he plunges into oblivion, despair and regret filling him as he reminisces about the only time Georgia came to him of her own volition.

Three days ago, Melbourne, Australia

"LET'S WASH IT OUT FIRST," *Ethan coaxed, taking Georgia's hand to unravel the soaked, bloody towel. There was blood everywhere. Her blood.*

"Jesus," he muttered.

49

What was he thinking, letting her make dinner? Georgia couldn't cook to save her life. She'd always been clumsy, and he wouldn't trust her with a knife at the best of times. He'd only sharpened it yesterday, for Christ's sake, and now she was probably going to need stitches.

But what was he to do when she showed up at his doorstep unexpectedly, demanding that they talked? Even though he was still pissed at her for not returning his messages after the night they spent together in Taipei, he was just so relieved to see her again that he'd folded as soon as she'd stared up at him with those big brown eyes. Besides, Georgia had never been the one to take initiative in anything that didn't involve her work. Especially when it came to matters of the heart.

He'd made her beg, of course, and she'd offered the bribe of a chicken sandwich. His favourite. He'd agreed, knowing it was the only thing she could make. But the news report of her being discovered in Taiwan had come on while they were in the kitchen, and both their eyes had been glued to the TV. Distracted, Georgia had cut her finger right open.

Tears welled now in her dark eyes and his chest clenched, fighting the urge to pull her close. He led her to the sink. He needed to clean the wound and see how bad it was, to decide if he had to take her to the hospital to get it sewn up. Guiding her hand under the running water, he watched as the blood washed away. Then he blinked at her unmarred finger. He turned her palm over and did not find a single mark on her perfect skin.

His laughter came out as a surprised snort, and he let go of her abruptly. She got him. Georgia rarely played pranks—it was always the other way around—but she got him good this time.

"Oh, very funny, George," he said, still chuckling. "Trying to win some sympathy points, eh?"

"What are you talking about?" Feigning ignorance, she

looked at her finger as the last traces of blood disappeared down the drain.

She blinked. Her mouth dropped open. She lifted her hand to study it, as if seeing it for the first time.

Then her entire face blanched, and Ethan's grin faded.

"George?" Ethan frowned. "You okay?"

She jerked her head up, as if she'd forgotten he was in the room with her. She stumbled back a few steps, bumping into the metal flask behind her and knocking it over. Water spilt across the counter and splashed onto the floor.

"Sorry—" she stammered. Her hands trembled as she fumbled to clean up the mess.

"Don't worry about it." He strode over to grip her by the shoulders, alarmed at her erratic breathing. "Are you okay? You're looking really pale."

The haunted expression she wore made him panic. She seemed like she was going to pass out.

"Come, sit down." He guided her towards the sofa.

"No, I have to go." She pulled away.

"What? No. Stay."

She shook her head vehemently. "I can't. I need to think—"

Georgia shrugged out of his grip and grabbed her bag, walking out of the kitchen and down the hall. She made a beeline for the front door.

Dumbfounded, Ethan felt his rising desperation with every step she took away from him. He followed her, reaching for her arm. "Don't. George. Please."

Georgia paused, her hand on the doorknob. But she didn't turn around. She wouldn't look at him.

"Don't leave, G," Ethan pleaded softly. He had never begged her before, but he was begging now. "Tell me what's happening. I can help. For God's sake, let me help."

She turned to peer up at him, and for a moment, she looked as if she was going to give in. Then something flashed in her features and her expression shut down. She said, "You wouldn't understand."

Those words broke something in him. He released her arm. He closed his eyes, fighting to calm himself. But he couldn't suppress the mounting outrage within him.

Before he could contain it, he accused with exasperation, "I wouldn't understand? I've known you since we were babies, George. I know you better than anyone else." He heard the bitterness in his own voice as he said, "I understand, alright. You're scared, and this is exactly what you do every single time. You run off whenever someone gets too close. You push people away as if you don't need them. It got even worse after Jacqui died. It's no wonder Lucas left."

Regret crushed him as soon as the words were out of his lips. But it was too late. Georgia flinched as if he'd slapped her. Her eyes full of hurt, she stifled a sob as tears slid down her cheek.

Ethan wanted to reach for her, to apologise and take it all back. But he didn't. He balled his hands into fists, and he kept them glued to his sides.

"I'm sorry, Ethan," Georgia whispered.

She opened the door and walked out into the waning after-noon light, leaving him staring after her from his front porch.

8

WHEN GEORGIA finally arrives at the address she was given, she's already five minutes late. Navigating the notorious Sydney traffic on a good day would have taken her forty minutes to drive here, but this is a Friday night. The number of traffic laws she broke was staggering, but absolutely necessary to make her deadline.

Georgia parks her car on the side of the street and hurries out of the vehicle. She can understand why the Russians chose this location. Nestled within a newly developed neighbourhood, it is surrounded by empty construction sites. Before her, the three-storey shell of a building is sectioned off with a wire fence. It looks like it's going to be a school. Everything appears to be dark inside, and with only the moon lighting her way, the place seems even more sinister in the shadows.

With the black case in her hand, she walks up to the gate but finds it locked. She follows the boundary line, looking for another way in, or a tree to climb up. She locates an entrance around the corner which is concealed by shrubbery: someone has cut a section of the fence, a hole just big enough for one person to get through. Squatting down, she pushes the large case through the fence, then crawls into the compound.

Georgia hurries up the few steps leading to the front door, hoping that she has the right place. The Russian woman only gave her an address and no further instructions. With nothing else to go on, she finds herself wandering in the building with the light of her phone guiding her way, jumping at every minuscule sound and echo.

Her phone suddenly shrieks in the dark, and she almost drops the device. She answers it, hearing her own unsteady voice. "Hello?"

"Professor Lee, how nice of you to join us. You're a little late," the woman reprimands.

"I got here as soon as I could." Georgia turns around, scanning her surroundings but seeing nothing. "Where are you?"

"Come upstairs to the top, end of the corridor." The Russian hangs up.

Georgia does as instructed, climbing the concrete steps two at a time. The room at the end of hall seems to be the only one with a door. It's open, and light emanates from inside, but is obstructed by the silhouette of a tall figure filling the entire doorway. As she gets closer, she sees that the man is leering at her. She stops a few paces away and frowns at him. The familiar woman's voice sounds from within the room, and after a brief pause, the big man steps back to allow her access.

Georgia comes to an abrupt halt as she spots Ethan, a tremor of horror and rage quaking through her. Her best friend, bound at the wrists, is hanging upside down outside the large windowless opening. His weight is supported by a rope around his ankles, which passes through a pulley system that is used to haul construction supply up to the top floor. Next to the window, an armed man is holding onto the other end of the rope.

Ethan is motionless and facing away from her. She cannot breathe as she watches his body swing gently from the rope, slowly turning towards the room in an unhurried revelation of what the Russians have done to him.

A strangled cry escapes her at the sight. Ethan's face is swollen beyond recognition. His t-shirt, bunched up around his chest and exposing his bruised torso, is splattered with blood. His arms, hanging limply under his head, are full of injection marks.

She rushes towards him.

"Hang on, Professor."

A hand grips her shoulder, stopping her in her tracks. She flinches, but the hold tightens on her, and that's when she notices the woman standing beside her for the first time. Tall and striking with beautiful auburn hair, she's assessing Georgia with a red-lipped smile.

"We haven't met before, but I know your work," the woman says, eyes travelling over Georgia in a slow sweep, then finally back up to her face. "I was surprised and delighted when Ethan told me I'd be meeting *the* eminent Professor Lee, world renowned archaeologist. I'm a big fan." She tilts her head to the side, smiling. "May I call you . . . Georgia?"

Goosebumps break out over her skin. Ignoring the question, Georgia points to Ethan and demands, "Take him off that rope."

The woman's smile broadens, and she extends her hand casually as if they've just met at a party. "You may call me Anya."

Georgia stares at Anya's proffered palm, at the pale, slender fingers and the carefully manicured nails in matching shade to her lipstick. There is something so creepy about the Russian, and Georgia can't decide which is more disconcerting: her strange, unaffected demeanour, her blood-red lips in startling contrast to her pale, translucent skin, or the way she is assessing Georgia as if she is something to be devoured.

Disgusted, Georgia thrusts the black case in the woman's direction. "I brought what you wanted. Now let Ethan go."

Anya releases her grasp on Georgia's shoulder, her brows twitching with a momentary frown. "There's no need to get so tense. If anyone should be upset, it's me. This was stolen from us. Mr. Akiyama is the one who has wasted all of our time."

Anya takes the case from her and strolls to a cluttered trestle table a few paces away, clearing the top with a sweep of her hand. A collection of tools and medical equipment scatter to the floor. Georgia spots a syringe amongst the debris, and she clenches her fists with anger.

She moves towards Ethan again, but the man by the window lifts his pistol at her, shaking his head with a silent warning.

Across the room, Anya opens the case, smiling when she sees its contents. Without lifting her gaze, she says, "Do you know how long I've been looking for this, Georgia? My entire life. All my life, I've been searching for this *sulde*, following one clue after another, rummaging through archives, historical records, government files. It took me two long years to gain access to the vaults, then another three to sift through the thousands of crates."

She looks up, meeting Georgia's gaze, her pale eyes

glimmering in the dim light. "The things I've uncovered there . . . oh, you wouldn't believe it even if I told you. Hell, you'd be just as excited as I was if you knew. Stalin had a knack for collecting things, that's for sure. But then the Cold War started, Stalin died, and everyone forgot about what was down there in the basement."

Anya returns her gaze to the *sulde*. "Not me, though," she continues. "I knew what I was looking for was in there, buried deep amongst all the junk and treasure. And I found it, even when everyone else believed that it was destroyed."

With quick, decisive movements, Anya shuts the lid and secures the latches with staccato clicks. Case in hand, she turns around to face Georgia.

"Thank you. For returning it to me." Anya touches Georgia on the arm, giving it a squeeze of appreciation. Georgia jerks away as if she's been burnt by the contact.

Addressing the two burly men present in the room, Anya says something brief in Russian. Then, with a lingering gaze at Georgia, she declares, "It has been a pleasure. For me, at least. It's a shame. I would have liked to meet you under different circumstances. No hard feelings, hm?"

She turns, marching out the door as she issues a sharp order in Russian. At the command, the man beside the window lets go of the rope, and Georgia watches with horror as Ethan falls, disappearing from view.

9

"ETHAN!" Georgia screams.

She sprints towards the window at full pelt, ready to leap after him. But the Russian man who was holding onto the rope tackles her before she reaches the opening, and the air is forced out of her as she slams onto the floor.

Suddenly, chaos explodes in the room. Georgia's assailant shoves her against the concrete as gunshots blast all around them, lighting up the gloom with short, deafening bursts. Her face is pressed to the cold, rough surface as she struggles against the man above her, but he tightens his hold, pinning her in position. Booted feet land all around, some dashing in the door's direction.

Men are yelling over the boom of gunfire, but she doesn't register their words. All she can hear is the thundering rush of blood in her ears as her mind howls with despair: *Ethan Ethan Ethan—*

She struggles to break free, bending her leg for a backward kick, and her foot lands on something soft. The man grunts in pain, momentarily loosening his grip. Then all at once his weight is gone, and she looks up to see him rising slowly with his hands behind his head. There is a gun pressed at his temple, and he's protesting, "Woah woah! Friendly here. Do not shoot."

Georgia scrambles up and darts towards the window, but someone else grabs hold of her from behind. Several ropes are dangling through the opening from outside, and she realises that the other men—whoever they are—must have abseiled from the roof. Before she is pulled away, she cranes over the ledge, catching a momentary glimpse of the sight below: beams of torchlight sweeping through the darkness, and two figures crouching over Ethan's limp, twisted body in the dirt.

"Oh my God," she sobs.

She fights to break free again, wanting to hurtle towards the door, to get to Ethan's side. Charlie and Wang Jian's words fill her mind, and she knows that if she gets to Ethan in time to give him some of the elixir—*some of her blood*—it could save his life. But she is restrained within a vice-like grip, and she suddenly stills when handcuffs are slapped around her wrists.

For the first time since the mayhem erupted, she takes stock of what's going on around her. The Russians are gone, except for the one who attacked her. She counts three others, not including the man holding her, all wearing combat gear and armed with semi-automatic rifles. They are wearing helmets and black bullet-proof vests, and the word "police" is printed in bold over their chests.

A few metres away, the Russian man is raising his voice, the control on his temper tenuous as he snaps at the policeman who's cuffing him. Dressed in black, the Russian's blond hair is cropped short, his face cleanly shaven, his frame dominant and imposing. Everything about him, from the way he looks and moves to the determination in his features, screams *military*.

"Of course I can verify it!" he's saying to the police officer. "Call the US embassy. Tell them to contact the deputy director at the DIA."

"Your name?" the police officer asks half-heartedly.

"Miller. Agent Brandon Miller. I'm the one who called this in."

Georgia finally detects the man's Southern American drawl. Her mind whirls with confusion. *What the hell is going on?*

"Maybe you are, *Agent* Miller," the policeman retorts with sarcasm. "But before we can confirm that, everyone is under arrest."

The crackle of the radio echoes through the room. "All clear," a voice says.

The men immediately move as a unit, and Georgia is pulled out the door and ushered down the wide corridor towards the stairs. They encounter two injured officers being attended to on the way. Her mind is reeling, and she's willing herself to wake the hell up, for the bizarre nightmare to end. But as they fly down the steps and exit the construction site, she falters at the sight of the stretcher being carried by two men in uniform, heading towards one of four vans parked in the street. The body on the gurney is covered with a white cloth.

No.

She thrashes ferociously with all her might, breaking out of the clutch of her accompanying officer and bolting towards her goal. Ignoring the warnings being screamed at her, she stumbles to a stop in front of the stretcher. The men carrying it halt and jump back in shock, causing the loosely draped cloth to flutter to the ground.

The air whooshes out of her lungs.

Ethan's discoloured, bloated face is unveiled before her. His left eye is dark purple and swollen shut, and there's dried blood smeared all over his engorged lips and crooked, broken nose. His skin is a sickening shade of bluish-grey.

He's so frighteningly still.

He's not breathing.

Georgia's chest tightens to the point of pain. She can barely recognise him but for the messy, sandy blond hair and his soiled t-shirt with Dali's face.

"No," she murmurs with a sob. "No no no no no . . ."

This cannot be.

Images of her life with Ethan explode in her mind like the birth of a thousand stars. Every childhood moment. Every joke he ever uttered. Every look, every touch and caress he gave her. Every possibility that could have been between them.

All of it blurs and disappears as tears flood down her face, replaced by pinpricks of light filling her field of vision as her world spins out of control. Her legs give out from under her and she collapses to the ground.

"Fuck!" Someone yells in the background, his voice faint against the pounding in her head. "She's going into shock."

Her surroundings fade away, and she barely registers what happens next. The sensation of being lifted. A blanket being wrapped around her, doing nothing to thaw the chill in her body. The croon of soothing words whispering in her ear. None of the words makes sense to her, though. Nothing in her life makes sense anymore.

Ethan's dead.

The thought repeats itself, over and over again in her

mind, haunting her relentlessly like a possessed, angry soul. She cannot shake it off. She doubts she'll ever be able to shake it off.

Seeking escape, Georgia curls her body into a tight ball, rocking herself slowly as she drifts out of consciousness.

10

THE INTERVIEW ROOM is nothing like what Georgia expected. Bearing no resemblance to the ones that are normally shown on television, there's a couch and two lounge chairs, a wooden coffee table between them, and a computer on a small desk against the wall. It looks more like a doctor's waiting hall than a place for interrogations.

Is she being interrogated? She's not entirely sure. As she fidgets on the couch, eyeing the man and woman sitting in the lounge chairs across from her, she wraps her fingers around her coffee mug—now completely cold—and tries to comprehend everything that transpired in the last twenty-four hours.

The woman, Sergeant Heather Nguyen, is the one who's been asking questions while her colleague, Senior Constable James Wilson, jots down notes on a pad. The pair have been brought in from the Australian Federal Police after Georgia gave her initial statement. They've been talking to her for hours, going through every minute detail of all that has happened since she arrived at Ethan's parents' home. Despite the casual approach of the interview, Nguyen and Wilson now know many intimate specifics of Georgia's life, from her relationship with Ethan, and their friendship with Hiroshi, to what she had for breakfast this morning.

"So, what I'm hearing, Georgia," Senior Constable Wilson speaks up, "is that you lied to the police when you gave your statement at Ethan's home."

"Only about the Spirit Banner," she stammers, wringing her hands. "I told the constables at the time that the Russians had taken it, but I'd actually stashed it in the neighbour's yard."

"Why?"

"I . . ." She rubs her wrists, her fingers going over areas where the handcuffs had dug in when she was arrested. "Ethan told me Hiroshi's dad had warned him to be careful about whom to trust. Mr. Akiyama worked for the Japanese government, but he was betrayed by someone on the inside. Plus, I thought if the Russians took Ethan, then the Spirit Banner was the only thing I had to get him back."

Wilson's expression is stern. "Do you have experience in hostage negotiations?"

"No . . . I . . ." Georgia feels the blood draining from her face.

They think this is all her fault.

Is it my fault?

Nguyen throws Wilson a look, and the senior constable purses his lips, returning his gaze to his notes.

"What my colleague is saying," the sergeant explains, "is that it's always best to leave such matters to the police. Trying to deal with it yourself puts you and others in unnecessary danger. Three policemen were injured during the incident today, and one of them is in a critical condition. The Russians have gotten away, and Wilson and I are trying to track them down. But in order for us to do our jobs, we need your full cooperation. And that means being honest with us regarding the case."

"But I am," Georgia protests. "I've told you everything I know, and I swear it's the truth. The Spirit Banner was the only thing I hid from the police earlier."

Sergeant Nguyen scrutinises her with a steely, penetrating gaze. After a few moments, she leans back, seemingly satisfied by Georgia's response. "Okay. I think we've got everything we need here. You have our contact details. Call us if you think of anything else."

"Do you . . ." Georgia says, gripping the arm of the couch as guilt rips through her heart. "Do you think if I'd given the Spirit Banner to the police, then things could have turned out differently for Ethan?"

Nguyen frowns. Then she sighs, compassion softening her eyes. "Maybe. It's hard to say. But I'll tell you something, Georgia. Ethan was long dead before you showed up at that construction site."

"Already . . . dead?"

The sergeant nods. "It's what Agent Miller told us. The coroner confirmed it after examining the body."

"Agent Miller," Georgia repeats the name, furrowing her eyebrows. "He was the one who jumped on me, the Russian man holding the rope. He let Ethan go."

"Miller's no Russian," Nguyen says. "He's DIA."

"DIA?"

"He works for the Defence Intelligence Agency, which is like the American military's CIA. He anonymously alerted the police to what was going on, hoping he could save you and Ethan."

65

11

CAPTAIN BRANDON MILLER slaps his laptop shut, emitting an aggravated growl. Leaning forward on the small hotel desk, he scrubs his face with calloused palms.

What a fucking mess.

Two years of undercover work gone to hell. And all because of one crazy-ass professor who decided she was going to leap out of the goddamned window.

Miller still cannot believe it. He has witnessed countless horrific incidents—the stuff of nightmares—and he learnt long ago that you can never predict how someone's going to react in such situations. In fact, it is those very rare moments that reveal who you truly are. And what the professor did when she saw Ethan fall was *not* a normal reaction.

He questions if he should have let her jump. Then he shakes his head, chastising himself. No, he did the right thing. After all, the civilian casualties were starting to pile up.

In all honesty, he's been unbelievably stupid, naively hoping he could pull this off by alerting the local officials while maintaining his cover at the same time. But to be fair, if he didn't have to stop that broad from going out the window, he'd probably still be undercover. Hell, he and the Russians might have even made a clean escape, leaving the Australian authorities none the wiser about an unsanctioned DIA operative on their turf, a fact that both the AFP *and* ASIO are chewing his ass over. These two local national security agencies are seriously pissed, especially because he sneaked into the country under a Russian alias.

It's only been a couple of hours since his boss managed to get him out of prison and transferred to this hotel room. He's also had a brief visit from the US diplomat, who brought his laptop and essentials, with strict instructions to keep his trap shut about the case and let Washington do damage control from their end. The entire thing is a colossal disaster, and he imagines he'll be escorted onto the plane home first thing in the morning.

Miller grinds his teeth, thinking about the valuable time he's losing as he waits this shit storm out. He wonders where the Russians are now.

Then he sighs, knowing that the case is pretty much lost to him anyway.

Unless . . .

With a sudden flash of inspiration, he flips open the laptop, bringing up the latest intel that was sent to him. He goes over the dossier again carefully, and an idea of involving Professor Georgia Lee begins to piece together in his mind.

She was a child prodigy, beginning her career as an archaeologist before she even turned twenty. Miller marvels at her extensive, impressive list of academic and professional achievements. Her IQ, last tested in high school, was off the charts. And it looks like she's done some high-profile side jobs over the years too, with the latest one funded by the recently deceased billionaire, Mark Lambert, no less. Divorced and with no dependents, she could very well be the most qualified person to finish the job. In fact, she's probably the only person who can help him now.

He has no doubt she's physically up for it. In fact, her speed and agility are astounding. Miller barely managed to stop her before she went flying out the window. He reflects on how she fought him off, not once but twice now: first when she kicked him in the balls at Ethan's house, and then again in the kidneys while the police's Tactical Operation Unit mounted their attack. Miller hasn't considered having kids thus far, but the professor's probably made sure he's never going to have any now. That savage blow had him limping for an hour afterwards. He absently wonders if she has had any combat training.

He shuts the laptop when a knock sounds at the door. He crosses the small hotel room to open it, and his brows arch with surprise when he finds the woman in question standing in front of him. Her large eyes are bloodshot and swollen from crying, and she glances nervously at the brawny man seated outside the door, charged with watching Miller until the AFP decides what to do with him.

"May I come in?" she asks.

He steps aside to give her access. The young AFP constable gives him a stern glare of warning as Miller nudges the door closed.

Professor Lee sits down on the only lounge chair in the room. She crosses her legs, uncrosses them, then crosses them again. Her hand trembles as she flips back her long, jet-black hair.

She looks too young to be a professor. She's so diminutive in her frame and seems so meek in character. Even though Miller knows from her file that she's now well into her thirties, the woman can easily pass as a recent college graduate.

"Professor Lee—"

"Call me Georgia, please." Her voice is hoarse.

"Okay, Georgia."

She clears her throat, regaining some confidence as she says, "And you're Agent Brandon Miller. From the DIA."

"That's right."

"You're the one I kicked in the crotch at Ethan's house."

Miller is surprised by her recall. Most victims of attack cannot remember their assailant's faces with such clarity, especially when things happen that fast.

"Sorry about that," she says, not waiting for him to confirm it. Her gaze drops to her clasped hands.

His brows lift even higher. "Are you?"

"Not really." Her eyes flit back to his face. "You're also the one who let Ethan fall."

Miller sucks in a breath when he sees her expression. He briefly wonders if she's going to kick him again. The professor is obviously not as demure as she appears.

She looks down again, wringing her hands. Her voice is softer when she explains haltingly, "I just came from my interview with the AFP. They said I could . . . talk to you about what happened to Ethan."

Tears suddenly well in the professor's almond-shaped eyes, and Miller draws back with alarm. He fidgets with discomfort as panic rises to his chest, now regretting the decision to let her in. He can't do this, if all she wants to do is cry about her friend. Miller hates it when women cry. He just cannot deal with it.

"Shouldn't you be . . . at home, resting?" he suggests. *Or speaking with a shrink?* He tries to not sound too harsh as he thinks of ways to get the professor and her tears out of his room. "You went through a lot last night."

She shakes her head, blinking back the moisture in her eyes as she takes a deep breath, and Miller is intrigued as he watches her visibly regain her composure, the distress in her features gradually transforming into resolve.

"That's what the AFP said too," she says, sniffling. "But I insisted. I've slept enough in the van and in the hospital. The doctors checked me out and cleared me. I just need . . . I need—"

"Closure?"

She nods. Sympathy stirs in Miller's chest as he sits down on the edge of the bed. From the files, he's deduced that Ethan and the professor were childhood sweethearts.

After a silent moment, she asks in a bare whisper: "He was already dead before I got there? You're sure?"

"Yes," Miller confirms. He pauses, then decides to be honest with her. "Ethan must've had a reaction to the drugs that the Russians gave him. He stopped breathing shortly after I had a chance to call the police for help. I tried what I could, but nothing helped."

He doesn't tell her the gruesome details of how Anya toyed with the poor man like a cat playing with its prey. How she seduced him, tortured him, then upped the dosage of the shots until his heart gave out.

"What happened to Hiroshi?" the professor asks.

Miller hesitates, then says, "Two of the Russians went after him at his hotel. I don't know the specifics, but by the time they brought him back, he was already dead. The AFP is recovering his body now. I'm sorry."

Georgia closes her eyes as she absorbs the information. When she opens them again, Miller is amazed to see that her dark eyes are full of fury.

"I want to know what's going on," she declares.

Miller contemplates her request. He ponders on whether the AFP has unleashed the unsuspecting professor on him to extract more information. He certainly wouldn't be surprised if they're listening to this very conversation right now.

All the more reason to win her over. She needs to be working on my side.

A thousand iterations of how this could go wrong cross Miller's mind, but his gut tells him otherwise. And in the field, he almost always goes with his gut. After all, it is what has kept him alive all these years. Miller now sees the chance to salvage the case and his career, and he decides to seize it. He'll worry about the repercussions later.

"That is not something I am at liberty to discuss," he states firmly as he reaches for his laptop, opening it again and bringing up a track of white noise on the media player. He turns the sound level to the maximum.

"But—"

He bends forward and gestures for her to keep her voice down. She frowns, copying his posture as she leans towards him.

He whispers, "Before I begin, it's important for you to understand that what I'm about to tell to you is considered classified information by the United States government. However, time is running out for me in this country, and it's become clear that without your help, I'm unlikely to make any more progress on this case."

She nods mutely, waiting for him to go on.

With an exhale, he reveals: "For the two past years, I've been on a deep undercover assignment in Russia. Through a contact, I was recruited as one of the security details for a privately funded team—the team that Anya started putting together when she finally uncovered the Spirit Banner. But soon after, the artefact was stolen by the Japanese."

"By Hiroshi's dad."

"Yes," Miller replies. "Hiroshi's father was working for the Japanese government. The Russians chased him all around the world for months to get the Spirit Banner back. But things started getting out of control when it ended up in Hiroshi's hands, and then in Ethan's. We never expected civilians to be involved."

He pauses, then tests the professor's knowledge: "How familiar are you with Stalin's interest in Genghis Khan?"

"*Chinggis* Khan," she corrects him.

Miller stares at the professor, deadpan. He couldn't care less what the proper pronunciation is.

"I know enough," Georgia finally answers. "I know that Stalin developed a strange obsession with the Mongol Empire in the years leading up to the Second World War. He was particularly interested in Chinggis Khan and Timur Khan, and their unsurpassed military tactics. I know that in the late thirties, Stalin had the remains of Timur Khan exhumed, hoping that by doing so he could understand the fourteenth-century conqueror better. Timur claimed to be a descendant of Chinggis, and even though there was no proof, he was a formidable military leader in his own right. Stalin also sent several expeditions to Mongolia to find the body of Chinggis Khan, but none of them was successful."

Miller is impressed with her concise description. "That's right. And at the same time, Stalin was searching for the Spirit Banner, because it was rumoured to contain vital clues to Genghis' final resting place."

The professor doesn't miss a beat. "This is why your team was after the *sulde*? They're grave hunters after buried treasure?" She says with disgust, "This is why Ethan died?"

"The second phase of our mission was to locate the tomb, yes," Miller confirms. "But the Russians are not just after treasure, Georgia. Their real objective is what was said to be buried with the Khan: his final legacy, *The Secret History of the Mongols*."

12

CONFUSION OVERTAKES Georgia as she processes the information. "You're telling me that the Russians have done all this for a *book*? But there are plenty of copies of *The Secret History* out there now, in several languages."

"Yes. But those have all been translated from an edited Chinese version. The original that was written in Mongolian script was never found," Agent Miller replies.

A sudden realisation sweeps through her. Astounded, she leans back in her seat, finally understanding why the Russians are going to such lengths to retrieve the *sulde*. They are not after the legendary wealth of Chinggis Khan, after all.

What they seek is his unrivalled power.

"Tell me what you know about *The Secret History*, Georgia," Miller now says.

Georgia stares at the agent, noting the seriousness of his features, the permanent crease between his brows. His prematurely greying hair is razored close to his scalp, and his eyes shine a deep blue in this light. She guesses that Miller is probably younger than her, but has a lot more mileage on him. She also gets the feeling that he is testing her, leading her on with clues to see what she actually knows.

With a shrug, she gives him the basics: "*The Secret History of the Mongols* is the oldest surviving literary work in Mongolian. It was commissioned by the Mongolian royal family, known as the Golden Family, and was completed a year after their Golden Khan's death in 1227. The text was the most significant native account of his life, and the only one that was written close to the Khan's time. Apparently, there were only two original copies ever made: one was buried with Chinggis, and the other was kept in a locked vault and guarded by Mongol scholars. It was accessible solely to the most important members of the Golden Family."

She then addresses the most relevant points at hand: "Because of its secrecy, rumours began to spread about the book. Some said that with proper interpretation, the contents would unlock a detailed blueprint to Chinggis' genius military tactics and instructions to his successors for world domination. To many people, these rumours were proven to be true by the unprecedented success of the Mongol Empire. When Chinggis died, he left behind an estate that was twice the size of Alexander's and almost three times the size of Rome's. He had conquered more lands and more people in two decades than the Romans did in four centuries. Then, his descendants took over and almost doubled the size of his conquests, creating the largest contiguous land empire ever known."

She looks out the small window of the hotel room, contemplating the sheer military might of the Mongols back then. Many have tried to emulate it since.

And it appears to be happening once more.

The DIA agent looks at her expectantly, waiting for her to go on.

"The original copy in the vault was destroyed after the Golden Family was thrown into chaos when different factions fought against each other," she says. "Then, in the late nineteenth and early twentieth century, several copies transliterated into Chinese were uncovered one by one. As World War Two approached, the Soviets, the Japanese, and the Germans all raced to translate the document, believing that its secrets would be the key to prevailing over Eurasia.

"It turned out that the surviving editions contained very few military details, though. They'd been edited several times over and heavily redacted, and other than an intimate account of Chinggis' life, there was really nothing Hitler or Stalin could use for the war."

Agent Miller nods quietly. From the way he is looking at her, it would appear that she has passed his test.

Georgia dismisses it all with a derisive snort. "So the Russians think that by finding the last original copy of *The Secret History*, they're going to be able to . . . what, *take over the world?*" Then, remembering Hiroshi's father's involvement, she adds, "The Japanese, too?"

"Both the Soviets and the Japanese were big, ambitious players in World War Two," Agent Miller says.

Georgia frowns at the agent's version of history. That is not how she would describe it—not for the Soviets, at least. Her professorial urges kick in, but she decides not to interrupt him.

Miller continues: "Since then, both countries' political and economic roles in the world have dramatically declined. The Russians in particular have been trying to reassert their dominance since the Cold War. Officially, their government isn't involved in the project, even though it's supported by military personnel as well as civilians. It was easy for Anya to get the backing—she'd sold them on the buried treasure alone. We suspect that Russia's current head of state has even invested his own funds into the project. He was a former KGB intelligence officer back in the eighties, so it's possible he came across some files from the extensive research that the Soviets did during Stalin's time. We believe it's all part of his ploy to expand his influence and control."

"That's insane." Georgia shakes her head. "And you? Why is the DIA even remotely interested in this? Surely you don't believe in all the myths and legends . . . or is it about the gold?"

Agent Miller hesitates, studying her as he considers the question. Finally, he reveals, "In the eighties, the US Military started a covert division with the intention of conducting paranormal experiments. The goal was to create a breed of 'super soldiers'."

Georgia's forehead creases at the direction the conversation is headed. "I've read a book about this. It was later made into a film." She narrows her eyes, having a momentary mind-blank on the movie's title. "It's the one with George Clooney. And . . . a goat."

"Yeah, but that movie was mostly Hollywood bullshit. The specialised division did exist, though. Its role was to research and investigate the supernatural and the unexplained. In the nineties, these experiments were declassified and shut down because of media leaks, but after 9/11, the program has been reactivated. It's now part of the DIA."

"And you work for that program."

"Yes. Ours is a very small, very self-sufficient covert

unit, but our projects are considered top priority by the agency."

He leans forward and rests his elbows on his knees, explaining, "For centuries now, people have speculated on what *The Secret History* might contain. It was said that decades of campaigning had allowed Genghis Khan to distill his strategies down to one or two eternal truths, secrets that would allow anyone to manipulate and dominate one's opponents. Others talked about how Genghis embraced new technology and inventions, and supported the work of esteemed foreign engineers and scientists. They believed that before the Khan died, he had commissioned the design of a weapon so powerful it would obliterate any enemy. Some even suggested that the Black Death was part of this weapon, the plague that swept from China to Europe towards the end of the Golden Family's reign, killing hundreds of millions in its wake."

When Georgia stares at Miller as if he's gone mad, he says, "I understand that all of this may seem . . . outlandish to you. But to us, what the legends describe could be a biological weapon—a weapon of mass destruction. If there's even a modicum of truth in this, then it is imperative we go after the Russians *now*. What you have to realise is that when it comes to intelligence and chemical warfare, the United States government simply cannot afford to take any chances. It's a different world out there these days, especially after everything that's happened to American citizens on our American soil. Between the War on Terror, the Chinese rising to power, and the psychopathic child-king building nuclear and biological weapons at the expense of starving his own citizens in North Korea, we cannot allow the Russians to complicate things too. The United States of America *must* hold on to our status of power. Being the greatest nation on Earth means that we have a role—a *responsibility*—to oversee the stability of the Western world order. We take our duty to protect the good guys very seriously. And that means we have to stay on top of everything—every piece of technology and information—our enemies have access to, no matter how far-fetched it may initially seem."

Georgia fights the urge to roll her eyes at the agent's zealous spiel, biting her tongue to keep her opinions to herself. She can tell that Miller is a brainwashed patriot, but it's neither the time nor place to get into a debate now. The agent's conceited sense of grandeur about his country's political interests aside, this is exactly the sort of ludicrous, superstitious interest she has tried to avoid her entire academic life. Too many times she's had job offers from wealthy collectors who've been seduced by fantasies and legends of the past, with complete disregard for scientific facts. Mark Lambert was one such hobbyist, lusting after the elixir of life.

And look how that turned out, she reminds herself. *Lambert ended up being right, and you are now an aberration of nature.*

She runs her hand through her hair, suddenly feeling exhausted. It has been a hell of a week. And it just keeps getting shittier.

"What you're saying doesn't make sense," Georgia argues weakly. "Myths and hearsay aside, how could a thirteenth century text possibly be relevant to contemporary military applications?"

"Well—we don't really know."

"You don't know?"

"Not exactly, no. But Anya does. That was my primary mission: to find out what the Russians know that we don't," Agent Miller explains. "My deduction is that the Spirit Banner wasn't the only thing Anya found. That's why she's so fixated on getting to the tomb. Maybe there was something else in that vault—something which proves all the legends to be true. Whatever it is, we must find out why Anya's so obsessed with the book. We can't just stand by and observe until it's too late. We can't risk the Russians getting their hands on something that we don't have access to."

He pauses, holding her gaze intently as he says, "And this is where we need your help, Georgia."

"No." Her voice is firm. "I'm hardly an expert in this area. There are other scholars out there who've spent a lifetime studying Chinggis Khan."

"I'm aware of that. The Russian team is led by the best of them. Dr. Mihailovich."

"Mihailovich . . . Dr. *Anya* Mihailovich?" Georgia gasps, finally recognising the name. The Russian woman's gushing comments about being an admirer of Georgia's finally make sense. "She's well known in the academic circles. Her work is brilliant, in fact."

"Yes," Agent Miller agrees, "and the woman is cunning and manipulative, too. My assessment is that she won't stop until she gets what she's after." Rubbing his palms over his thighs, he straightens. "Look, I realise there are other specialists we can approach. But we are short on time. My cover is blown, and for all we know, the Russians are already on their way to the tomb. Besides, when it comes down to it, you're already involved. My men have checked your track record. They believe if anyone can outsmart Mihailovich, it'd most likely be you. The Russians are well funded and highly organised. They're backed by a full team of historians, geophysicists, and linguists. And now that Mihailovich has the Spirit Banner, it's only a matter of time before she finds *The Secret History*."

Georgia leans back with escalating unease. Her head throbs with the thought of it all. This is something she should never get involved with. She needs to stay as far away from the DIA and its Russophobia as possible. Everything she's dealing with now—her newfound healing abilities, her speed and strength—they are exactly what the DIA is after. *Super soldiers.* If Miller finds out about her condition, he is likely to lock her up and experiment on her until he figures out how to replicate it. This is precisely what Charlie warned her about.

But then he says, "Help me bring Anya and Lev to justice, for what they did to Ethan and Hiroshi. You're the only one who can help us."

Georgia's breath catches. Her throat goes dry. Ethan's blood-streaked, disfigured face swims into her mind, and she chokes down a sob. In that single moment, all the resistance leaves her body.

She drops her gaze, and before considering it further, she blurts out what she's kept from the DIA agent in a whisper: "There was some concealed text on the Spirit Banner. I managed to find it before giving it back to the Russians. It's being translated by my colleague now."

13

"I'VE BEEN CALLING you all day," Sarah complains as soon as Georgia walks into their office. "Where the hell have you been?"

Georgia drops into her chair without a word as she wrestles with emotions that are threatening to break out of her chest. After leaving Agent Miller at his hotel room, she rushed home to pack, and she's only dropped by at the university for a vital piece of information before heading for the airport.

She reaches for the desk phone to contact the Asian Studies department. It rings twice before the call is answered.

"Hi Lena, it's Georgia," she says. "I was wondering if you've had a chance to translate the text I sent to you?"

"Just barely," is Lena's answer. "This is thirteenth century Mongolian, Georgia. I had to send it to Linguistics for their help. Anyway, I can come up to your office to have a chat about it, if you like."

"That'll be great, thank you." She hangs up.

"What is going on?" Sarah demands. Her face drops when she sees Georgia's expression. "Are you okay?"

Georgia opens her mouth to reply, then closes it again. On her way here, she has gone through different iterations of how she should reveal to Sarah all the events that have happened since they last saw each other. But the only two words she manages are, "Ethan's dead."

For a few moments, Sarah says nothing. Her face scrunches up with confusion, the expression so rare on her it almost appears comical.

Finally, she exclaims, "*What*?"

Georgia hesitates before replying. Her mind goes back to Agent Miller's warning about confidentiality, but at this point, she couldn't care less about being discreet for a government agency she neither trusts nor has faith in. Besides, Sarah has always been her closest confidante. Sure, the woman can be nosy, confrontational, and unbelievably exasperating at times, but she knows how to keep a secret when necessary.

She takes a deep inhale then gives Sarah a quick, abbreviated rundown of everything that happened in the past two days. She keeps her voice detached, for the fear of delving into the crippling grief that would drown her if she were to allow herself the luxury of feeling. Finishing her story at the DIA's involvement, Georgia summarises what Agent Miller has requested of her. With any luck, the inscription on the *sulde* would give them clues to locating the tomb, and hence where Anya will be heading next.

"Fuck," Sarah swears, reaching for Georgia's hand. "Jesus-*fucking*-Christ. I'm so sorry, Georgia."

Georgia nods, silent.

Her assistant's hand clasps tightly over hers, reading

her mind as usual. "It's *not* your fault. You know that, right? Don't you go feeling guilty over this."

"I could have saved Ethan. I *should* have—"

"What the hell are you talking about? There's nothing you could've done. If you want to blame someone, blame it on the Russians. Blame it on the DIA. Those bloody arse-holes. What a colossal cock up." Sarah tugs on Georgia's hand when she drops her gaze. "You hear me? Don't you bear this cross too. What happened to Ethan is not your fault. It's a miracle you got out of there alive."

Georgia exhales heavily, refusing to accept any of what Sarah is impressing upon her. As far as she's concerned, this *is* her fault. Ethan was captured while trying to save her. The irony is that she didn't need rescuing. In fact, she was in no danger at all.

She purses her lips as she considers sharing the truth of this with her assistant. The burden of her secret is becoming more tiresome by the day, and she finds herself in uncharted territory, navigating without the light of insight.

"Look, Sarah," she finally says, "there's something else I've been meaning to tell you—"

"Tell me later. What I need to know right now is: you're not going to help the half-witted Americans with their mission, are you?"

"Well—"

Sarah huffs with outrage, and she stops Georgia with a raised hand. "Let me get this straight. The Russians are looking for this book, because legend says that it'll allow them to dominate the world. The Americans don't quite believe the rumours, but suspect that there's something they're missing, a piece of information Anya has that they don't. They don't know for sure what the book is, or if it was really buried with Chinggis Khan, or if it even has any relevance to today's military applications. But they're going after it too, because Russia might end up with a new toy America doesn't get to play with? Are you fucking *kidding* me?"

"This is about getting justice. For Ethan. And for Hiroshi."

"Bullshit. Bull-*fucking*-shit. Miller might have manipulated you into believing that, but this is about stupid boys playing their dumb war games. And I'll bet my arse it's about the gold, too. Even if the book exists, if you work with the Americans you'll just be keeping *The Secret History* from one lunatic and giving it to another. Everyone knows that the current president of US is batshit crazy. You'll be helping him to *make America great again*," she says in a mocking tone.

Georgia pinches the bridge of her nose, all at once irritated by the sound of Sarah's voice. Even though she doesn't want to contribute to Miller's nationalist causes, she cannot listen to this. She won't. To her, it doesn't matter why the Americans are going after *The Secret History*. Right now, all she wants is revenge. Getting involved with this mess was the last thing she wanted, but her desire for Anya to pay for what she's done has eclipsed all the reasons she should stay away from the case. Georgia can feel the simmering anger in the seat of her belly, an insidious rage that she's never experienced before. Events of the last two days have replayed in her mind over and over again, torturing her with every choice she made. She is furious with her own stupidity, for naively believing that by giving the *sulde* back to the Russians, it would somehow buy Ethan's safety. She doesn't want Anya to have the satisfaction of achieving her ultimate goal, too. Whatever chance she has in bringing the Russian murderers to justice, she will take it.

"Ethan was my best friend. The only real friend I've ever had," she says curtly as a way of explanation.

To her surprise, Sarah doesn't come back with anything and when Georgia finally looks up, there is a dark look on the older woman's face. Georgia's only seen this expression on her assistant once, when she found out that her son had secretly eloped with his long-term girlfriend, without the consent or blessings of their families.

Sarah's voice drops to a deathly whisper. "Best friend? *Only* friend? What the fuck am I? Chopped liver?"

Georgia rolls her eyes. "That's not what I meant—"

"Oh really? What did you mean, then?"

Ire erupts, exploding through her veins. She throws up her hands in exasperation. She can barely recognise her own voice when she snaps, "You know what? This doesn't even concern you. I don't even know why I'm telling you all this because I've already made up my mind. Agent Miller is being deported to Singapore today and I'm meeting him there. And as my *assistant*, I expect you to support and respect that decision."

Sarah flinches as if Georgia has slapped her. Her face contorts with shock, hurt etched in her features. Georgia has never spoken to her that way before.

Regret lances through Georgia's chest. What the hell has come over her? She didn't even mean any of it, and she knows she should apologise. But she's never been good at dealing with this kind of drama, and right now, she doesn't have time for it.

To her relief, Lena Jones walks in the door, a piece of paper in her hand. Lena joined the Asian Studies department around the same time Georgia became a professor at

Sydney University. She teaches a variety of topics within the curriculum, but her real passion lies in the Heartland of Asia, namely, Mongolia.

"Hey guys," Lena says brightly, oblivious to the tension in the room. She places the document in front of Georgia. "Here you are. Between me and Linguistics, this is what we came up with. The translation isn't perfect. Really, you need someone with a deeper understanding of all the Mongol symbolism to do that. Do you have the rest of the passage?"

"The rest?" Georgia asks, puzzled as she picks up the piece of paper.

"It's incomplete. The message is cut off mid-sentence, in fact. Where did you get it from?"

Lena's voice fades into the background as Georgia reads over the two lines of text:

> *When the spirit and the seat of the Golden Khan are*
> *together again,*
> *Then shall the truth be revealed . . .*

14

Singapore

"WHAT DOES THIS MEAN, GEORGIA?" Agent Miller asks, his finger tracing across the lines on the page. "The *spirit* and the *seat* of the *Golden Khan?*"

They're sitting at the hotel foyer in Singapore, at which Georgia arrived only moments ago. Her hefty hiking backpack is on the floor by her feet, and she hasn't even checked in yet. With the information she has at hand, she doesn't see the point of staying the night. She is pretty sure Agent Miller can pull the strings to get them to their destination on the next available flight.

After muttering her thanks to Lena for the translation, Georgia rushed out of her office and jumped into a taxi for the airport. The trip from Sydney to Singapore took over eight hours, during which she had plenty of time to review her research and to ponder upon the cryptic message.

It didn't escape her notice that Sarah failed to say goodbye on her way out. When Georgia left, her assistant was still sulking at the desk, arms crossed stubbornly over her chest. The memory gnaws at Georgia, making her uneasy. She and Sarah have argued on plenty of occasions throughout the years—in fact, sometimes it seems that it's all they do—but this feels different somehow. This time, Sarah seems genuinely wounded.

Georgia pushes the thought aside. She won't worry about it now. There are more pressing matters at hand. She'll deal with it all later, once she's figured this thing out with Agent Miller.

"I've been going over it on the way here," she says. "'Golden Khan' is obviously Chinggis Khan. And the 'spirit' is probably the *sulde*. The Mongols believe that the Spirit Banner is the repository of its owner's soul."

"And the 'seat'? Is that Genghis Khan's throne?"

"I doubt one ever existed," Georgia replies. "Chinggis was a nomad. He despised the filth of cities and being confined by four walls. He was always on the move with his mobile *ger*—the Mongolian felt tent—and he always ruled from the mount of his horse."

"So the seat . . . must be his saddle?"

"That's what I'm thinking, yes." She nods. "Chinggis died during a campaign against the Tangut in the south. His body had to be transported back to the Mongol homeland for burial. Sources say that the *sulde* led the cortege of mourners, followed by Chinggis' horse with a loose bridle and an empty saddle."

"So his saddle probably has as much meaning to the Mongols as the Spirit Banner," Agent Miller speculates.

"Yes. As well as his bow and quiver, since the Mongol Empire was built on horseback and with bow and arrow," Georgia adds.

"Okay." Agent Miller sits back, looking pleased.

"Seems like we're finally getting somewhere. But what about the way the message is cut off, mid-sentence?"

She frowns. "I had very little time to examine the *sulde*. It's possible I could've missed something."

"Then we have to get it back," Agent Miller says. "And to do that, we need to know where Anya is going next. We'll assume she's found and deciphered the inscription by now, so she must also be looking for the saddle. Do we know where that may be?"

"Yeah," Georgia says. "It's at the Mausoleum of Genghis Khan."

Miller stares at her with confusion. "Mausoleum? Where he was buried?"

"No, he wasn't buried there. It's a long story. This mausoleum is in China."

"China? Not Mongolia?"

"No, that's an even longer story." Georgia rises to her feet, impatient to return to the airport. She reaches for her bag. "C'mon, I'll explain it to you on the way."

15

Mausoleum of Genghis Khan, Inner Mongolia, China

MILLER GAZES at the looming gateway of the mausoleum as he climbs out of the hired vehicle. The highly popular tourist site has just opened for the day, and already the sprawling car park is at full capacity. Miller and Georgia have come here under the guise of sightseeing travellers, and the professor has requested that they hire a tour guide, insisting that much can be learnt from the local perspective. The guide approaches them now as they walk up to the gates, welcoming them and introducing himself as Bataar.

Bataar is a portly man with a bubbly personality and crooked teeth. Ethnically Mongolian, he was born and raised here but speaks perfect, if accented, English. Miller is surprised to find out that today more Mongolians live in China than in the country of Mongolia.

On the way here, Georgia has given Miller a brief introduction of the place. The Inner Mongolia Autonomous Region has had a tumultuous past, alternating in control between the Chinese of the south and the tribes of the north. The entire area, including China itself, became part of the Mongol Empire during the reign of Khubilai Khan—Chinggis' grandson—who established the Chinese Yuan Dynasty in 1271. But when the Han-led Ming Dynasty overthrew the Khans in 1368 and drove them back to their Mongol homeland, the bordering region of Inner Mongolia became a place of constant conflict. Since 1945, however, it has remained part of China, and is often confused with the neighbouring independent country of Mongolia.

Even though they've barely begun to work together, Miller is already impressed with Georgia's wit and progress. He took no small risk in getting her involved in the case, something which could have possibly gotten him fired, especially after everything that went down in Sydney. But when the professor presented to him the hidden inscriptions on the Spirit Banner and her interpretation of the message, Miller knew that he had been right about her. His boss grumbled somewhat when she was updated, but she has allowed him a long leash while he chases down the lead. An eventual inquisition over his conduct is inevitable, however, when he finally returns to Washington, something which Miller is not looking forward to.

All the more reason to ensure the success of this mission, he thinks. Miller desperately needs things to tip in his favour, and right now, the professor seems to be the solution to that.

The three of them pass through the gates into a giant courtyard, and Miller listens to Bataar's enthusiastic explanations as they climb the flight of ninety-nine steps, an auspicious number for the Mongols. Also known as the Lord's Enclosure, the Mausoleum of Genghis Khan was completed in 1956 after a long and fretful history of the Khan's relics being transported from one place to another, roaming all over the grasslands of the steppes and through vast regions of China.

"But I thought this mausoleum has nothing to do with Genghis Khan's remains," Miller says, thinking about what Georgia told him on the way here.

"His bodily remains are not here, no," Bataar explains. "But some of his things are kept in the mausoleum. The Khan was buried in a secret location in Mongolia where no one had access, so to allow his people to honour him, a shrine of movable tents was set up."

"A mobile shrine for a nomad king," Georgia chimes in.

"Exactly." Bataar beams.

Up the hill, the stairs lead through a triple archway and continue over the hill crest, where three tiled domes of yellow and blue glisten in the early morning sun. The domes sit atop pagoda-style buildings adorned with crescent eaves, which according to Bataar, are a blend of inspirations from the iconic Mongolian *ger*, Tibetan Buddhism, and Chinese architecture. Linked by long white corridors, the three buildings are fronted by another huge courtyard. Tourists roam around the grand site, taking pictures with their phones on selfie-sticks.

"Over the centuries," Bataar says as they head towards the entrance of the central dome, "the tents travelled from place to place, guarded by an elite clan known as the Darkhats, descendants of one of Chinggis Khan's greatest generals, who was charged with protecting his relics. The Darkhats, also called the 'Untouchables' or the 'Protected Ones', moved the shrine across the great steppes, allowing the Mongolian people to worship their founding forefather. They finally settled here, in the Ordos region of Inner Mongolia. Then, when China was invaded by the Japanese in the thirties, their soldiers came for the relics."

"The Japanese? Why?" Miller asks.

This time, Georgia speaks up: "According to the theories of geopolitics and geostrategy, Mongolia was a crucial spot in gaining control over Eurasia. In the years leading up to World War Two, Japan increasingly saw itself as the new leader of Asia. They believed that securing the Lord's Enclosure was the key to controlling Mongolia, a base from which they could secure both China and Russia. Possessing Chinggis Khan's relics would have given the Japanese a greater claim over his heritage and people, and over the lands he'd once ruled."

"Someone has done her homework." Bataar smiles, looking impressed. Miller can tell by the way their guide is staring at Georgia that he is fast developing a crush.

Miller clears his throat, arching an eyebrow at the Mongolian man. "The Japanese came for the relics and . . .?"

Bataar snaps his gaze back to Miller. "Oh. Yes. When the Japanese came, we asked the Chinese to help us protect the shrine. The Nationalist Party of China, also known as KMT, enlisted the help of their rival Communist Party, and together they moved the tents all over China, evading Japanese troops until the war ended. Then the tents travelled back here, and a more permanent temple was built in Chinggis Khan's honour, which is what you see today."

The entrance to the temple is flanked by Darkhat men wearing trilbies and traditional Mongolian *deels:* long robes bound at the waist with sashes. Inside the building and beneath a frieze of ornate dragons, a five-metre-high jade sculpture of the Khan is seated before a huge map, displaying the vast extent of the Mongol Empire. Locals and tourists alike pay their respects, lighting incense sticks and murmuring prayers. More Darkhat men are posted within the shrine, keeping watch on the visitors and stopping them from taking any photos.

Miller surveys the hall, noting the locations of the guards and memorising all exit points. The history lessons, interesting as they may be, are starting to fry his brain, and he's anxious to get to the point of their visit. Georgia seems to be engrossed in the details of what Bataar is saying, but as far as Miller's concerned, this is a reconnaissance operation. The mausoleum is too public a place, with too many visitors and Darkhat men around, for him to make a move on the saddle in broad daylight. He has to scope out the site and locate the artefact first, then plan for a retrieval mission later tonight.

That's if the Russians haven't beaten him to it already.

He turns to Bataar. "Where are these relics you keep talking about?"

"The Mourning Hall is this way," Bataar says, leading them past the marble statue and towards the back. "There are three tents in the Hall: one for Chinggis Khan, the other two for his wives. His Sacred Bow and Quiver and the Holy Saddle are also in there."

They come to an abrupt stop at the taped-off entrance. Two Darkhat men stand on either side, their countenances dour. Bataar approaches the guards with cheerful familiarity, and Miller observes as the three speak in Mongolian at length.

Beyond the doorway, Miller can see three small Mongolian *gers* on an elevated platform, decorated with blue ceremonial silk scarves. Georgia stands on the tips of her toes beside him, peering into the Hall curiously. Miller's not sure what she's looking at, but he knows by now that the professor doesn't miss much.

Bataar looks increasingly upset as the conversation between the men continues. Finally, he turns back to them with a grim expression.

"What's going on?" Miller asks, already dreading the news.

"This is devastating." Bataar drops his head. "The Mourning Hall is closed. There was a break-in here last night, and some of the Darkhat men were seriously hurt. They won't let anyone in here, not for a while."

Miller throws a quick glance at Georgia before asking Bataar, "What happened? Did they see who did it?"

"They don't know. The police are still investigating the case." Bataar's face is ashen. "The thieves took the Holy Saddle. It's gone."

16

"Fuck," Miller growls with frustration, slamming his palm down on the hood of the car.

Moments ago, they said goodbye to Bataar and watched him saunter off to greet other customers. Miller has kept his cool all the way until this point, but that facade is quickly crumbling as he considers their situation.

The Russians now have both of the vital components to the puzzle. And he's got nothing.

"Back to square one," he snarls, wondering how he's going to report to his boss about this.

"Not necessarily," Georgia murmurs, looking thoughtful.

Miller turns to her, waiting for her to elaborate.

"C'mon, I'll explain in the car," the professor says as she opens the door, getting into the black sedan. "We need to head back to the airport."

Intrigued, he climbs into the vehicle, starting up its engine. As he pulls out of the car park, he asks, "Care to enlighten me?"

Georgia stares out of the windscreen as she chews

thoughtfully on her lower lip. After a long moment, she says, "Something bothered me the entire time Bataar was explaining the history of the place: the mobile shrine, the involvement of the Japanese, the Chinese Nationalists, and the Communists. All of it just doesn't seem right."

"How so?"

She opens her mouth to say something, then shuts it again, thinking on it further. She frowns. "I'm not sure yet. Look, it's only a hunch at the moment, and I don't really want to talk about it in depth until I have something more concrete, but I have a feeling we'll be able to find some answers elsewhere."

"Where?"

"In Taiwan, at the National Palace Museum," she replies. "Let's just get on the plane first. I have to do some research on this. I promise I'll tell you everything once I have the information I need."

Miller throws a surprised glance at her, wanting to ask more, but the professor is already opening her laptop. Her long, slender fingers fly over the keyboard as she types rapidly. The frown deepens between her brows, and from the set of her lips, Miller can tell she is now completely absorbed with the task at hand. From his limited time with her, he knows that she would most likely ignore any further questions from him.

It would appear that the conversation is over.

Fuck it. Frustrated but holding back further grumblings, Miller stabs at the car's navigation system, programming it to the nearest airport from which they drove only hours ago.

As it is, he's out of options, so he'll go along with whatever the professor's cooking up. For now, anyway. Georgia is living up to the image of the eccentric genius with the appalling way she works with others, and even though Miller is itching to dominate and control the situation, something tells him he should give her some space while she buries her nose in her books. It's a relatively short flight to Taiwan, and if she's really onto a lead, maybe he'll have something decent to report back to Washington in time for his scheduled call in forty-two hours.

The professor better damn well deliver. He runs a palm over his scalp. There is so much that hinges on this case—his first major assignment that could either make or break his new career at the DIA. The Deputy Director has pulled no shortage of strings to get him out of the shit show in Australia, and he cannot possibly fail her now. Miller still has no idea how his boss did what she did, or what she used to bargain her way out of trouble for them both, but she has pulled it off beautifully. The woman has a talent for making circumstances and people disappear, and Miller is not exactly sure he wants to know how. He's certain of one thing, though, and that is he will do anything to not get on the wrong side of her.

Settling in for the journey, he stretches his arms over the steering wheel as he emits a long-held breath, observing his travel companion from the corner of his eye. The woman is an enigma. Throughout their travels, she has barely said anything other than what is necessary. She scarcely eats and, from what he can tell, hardly sleeps either. Each waking moment of hers is devoted to research, and she is always on her laptop or reading a book. Every so often, though, Miller would catch her gazing into nothing, and whatever is on her mind would make her face contort with sadness. She'd then shake her head, blinking a few times to bring herself back to reality, and refocus her attention on her work again.

Miller frowns. He worries about her state of mind. He knows the symptoms of grief well, and if protocol had a say, he'd have a shrink assess her first before getting her involved in the mission. But that is a luxury they do not have, and he just prays that the adrenaline of the chase and the drive for revenge will tide her over until their task has been completed.

The professor looks up from her laptop now, staring out the window, deep in thought. Miller glances at her, concerned about her blood-shot eyes. He asks, "How's the reading coming along?"

She blinks as if startled by his presence. Returning her gaze to the screen, she answers without looking at him, "Fine. There's a lot of information to digest. Some accounts are conflicting, some in agreement. It's a matter of making sense of it all."

"What I don't understand is, why hasn't anyone found Genghis Khan's tomb yet?" Miller asks. "He was probably the most famous conqueror of all time, so why is the location of his grave still a mystery? What does *The Secret History* say about his death?"

Georgia finally looks over at him. "*The Secret History*— at least, the version that's available to us—doesn't reveal much about his death. It only says that he 'ascended to heaven.' There's no mention of how he died or what happened to his remains."

She shuts her laptop and addresses his other question: "There are several reasons why his tomb remains undiscovered. When Chinggis Khan died, it was kept a secret for strategic purposes. The Mongols were in the middle of a campaign when he fell ill. They were on the cusp of annihilating the state of Xi Xia, the base from which Chinggis would have conquered the rest of northern China. His illness came at a very inconvenient time, because if things worked according to plan, the Mongols would've soon controlled the entire trade route from the Pacific to the Middle East. But their newly defeated enemies would have revolted if they heard about the Khan's death. That's why the royal family kept the whole thing under wraps, and no one even knew about it until long after the burial."

"And the other reasons?"

"Mongolia is a huge and mostly undeveloped country, and not much archaeological work has been done until recently," Georgia explains. "For a long time, the Mongol homeland was closed off to outsiders, firstly by the Mongols themselves, then by the Soviets. Too much time has passed, and there is just too vast an area to cover. There are, actually, many places Chinggis could have been buried. Some even claim that he was entombed near where he died, in modern day China. Added to all of this is the fact that the Mongolian government is not cooperative at all with the excavation of the grave of their founding father. In fact, many speculate that the high officials already know where it is, but would never reveal their state secret. They just don't want him found."

"What about you?" he asks. "Where do you think the tomb is?"

She pauses, thinking on this. "I think to find where he was buried, we need to go back to where he was born. In Mongol folklore, there's a belief that you should be buried near where you came into being in this world."

She rubs her red eyes, suddenly looking exhausted.

"When was the last time you slept?" Miller asks.

She shrugs.

Shaking his head, he orders more sternly than he

intends, "Get some shut-eye. I'll wake you when we arrive at the airport."

He's expecting her to argue, but for once, she doesn't. She frowns with annoyance as she stares out the windscreen, leaning back in her seat. In the periphery of his vision he observes her, noticing the faraway look again and the sorrow in her expression. As he drives on, her eyes eventually flutter to a close, and the professor falls into a fitful sleep, murmuring about Ethan and someone named Charlie.

Six weeks ago, east coast of Taiwan

"TELL ME AGAIN," Georgia said to Charlie as she trudged through the dense thicket, "what exactly are you going to do if we find the elixir?"

Dawn came only an hour ago, and they were already navigating the treacherous terrain in the lush forest, beginning another day of search in the Taroko Gorge of Taiwan. Georgia's entire body ached from the strenuous efforts of the last few days, and her feet were covered in blisters. She wondered if they were ever going to find Naaya's elusive cave at all. She and Charlie walked side by side as they traced a path up and down the valley methodically, using the surface survey technique to look for an entrance to the system of caves that must be beneath them.

Charlie turned briefly at her question, casting a puzzled glance at her. Then he shrugged and continued to scan the forest bed in front of him, saying, "I am planning to take a sample of the water back with me. I would like to study it, to figure out how it made me . . . what I am. The elixir is a curious thing, you see. I know from comparing my blood with others that there has been a fundamental DNA change in me. It works almost like a virus, infecting the host and taking over cells to insert its genetic material into the genes. But there is a missing link to under-standing this transformation, and the way to reverse it. What is even more baffling, is that the effects stop with me. It did not pass onto any children I had. It is almost as if the DNA change cancels itself out in the offspring."

Georgia nodded thoughtfully. "You really think you can reverse the effects of the elixir?"

"I suppose there is only one way to find out." He smiled, turning again to assess her, his expression contemplative. After a quiet moment, he asked softly, "Tell me, Georgia, what are your plans for the elixir?"

She faltered in her steps, feeling caught out all of a sudden. "I don't have any plans. We're on this search for you."

"Uh-huh." Charlie chuckled with a knowing look, the lopsided smirk on his face making him seem younger than his apparent years.

She flushed, feeling embarrassed by his perceptive observa-tion. "Well, it's hard to not entertain the thought," she said in self-defence. "I mean, just the sheer potential of it . . . An elixir of life would change our world, and the course of our history."

Despite Charlie's warnings, her mind had roamed over all the wonderful possibilities that a cure for all physical ailments could bring. The idea was too momentous to dismiss, and as a scientist, she was fascinated not only by the physiological effects it had on the body but also by what it could mean for human civilisation, especially at a critical time such as this, when every day on TV there was more news of disasters happening around the world. Drought, hurricanes, rising seas, mass extinction, and widespread pollution—the list went on and on. Earth was teetering on the edge of survival, where decisions made today could forever determine its fate. If people knew they would live *indefinitely, Georgia reasoned, it would mean they'd take care of the world that they lived in. Politicians and leaders would act with more foresight, rather than leaving a mess for future generations to clean up.*

Besides, she couldn't in good conscience walk away from the thought of being able to save men, women, or children from whatever horrible illnesses they were suffering from. As a mother who lost her own daughter, she knew that death did not only strip away life; it crushed souls and destroyed families, too.

"Yes," Charlie was now saying, his face suddenly sombre. "There is no doubt that it would change everything."

She shook her head, knowing what he was referring to. Charlie's friend Naaya was the first to discover the elixir in the cave they were searching for, but the gift of healing did not bring prosperity to her people. It caused madness and destruction instead, ultimately wiping out her entire tribe in the most horrific fashion.

With this example, Charlie had asked Georgia to consider one question, over and over again:

Is humanity ready?

"What happened to Naaya's tribe isn't necessarily going to happen to us," Georgia argued. "We can warn people about it and put measures in place so that we don't end up with the same outcome."

Charlie listened in pensive silence as Georgia rambled on in a brainstorm over what they could do to ensure immortality was used to society's advancement, rather than a catalyst to its demise. Naaya's world was so different from their contemporary one, and there were technologies, treatments, and therapies that were available now which were not around before. Naaya's people's descent into hysteria could very well be prevented, she argued, if the right systems were put in place.

"Have you ever considered that insanity could be a physiological side effect of the elixir?" Charlie suddenly asked.

Georgia's forehead creased. "But that didn't happen to you.
Or Naaya."

"No, but we were only two out of thousands. The point is,
we do not understand enough about what the elixir does to the
human body or mind. And do not forget, I fought very hard
against despair over the years. I had to confront my own inner
demons, and the process was far from easy. If it were not for the
teachers I studied with, or the devotion I had towards this ascetic
lifestyle, I could very well have lost grasp of my own reality.
And you know, sometimes the distinction between lunacy and
sanity is not so clearly defined." Charlie grinned, his green eyes
dancing with humour, and in spite of herself, Georgia mirrored
his smile. He gestured around him. "Look at me now, tramping
through the mountains of Taiwan to find a magical cave, just so
it may allow me to finally die a natural death."

Georgia's smile twisted into a grimace, her heart clenching
unexpectedly. She didn't like the thought of Charlie dying. In
fact, after losing her daughter Jacqui, she'd be glad if no one ever
died in her life again. She was only just getting to know this new
friend of hers, and if she was being honest, he'd grown on her
over the past few weeks. She felt some intangible sense of connection with him, a strange recognition between kindred souls,
something which transcended what words could describe. The
possibility of losing that made her entire chest ache.

Jacqui's face swam into her mind, and Georgia pushed the
image away along with the accompanying swirl of emotions. She
was suddenly acutely aware of Charlie studying her closely.
Sensing his imminent question and not wanting to go into a
lengthy discussion over it, she picked up her pace, waving her
hand dismissively as she said, "Anyway, it was just a thought."

Charlie widened his steps to catch up to her, and they walked *on without speaking again, immersed in the sounds of the forest. The chorus of the cicadas rose and fell like waves, the birds chirped sporadically in the trees, and the leaves rustled softly as a breeze swept through the valley.*

When the sores on her toes began to rub raw in her boots, Georgia called for a break. She sat down on a rock by the river, removed her shoes and socks gingerly, and winced at the ugly sight of her feet. Swollen and bruised, there were inflamed red blotches all over her skin. Despite her best efforts with the band-aids, some of the blisters had ruptured, leaving spots of raw, exposed flesh. She dipped her abused feet into the cool water, hissing at the sting of the initial contact.

"Bet this never happens to you," she joked with mock jealousy as Charlie sat down beside her.

He smiled wryly. "It does, and it still hurts just as much. The only difference is that I heal faster. And I can still die—if you cut out my heart, saw off my head, or crush all my vital organs."

Georgia cringes at the ghastly image.

Charlie gave her a gentle smile and pursued the subject she was trying to avoid. "Tell me something, Georgia. What is the first thing that pops into your mind when I mention the word 'death'?"

Georgia knew where this conversation was headed, and she did not want to go there. She joked again, "Death is my arch nemesis. It's Paris to my Achilles. It's Darth Vader to my Luke Skywalker."

Charlie chuckled at her geeky humour. "And what is your Achilles' heel?"

"Love," Georgia blurted out without thinking. She frowned, pursing her lips and pressing her fingers against them as she inwardly chastised herself for what she'd revealed. Her eyes

welled unexpectedly, and she looked upwards towards the sky, trying in vain to stop the tears from spilling down her cheeks.

"No," Charlie said softly as she turned away. "No, Georgia. Love is your lightsaber. It is the only thing that wins in the end, the only thing that can transcend death."

17

Moscow, Russia

DR. ANYA MIHAILOVICH lets out a guttural growl of exasperation. Grabbing the nearest thing on the table, she hurls the glass paperweight at the wall. The solid sphere smacks into the plastered surface with a clunk, then plummets to the floor with a heavy thump. It rolls a few metres before stopping, not even giving her the satisfaction of seeing it shatter to pieces.

She snarls.

Then, realising that all the staff in her laboratory have stopped to look at her, she straightens to her full height, tugging on her black silk blouse and smoothing over her charcoal pencil skirt.

"What the hell are you looking at?" Anya snaps in Russian as she flicks her hand with scorn. "Get back to work."

Men and women scramble to return to their tasks, and Anya turns her attention to the wood and leather saddle mounted on the custom-made stand. Tools and instruments are scattered all over the workbench, and the large computer screen in front of her reveals the truth that she cannot ignore.

She had her suspicions when she first saw the saddle at the Mausoleum of Genghis Khan, but she brought it back to the laboratory anyway. And now studies have confirmed what she already surmised.

Mongolian saddles usually bear the mark of the owner. This one doesn't. Carbon dating also places it as being much more recent than it should be.

It's a fake.

Anya drops into her seat with frustration, reevaluating the situation anew. The entire project has been riddled with one obstacle after another ever since she uncovered the *sulde*. First, it was losing it to the Japanese. Then, the many wasted months of trying to recover it. Anya was ecstatic when she finally got it back again, but the joy was ruined when they were betrayed by a member of their own team. They barely managed to escape when the Australian police ambushed them in Sydney, and then there was the complication of leaving the country when images of their faces were all over the border control database. Russian intelligence had to get creative to come up with an exit strategy, a fact that her superiors are not happy about. Already, there are too many parties and too many governments involved.

Infiltrated by a mole from the very beginning. Anya clenches her jaws with anger. And he was such an integral part of the team too, being one of four who were deployed to retrieve the *sulde*. Only a few hours ago, the Russian intelligence advised her that the man is likely an operative of the American Defence Intelligence Agency, and the intel leak is potentially cataclysmic.

Anya shakes her head, casting the thoughts aside. Let the government worry about it all. Her number one priority is the tomb. It has always been, for as long as she can remember.

Her grandfather was the one who sparked her interest in the first place. One of her earliest memories is of Deda Dmitry seated in the study of his home, hunched over books and maps sprawled across the enormous mahogany desk. When Anya asked what he was doing, he picked her up, sat her on his knee, and told her a story so remarkable that she was instantly bewitched. After that day, whenever Anya and her mother visited Deda Dmitry, she and Deda would spend hours in his study, puzzling over the mystery together.

She later found out that her grandfather was a decorated soldier in the Russian military, a war hero who answered directly to Stalin himself. He was the officer who uncovered Chinggis Khan's *sulde* in Mongolia, and the one who led the team that exhumed Timur Khan's remains at Stalin's command. At Deda Dmitry's deathbed, only a few days shy of ninety-five, he finally revealed to Anya the shocking secret he'd unveiled at the Mausoleum of Timur Khan, and the true reason for his personal obsession ever since. Then, his last words to her were a prophecy of sorts. At least, she's always thought of it that way. Deda said that one day, she would be the one who finally finds the tomb of Chinggis Khan, and that the discovery would bring Mother Russia back to its former glory again.

Later on, as an adult and a scientist, she has often questioned the reality of what Deda told her. Her logical mind would argue vehemently against the legitimacy of his claims. But those arguments would always be silenced by one question. *What if?* What if everything he said were true?

Anya simply has to find out. Not knowing the answer has haunted her existence, monopolising her thoughts in every waking moment. Her interest has never been to serve her country. After all, politics are for men with engorged egos and shrivelled cocks, neither of which Anya has the time nor the patience for. Rather, she has been motivated by the simple yet obsessive fascination of the potential of such a find. She decided at an early age that she would devote herself to hunting down what her grandfather could not in his lifetime.

Her gaze falls on the *sulde* a few feet from her. Deda Dmitry told her it is the key to locating the tomb, and amongst the Mongols there's always been the belief that it contains crucial clues. She was hopeful the artefact would at least give her some guidance in unearthing the site more quickly, but it seems to have only wasted more of her time.

When she first saw the inscriptions that Professor Georgia Lee had exposed, she was astounded. Granted, Anya barely had a chance to study the Spirit Banner—let alone authenticate it—before the Japanese stole it, but Georgia had even less time before she was summoned to trade it for Ethan. This realisation fills Anya with regret anew, an emotion she is not accustomed to. She wishes she met the professor under happier circumstances.

Smart and *beautiful, not a combination you meet every day.* All her life, Anya has longed for an equal. It is a lonely existence, being surrounded by people who are far less intelligent than you are. The image of Georgia comes to her mind now, and Anya recalls with great detail the professor's petite frame, her delicate Asian features, and her long dark hair. She imagines with longing what they could have achieved if they teamed up together.

Or perhaps there's still a possibility?

Anya sighs, knowing it is highly improbable. Ethan's death most likely ruined any chance of that. People tend to get overly emotional about such matters. Not that Anya has ever understood why.

All around the laboratory, her minions mill about like ants, busily packing equipment for the expedition. Anya watches them with a growing sense of powerlessness, and a pressure builds between her temples—the early warning signs of an oncoming migraine.

She has no idea where to lead her team.

"Doctor." One of the men approaches her. "Would you like me to pack the saddle, too?"

"No." She glares at the object with disgust. "That one's useless to us."

She rises to her feet, her eyes falling on her open note-book. Scribbled in her own handwriting is the beginning of the message on the *sulde*:

> *When the spirit and the seat of the Golden Khan are*
> *together again,*
> *Then shall the truth be revealed . . .*

Annoyance surges through her and she tears the page from the book, screwing it up into a tight ball and tossing it into the waste bin. Damn this cryptic bullshit. She is a scientist, for God's sake, and she's not about to go on an archaeological expedition by following obscure, poetic riddles. No, Dr. Anya Mihailovich is going to unravel this mystery with hard, scientific facts—it is what she has always relied on, and it is what she trusts above all else.

She has already narrowed it down to a handful of potential sites, and it's a matter of eliminating them, one by one.

"What about this one, doctor?" A woman asks, pointing at the Spirit Banner.

Anya walks over to the *sulde*, examining it again from end to end, noting the inscriptions of vertical script along its length. Her team has stripped the black paint down, revealing everything that has been etched into the wooden rod. Her attention moves to the base of the shaft where an abstract symbol has been carved deep into the surface:

Anya's gaze travels over the grooves of the design. She memorises its shape. Then, straightening, she turns to the woman beside her.

"Pack this one," she declares. "It's coming with us."

18

National Palace Museum (NPM), Taiwan

As GEORGIA WALKS up the wide boulevard, she gazes at the sprawling, Chinese-style buildings of Naples yellow walls and turquoise blue roof tiles, once again marvelling at the thought of the immense riches contained within. Home to the finest permanent collection of ancient Chinese arte-facts, the National Palace Museum is considered the legacy of Chinese culture, encompassing eight thousand years of history with high-quality pieces that were procured and passed down by generations of emperors, including those acquired during Mongol reign.

It has also been a constant source of reliable informa-tion for Georgia's work.

She has called ahead to meet with her friend, Ling Ling Hsia, who works as head of the conservation department at the museum. The two women met at a special excava-tion project in the Bali District of northern Taipei three years ago, striking up an instant friendship over common passions and interests. Agent Miller wanted to join

Georgia for the visit, but she suggested that she attend to this alone.

The National Palace Museum is probably the most secretive museum she knows, with state-of-the-art surveillance systems covering every inch of the grounds and a vault with such restricted access that most employees, no matter how long their service, have never seen the inside of it. Even members of the government of the highest rank would have trouble gaining entry. To bring someone unknown in the academic circles—not to also mention foreign—into the back offices would require months of working through mountains of paperwork and navigating a complex web of bureaucratic red tape, none of which do they have the time for. As it is, Ling Ling is already doing Georgia a favour by granting her a meeting at such short notice.

Before coming here, she finally explained to Agent Miller the reasons for her visit. Something struck her as odd when their guide, Bataar, described the history of the Mausoleum of Genghis Khan in China. Then, when she saw the Mourning Hall and what was in there, she had a stark realisation. From where she was standing, some of the "relics" looked suspiciously in good condition.

A bit of digging around gave her the answers she expected. The mausoleum was built in 1956. Ten years later, Mao unleashed the Chinese Cultural Revolution, calling on the Red Guards to destroy everything connected to bourgeois ideals. Inner Mongolia was one of the places that got hit the hardest, because Mao feared its desire for independence, and a new wave of xenophobia towards the Mongols began. In Mao's mind, he was about to usher in an era so significant that even Chinggis would appear petty next to him. Any kind of study or worship of the

Mongolian idol was a threat, and the newly built Mausoleum became one of the biggest targets in the region. Whatever authentic relic it had of Chinggis Khan would have been destroyed by the Red Guards.

"But Bataar seemed to believe they were real," Agent Miller countered after she explained her theory.

"Yes, and he and all other Mongolian people would be deeply offended if you suggested otherwise. What you have to understand is that to the modern-day Mongols, Chinggis Khan isn't just the founding father of their nation. He's also worshipped as a deity. *Anything* associated with him or his name is considered sacred."

"But if the saddle was destroyed during the Cultural Revolution, then what the Russians took . . . was a *fake?*"

"I believe so. At least I hope so," Georgia said.

"But that means the clues on the saddle are lost to us. And we'll never know the location of the tomb."

"Maybe, maybe not."

At his confused frown, Georgia reiterated the information Bataar gave them with greater detail, explaining that during the Second Sino-Japanese War, the KMT Nationalists and the Chinese Communists cooperated together to keep Chinggis Khan's mobile shrine away from the Japanese. Despite the ongoing conflict between the two factions, the Nationalists and the Communists put aside their differences to work towards a common goal. Chinggis' revered tents were transported by a fleet of vehicles which travelled over a thousand kilometres and across areas that belonged to either one party or the other. When the convoy would arrive at a Communist territory, it was passed from KMT possession to the Communists, and then back to the KMT again when it reentered Nationalist land.

Bataar's explanations raised strong suspicions in Georgia. She was immediately reminded of the similar way in which the treasures of the Palace Museum were carted around China on a ten-thousand-kilometre journey to prevent the collection from being destroyed by aerial bombardment or falling into Japanese hands. Sixteen thousand crates of museum pieces were hauled on trains, in lorries, and on boats in an unprecedented mission to preserve the essence of Chinese culture from constant threat. A dedicated group of escorts moved the treasures over and over again, whenever the war got too close.

The Japanese were eventually defeated, but war erupted again between the Chinese Nationalists led by Chiang Kai-Shek and the Communists headed by Mao Zedong. Then, Chiang lost the civil war to Mao, forcing his KMT army to retreat to the nearby island of Taiwan, from which Chiang planned to relaunch an attack to claim back the mainland. In the process, he took the best pieces of the imperial collection with him. So powerful was the meaning of these precious items to the Chinese, that Chiang believed by possessing the legacy of Chinese history, he would ultimately have a legitimate claim over China itself.

The vast amount of artefacts needed to be stored somewhere once Chiang got to Taiwan. Fearful of imminent air raid attacks from the Communist army, he ordered for long tunnels to be dug into the mountains of Taipei, serving as cave vaults. In 1965, a museum was built at the head of the tunnels, and the National Palace Museum was thus born. Of course, China has long claimed that these treasures were stolen from them, but Taiwan maintains that it was a necessary act to protect the pieces from destruction, especially when so much was lost during the Cultural Revolution.

The similarities between the treatment of National Palace Museum's collection and Chinggis Khan's shrine are just too significant to ignore. Georgia cannot help but wonder if some of Chinggis' relics were also removed for "safe keeping" by the Nationalists when they escorted the shrine through their designated territories, replacing artefacts with fakes to deceive the unsuspecting eye. If so, it is very probable that despite everything, the Holy Saddle could have survived.

She knows it's a long shot, but it's a hypothesis worth investigating. The idea is actually not that inconceivable, considering the clandestine things the KMT got up to back then. Despite the museum's new policy of transparency and its efforts to digitise its entire inventory, it has been pointed out that a vast majority of its expansive collection has never been exhibited. The secrecy is a necessity, perhaps, due to its controversial history and the ongoing cross-strait political tension between Taiwan and China. Georgia speculates that there are probably some prized relics that the National Palace Museum never wants the world to know about.

Now, as she enters the administrative building, she finds Ling Ling waiting for her behind the security counter. Ten years her senior, Ling Ling has a boisterous nature and the most infectious laughter Georgia has ever come across. She's half a head taller with quite a bit more weight on her, and her presence and her personality dominates every room she walks into.

"Georgia!" The older woman's eyes light up with a beaming smile, and she rounds the counter to engulf Georgia in a warm embrace. She talks rapidly in Mandarin: "So good of you to visit us again! How are you? How is your excavation going in China?"

Georgia's face falls. "It's a long story, but we're no longer on the team."

"What? Oh dear. Come, tell me all about it," Ling Ling says.

She gets Georgia to sign in, trading an ID for a visitor's pass with the guard. Then, linking her arm with Georgia's, she guides her through the security doors and down the corridor as Georgia tells her everything that has transpired with the project in China.

Ling Ling pauses before entering the laboratory, commiserating with Georgia. "I am so sorry to hear this. It is really unfair and you deserve better."

Georgia nods. "Thank you."

"Well," Ling Ling says, smiling as she gestures to the door. "Let's see if we can brighten your day by showing you what you came for."

Turning to the entrance, Ling Ling waves her security card over the lock. The door clicks open with a beep, and she ushers Georgia into the bright, white-washed room, furnished with work benches and stools. On one of the central tables is a large blue box.

Ling Ling moves to the container as she pulls on a pair of white conservator's gloves. "It's good you've requested to see this now. It reminded me that we should really schedule a Yuan Dynasty exhibition soon, in celebration of the eight hundredth birthday of Khubilai Khan. The new director seems to be on board with that, and she's asked me to start going through our Mongolian collection. Do you know much about this particular piece?"

Georgia shakes her head, watching quietly as Ling Ling opens the box, revealing a book nestled into the soft, yellow interior lining. The volume has traditional Chinese stitch-binding and an unremarkable, yellowed cover smaller than an A4 sheet of paper. A single column of vertical Chinese text is printed in the centre of the cover: *The Secret History of the Mongols.*

Ling Ling gives Georgia a quick explanation as she gently lifts the book and places it on the soft cloth laid out on the worktable.

"Unfortunately, what we have is only a fragmentary copy," she says. "Apparently it was discovered in a waste paper heap in the storage facility of the imperial government at the time. It's one of the Chinese-transliterated editions that was produced in the late fourteenth century."

"How much of the book is missing?" Georgia asks.

"Well, *The Secret History* has twelve chapters in total," Ling Ling replies. "Ours has only four, and some sections are also missing half the text." She demonstrates by flipping through the book carefully. Many pages of the original were torn or rotted, and the museum has salvaged the piece by mounting what remained onto new paper, then re-binding it into a softback.

"You don't have any other copies in your collection?" Georgia asks.

Ling Ling pauses, an almost imperceptible frown appearing between her eyebrows. Then she says, "No. Sorry. This is all we have. But I can ask a friend at the university to send you the digital version of a complete copy, if you like."

"No, that's fine. I'll get my assistant to do that." Georgia smiles. She doesn't want to trouble Ling Ling much further. After all, the book is not really why she came to the museum. She decides to finally get to her true purpose, saying, "I had a quick look at the online catalogue before coming here. I was wondering . . . is there anything in your Mongolian collection that hasn't been documented digitally?"

Ling Ling cocks her head, giving Georgia a quizzical look as she sees straight through the implied question. "Are you asking if the museum is hiding any secret treasures the public doesn't know about?"

"Uh, well—"

Ling Ling laughs, a hearty guffaw that wobbles her ample bosom. At her friend's amused reaction, Georgia flushes red, suddenly feeling embarrassed about her conspiracy theory.

"No, Georgia," Ling Ling finally says, "all that secretive business from the KMT days is finished. So many people still believe the rumours that the museum has some obscure gems we haven't shown or told the public about. It's utter nonsense. We've been operating transparently for decades now, and the only reason some pieces haven't been exhibited is because they are just too fragile. But as you can see from the online catalogue, we've been making all the information available to the general public as we work to document the entire collection. Everything we have in the Mongolian section is already on there."

Georgia nods. "I guess I was hoping that some of the original Chinggis Khan relics might have been saved somehow." She explains to Ling Ling her reasoning, speaking of her recent visit to the Mausoleum of Genghis Khan in China, and the KMT's efforts to save the shrine from the Japanese. She leaves out the true motivations of her interest and the Russians' involvement, telling Ling Ling that the research is for a new paper she is working on.

"So you were hoping that the KMT stole the real relics

of Chinggis Khan and brought them to Taiwan when they retreated from China?"

Georgia shrugs, flushing red again.

Ling Ling smiles. "Well, I'm sorry to disappoint, but we don't have any of those items here. I wish we did. Chinggis' shrine and his relics were just some of the countless number of important things that were lost during the Cultural Revolution. The only pieces we have here that are close to what you're talking about are the portraits of the Golden Family."

At this, images of the paintings spring to Georgia's mind, and her lips part as a sudden idea emerges. Her thoughts return to the words that were inscribed on the *sulde*:

> *When the spirit and the seat of the Golden Khan are*
> *together again,*
> *Then shall the truth be revealed . . .*

Like *The Secret History*, messages in thirteenth-century Mongolian are usually full of hidden meanings and shamanic symbolism. What if the *seat of the Golden Khan* is not an actual seat, in the literal sense?

Her scalp tingles with excitement as she turns to Ling Ling, asking urgently, "The portrait of Chinggis Khan . . . can I see it?"

Her friend raises her brows with surprise. "Georgia, you really need to put in another official application for that—"

"I know," Georgia says. "But I'm leaving Taipei tomorrow so there isn't enough time. Are you able to make an exception? I'll file all the necessary paperwork on the way to the airport. Please?"

Ling Ling purses her lips as she considers it. Then, hunching up her shoulders, she says, "Alright. I'll have to call the director for her approval, though. But since you're in her good books, she'll likely say yes. It's being repaired in the other lab right now anyway. I suppose there's no harm in letting you have a quick peek while it's being worked on."

19

"Georgia, this is Mr. Fang," Ling Ling makes the introduction as they enter the laboratory, a bright, utilitarian room much like the one they've just been in.

There are several men and women dressed in lab coats and seated at the benches, working on a variety of artefacts. Next to each of them is a collection of tools, fine brushes, and small wells of ink colours meticulously mixed to precisely match the palette of the artwork they are restoring.

Mr. Fang is an older gentleman with thick glasses, a slender face, and a thin-lipped smile. Georgia shakes the man's hand, and he moves aside to allow her a better view of the piece he is working on. A large, open album rests on the workbench, roughly the size of an A1 sheet of paper. Mounted on the right-hand side of the folio is an ink painting on silk, portraying Chinggis Khan in his old age. Dressed in a white robe with a matching hat, his hair is styled in the traditional Mongolian *pojiao* fashion, where the top half of his head is shaved clean, leaving only a tuft on the forehead and long braids tied in loops behind the ears.

The painting is framed by strips of golden silk with decorative patterns, and some discolourations are apparent due to age, especially in the background of the subject. On the left page are five lines of Chinese text.

"Beautiful, isn't it?" Ling Ling says proudly. "There are eight portraits in this folio. Each leaf depicts an emperor of the Yuan Dynasty, when Mongolians ruled over China. But the most notable and famous work, of course, is this one of Chinggis Khan."

"A family album for Mongol royalty," Georgia murmurs, thinking of the long line of rulers of the Yuan Dynasty, which was posthumously founded by Chinggis Khan after his grandson, Khubilai Khan, took over China under the Mongol Empire. It would appear that not all of the monarchs were included in the folio.

Ling Ling chuckles. "I guess you could call it that, yeah. But the paintings weren't always collated together in this form. They were created during the thirteenth and fourteenth century, and then remounted into this folio much later in the eighteen-century, during the Qing Dynasty. The explanatory text on the left was added at the same time, identifying the emperor and the years of his reign."

"This piece was commissioned by Khubilai Khan, right?" Georgia asks, pointing to the portrait of Chinggis Khan.

"Yes, created by an unknown artist sometime around 1271," Ling Ling confirms. "It's still widely recognised as the most accurate image of the conqueror."

Georgia nods, knowing that there have been countless other versions based on this original. Unlike other rulers of his calibre, who compulsively commissioned paintings and sculptures in their image and imprinted their names and faces on coins, there were no pictures made of Chinggis Khan during his lifetime. The only thirteenth-century portrait of him is the one in front of Georgia now, which was created half a century after his death in 1227.

The Seat of the Golden Khan.

When Ling Ling mentioned the portrait, Georgia was reminded of the symbolic meaning of the head in Mongolian culture. To the Mongols, the head is the seat of the soul. This portrait, therefore, would be an image of the seat of Chinggis' spirit.

> *When the spirit and the seat of the Golden Khan are*
> *together again,*
> *Then shall the truth be revealed . . .*

The riddle on the *sulde* is cleverly deceptive. Anyone who is in possession of the Spirit Banner would immediately interpret the 'seat' as Chinggis' saddle, given that both artefacts were vital instruments in battle during the Khan's time. But this portrait is by far the most elegant and poetic solution to the puzzle.

Georgia leans closer to study the entire surface of the artwork. Upon first examination, she finds nothing she doesn't already know. She has seen a digital version of this piece many times, and the physical work itself presents no new information other than the clear, sketch-like marks in the painting strokes.

When she points this out to Ling Ling, her friend explains, "We believe that these paintings were most likely first drafts, shown to the sovereign for approval before the actual larger commissioned works were made, which were then hung and worshipped in the imperial shrines."

Georgia returns her gaze to the portrait. She is becoming more and more certain of her hypothesis. The *sulde* and the portrait—or, the *spirit* and its *seat*—would have once been placed side by side for worship in the Imperial Ancestral Temple built by Khubilai Khan. According to the inscriptions on the Spirit Banner, if she brings the two together once again, then the answer she seeks shall be unveiled.

But how?

She smiles at Mr. Fang and moves out of the way to allow him to continue restoring the work. The museum has done an excellent job of preserving the picture, retaining the quality of the image while keeping the authenticity of its age. Ling Ling has explained to her before that there is always such a fine balance when conserving ancient relics, and one has to be very careful not to end up "re-making" the piece itself. On this occasion, sections of the golden silk mount have peeled off and Mr. Fang is slowly and painstakingly adding glue, dot by dot, to paste the fabric back in place. Georgia's eyes follow his movements as he makes his way around the work, until her gaze lands on the bottom left of the painting.

She squints at the spot, her breath catching in her throat.

"Ling Ling," she says, pointing. "What is that?"

"What?"

Mr. Fang moves away again as Ling Ling scrutinises the area Georgia is referring to. The older woman pulls over the swivelling magnifying lens attached to the work-table to look through the large scope. As Georgia peers over Ling Ling's shoulder, her pulse quickens at the expanded sight of her discovery. At the bottom left edge of the painting, there are very faint brush marks over the sleeve of Chinggis Khan's white robe.

"Did you know that was there?" Georgia asks. "I never saw it in the digital file."

But her friend seems unsurprised. Looking up from the scope, she says, "Yeah, of course. It's hard to capture everything with photos and scans, especially subtle details like these. That's why it's always better to see the real thing in the flesh."

"It's written in Mongolian script," Georgia's voice is at a whisper as she recognises the familiar strokes. "Have you had it translated?"

"Sure," Ling Ling replies. She pauses to think on this, then shakes her head. "I can't remember exactly what it said, only that the translation made no sense. You know what the Mongols were like, always full of poetry, metaphors, and whatnot."

Georgia is surprised at her friend's apparent disinterest. "Are there similar texts on the portraits of the other emperors?"

"I don't think so." Ling Ling asks Mr. Fang to flip through the folio with gloved hands, confirming her hypothesis as they look through the other paintings.

"May I take a picture of the writing?" Georgia gestures to her camera.

Ling Ling shrugs, giving her a smile. "Sure."

20

Back at her hotel room, Georgia sits by the large window with her books and papers scattered across the small desk and the carpeted floor. The sky is darkening outside, and thousands of pinpricks of light appear all over the city, illuminating the streets of Taipei. She reclines in her chair and stares at the digital copy of Chinggis Khan's portrait on her laptop screen, working over the mystery in her mind.

She returned from the National Palace Museum earlier in the day to share her findings with Agent Miller. The photographs she took of the text on the painting were immediately sent to Washington, where it is now being translated by DIA's linguistic experts. After some discussions over the case, Miller left her to work on some reports of his own, giving her strict instructions to get some sleep. She got none, of course, and has been spending the hours reading academic papers on the Mongolian founding father instead.

A quick knock sounds at the door, and she rises, walking over to open it. Georgia finds the agent standing outside, his laptop in hand and his brows pushed together. She moves aside to give him access, and Miller strides over to the desk, dodging the books strewn over the floor.

"I got the translation back from our linguistic guys," he explains as he piles her documents to one side, making room for his computer.

Georgia glowers as she joins him, annoyed that he has messed up her workflow with the manoeuvre. "Do you mind?"

"What?" He looks up, confused.

"Forget it," she huffs.

She peers down at his screen. The email shows two lines:

And only one who possesses the truth of our history
May find his eternal resting place . . .

"It's still incomplete," Miller says, the frustration in his voice clear. "Where's the rest of it?"

"I don't know." She's sure there wasn't anything else written on the portrait. She checked every inch of that painting before leaving the museum.

"Do you think there was more on the *sulde*?"

"It's possible."

"Then we need to get it back from the Russians." Agent Miller straightens, crossing his arms over his broad chest. He lifts his chin in the computer's direction and asks, "Any idea what it all means?"

Georgia reads over the lines again, then reaches for her notebook and writes down everything they have so far:

*When the spirit and the seat of the Golden Khan are
together again,
Then shall the truth be revealed,*

*And only one who possesses the truth of our history
May find his eternal resting place . . .*

She runs a finger back and forth over her lower lip as she considers the words. The lyrical tone of the verses reminds her of the ancient system used by the Mongol army to transmit important messages during their campaigns. With most of the military personnel illiterate and spread over vast areas of land, orders and commands had to be repeated orally from rider to rider in a relayed chain of communication. Any errors or changes could break that chain and result in devastating consequences. So the officers composed their instructions with a standardised structure of poetic styles and melodies that were known to each soldier. In effect, memorising a directive was like learning a new verse to a song that every Mongol warrior was familiar with.

A chill travels down the back of Georgia's neck. It's as if the message in front of her is a communique by an unknown Mongol official from a time before.

But who is it for? And why?

She tears her eyes away from the page and finally answers Miller's question: "I can't say for sure, but I have a feeling it has something to do with *The Secret History of the Mongols.*"

"Why?"

Georgia points to the third line. "Here, it refers to *the truth of our history*, implying that the history known by the general public is false."

When Agent Miller shows no signs of comprehension, Georgia asks: "What is the first thing most people say when they're asked to describe Chinggis Khan?"

He shrugs. "He was a savage barbarian who raped and pillaged the civilised world and massacred millions of people."

She nods. "That's what most people believe today, especially in the West. But that opinion was shaped by centuries of anti-Mongol propaganda. Chinggis Khan was far from a savage barbarian."

Miller leans against the wall, looking unconvinced as he silently waits for her to go on.

"Think about it. There is no way a barbaric idiot can outsmart and outfight so many well-established cultures and create an empire so large we have not seen the likes of it since," Georgia says.

Sitting down on the edge of the bed, she explains, "History is usually written by the victors, but in the case of the Mongols, their story was documented by the vanquished. And it was only natural that they painted Chinggis Khan in the worst possible light, describing him as a ruthless, bloodthirsty demon. The devastation he caused was undeniable, of course, but what he and his descendants also built was ignored."

"What did the Mongols build? They were nomads living in *yurts*."

"Yes. But what they constructed was something far greater than cities. Much of it laid the foundation to our modern world of secular politics, meritocracy, religious coexistence, free commerce, and universal law," Georgia replies. "When you peel back the layers, Chinggis was actually a revolutionary leader for his time. At a moment where all other cultures considered their monarchs and aristocrats to be above the law of common men, he decreed a Great Law over everyone, including himself. While Europe still operated a feudal system, where titles and privileges were passed down by blood, he appointed his members of court based on skills and loyalty. When Christians were burning and executing Jews in the West, Chinggis' was the first empire to embrace all religions and accept multiculturalism. He also invented the concept of diplomatic immunity, and opened the routes of exchange from Asia to Europe, trading not only goods but also culture, knowledge, and technology."

Miller seems confounded by this apparently revolutionary idea. He lowers himself onto the seat beside the desk, and it takes him a few moments to ask, "Then why wasn't any of this taught to us in school? How come everyone is still told the complete opposite of what you just said?"

"Well, after the Mongol Empire declined, Europe rose to power. The documents containing the truth of Chinggis were lost, and the only information we had were accounts written by people who hated him and hated Asian people. The image of the Golden Khan became more and more distorted over time until he was a mere caricature." Georgia pauses, then says, "But, against this dominant trend, historians had been struggling to write about the real man behind the Mongol Empire for centuries. They wondered: under the veil of a feared military leader, who was Chinggis Khan? Even though practically everyone on earth knew his name, very little was known about who he was as a person."

She turns her gaze to the portrait of Chinggis on her screen. In this image, he appears more like an elderly Chinese scholar than a Mongol warrior. "As the search for truth continued, rumours began to spread among scholars that there was a secret document written about Chinggis soon after his death. It was said to have been written by someone close to him, containing information about his private life. Finally, in the late nineteenth century, a few copies of the document were uncovered."

Understanding dawns in Miller's eyes. "It was *The Secret History of the Mongols*."

"Yes," Georgia confirms. "The Golden Family wanted an authentic and truthful account written, so they didn't try to glorify Chinggis in the book. They included the good as well as the bad, even if it portrayed him in an unflattering way at times. Growing up, Chinggis was afraid of dogs, cried a lot as a child, and was often chastised by his mother. He was abandoned by his clan after his father's death and left to starve in the punishing landscape of the steppes. He murdered his own half-brother before he became a teenager and was then enslaved by a neighbouring tribe. He adored his wife, but her first child was another man's. He loved his best friend, but was betrayed by him. Within this cruel environment of injustice, treachery, and disempowerment, Chinggis fought, struggled, formed allegiances, and campaigned until the day he died.

"At its core, *The Secret History of the Mongols*—at least, the edition that's available to us—is the tale of a beggar king, of a man's aspiration to be more than who he was born to be. It is a psychological profile of what it took for an outcast to climb the tribal ranks and ultimately become an emperor. It tells of how an underdog reached his full potential and ended up with something greater than any man had imagined. And if you think about it, it's probably the first ever account of what many would describe as the great American Dream."

Miller's eyes widen with disbelief. It is obvious that this is a version of Mongol history that is completely new to him. He mulls over the revelation for a long while, then gestures to the verses in her book. "So to find the tomb, we must know the truth of Mongol History. I can get an English copy sent to us."

"It's not that simple," Georgia says. "The only editions ever found were all transliterated into Chinese."

"Transliterated? You mean translated?"

"No. They were *transliterated* into Chinese phonetics. The entire book was written with each Mongolian syllable matched with the Chinese character that sounded most similar. Reading it aloud would be . . ." she pauses as she tries to think of an analogy to best explain it. "It would be like someone trying to speak thirteenth-century Mongolian with a bad Chinese accent. It'll be near impossible to understand. Imagine playing the Telephone Game with people who don't speak the same language. Meanings get horribly muddled and confused. Scholars have been struggling to translate it ever since it was uncovered. Every few years, someone comes up with a new interpretation of what it all really means."

"Why? What was the point of transliterating it if no one could understand it?"

"To hide the contents, I suppose," she speculates. "The Golden Family conducted the most secretive government ever known. They flaunted their enormous wealth and spent lavishly—often irresponsibly—but they kept all of their written records locked in the treasury and away from foreign eyes. Knowledge was valued above all else. It was what gave them the most power, and they held onto the control of information like it was their lifeline. All the great seals of the Mongol dynasties were never disclosed, and all the Khans were buried in secret locations. Everyone was on a need-to-know basis, about *everything*."

Georgia rubs her forehead, then continues: "To make things even more complex, the difficulty of translating *The Secret History* is not just limited to language issues. When the Mongols wrote it, they were strongly influenced by shamanism. The book is full of hidden symbols and metaphors. To accurately interpret the full meanings of the text, and to pinpoint the places mentioned in there, you need to have a good understanding of the shamanic practices of the Mongols. And you need to be on site, at the locations where the actual events within *The Secret History* occurred."

Agent Miller's left leg jiggles as he thinks on this. "We can get you to Mongolia. And we can find a linguist to help with the interpretation. You can work on deciphering *The Secret History* while we try to locate Anya and the *sulde* at the same time."

Georgia frowns at the agent's naive enthusiasm. Clearly, he just wants the case to be solved regardless of the enormity of such an academic feat. "I don't just need *any* linguist. I need someone who's an expert in Daur, a dialect of Mongolian."

Miller looks surprised. "You need a Daur Mongol?"

"Yes," she confirms. "The Daurs are the only people in Mongolia who haven't been influenced by the influx of Buddhism or Confucianism. They've retained their shamanic knowledge since the thirteenth-century, and their old dialect is the one which most resembles the language of *The Secret History*."

The permanent line between Agent Miller's brows

deepens, and Georgia is certain that he's going to tell her it'll be near impossible to find someone with such a specialised skill.

Then the trace of a rare smile crosses his face, vanishing as quickly as it appeared, and he surprises her by saying, "I think I may know someone who can help."

21

Two days later, Mongolia

BEN EMERGES from the warmth of his *ger* and squints at
the sun low on the horizon, taking a slow inhale as he
gazes upon the broad open plains reaching as far as the
eye can see. The early morning frost tints the pasture with
a silver veneer, glistening in the light like a bejewelled
carpet.

He tilts his head upwards, awed by the infinite stretch
of cerulean blue sky spanning over him. There's not a
cloud in sight. A hawk glides across his field of vision,
circling lazily in a helix as it searches for prey.

Ben smiles. There is a deep silence in this land, a pervasive sense of tranquillity that has infiltrated his heart and
mind, and he feels a contentment he has not experienced
in years.

Whistling an unknown tune to himself, he ambles
towards his chestnut horse grazing nearby. It looks up at
his approach, snorting with affection when he strokes its
face and coos fondly in its ear.

"Wanna go for a run, boy?" he murmurs. "Down by the river?"

He gives the animal a lingering pat and turns, heading for the wooden shed to retrieve the bridle. He's about to open the door when he spots a trail of dust in the distance.

Ben frowns. He fishes out the binoculars nestled in the large pocket mid-way down his thigh to get a proper look. *A vehicle,* headed straight for him. Out here, and so early, too. He purses his lips. This is not going to be good.

Ben has been living on the Mongolian steppes for three years now. As the only medical specialist available within a two-hundred mile radius, he's always the one who makes the rounds to the nomad families dotted across the plains. It's highly unusual for the herders to call on him at his place, given how busy they are with their daily chores. It's a tough life around here, and with the devastating *zud* that happened only two winters ago—the widespread animal famine that killed millions of livestock—everyone is struggling to make ends meet. Something must be very wrong to warrant this visit.

His sense of calm now gone, he marches back into the *ger*. At his entrance, Indi, his dog, sits up and watches his movements intently from her cot. He paces about, checking his medical supplies and making sure that everything is ready for whatever is coming. His stock is down, and he really ought to drive to the capital to replenish many of the much-needed medicines, but what's the point when he doesn't have the money?

Too soon, he hears the distinct crunch of tyres on the dirt path, and he heads out the door with Indi trotting along at his heels. His gut twists when he sees that the car pulling up is a brand new black Land Cruiser.

His fists clench by his sides. This is not a visit by some

local nomad seeking medical help. Ben has chosen to live off the grid all this time for a good reason, and that reason has just caught up to him.

Indi senses his escalating unease and emits a high-pitched whine, pressing her muzzle into his hand and licking his palm. At her cue, he lets out a sigh and pats her on the head, muttering, "I'm okay, girl. Sit. Stay."

The van rolls to a stop in front of him, its heavily tinted windows obscuring the identity of the driver. He eyes the large axe leaning against the shed to his left as he briefly contemplates picking it up to chase the intruders away. But he doesn't. He folds his arms across his chest and gnashes his teeth in anticipation instead, waiting with growing agitation as the engine cuts off.

His pulse thuds rhythmically in his neck.

The driver's door finally opens, and Ben's brows lift with surprise. The man emerging from the Land Cruiser is the last person he expects to see in the middle of nowhere in Mongolia.

The American golden boy. Brandon *fucking* Miller.

The last Ben heard, the Special Forces captain was recruited by the DIA. This is a low blow for them to send him here. Whatever the DIA's after, they must be desperate.

"Doc!" Brandon calls, two rows of perfect teeth glinting within his wide grin as he slings a backpack over his shoulder. "You're a tough man to track down."

"That was the idea," Ben growls.

Brandon ignores the surly remark and strides up to him with an almost boyish bounce. "Come 'ere, big guy." He pulls Ben into a tight hug, giving him an affectionate slap on the back. "It's been way too long, bro."

Brandon's genuine delight is near infectious, and Ben

unclenches his fists with a sigh of resignation. He says with a low grunt, "How'd you find me?"

"We like to keep tabs on our assets. You know that." Brandon raises his finger.

Of course. Ben tips his face towards the sky, its colour so deep it's like staring into the ocean. For a brief second, he thinks he sees a faint sparkle of light.

Fucking drones.

"*Ex*-asset," Ben corrects Brandon, dragging his gaze back to him. "I don't work for the US military anymore."

Brandon snorts. "C'mon, bro. Folks like us, we got it in our blood. You can run to the ends of the Earth, but it'll still be right here," he declares proudly, thumping the centre of his chest.

When Ben glares at him without a reply, Brandon smiles and walks over to Indi, squatting down to pat her on the head. The German Shepherd leans into his hand as she pants with ardour, soaking up the attention.

Ben narrows his eyes at his canine companion. *Traitor.*

"So." Brandon gives him a pointed look. "You kept the dog."

"Of course I did." He frowns. His voice is tight as he says, "What the hell are you doing here, man?"

Brandon's smile fades. "Can we talk? Inside?" He nods at the *ger*.

Ben considers this. He's sure he is going to regret it, but for reasons he doesn't want to admit to himself, he gives Brandon a terse nod, opening the wooden door to his *ger*.

"Fine. But leave your shoes outside."

Brandon complies, removing his dusty boots and stepping into the round, felt tent. He nods with approval as he looks around. "Cool place. Nice and cosy. Kind of like a man cave, huh? I can see the appeal."

Ben remains silent. He follows Brandon's gaze, trying to see his home in the other man's eyes. Despite the modest furnishings, it is considered luxurious by local standards. There's a large, custom-made double bed to the right—its size chosen for the practical reason that he physically cannot fit in a normal single-sized mattress. To the left is a long wooden bench over which his medical supplies are neatly laid out. Next to it is a small kitchen cabinet, filled to the brim with provisions. A rectangular wood stove stands in the middle of the tent, its chimney extending through the central hole at the highest point of the *ger*, which also admits light inside. Behind it is a sizeable Persian rug with colourful cushions scattered around a low coffee table. Minimalistic and utilitarian, there's not a single thing that isn't used on a daily basis. The sum total of Ben's worldly possessions are in here and in the shed outside, or grazing on the grass nearby.

He stalks around the stove, grabbing a jug and two bowls from the kitchen cabinet. Setting them down on the coffee table, he lowers himself onto the rug, pouring white liquid from the container into the deep dishes. Brandon settles down opposite him, sniffing at the contents in the bowl as he looks questioningly at Ben.

"It's *airag*," Ben explains, "a traditional Mongolian drink. Something every host offers to his visitors. As a guest, you're expected by custom to drink every drop."

He demonstrates by taking long swigs of the slightly alcoholic beverage, savouring the soft fizz on his tongue and the mildly sour, refreshing taste. Brandon wrinkles his nose after a tentative sip. It's clear he doesn't like it. But the man is a good sport, and he finishes his portion with a few hearty gulps.

"What's it made of?" Brandon finally asks, wiping his mouth with the back of his hand.

"Fermented mare's milk."

Brandon blanches, looking as if he's going to be ill, and Ben chuckles, the knot loosening somewhat in his gut. He doesn't tell the agent that to a novice the *airag* can sometimes be a strong laxative.

"Alright," he says as he readies himself for the reason of Brandon's visit. "Let's hear it."

Over the next half hour, Brandon gives him a full briefing. He describes in detail the covert DIA division he has joined, the undercover assignment in Russia, the ambitious project led by Dr. Anya Mihailovich, and the accumulating casualties as they progressed in their mission. With growing distress he recounts how his cover became compromised, and the resulting diplomatic fallout. Brandon's contact who helped to get him recruited for Mihailovich's team has gone MIA as the Russians conduct a "clean-up" operation after they realised there was a mole within their circles. It seems Brandon is going to be in some trouble when he returns to Washington, even if the DIA is keeping him on the case for the time being.

"What Professor Lee needs now," Brandon says, finally getting to the point, "is someone like you to help her finish this mission. We need to catch up to the Russians and get the Spirit Banner back while the professor deciphers *The Secret History* for clues to the location of the tomb."

Ben is already shaking his head, wary of what Brandon is asking. "No way. Find somebody else."

"There *isn't* anyone one else, Doc. This is a highly sensitive, skill-specific mission. We can't just send in *any* agent. You know why no one's found Genghis Khan's tomb yet?

Because the Mongolians consider it a state secret. They don't want it dug up, or to have a foreigner meddling with the original copy of *their* Secret History. Access to the Mongol homeland has been restricted by the government. The Russians are probably gonna approach from the Siberian northern border, but we don't have that option. We need someone local, someone who can blend in. There ain't nothing that attracts attention like a tall, white male with a military buzz-cut in this part of the world." Brandon points to his greying blond hair.

Ben lets out a sardonic snort. "Or the brand new, shiny black van you've got outside."

"It's what they gave me."

"Exactly. Standard government issue."

Brandon shrugs, continuing, "Anyway. The point is that you and Professor Lee will blend in here. With a change of clothes, she could even pass off as a local."

"You can't stay?"

Brandon shakes his head. "Low profile is the key, bro. The less people on the ground, the better. We don't want the Mongolian government on our case when we're already gettin' chewed out by the Australians." He sighs. "Plus, I gotta get back to Washington and have my ass handed to me, man. There's an enquiry into how I've handled things, with the two dead civilians and the shit storm with the Australian government, and for involving the professor before she was properly sworn in."

"Fuck."

"Yeah. I fucked up. But there wasn't enough time, and I had to get her committed to the case while I still had the chance to speak to her. I was about to be booted out of the country, and she was probably gonna be the only person who could help me salvage the mission. Turns out I was right—the professor is some kind of a genius. Besides, I had her full file in front of me and she was squeaky clean. I weighed it up, and as far as I was concerned, she was low risk." He scratches the side of his head, frustrated. "Honestly, navigating all these protocols and reports and fucking politics got me missing our time in the Special Forces. The only way for me to redeem myself now is to make sure the Russians don't get to the tomb before us. My boss . . . she's a results-driven kinda gal, you know that. If I get the job done, it'll be easier for her to overlook the mistakes I made in the process."

"How is Susan?" Ben knows the Deputy Director of DIA well and does not envy Brandon's position.

"Same. Being a giant pain in my ass, as usual. You know how she can get sometimes." He drags a hand down his face, his vexation obvious. "That's why I need your help to dig me out of this mess before she feeds me to the dogs. There's no one else I trust more, Ben."

Brandon pauses, letting his last point sink in. Then he adds: "And also, the professor needs someone with linguistic skills, ideally with Daur Mongolian background."

Ben levels him with an icy stare. "My mother was the Daur, and I was taken from her when I was eight. I lived in the States from then on. It hardly makes me a Daur expert."

"But you understand plenty, Ben," Brandon argues. "You still speak the language. And you've been back for three years now. I bet you're familiar with shamanism, too?"

Ben doesn't reply. It's true he's been reconnecting with some of his mother's side of the family since his return. They've embraced him with open arms like the long-lost kin he was, including him in every social gathering—

events that often involve a shaman giving a blessing of sorts. In fact, one of his aunties is a respected shaman herself.

"Bottom line is, you can't deny you're the perfect man for the job," Brandon continues. "You've got all the skills in one neat package: the military training, the linguistic background, the Daur and shamanist knowledge. And from what Professor Lee has described, to interpret the true meaning of *The Secret History*, we need someone who understands how herders think. Someone who can easily identify where their ancestors would have camped or which way they would have travelled, and what they could or couldn't have done mounted on their horses. This is the one thing that the Russians don't have. They're well-funded and highly organised, but they lack the local knowledge. It'll be hard for them to get a Mongol to cooperate, 'cause the locals are deadly loyal to Genghis Khan. It's the only advantage we have for the race we've already fallen behind in."

Ben's lips press together into a thin line. Every cell in his body is screaming for him to tell the DIA where to shove it, but he senses his resolve softening as he sees the angst in Brandon's eyes. He knows full well that the agent would not be here if he isn't desperate for the help, and Ben feels compelled to assist a brother in need. It's what has been instilled in him since an early age, and even more so when he joined the Special Forces.

But there's still an undeniable fact he cannot ignore.

His admission comes out at a bare whisper: "I'm not ready, man."

Brandon stares at him. Then, with a long sigh, he says, "Yes, you are. I talked to your doctor yesterday, bro. He told me that after your last session, he cleared you for mission. That was over three years ago. But you still left the army, anyway. Why the hell didn't you tell me?"

The muscles in Ben's shoulders tense. "That's doctor-patient privilege."

"Not when it comes to intelligence and security interests, it ain't. Look, I realise you're probably feeling a little rusty. Getting back in action might make you jittery at first, but it's just like riding a bike, man. And what better way to get your feet wet again, right here in Mongolia, where you are most comfortable? Honestly, you can't live out in the middle of nowhere for the rest of your life."

Brandon leans forward, resting his arms on the table. His tone is sombre as he says, "Listen, Doc. I've said this before, but you need to hear it again. What happened in Syria ain't your fault. You gotta let it go."

Ben scrunches his eyes shut. This is not something he wants to get into. Not here, not now. Not with the man seated in front of him.

Changing the subject, he says, "What exactly do you think is in that tomb? Surely not the secrets to world domination?"

"I'm not sure. But doing what I do, I've seen enough to not dismiss any idea outright, no matter how crazy it may seem at first. Whatever you find, just make sure it doesn't fall into enemy hands. Destroy it if you have to. That's the primary objective. But if you can, bring what you find back to us. Lev Ivanov is the muscle head you gotta watch out for. Guy's got a few screws loose in his head, and I once saw him take on five men in a brawl. And Anya Mihailovich . . ." Brandon's voice drops to a grave tone. "Do *not* underestimate her. I cannot stress that enough. That woman is a chameleon, and one sick bitch. She's beguiling, she's sharp, and a hell of a convincing actress.

She adapts herself to any situation and anyone she's dealing with to extract what she wants. The witch can literately get away with murder every time. You cannot trust anything that comes out of her mouth, but it's hard as hell when she turns on her charm. You'll understand what I mean when you see her. Must admit I couldn't help getting a hard-on for the good doctor until I finally realised her game."

Ben glowers, protesting, "I haven't agreed to the job."

Brandon ignores his comment. "And keep your eye on the professor. I still haven't fully figured her out yet and there's something not quite right . . ." He stops, thinking on this. "I don't know, just don't let her out of your sight."

He reaches into his rucksack and produces a thick folder. "Here's the full brief. It's everything I've told you and more. You'll find a very generous offer in there. It'll buy you all the medical supplies you require for this . . . little project of yours." He gestures to the bench covered with Ben's equipment. "I'm well aware that the piddling amount of pension the army gives you is hardly enough."

Brandon gets up, slinging the bag over his shoulder. "Think on it. Please. I wouldn't be here if I didn't need this favour, Ben. As it is, we're out of options and on a tight timeline." He fishes out a satellite phone and places it on top of the folder. "I've programmed my number in there. It's secure. You can reach me at any hour."

Ben's nostrils flare as he works his jaw. Without another word, he rises to usher Brandon out of his *ger*. A light breeze has picked up and the vast sea of grass ripples gently, glimmering in the sunlight. The tantalising beckoning of the plains tugs at his heart, and he is desperate to go for a ride. He needs to think over everything Brandon has said.

Brandon gets into the van, rolling down the tinted window and shaking Ben's hand with a firm grip.

"It's good seein' you, Doc," he says, giving Ben a once-over. "I realise you're done with the military, but there'll always be a job waiting for you at the DIA whenever you decide to come home. We need someone like you on our team."

Ben grits his teeth, watching quietly as the van pulls away, throwing up a plume of dust as it gains speed. An irrepressible sense of helplessness and rage rises in his chest. He turns and kicks a stone in front of him, sending it flying through the air.

"*Fuck!*" he bellows, the sound of his outburst swallowed by the windy steppes.

22

Ulaanbaatar, Mongolia

SEATED at the hotel foyer with her large hiker's pack beside her, Georgia fiddles with her phone, fidgeting nervously as she waits for Agent Miller.

They arrived three days ago in the capital of Mongolia, the Land of the Eternal Blue Sky, named for its yearly average of two-hundred and sixty days of clear, azure heavens. This is the most sparsely populated sovereign state in the world, with humans being outnumbered thirteen to one by horses, and thirty-five to one by sheep. On average, less than two people live in every square kilometre of this vast, landlocked country spanning the size of Western Europe and wedged between Russia and China.

It is Georgia's first time in Mongolia. As their plane coasted towards its only real city, Ulaanbaatar, she saw below her a smooth, undulating carpet of ochre and green, completely devoid of tress and crisscrossed by pale wiry veins of randomised dirt roads worn by years of usage. It was the image of a true final frontier.

Not long after landing and checking into the hotel, Agent Miller disappeared for two days as he tracked down her local guide, and Georgia spent the time researching *The Secret History*. With Sarah's perfunctory help, she now has access to a full digital Chinese edition that was uncovered in the nineteenth century, as well as the multiple translations that have emerged since. She has already begun comparing the different interpretations, mapping out the differences and similarities between them.

Agent Miller has reassured her that the local contact would provide everything they need to travel to the most remote part of the country: the ancient Mongol homeland in the northeast, where Chinggis Khan was born, elected, and possibly buried. It is one of the most isolated places in the world, where the landscape has been virtually untouched since Chinggis' time almost eight hundred years ago. All Georgia has to worry about are her books and appropriate attire for the journey. The DIA agent is heading back to America this afternoon to report to Washington, but his replacement, who is soon to arrive, will keep him updated at all times.

She gazes down at her phone again, the restlessness in her leg intensifying as she stares at Sarah's cryptic email, which arrived yesterday. The correspondence is short and curt, delivering Georgia's requested information without the usual long-winded report on the latest departmental gossip or the customary bombardment of nosy questions. And that only means one thing: she wants Georgia to call her.

Georgia hasn't talked to her assistant since she walked out of their office in Sydney. It is probably the longest time Sarah has ever refrained from calling her. She must be really pissed.

She brings up Sarah's contact details, knowing she has to have the uncomfortable discussion to resolve their argument. Besides, there are still some important pieces of information she needs Sarah to send over. But every part of her is dreading the conversation.

She takes a breath to steel herself and presses the call button, then waits anxiously for her assistant to pick up.

"Hello." Sarah sighs.

"Hey, it's me." Georgia clears her throat. "I just got your email about Dr. Fujimoto . . . thanks for that. I think it'll be very helpful."

There's an uncomfortable silence as she waits for Sarah to speak. When she doesn't, Georgia searches desperately for something to say. "Listen. I'm in Mongolia right now, and I need you to look up some documents in the university archives."

"Mm-hm."

Perturbed by her assistant's less-than-enthusiastic response, Georgia rattles off the list she compiled earlier.

"They'll be in your inbox by the end of the day." Sarah sighs again, sounding like she's about to hang up.

"Wait." Georgia grips the phone, confused when the routine Sarah-style interrogation doesn't come. "Don't you want to know what we're doing in Mongolia?"

"Why?" Sarah snorts. "I'm just a lowly assistant to a professor, aren't I?"

"No. And I never said that."

"Oh, *really*?"

Georgia squeezes her eyes shut as she scrambles for words. "It wasn't what I meant. I . . . I need to do this, okay? For Ethan. I wasn't there for him when he was alive. I will not fail him now."

"No, Georgia. You *don't* need to do this," Sarah says

with exasperation. Then her voice softens a notch as she says, "Ethan died. The Russian mob and the DIA are pricks. Life's a humongous motherfucker sometimes. You're not the one who killed Ethan, and nothing you do will bring him back. It isn't your fault. The only thing you can do is to accept that. I saw what Jacqui's death did to you. Don't bring this on yourself too."

The mention of her daughter's name delivers a pinch in the centre of her chest. She stammers, "But it *is* my fault. And I *have* to fix it. You . . ."

She tries to think of how to explain it all, to describe the way she has gone over the events of Ethan's kidnapping in every detail, torturing herself for each decision she made which could have led to a different outcome. Why did she run? Why didn't she just give the Spirit Banner to the Russians and demand they leave them alone? Why didn't she let the Russians take her instead of Ethan, when he was the one who needed rescuing and not her?

But all of it becomes lodged in the depths of her throat, and the only words that scramble their way out of her mouth are: ". . . you don't understand."

There is an extended silence on the line. Then the icy tone in Sarah's voice is back as she snaps: "I guess I don't. Even though I'm the person who knows you best, and I'm the one who has stuck by your side all these years, I just don't know what the hell is going on with you anymore. You never let anyone in, you're always keeping people at arm's length, and ever since Taiwan there's just been something so off with you, it's like you're hiding something all the time—"

Across the foyer, Agent Miller marches towards Georgia with two large black cases in his hands. The permanent frown on his face deepens when he sees her expression.

"I'm sorry, Sarah." Georgia interrupts Sarah's tirade as Miller comes to a stop in front of her. "I have to go."

For a long time, Sarah doesn't speak. Then, with a sarcastic tone she says, "Fine, *professor,* the material you requested will be in your inbox by the end of the day."

The line goes dead.

Georgia frowns at her phone, regret filling her as she wishes she had handled that better. She looks up at Miller.

"Everything okay?" he asks.

"Yeah," she lies.

He hesitates, looking like he's about to ask more, but thankfully he doesn't. "Good. Let's get going. Ben's almost here."

They walk out the entrance of the hotel just as a grey, boxy van pulls up, the chugging noise of its ancient engine making Georgia's stomach churn. She has heard plenty of stories about these antiquated Russian *furgons* roaming the countryside, but she never thought she would be riding in one.

"You're in excellent hands," Miller says, as if sensing her uncertainty. "Ben's one of the very best. He's a tough nut to crack, but I trust him with my life. We served in the army together, and he's saved me . . . too many times."

Staring at his choice of transport, Georgia wonders who's going to be saving them out in the Mongolian wilderness when the mechanical beast breaks down.

The van rolls to a stop, coughing and spluttering as it shuts off, and Georgia's eyes widen further as she watches the driver step out of the vehicle. The man is huge, towering over her at over two metres tall. Even Miller is dwarfed by him. He's wearing a black t-shirt stretched taught across his expansive chest, tan cargo pants, and polished boots. His features are rough, his nose looks as if it's been broken more than once, and there's a jagged scar directly above his right eyebrow. The scruffy beard and dark, shoulder-length hair make him look like he belongs to a nomadic tribe of an ancient time, a warrior-herder who's seen a lot of hard work and too much sun.

Agent Miller's usual solemn face breaks into a brilliant smile, and he steps forward to shake the burly man's hand, pumping it enthusiastically.

"Ben, meet Professor Lee," Miller says as he turns to her.

"Call me Georgia."

She fakes a smile to hide her intimidation as her hand disappears into Ben's massive grip, feeling the roughness of his calloused palm. Ben doesn't say anything and doesn't return her smile. He gives her a curt nod instead, studying her with a dark, intense stare that makes her avert her gaze.

Miller gestures to the van and cocks a brow. "You sure that's gonna make it? How fast does it go?"

Ben pats the side of the vehicle with obvious affection. His voice is a deep baritone as he replies, and Georgia is surprised to hear a Southern American drawl not unlike Miller's. "They don't build things to last like this anymore. This all-wheel-drive is as reliable as they come, and much easier to fix out on the steppes where there are no garages. You can't travel that fast on the tracks out where we're going, anyway."

Miller shrugs, satisfied by his response. "You're the boss, bro. Here, everything you've asked for." He hands the black cases to Ben, and the two men exchange a knowing look.

With a few final words, the three of them utter their goodbyes, and Miller turns to disappear through the hotel entrance.

Ben picks up Georgia's large backpack as if it weighs nothing. He tosses it into the rear of the van with brusque efficiency and heads towards the driver's door. Georgia takes that as a silent cue that they are leaving and scurries to the passenger side just as he starts the engine, climbing into the spacious interior.

She cries out with surprise when something wet and furry presses against the back of her neck. Swivelling, Georgia comes face-to-face with a fully grown German Shepherd panting hot air onto her cheeks. The reek of its doggy breath makes her scrunch up her nose.

"Oh. Hello." She laughs, scratching the canine under its neck as it leans into her hand. "Where'd you come from?"

"You alright with dogs?" Ben asks.

"I love dogs," she replies. "What's its name?"

"Indi."

"Hi, Indi. I'm Georgia."

Indi responds by lapping at her cheek. She chuckles, but the sound tapers off when she feels Ben's stare boring into her profile. He doesn't seem happy about the affectionate exchange between them at all.

She lets go of Indi and turns back to the front as Ben pulls out of the hotel car park.

His voice is gruff as he asks: "Tell me where we're headed, Professor."

"Well, I don't know how much Agent Miller has told you—"

"I've been fully briefed. Assume I know as much as him."

"Oh. Okay." Georgia is taken aback by his clipped tone. Miller's right, his replacement is a pretty cantankerous guy. She just hopes his ill manner doesn't end up affecting their work together. "I think I've figured out where the Russians will be going first."

"Where?"

"Avarga."

23

BEN'S GRIP tightens on the steering wheel as he navigates the van through traffic. The streets are especially busy this time of the year, and dusty vehicles with deep-treaded tyres crowd the highways, all wrestling for a way out of the city.

His eyes dart up and down the road as they inch along, his anxiety piqued. When on mission, Ben's constantly assessing possible dangers, looking for points of vulnerability, sizing up every potential opponent in sight. But nothing he does can ever contain the risk inherent in crowds. The unpredictability of people has always been the wild card in his line of work, and the throng has him watching for probable threats at every turn. Even though most would argue that Ulaanbaatar is far from being populous relative to other cities in the world, it still accommodates over forty-five percent of the country's population, and compared to where he lives on the steppes it feels absolutely teeming with people.

He hasn't visited the capital in at least six months, and the past few hours have been a startling reminder of why

he hates cities. The chaos and filth of the densely populated metropolis is a permeating, odious atmosphere that
blankets everything in sight. It overwhelms all of his
senses at once, infiltrating his mind and chafing at the back
of his brain like a scratchy woollen sweater, waiting for
him to become accustomed to the constant assault of stim-
ulus, until he's finally manipulated into believing that all
of this is somehow normal. He's sure if he stays long
enough, he'll soon be wandering the streets like the other
zombies, taking selfies and mindlessly scrolling through
their phones.

All of it fills him with disgust. It makes him feel
tainted. It has him itching to get the hell out of this putre-
fied cesspool, to jump into a river and scrub until his skin
is raw.

He brings the van to a stop at a traffic light, and
seconds later, a black Mercedes G Wagon rolls up next to
him. The Wagon's passenger has his window down, and
loud music pumps through the powerful speakers: a track
of a high-pitched Mongolian woman's voice juxtaposed
with the low tone of deep throat singing and a background
beat of contemporary rap.

The muscles in Ben's neck bunch up. His pulse escalates to the booming rhythm of the song. He glares at the
driver and the passenger in the Wagon synchronously
bobbing their heads to the chorus, and he tries to determine if they are hostiles he needs to take out.

Behind him, Indi whines. She presses her muzzle to the
back of his neck, puffing warm air against his skin.

He squeezes his eyes shut. *For fuck's sake, Ben. Keep it
together. They're just a couple of rich kids having fun.* He takes
a deep inhale, then exhales slowly through his mouth.

The light turns green, and the G Wagon races off with a

screech. Feeling at once rattled and ashamed by the encounter, Ben puts the *furgon* into gear again and continues on down the road out of town.

You can do this. Remember what Brandon said. Just like riding a bike.

They pass a power station with looming cooling towers by the river, spewing out plumes of white steam and smoke as it struggles to meet the growing demands of the population. There are construction cranes everywhere, ceaselessly pushing the boundaries of the burgeoning metropolis outwards. Giant, identical residential blocks reminiscent of a recent Communist era dominate much of the city, each of them branded with a number like cattle in a herd.

Most tourists are surprised at how modern Ulaanbaatar is when they arrive. They come here with their romantic notions of Mongolia, dreaming of a last frontier with roaming horses, white *gers* puffing out smoke through their central chimneys, and nomadic herders with round faces and ruddy cheeks. But they never expect the clean and tidy bitumen roads, the towering high-rises, the ever-expanding presence of engineering firms attracted by the mining boom, the fancy condos and luxury car dealerships, and the snobby international schools to accompany it all.

The reality is that the capital is a clash of the new against the old, at times both fighting to gain dominance, other times intertwining to create a strange hybrid. On the outskirts of town are the *ger* districts, slum areas with leaning wooden fences, a clutter of brightly coloured roofs and large round *gers*. Cyrillic text appears side-by-side with traditional vertical Mongolian script. Chinggis Khan's image and name are everywhere you look, greeting visitors at the international airport and prevalent on posters, t-shirts and fridge magnets. There are even beers and vodkas named after him.

Ben eyes the professor seated to his right, who has been quietly absorbing the surrounding sights with wide-eyed fascination. It is obvious it's her first time here. Even though Ben has practically memorised the dossier on her, she is far from what he imagined in person. With her dainty frame, long black hair and elfin face, she looks hardly old enough to be involved in this case, much less to be a respected expert in archaeology. Large brown eyes dominate her Asian features, making her appear almost childlike and naive at first sight. But the palpable air of melancholy ages her somewhat, and Ben is reminded of the recent trauma she has experienced with the murder of her friends, Ethan Sommers and Hiroshi Akiyama.

He presses his lips together. For the hundredth time in the past two days, he questions whether he made the right decision in taking on this case. The calming influence of the steppes seems so far away now, and the last place he wants to be is driving through this madness as he babysits some academic with her own set of emotional baggage, while they head for some unknown danger that could get them both killed. Lord knows he's got plenty of his own demons to deal with.

He mentally curses Brandon Miller again, the devious little fuck with his disarming smile, who knew exactly the right things to say and the buttons to push so that Ben could not refuse him. The agent understands him too well and has used that to his advantage. He knows that Ben cannot turn a brother away who comes calling in need, that guilt would plague the ex-SF's mind until he finally gave in. And even though Ben was perfectly aware of the agent's ploy, he still could not for the life of him say no. *That* is how thoroughly the army has trained him.

Besides, he needs the money. Brandon has ensured that Ben will be more than well-compensated for his services. The sum offered by the DIA would fund his medical supplies for the next year and more.

Accepting his fate, he sighs with resignation and throws a glance to the right again, saying, "Tell me about Avarga, Professor."

She turns towards him, looking as if she's startled that he spoke. Faint lines appear between her eyebrows. *Did she forget I was in the car?*

"I prefer Georgia," she says, not replying to his question.

Ben resists the urge to roll his eyes. "Fine. *Georgia.* Tell me about Avarga."

Again, she doesn't answer him. Her gaze travels lower instead, and she points at his right thigh. "Is that really necessary?"

Ben stares at her accusatory finger, then at the pistol that's holstered above his knee. He had it concealed at his waist when he picked her up at the hotel, but as soon as they were away from prying eyes he moved it to where it was more comfortable for him—not to mention, more accessible while he's seated in a vehicle like this.

With a scoff, he returns his gaze to the road. "Of course it is. I carry it at all times when I'm on a mission."

Her frown deepens. "But we're just driving. I hate guns. They make me uncomfortable."

This time, Ben *does* roll his eyes. "That's because you're Australian," he retorts with barely disguised contempt. "You're working with the Americans now. I suggest you get used to it. Miller always keeps one in his shoulder holster or strapped to his ankle. Just because you didn't see it doesn't mean it wasn't there."

The professor's pretty mouth drops open at his abrasive response, and the corners of Ben's lips twitch as he pushes down an unexpected flutter of satisfaction in his chest. She sits there, fuming, then turns with a huff to stare out her window, apparently fascinated with whatever is going on out there.

So. This is how it's gonna be. Unfazed, he returns his attention to the traffic.

The van is silent as they edge out of the city, and Ben's hold on the wheel gradually relaxes as evidence of civilisation falls away. Out here, there are more animals and abundant open space, with fewer cars and people.

He tries again after an hour passes. "Tell me about Avarga."

Georgia releases a long sigh and turns away from the window. Her gaze falls on everything except him as she explains: "Avarga was the old capital during Chinggis Khan's time."

"I thought he was a nomad. Didn't he live in a mobile *ger* and rule from horseback?"

"Yes, but Avarga was his base camp," she replies. "The site was chosen because it was close to where he was born, and it was where his family stayed when he was away on long campaigns. As Chinggis' power grew and as he conquered more people and more lands, boundless treasure flowed in from all the Mongol tributary states. Chinggis needed somewhere to store and administer all that wealth. So he allowed some buildings to be constructed near the Avarga Stream. The complex was called the Yellow Palace, and it was where the succession of the Mongol Empire was decided, where Chinggis' son

Ogodei was eventually enthroned, and where *The Secret History* was commissioned and completed."

Ben nods as he understands what the professor is getting at. "The Khan was buried with his riches, so it makes sense that his grave would be where the treasure was stored."

"Yes," she confirms. "In fact, there have already been excavation attempts at Avarga. After the collapse of the Soviet Union and the fall of communism in 1991, Mongolia was finally opened to outsiders again. Archaeologists from all over the world flooded in, eager to solve the enduring mystery of Chinggis Khan's missing tomb. The Japanese got here first with their Three Rivers Project in 1992, and Avarga was one of the places they excavated."

"What did they find?"

"A few ditches, some remnants of stone walls." Georgia shrugs. "The report was superficial. But the archaeologist leading the team was almost certain that Chinggis' grave is in the area."

"And you think the Russians would be going to Avarga first because of this?"

"Well, yes. But there's also another reason, probably a more important one."

Ben throws her a questioning glance, waiting for her to go on.

"I keep asking myself what I would do if I were in Anya's position," Georgia says. "The saddle she took from China is most likely fake. The first verse of the riddle on the *sulde* doesn't reveal anything else that's useful. And she doesn't have the second verse we uncovered at the National Palace Museum, either. She might have extracted more information from the *sulde*. But maybe she hasn't. Really, the clues have been pretty cryptic so far, and I'll bet she's not going to solve it all straight away. There was something else Ethan told me, though, when he first showed me the Spirit Banner. He said that Mr. Akiyama had told Hiroshi to find Dr. Ken Fujimoto. He'd said Fujimoto would know what to do with the *sulde*."

"But Hiroshi couldn't get in contact with Fujimoto," Ben counters, recalling the detail from the case file.

"That's right. And I got my assistant Sarah to call around the academic circles to find out why. Turns out Fujimoto goes away every summer to resume his long-term excavation project in Avarga."

Ben arches his brows.

Georgia continues: "Fujimoto has been leading a Japanese-Mongolian team, and the project has been going on for years. Every August, the scientists would return to the site to uncover more of the ruined city. Dr. Fujimoto is the top on-the-ground expert on the latest archaeological findings in Mongolia when it comes to Chinggis Khan and the Mongol Empire."

"And you believe that Anya's going after him to find out what he knows about the *sulde*," Ben summarises.

"Yes." She chews on her bottom lip, suddenly looking worried. "How long do you think it'll take for us to get there?"

Ben shakes his head as he steps on the accelerator. "In Mongolia, we never ask that question. It's considered bad luck."

24

THE REASON behind Ben's comment soon becomes clear to Georgia as paved roads give way to makeshift trails and progress slows to a crawling pace. Their old Russian hunk of junk bounces and bumps its way over corrugated, pothole-ridden tracks, its innards making a cacophony of squeaking and thumping noises, filling the heavy silence between the passengers.

Ben rolls up his window, and Georgia follows his example to shut out the blooming cloud of dirt. It does little to prevent the infiltration, though. Everything is covered in a layer of dust.

The temperature in the van begins to climb.

She looks back to check on Indi, discovering that the dog has nestled herself in a custom-built hammock-style cot. The weighted canvas swings as the *furgon* jolts and jiggles, but keeps its occupant snug in place. Indi is snoring, completely unfazed by it all, obviously accustomed to the entire process.

Driving in Mongolia is evidently an experience in its own

right, and Georgia can understand why nobody likes to commit to a time frame. The roads are made in true DIY fashion here, a sort of Choose-Your-Own-Adventure escapade as dirt tracks separate into lanes of three or four or five, snaking along the great plains for miles on end before rejoining again at a later point. Sheep, cows, horses, and goats sprinkle across the steppes, roaming and grazing freely, and Ben has to honk and bark at them to clear the way.

With no landmarks in sight, the landscape looks exactly the same to Georgia in every direction. But her companion seems to know the land well, and he navigates the journey without the aid of a map, handling the drive with expert confidence.

They travel in silence for hours, inching along at thirty kilometres an hour. As the sun descends in the sky, they pass a creek, next to which a family has set up camp. The adults are bathing their children in the water as the youngsters splash about with delight. Ben drives on, and soon they encounter a collection of cars and groups of locals gathered around a small wooden shed. Up ahead on the gentle slope, Georgia spots a large, empty, fenced-off area, and beyond that, a single-storey building in the far distance.

She straightens in her seat. "Is this it? Are we here?"

"Looks like it," Ben grunts.

He guides the van along the steel fence line, spanning about five-hundred metres on one side and a kilometre on the other. As he brings the chugging vehicle to a stop at the gate, Georgia jumps out, grateful to be on her feet again. There are tiny holes all over the dry, dusty ground, and gophers leap between the burrows as she strides over to the perimeter of the enclosure. Flies instantly gather like a veil, and she swats to drive them away with little success.

She notes the erected sign to the left of the entrance, which confirms the location as the archaeological site of Avarga in both Mongolian and English. Within the boundary, the ground is covered with overgrown grass. It appears there hasn't been an excavation here for a while.

Where is everyone?

Her eyes scan the entire area again, her heart dropping as she takes it all in. Something doesn't feel right.

This cannot be the location of Chinggis Khan's tomb.

BEN GLANCES at Georgia as they get back in the vehicle. Her bottom lip caught between her teeth, the professor seems to be deep in thought. She must have seen something revealing at the Avarga site, because he can practically hear the cogs of her mind working. Whatever it is, he hopes it's going to be helpful to them.

He takes the van further up the slope towards the single-storey brick building, the first construction they have seen since leaving Ulaanbaatar. It's a modest-sized, rectangular dwelling surrounded by a low picket fence. To the rear, there's a row of five *gers* and a twenty-foot shipping container, probably used for storage. The only vehicle in sight is the old motorbike parked outside the *ger* to the right.

Ben stops in front of the white felt tent, scanning the whole compound. There's no one around. Still, as a precaution, he remains inside the van until a middle-aged man walks out the door.

"I'll ask the questions," Ben says to Georgia. "You have a look around and see if you can find any information."

She agrees with a silent nod. Tucking his weapon out of sight, Ben exits the *furgon* with Georgia and Indi following closely behind.

The Mongolian man tips his head at Ben in greeting, then stares at Georgia for a beat too long. His dark, leathery skin is roughened by exposure and Ben suspects he's actually much younger than he appears. As Ben approaches, the older man says in Mongolian, "Here to see the museum?"

"Yes." Ben improvises, hiding his surprise. He had no idea there would be a museum on the broad open plains out here.

Ben introduces himself and Georgia, explaining that he's her guide, a professor who's here to conduct some research on the surrounding area.

"Erden," the caretaker says as he gestures to himself. Again, his eyes linger on the professor. "The museum closed at five. But I can still take you through if you like."

Erden guides them to the brick building, taking out a bunch of keys to unlock the front door. A sign on the wall reads:

Archaeological Research Centre
Museum of "Khuduu Aral"

As Georgia disappears into the dwelling behind Erden, Ben turns to his dog, pointing to the ground with a firm command: "Stay. Keep an eye out."

Indi huffs in response, circling the spot as Ben steps through the entrance.

Erden conducts a very succinct, very underwhelming

tour of the establishment. To the rear, there are accommodation quarters and offices for the archaeologists. In the front two rooms, some of the artefacts and photographs from excavations of the nearby sites are displayed.

Georgia ambles off, the exhibits already capturing her interest, leaving Ben to talk to Erden.

"We heard that there may be a dig going on out there," Ben says, pointing through the window.

"Yep, every summer," Erden confirms. "Season's about to start soon. The team arrives in three days. Dr. Fujimoto is here already, though."

"Dr. Fujimoto?" Ben feigns ignorance.

"He's the one leading the team. He always gets here a week early, before everyone else arrives."

"Can we meet him?" Ben gestures to Georgia. "The professor would probably like to ask him some questions about his work."

Erden shakes his head. "He's not here right now. He's gone to another site. The team may be doing some investigations there this year."

"Where did he head to? Maybe we can find him there."

"Öglögchiin Kherem," Erden tells him, pointing to the location on the map.

"He's on his own?"

"Yeah, just checking out the site before the others arrive."

"What kind of car does Dr. Fujimoto drive?"

Erden looks surprised by the question. But with a shrug he answers, "Same thing everyone else drives around here, a Toyota Prius."

From the corner of his eye, Ben spots the professor wandering around the exhibition room, studying the displays on the walls and taking photos of almost everything in sight. She seems fascinated by what's on show here, studying each item with careful attention.

Ben frowns, taking note of the peculiar way she moves. Graceful and ethereal, she looks as if she weighs nothing and is walking on air. Nothing she does seems to take any effort. He's never seen anything like it.

Strange.

"You know, you're not the only ones who have been looking for Dr. Fujimoto," Erden says, snapping Ben's attention back to him.

"Is that so?"

"Yesterday another couple came 'round here. Russians, I think they were. Told me they were fans of Dr. Fujimoto's work." He nods, smiling. "Good-looking woman."

25

"WE SHOULD GO AFTER THEM NOW," Georgia says as she paces in front of Ben, a sense of urgency and unease bubbling through her.

"No," Ben retorts, retrieving the tents out of the van. "It's too risky."

They're parked by the stream with a handful of other local families, who have all made the pilgrimage here for the healing water that springs from deep in the ground. The small shed next to the creek houses a pump which draws the water out, and visitors come with plastic containers to bottle the naturally fizzy drink. Bathed in the orange light of dusk, children run around in the shallow brook while adults sit by small fires, chatting and laughing as they chug back bottles of vodka. Indi canters around the rowdy kids with her tongue lolling about and her fur slick with moisture. The days are long here; it is now almost nine o'clock but the sun still hovers over the horizon.

"But Fujimoto could be in real danger," Georgia argues, watching the burly man set up camp for the night.

"He could be dead by now for all we know," Ben says, not looking at her as he performs his task with efficiency. "But as soon as that sun sets, we'll be blind out there. It's going to be a moonless night. I won't be able to see a thing, and we'll most likely end up in some ditch. Worse, we might run into a stray herd. And with our lights on, our enemy would spot us coming from miles away." He shakes his head. "No. We stay here tonight. It's much safer. We'll leave at the crack of dawn, and with any luck, we'll catch the Russians before they wake for the day."

Georgia falls quiet, hating that he's right. She can't shake the feeling that they're wasting valuable time. Her chance to avenge Ethan's death seems so tenuous now, an infuriating thought when Anya is merely a few hours' drive away. But from the expression on Ben's face, she knows he's unlikely to change his mind.

With a frustrated sigh, she walks over to help him set up the tents. The sky darkens quickly, but before long, Ben has raised a fire and is cooking dinner. Children retire for the night, and Indi comes back to join them by the fire. Ignoring the loud protests of both Georgia and Ben, she wiggles her backside like a young pup, the quake spreading along her body as she shakes off the water in her coat, dousing her human companions.

They eat in silence, the unceremonious affair over within minutes. Ben gets up to perform a few checks on the van's engine, and Georgia scoots closer to the fire, pulling on the blanket around her as she studies her stack of academic papers. She's surprised at the drastic drop in temperature as soon as the sun has disappeared. At midday, she was burning up in the oven-hot, fly-infested *furgon*. Now, she's cold even with her thermals on.

She senses Ben's sudden presence behind her, wrapping her in another layer of blanket. He hands her a hot-water bottle swaddled in felt.

"Here," he says, his voice low. "This will keep you warm for the night."

Surprised by the kind gesture, she accepts it, murmuring her thanks. He settles down by the fire with Indi snuggling up to him.

"Do you know anything about the site of Öglögchiin Kherem, where Dr. Fujimoto has gone?" Ben asks.

Georgia nods. "It was another place excavated by the Japanese Three Rivers Project. Öglögchiin Kherem is more commonly known as 'Almsgivers Wall,' or 'Chinggis Khan's Castle.' It's also high on the contenders list for Chinggis' burial site. Archaeological digs have uncovered at least sixty ancient graves in the area, leading to the rumour that the tombs of The Great Khans could be located there."

"The tombs of The Great Khans?"

"Yeah. 'The Great Khan' title didn't just belong to Chinggis, it was also bestowed on each succeeding Khan who ruled over the greater empire. When a Great Khan died, he was transported back from wherever he died to the Mongol homeland for the funeral. It's believed that the Golden Family members were all buried in the same location, because none of their tombs have ever been discovered."

"So what we're looking for isn't just Chinggis' grave, it's actually his family mausoleum?"

"Yes."

Ben scratches his beard, then asks, "And what do you believe? Does Almsgivers Wall contain the tombs of The Great Khans?"

"I don't know." She stares at the fire, contemplating this. "Dr. Fujimoto would be the best person to ask about it. He's had a lot more experience on the ground than me." She gestures to her pile of reading material. "I really need to go through more of the research papers on the area. And I have to see the site first. There's a large rock formation there, known as 'Chinggis Khan's Saddle'. It may be significant since the clue on the *sulde* mentions *the seat of the Golden Khan*."

"Haven't you already disproved the saddle theory?"

"In a way, yes. The riddle seemed to refer to the 'seat of the soul', the portrait of Chinggis. But Mongolian writing is full of double meanings. I believe it's still worth checking out."

"And what about the site here, Avarga?"

"I had my suspicions about this place when we first arrived. I don't think this could be where Chinggis Khan was buried."

"Why not?"

"The exhibits at the museum indicate that Avarga was the town centre, where Mongol families stayed while their warriors were away on campaigns. The geography of the location just doesn't fit the requirements of an imperial tomb. Mongolians don't like having their graves walked over, and this area is too open, too exposed, and too accessible to people and animals alike. The topography of the region is mostly flat. Even dogs, considered as guardian angels in Mongolia, are buried high in the hills so people don't trample over their remains. The Mongols would have chosen a higher, more sheltered place for their Great Khan's grave."

"Makes sense," Ben says, absorbing the information. "It seems Dr. Fujimoto is our best bet in getting some answers. Let's hope he's still alive, and that we catch the Russians by surprise in the morning."

Georgia murmurs her agreement, watching him as he twists open a small bottle of Chinggis Khan Vodka. Ben takes a long swig, then offers it to her. When she declines, he says, "It'll warm you up."

She accepts the liquor, taking a small sip and feeling the alcohol burn down her throat. Coughing, she hands the bottle back, grimacing at the sharp taste as she swipes at her lips.

Nasty.

Ben chuckles, the sound deep and resonant in his chest. He takes another drink and replaces the cap. Georgia gives him a wan smile. This is the most relaxed she has seen him. She was beginning to think that the expression of scorn was permanently etched on his face.

Without thinking, she blurts out the question that has been on her mind: "How does a US Special Forces guy with a Purple Heart also have a background in linguistics?"

Ben tenses visibly at the sudden enquiry, his sharp gaze cutting to her. "Miller told you I have a Purple Heart?"

Georgia chides herself for her unexpected curiosity. Why the hell did she even ask? She should really just focus on reading her papers. Or go to bed. It's best to minimise any kind of interactions with these mercurial Americans. But Ben pins her in place with a fierce glare that she's quickly associating with his personality.

Licking her lips, she admits, "Yeah. He did."

His nostrils flare. "What else did *Agent* Brandon Miller tell you?"

"He said . . . that they ran out of medals to give you in

the army, that you saved his life many times, and that he trusts you as if you were his own brother."

Ben's chest rises and falls as the muscles of his jaws tick. "That's all he said?"

"Yeah. Pretty much."

He exhales, and when he speaks again, his voice is softer. "I studied foreign languages at college before enlisting. I've always had an interest in it, I guess, maybe because I grew up bilingual."

"How many languages do you speak now?" She frowns, annoyed at her piqued interest.

Stop asking him questions, Georgia.

"Six," he says, then adds, "Bits of Russian too, but my brother's the Russian expert."

Georgia is impressed. "Miller said that you're a Daur Mongolian?"

"Half. My mother's side. I grew up with her nomadic family as a kid. Then I was sent away to live with my father's family in the States."

"I bet your mum is happy that you're back in Mongolia."

"I never saw her again. She died a few years after I left."

"Oh. I'm sorry."

Ben hunches his shoulders and drops his gaze, his expression undecipherable. He strokes Indi's head as she leans against his leg. The dog stretches open her maw with a languid yawn.

Clearing his throat, Ben's voice is brusque as he says, "It's late. Get some sleep."

Without another word, he rises and disappears into his tent with Indi. Georgia stares after him, unsure of what to make of his abrupt departure. The fire begins to dwindle. With a sense of resignation, she picks up her belongings and trudges to her own tent, knowing that it'll be another sleepless night for her.

26

ANYA COCKS HER HEAD, watching Dr. Fujimoto's ashen face with profound fascination as Lev shovels dirt over the man's lifeless body. Fujimoto's vacant eyes stare up into nothing, his blue lips parted in a silent sigh.

There's something remarkably intriguing about observing the end of a life. No matter how many times she's seen the myriad ways a person takes his final breath, she never tires of the experience. Anya's hardly the romantic type, but she finds the process inexplicably poetic, as if she is witnessing the dissolution of an entire universe in a single, insignificant being.

In the shallow grave, the Japanese archaeologist's face begins to disappear under the mounting soil. Anya slowly rises to her feet, stretching out her weary, yet satisfied, body. They've been up all night, extracting all manner of information from Fujimoto while he screamed, cried, and begged for mercy.

And it has been a fruitful effort.

Anya had her short list of potential sites to visit before

her team arrived in Mongolia, but she knew she had to make quick decisions on each location to eliminate them, one by one. There is no opportunity for extensive investigations and time-consuming digs. Even though the country is sparsely populated with not much law enforcement about, she's still wary of drawing too much attention to themselves. She has reduced her team to the essential three: herself, Lev Ivanov for security, and Alexey Morozov as the expert in scientific imaging. The fewer people involved, the easier it is for her to maintain control. She is loath to repeat the drama of what happened in Australia.

Fujimoto was her shortcut, and the man has been extremely helpful indeed. With his last breaths he even whispered in her ear where he thinks the tomb really is. Anya smiles at the memory now, knowing it's only a matter of time before she achieves her ultimate goal. For the first time since the Spirit Banner was stolen by the Japanese, she feels her objective within grasp. It's so close, she can almost smell the ripened fragrance of sweet success.

From her elevated viewpoint, she surveys the entire site of Almsgivers Wall below her and can understand why this place is also called Chinggis Khan's Castle. Situated on a steep hillock and sheltered by trees and boulders, there are fir-lined hills flanking both sides of the valley leading up to the site, making the place an ideal location for a fortress. You could see the enemy coming from miles away.

She gazes out towards the horizon, yawning as fatigue takes over. The sky is a deep shade of mauve as dawn approaches, and a morning mist hovers low over the grassy plains. A faint glint of light in the scanty woodland catches her eye, and she reaches into her bag for her night vision binoculars. She frowns as she zeroes in on the vehicle, which goes in and out of sight as it weaves around the trees.

The notion of sleep quickly dissipates. She barks at Lev. "We got company."

The soldier comes to her side, peering through the scope of his semi-automatic rifle.

"It's a van," he reports in Russian. "I can make out two subjects."

The faces of the driver and passenger become clearer as Anya zooms in. Her heart flutters with delight when she recognises the woman.

She smiles.

"Aw. Professor Lee," Anya murmurs. She has suspected—or rather, hoped—that Georgia would come looking for her.

A little quiver travels down to her navel and beyond as she stares at the Asian woman.

She swallows.

She trains her focus on the driver, but does not recognise him. In fact, he looks like a local, and is not the DIA operative who infiltrated her team.

"I can take them both out now," Lev says with his eye to the scope, leaning on a boulder to get into position.

"No." Reaching over, Anya presses the end of his rifle down. "Get Alexey. Pack up the truck. We're leaving."

"But—"

"Now," she orders sternly.

The big man sulks, grumbling low in his throat. He stalks away, yelling at Alexey to get his shit together.

Anya smiles as she takes one last look at Georgia through the scope. She's curious to find out if the esteemed archaeologist will live up to her reputation.

"Time to see if you're up for a little race, Professor Lee."

27

BEN STOMPS ON THE BRAKE, bringing the van to a halt.

"What's wrong?" Georgia asks. "Why have we stopped?"

He holds up his hand, gesturing for her silence as he squints at the hillock ahead through the fir tree branches. He lifts the binoculars to his eyes, scanning the entire area.

Nothing moves.

The site looks abandoned. There's not a vehicle in sight, not even Dr. Fujimoto's Toyota Prius. But the tension in his gut does not ease. Something has made him stop, and he doesn't know what it is.

He doesn't like it.

Their destination is located on a hill, giving the enemy a higher vantage point. On approach, Ben steered the *furgon* into the forest and switched off his lights to avoid detection. And even though he cannot find a soul out there now, he can't ignore the angst rising within him.

"Stay." He issues a firm command to Indi as he switches off the engine. Then, looking at Georgia, he orders, "You stay, too."

Judging from Georgia's expression, she's not accustomed to being told what to do, but Ben gets out of the vehicle before she has a chance to argue. He quickly covers the remaining distance with his Glock drawn, approaching the edge of the woods. He looks out to the hillock again. A long, dry-stone wall marks the boundary at the bottom of the ridge, giving Almsgivers Wall its famed name. The place is covered with long grass, dotted with trees and boulders, and a thin blanket of morning mist floats just above the land. He sees no movement or evidence of the Russians, but there are plenty of places to hide.

Crouching low, he leaves the protection of the woods and approaches the wall with caution. The sky has changed from a deep purple to a spectrum of peach and blue, and the frosty grass crunches beneath his boots. When he's almost reached the stone boundary, he halts as the hairs at the back of his neck stand on end.

He spots a hearth to the right over the erected barrier. Small tendrils of smoke rise from the centre in the chilly morning air. The fire hasn't been out for long.

He ducks behind the wall quickly, pressing his back against the rocks. A few hundred yards away, he sees Georgia standing by the edge of the forest.

Fuck.

"Get down!" he bellows, as the first of the gunfire bursts through the silence.

He curses as one of the bullets hits Georgia, sending a spray of blood onto the tree trunk. She screams as she staggers, falling to the ground.

"Get cover!" he yells again, returning a few rounds over the wall.

The shooter aims for him, bullets ricocheting off the thick barricade behind him. Ben returns fire, shooting blind, spraying slugs in the direction of the giant boulders on the hill. Looking back towards Georgia, he sees with relief that she's crawled behind a tree, leaving a bright trail of red smeared across the frost-tipped grass.

Shit.

Ben didn't see where she was hit. She could be bleeding out right now. His training as an army medic kicks in, and he can barely stop himself from running towards her. His heart catapults into overdrive, and he teeters on the verge of panic. All he hears is the clamorous rush of blood in his ears.

Fuck. Fuck. Fuck.

He cannot lose her. He cannot have another casualty on his watch.

He takes a deep breath. He closes his eyes. Then he snaps his eyes open again once he's got his priorities straight.

Get the shooter, Ben. Take him out.

The professor needs you.

28

GEORGIA CRADLES HER LEFT ARM, wincing in pain. Echoes of gunfire reverberate through the air and her ears start ringing. Several hundred metres away, Indi is barking wildly in the van.

She looks down at her injury, peeling back the torn fabric of her shirt. There is blood everywhere. At the sight, her limbs tingle and go weak as darkness crowds the edges of her vision, threatening to close in. Her breath comes in short, panicked gasps. She shakes her head and blinks a few times, fighting to stay focused.

She cannot pass out now.

Taking a deep inhale, Georgia examines the gash on her upper arm. As far as she can tell the bullet has only grazed her flesh, making a superficial yet gaping wound that is bleeding profusely. Dark blood oozes out of the long, open hole, streaming down her skin.

Ripping off the damaged arm of her long-sleeved shirt, she winds it tightly around the laceration. She turns back to check on Ben, who has now risen to his feet, returning fire at the enemy. Up the hill to the far right, a black truck speeds out of the cover of some trees, heading straight over the ridge. Its passenger window is down and bright orange sparks burst through in the dim twilight. A few bullets whistle over her head, and she quickly ducks down, pressing her face to the ground.

Then, silence.

Indi continues her barking, alternating with intervals of high-pitched whines. Footfalls rush towards Georgia, and she looks up to see Ben drop to the ground beside her.

"Where're you hurt?" he asks, his voice frantic. "Where'd you get hit?"

Ben helps her up to a sitting position, reaching for her left arm. She flinches back with alarm, holding it protectively. The area of the wound has already gone numb, and she suspects it's begun to heal under her makeshift bandage.

She cannot let Ben see it. If he finds out about her healing abilities, he'd hand her straight over to the DIA. Miller's admission rings clear in her mind: the covert intelligence unit he works for, and their interest in creating super soldiers. Georgia has no doubt they would go to great lengths to get what they want. She would become their latest test subject until they can replicate her condition.

Her gut clenches. She will not allow her condition to be weaponised.

"Let me help, Georgia," Ben says sternly, reaching for her again. "I was a medic in the Special Forces. I can get the bullet out for you."

"No." She turns so that her arm is out of his reach, pushing his hand away. "It's just a graze. The bullet scraped me, that's all. I'll be okay."

"Let me dress it, then. We have to stop the bleeding. You'll probably need stitches. And I must sanitise—"

"I said I'm *fine*," she snaps.

At her harsh tone, Ben draws back sharply. He stares at her with his dark eyes, the muscles of his jaw working, the veins popping in his neck. He looks as if he's about to lose it, and Georgia doesn't miss the twitch in his fingers before he quickly balls his hands up in fists.

He stands abruptly. A long moment of heavy silence falls between them as they glare at one another, each waiting for the other to give in.

After what seems like minutes, Ben finally breaks eye contact, letting out an aggravated growl. "The Russians are gone," he clips coldly. "I counted three in the car, but I could be wrong. I couldn't see if Fujimoto was with them."

Georgia nods, looking up at him with her arm still cradled. It doesn't hurt anymore, but she has to keep up the pretence for Ben's sake. And she needs to clean up, to wash all the blood off her arm.

A sudden thought hits her, and she asks, "Do you think they might come back?"

"The way they raced out of here? I doubt it. But I'm not taking any chances. I'm going to set up a perimeter to make sure we don't get ambushed again." He pauses, staring at her arm once more. He looks like he's about to say something else, but doesn't.

Without another word, Ben stalks over to the van, letting his still yawping dog out of the car.

29

"WHAT THE *FUCK* WAS THAT?!"

Lev Ivanov ducks his head at Anya's belligerent erup-
tion, half expecting the doctor to attack him from the back
seat of the truck. The woman is on a rampage, her
dramatic outburst more impressive than he's ever
witnessed.

Lev has never liked to retreat when the enemy makes a
move, not while he's got the advantage. He prefers to face
conflict head on, to take the offensive front and show the
adversary exactly where he stands. He knew that a few
bullets in the air would deter the professor and her driver
from coming after them as they made their exit.

He also had to see what they're up against. It is clear
now that the professor's companion isn't just an ordinary
local driver. In fact, they're lucky the man didn't put a
bullet through one of their tyres. Or the windows. From
the look of him, Lev guesses that the guy is probably
another intelligence operative, or military.

Plus, Lev was itching to see what Anya would say if he

nipped the professor. Just a little. Anya's over-the-top reaction confirms his suspicions.

She has a thing for the Asian broad.

And Lev does not like it.

Over the past many months of working together, Anya has been alternating from being an exasperating cocktease to a screaming, psycho bitch. She swings back and forth between the two any time it suits her and however she pleases, and the switch is always so abrupt it makes Lev's head spin. Whenever Anya decides to turn on her seductive charms, though, she never, ever gives him relief or satisfaction. It's got him so wound up—mentally, emotionally, sexually—he fears he may explode.

But Lev cannot help but play into her mind games. However screwed up it is, deep down, he's still hoping that she would finally fuck him after all this bullshit is over.

"I told you to leave Georgia alone," Anya shrieks again. "What part of that simple command did you not understand?"

"Jesus. Relax, will you? It was a little warning for them to back the hell off. If I wanted the professor dead, she'd be cold by now. I knew what I was doing. The bullet barely grazed her arm. No big deal."

His remark earns him a solid smack on the back of his head. Lev flinches, the assault inflicting more shock than pain. Then indignity overtakes everything else, and fury boils over. He has to white-knuckle the door handle to stop himself from turning around and unleashing his rage on his superior.

"When I give you an order, I expect you to follow it." Anya's voice is frosty as she bites out the words. "Do *not* disobey me again. Otherwise, I'll report your insubordination as a sign of treason. After that DIA mole, I can't be blamed for being too careful."

Lev snaps his mouth shut, chewing the inside of his cheeks until he can taste blood. He knows better than to retort. Even Alexey looks chastened as he manoeuvres the truck over the bumpy tracks.

From the rear-view mirror he sees Anya huff in frustration. She straightens her leather jacket, then turns her attention outside the window.

Within seconds, her expression is calm and controlled, and she issues her next directive to Alexey with authority: "Head north. We're going back to Siberia."

30

GEORGIA WATCHES from a distance as Indi leaps out of the van, circling Ben a few times before burying her nose in his open palms. Even with his back to her, Georgia can see the tension seep from his posture as he stoops to pat the canine, murmuring things she cannot hear.

Her heart softens at the sight. It is clear the man and his dog have a special bond.

She remains seated in the same spot with her back against the tree, taking some time to gather her wits as her mind goes over the events that have just unfolded. They've come here, hoping to take the Russians by surprise and to save Dr. Fujimoto at the same time. But Anya was clearly a few steps ahead of them and has got away yet again. They have no idea where Fujimoto is, or if he is still alive. The only positive outcome from all of this is that Ben and Indi are unhurt. She shivers at the thought of either of them being wounded instead of her.

The memory of Ethan's needle-marked arms and bruised face resurfaces in her brain, and anger swiftly consumes her. She gnashes her teeth as the acrid burn of hatred pumps through her veins, making her want to scream, to punch something with her bare fists. She realises she's never felt this way about anyone else before: this deep-seated loathing that clouds her mind and heats her blood with a murderous rage, dominating her head with fantasies of revenge.

She has a desperate urge to jump in the *furgon*, to go after the Russians like a woman possessed. To take Ben's gun and . . . No. She wants to make Anya suffer the way Ethan did. She wants to stab the woman with all the needles she can find—

Georgia blinks at the gruesome image. Horror and shame overcomes her, and she quickly shakes her head to dispel the notion. What the hell is she thinking?

Jesus, Georgia. What would Charlie say?

But her dear friend Charlie feels far away from her now. Instead, thoughts of Wang Jian crowd her mind: his contorted face in the gloomy light of the cave, the fury that radiated from him as he described how rage had driven him to cross oceans and continents in pursuit of retribution for his son's murder. Back then, Georgia couldn't fathom how anyone could harbour such hatred for centuries, or become so obsessed with vengeance that every action he took was for that end. She wondered if Charlie had been right, that perhaps madness was a possible physiological side effect of the elixir, evidenced also by the way Naaya's people had descended into lunacy.

But now, sitting in a forest in the middle of nowhere in Mongolia, with blood congealing over her arm and a gaping void inside her chest, she finds herself beginning to relate to the vindictive general.

From afar, Indi comes over to her in leaps and bounds,

breaking her out of reverie. The German Shepherd skids to a stop beside her, tentatively sniffing at her bandaged, bloody arm before letting out a soft whine. She then lavishes Georgia's face with a series of long licks.

"Hey," Georgia protests. She chuckles reluctantly as her sombre mood dissipates. "Stop that, Indi."

Indi emits a short bark, then steps back and waggles her tail as if waiting for Georgia to get up. Georgia rises to her feet, and with Indi at her heels she trudges towards the van to look for some water. She needs to wash the blood off her arm, as it is already encrusting over her skin. Ben is nowhere in sight, and she assumes he has gone to set up a perimeter like he promised.

The grey vehicle's rear door is left open, and she arrives to discover that the man has neatly laid out contents of the first aid kit for her to sanitise and dress her wound. Her heart skips a beat at his thoughtful gesture. Then she frowns, pushing the sentiment away.

Looking to check that he's not around, she sits down and removes her ruined shirt, cleaning the blood off her now perfectly healed arm. Her thoughts trail back to the day she met Wang Jian, as it has done countless times since. But today, she is seeing everything differently. She is beginning to view what happened in that cave in another light. Having lost Jacqui, and now Ethan, she can really empathise with the suffering he went through.

Eight weeks ago, east coast of Taiwan

GEORGIA COULD NOT MOVE.

She stared down at Mark Lambert's convulsing body on the

cave floor, horrified at the gurgling, strangled sounds bubbling out of his throat. The pungent scent of blood filled the dank chamber as inky liquid pooled around him. Charlie gripped her arm, drawing her back as the blood approached their feet.

Tears streamed down her cheeks as her attention moved to Mark's murderer, Wang Jian. Wang Jian's head was cleanly shaven, and his round face sported a goatee, the well-trimmed facial hair partially concealing a long, deep scar down the side of his right cheek. Short and stocky, his broad chest, sturdy build, and bow-legged stance made her think of a menacing bulldog. His dark, beady eyes had a brutish glimmer that would unnerve anyone he trained his gaze on.

This was the general who was sent by Emperor Qin over two thousand years ago to hunt down the imperial alchemist—Hsu Fu, now known as Charlie—when he never returned with the elixir.

She turned to Charlie. He looked as shocked as she was.

"I thought you told me Wang Jian died the night he killed your friend, Naaya," she said.

But Charlie wouldn't look at her, wouldn't acknowledge her remark.

Wang Jian chuckled, the eerie sound giving her the chills. Then he began to recount his story: a tale spanning two millennia, detailing his single-minded pursuit of Charlie, who had brutally murdered his only son. In spite of herself, being a mother who had also lost a child, Georgia could feel his pain in the most palpable way. Anguish and rage were clear on his face as he recounted the events. Charlie had cleverly evaded capture for centuries, but Wang Jian was able to use Georgia as a pawn in his elaborate scheme to at last lure out his prey.

That was the day she found out that her dear friend Charlie, who had found perfection and wisdom through centuries of meditation and study under sages, was not so perfect after all.

31

THE SUN IS high in the sky by the time Georgia hikes up the hill of Almsgivers Wall with Indi strolling by her side. The steep mound is covered by granite rocks and boulders, and wild flowers all shades of blue, red, orange, and purple grow in abundance in the tall grass. Horse flies as large as her thumb hover about, stinging her neck and any other exposed bits of skin. The giant pests attack Indi's ears too, making her bark and snap her jaws at them to no avail.

As they arrive at the foot of the huge rock formation known as "Chinggis Khan's Saddle," Indi lets out a yelp, crouching low to bat at her ears with her paw. She waggles her head and growls with crazed fervour, then, seeing Ben several hundred metres away, she bounds towards her owner, barking her protest.

Georgia smiles as she watches the bulky man tend to his dog's injuries. Then she looks at the pile of granite boulders looming over ten metres tall, and begins to climb up, finding petroglyphs etched on the surfaces of the rocks as she goes along. Some appear prehistoric, others probably less ancient, with most depicting hunters and their game. But there is one symbol she's never seen before that stands out from the rest:

She takes photographs and jots down notes for all of the images, making a mental note to send them to Sarah for clarification.

It doesn't take her long, and she's not even winded when she reaches the top. The view from here is majestic, and she can see the entire site below her, opening out towards the valley beyond. An impressive dry-stone wall of a few feet high partially encircles the ridge, spanning roughly three kilometres in length.

It is understandable why many would believe this place to be a potential burial site for Chinggis Khan. But after studying some of the research papers from Fujimoto this morning, she found conflicting evidence that suggests the wall may have been constructed during a pre-Mongol era, possibly dating back to the ancient Hun times. It would appear that the sixty graves uncovered here were also from the same period. Georgia now has strong suspicions that whatever the Russians found, it must have shown that the tomb isn't here. Especially since they abandoned the site so quickly.

A sharp whistle rings through the air, and Georgia peers down to see Ben waving at her from below, gesturing for her to join him. She clambers down with haste, and when she reaches him she sees that Indi is digging at a fresh pile of dirt.

"Stop that, Indi," Ben barks, grabbing the dog around the neck and pulling her aside.

As they move out of the way, Georgia finally sees the greyish skin of a face protruding out of the hole.

"Oh my God," she whispers.

With a grim expression, Ben says, "I think we may have just found Dr. Fujimoto."

32

LAPTOP IN HAND, Georgia lowers herself into the camping chair. She manages to establish an internet connection using Ben's satellite phone, quickly emailing images and information to Sarah and requesting her to do some research at the university archives.

She wonders what her assistant is doing now, and if she is still angry with everything that was said between them. *Most likely*, Georgia thinks. It is typical of Sarah to hold grudges.

But then again, Georgia reminds herself, Sarah is usually quick to forgive whenever an apology is offered. Sighing, she finally admits to herself that it is what needs to be done, even though she knows making amends would trigger another interrogation from Sarah regarding the strange way she has been behaving lately.

Georgia's not sure what she'll tell her assistant when the questions come. With the secret she's been harbouring, it's been difficult to be forthcoming about anything, making her feel like she needs to be more defensive than ever. She has never been good at dealing with personal conflicts, and she probably should have been more sensitive to Sarah's feelings, even though the woman has always appeared too robust to suffer any injury. But the reality is, Georgia knows she's been taking Sarah for granted all these years, expecting her reliable assistant to always be by her side, no matter what.

And as soon as she returns to Sydney after all this business with the Russians is finished, she decides, she is going to talk to Sarah about it.

Light begins to wane as the sun sets over the hill. Ben has decided that they will camp overnight at Almsgivers Wall because he feels that there's no other location in the area that offers better shelter. He has set up their tents behind some boulders by Chinggis Khan's Saddle, giving them a good view of the valley in case anyone approaches. With Fujimoto now dead, and judging by the way the Russians raced out of here, it is unlikely they'd be back. As a safe measure, though, Ben has set up some traps and trip wires that would alert them if someone gets close to the site.

Soon after uncovering Fujimoto's body, Ben found the deceased doctor's car abandoned in the woods behind the hill, most likely moved there by the Russians so as to not attract any attention. Georgia and Ben searched the vehicle, hoping to find some notes or clues left behind by Fujimoto, but came up with nothing.

Ben and Indi return to the camp now, and the man crouches down in front of Georgia to prepare a fire. Indi nestles against her, licking her bare toes. She smiles, scratching the dog on the neck affectionately.

"How's your arm?" Ben's voice is a low grumble, his back turned to her as he busies himself with the kindling.

"Fine," she replies. All day, she's had to be conscious of

limiting the use of her left arm, in case Ben became suspicious. She's assured him many times that the wound is clean and no longer bleeding, but he still seems unconvinced.

"Out here, there aren't any hospitals within at least a day's drive." Ben works on the fire, still not looking at her. "You really need to be careful about festering wounds. An infection can spread to the bloodstream and kill you pretty quick."

"You know, I didn't pick you to be the nagging type."

Ben freezes at her remark. Even though she cannot see his face, the muscles bunching in his shoulders are obvious, the tension oozing from him palpable.

Feeling bad about poking fun at him, she reassures him before the man gives himself an aneurysm. "It's not festering. I'm keeping it dry and clean. But if it starts looking funny, I'll let you know."

"Might be too late by then," he mutters like a grumpy old man. Finally turning around, he gives her a heated glare. "What's the deal, anyway? Why won't you let a trained medic look at your injury? I've treated plenty of men and women with gunshot wounds out in the field."

"I—" She fumbles for an excuse. "I'm . . . shy about my body. I don't like to be touched," she lies.

A deep frown forms between his eyes. He doesn't seem satisfied with her answer, but says nothing further.

"You were a medic in the Special Forces?" she asks, changing the subject. "I thought you specialised in linguistics."

"Both." He turns back to the fire, stoking it with a stick. "It's not uncommon for us to have more than one skill. Like I said, I studied foreign languages at college, then trained as a medic once I enlisted. Medics usually get some language training in the SF, anyway."

"How did you end up in Mongolia, then? Does the US army have a base here?"

"I'm not part of the army anymore."

Georgia tilts her head with surprise. This is news to her.

Ben settles into the camping chair a few metres away. Indi rises and trots over to lie by his feet. "I left after my last deployment in Syria. Been here ever since. Three years now. The military hires contractors sometimes, when their personnel don't have the required skills or profile for a specific mission," he explains.

"So the DIA does the same too?"

"Well . . . this is a special case."

Georgia nods slowly, then returns to her previous question, "What brought you back to Mongolia, then?"

He shrugs with apparent nonchalance. "I wanted to do something different with my life for a while. Thought it'd be good to come here, find my roots, reconnect with family, give back to the community, that sort of thing."

At Georgia's questioning expression, he explains: "My training as an SF medic was quite extensive. It's much more than what the nomadic people out on the steppes have access to. So I travel around, offering some basic medical services to the families who live here."

"Like a barefoot doctor?"

"What's that?"

"Someone who provides healthcare to rural areas where there are no doctors. It's something that was common in China during the Cultural Revolution."

"Yeah, I guess it's a bit like that."

Georgia is fascinated by his background. "So this is the first time you've been back, since you left as a kid?"

"Yeah." He stares into the fire which is now burning earnestly.

"What made you leave the army?"

He suddenly looks up, as if startled by the question. The piercing glare and scowl return instantly. "I reckon that's enough questions for tonight."

Alarmed by the drastic change in his demeanour, Georgia leans back in her chair. Next to Ben, Indi whimpers. She raises her head to seek his hand, pressing her muzzle against his open palm. At this, Ben visibly relaxes a notch. He scratches the dog under her neck.

"She . . . is a calming influence," Georgia says softly.

Ben is quiet as he strokes Indi's fur. He doesn't look up, doesn't meet her eyes as he says, "Yeah. Indi's a PTSD service dog."

"Oh."

The implications of his remark settles in. PTSD service dogs are trained to detect signs of anguish in people with post-traumatic stress disorder, helping them to cope with anxiety and panic attacks as a result of what they've been through. With that one sentence, Ben has revealed so much to her. She realises that this must be the reason that he left the army. Everything begins to make sense now: how Indi would whine and press her nose in Ben's hand every time he looks tense, the way she even helped to lighten Georgia's mood when she was distressed.

His answer triggers so many more questions in her, though. How did he get PTSD? Has he recovered now? She assumes so, if he's now back in active duty. But why is Indi still with him, then?

From the set of Ben's jaws, though, it is obvious he's

not in the mood to elaborate. So Georgia chews on her bottom lip, stopping herself from asking anything else.

Silence falls between them, and she listens pensively to the crackle of fire and the rustle of trees in the evening breeze. The bruised sky darkens further, giving way to the first few stars in the sky.

"What do you reckon the Russians found out from Fujimoto?" Ben asks after a long while. "Where will they be headed next?"

"I don't know." Georgia sighs. "But I've been thinking over the whole thing today and I feel like we're going about it the wrong way."

Ben gives her a puzzled look and waits for her to explain, so she opens her notebook, finding the page with verses from the *sulde* and the portrait of Chinggis Khan:

When the spirit and the seat of the Golden Khan are together again,
Then shall the truth be revealed,

And only one who possesses the truth of our history
May find his eternal resting place . . .

She explains: "We've been racing from site to site, chasing after the Russians so that we can get the *sulde* back. But we're always one step behind, forever playing catch-up to them, when we really should be focusing on these clues instead, because the second verse from the portrait is the only thing we have that Anya doesn't."

Ben nods, catching her meaning. "We need to figure out *The Secret History of the Mongols* to get ahead."

"Yes." She gestures to the pile of books sitting on her bag and elaborates: "The only surviving copies are problematic, since we're working with fourteenth-century Chinese to restore a thirteenth-century Mongolian text. I've been going over the English translations by different academics, and each has his own interpretation of the similes and metaphors, and the misleading homophones. Taken at face value, the text itself is nothing more than an account of the Mongol tribe's genealogies, and of Chinggis and his son Ogodei's life. The second section has been edited and re-written by later scholars who copied the text. Parts of the document have been erased and redacted, and the vital political role of Mongol women has also been censored. It's full of confusing and conflicting dates, and the lack of military details leads many to believe that it is incomplete, and that the original Mongolian version buried with Chinggis is the only one that contains the blueprint of how he conquered the world."

Ben shakes his head. "I still don't get the point of transliterating the text. Why not just translate it? Why put it in some strange code no one can understand?"

"That's just it," Georgia says. She grabs the Chinese transliteration of *The Secret History* she printed out in Ulaanbaatar, flipping through its pages. "I believe it *is* a code. If I'm interpreting the clues on the *sulde* and the portrait correctly, then what lies within these pages are the most protected secrets of the Golden Family, *in cipher*. Why else would you transliterate it, when it hardly makes any sense in either Chinese or Mongolian? The Mongols would have never allowed any outsiders to understand its contents, should the book fall into wrong hands. What if the way to find the original version is encoded in this obviously erroneous edition? What better way to mask the truth in plain sight, than to have one text that portrays multiple meanings?"

Ben is quiet as he contemplates her theory. Finally, he asks, "So how do we get started?"

"We go back to the surviving version written in Chinese," she says. "Every cipher has a key, and I suspect it has only remained undiscovered for so long because no one thought to search for it. Scholars became overwhelmed with translating the entire text, when maybe all they needed was one crucial detail. With your knowledge of Daur Mongolian, shamanism, and the geography of the Mongol homeland, perhaps we can find the critical clue to interpreting the document."

"So if we find the key to the code, it'll help us to unlock the secrets of the text?"

"That is my hypothesis, yes."

Ben's piercing stare stays on her as he absorbs this, and for the first time, Georgia detects something else in his eyes. She can't tell for sure, but the man seems to be looking at her with less disdain than before.

After a long while, he says, "Let's talk more about it in the morning. You seem tired. Get some sleep." Rising to his feet, he looks down at her. "And wake me if your wound bothers you," he adds, his request sounding more like a command.

Without another word, Ben walks off to his tent, followed by Indi, who never stops wagging her tail.

33

Four years ago, Syria

BEN BLINKED WITH SHOCK, *unable to believe his own eyes. Bodies—hundreds of them—filled the streets. Men, women, young children lay dead, faces bloated, lifeless eyes staring, skin turned blue. Trails of blood emanated from their mouths and noses. The reek of vomit, urine, faeces, and rot permeated the air. The buzz of flies droned ceaselessly.*

"Jesus fucking Christ," one of the men behind Ben whispered.

Some others on his team retched, emptying half-digested breakfasts onto the dusty ground. Ben swallowed against the sudden dryness in his mouth, swiping at his lips as if the action could remove the sour, burning taste at the back of his throat. He lowered his rifle, wrestling with shock and powerless rage.

The intel was wrong. There were no enemies here. Just dead civilians. Innocent women and children among them.

"What in the goddamn hell happened here, Doc?" Williams asked, his voice startlingly loud in the eerie silence of the village.

A. H. WANG

Ben turned to his team leader. "Chemical weapon, Cap'n. Some kind of gas, I think."

"Sarin?" Williams said, referring to the god-awful nerve agent.

"I hope not, or we're all fucked," Ben replied, now feeling alarmed as the initial shock wore off. "Let's get the hell outta here. These people look like they've been dead a few days now, but we shouldn't take any chances, in case there are still trace elements in the air."

"Fuck." Williams spat on the ground, yelling for the team to haul ass back to the truck.

From the corner of his eye, Ben spotted movement. Some of his teammates did too, and they jerked their weapons towards the door of the ramshackle building down the street.

"Hold your fire!" Ben yelled when he saw the young woman in the black hijab. He was already running towards her as she stumbled out onto the road.

He caught her just as her legs gave out. She was convulsing in his arms, wheezing and coughing as she fought to breathe. Foam oozed out of her mouth, and she spluttered as she tried to speak.

"It's okay. It's okay. I got you," Ben reassured her in Arabic.

The woman shook her head, frantic. "No. No," she was saying in between heaving air into her lungs.

"Shhh. Try not to talk." Ben checked her blood-shot eyes, noting the pinpoint pupils.

She thrashed in his arms again. Ben struggled to keep her on her side so she wouldn't choke on her own tongue. Her face was turning blue from the lack of oxygen.

"Need some help here!" Ben yelled.

One of the men was by his side instantly. "What do you need, Doc?"

"Atropine. In my bag. The small compartment to your right. That needle, yes. Hurry."

As he injected the antidote into her vein, the woman was still shaking her head, trying to talk to him. Ben's entire body stilled as he read her lips, finally understanding her meaning.

"Save my baby, save my baby, save my baby," she was saying in Arabic, over and over again.

Ben finally looked down and noticed the bulge under her shawl. He peeled the fabric back and saw the child swaddled against her body. It was a girl, barely six months old.

Her eyes were closed, and her blue lips were parted as blood trickled out.

Fumbling, Ben felt for a pulse in her neck.

He detected none.

It was then that the first of the explosions erupted, the blast knocking Ben flat on his back. The shock of it winded him, and when he finally remembered to breathe again he was gasping and coughing from the dust in the air. He blinked a few times to clear his vision, groaning at the sharp pain in his ribs. Ears ringing, he could hear the muffled sound of Williams' roar, "Ambush! Go go go! Get back to the fucking vehicle!"

Ben struggled to sit up, and it was then he realised he was still holding the woman in his arms. He looked down to check on her, but she had gone deathly still, her dark, unmoving eyes staring up at him, her lips parted mid-sentence.

BEN WAKES WITH A JOLT. Memories of Syria and his nightmare tangle and meld together, fogging his confused mind and dragging him back to a time of terror and impotence. Panic rises, tightening his throat and squeezing his chest. Sweat trickles down his face, neck, everywhere.

Indi's already up, licking his cheeks, reminding him to breathe. With effort, he focuses on his respiration: four seconds in, four seconds out. He concentrates on this agonising pace despite the wild hammering of his heart.

Long moments pass, and he slowly reels his pulse back under control. He's drenched with sweat, the sleeping bag soaked. He throws off the covers. Indi nuzzles her snout to his neck, puffing warm air against his skin.

"Thanks, girl," Ben finally says. He strokes her on the head and buries his face in her fur. "Haven't had one of those in a while, have I?"

It's those damn Russians that have brought this on again. Being shot at and having the situation spiral out of his control is a major trigger for him. And the fact that it's all happening on his home turf just makes it all that much worse.

Mongolia was his last frontier, the only place that was protected in his heart, a country he associates with serenity, healing, and safety from the threats of his own memory. Being on mission here has effectively brought war into his home, and he is now devoid of a safe haven.

His stress levels have already been elevated by the fact that he's travelling with the infuriatingly stubborn professor, who's been pressing all the wrong buttons in him. The last couple of days he's had to constantly keep himself in check from the roller coaster ride of reactions she's provoked in him: from general irritation, to a protectiveness that's creeping towards borderline possessiveness, to an irrepressible exasperation that threatens to make him lose his shit. It doesn't help when she stares at him with those big brown eyes, asking him all sorts of intrusive questions that he doesn't want to answer, but cannot stop responding to. And it frustrates him that she has continuously refused to let him see her gunshot wound. He hasn't seen that kind of obstinate nature in anyone else except . . .

Well, except himself.

All of it rolls up into one big stinking clusterfuck that has catapulted him back to the events of his last deployment in Syria and how it all went horribly wrong, triggering emotions he thought he'd long moved on from. This is precisely why Ben did not want to take the job. He just knew some horrible shit was going to go down, and he wasn't going to be able to do a damn thing about it. But a part of him was deluded enough to think that he was better now, that maybe he was cured after years of not having an episode. A part of him wanted to prove it to himself, and perhaps to Brandon Miller, too.

Yet as much as he still wants to believe in his recovery, the familiar nagging sensation gnaws at his innards now, something he hasn't felt since returning to Mongolia. It's the sense of inevitable doom that sits low in his gut, making him want to heave.

The contents of his stomach rise to his throat, and he bolts upright, rushing out of his tent on his hands and knees. He gags and coughs, but produces nothing. Spittle and perspiration drip down his clammy skin.

Ben wipes the mess away with the back of his hand, disgusted with himself. Four years ago, he had the strongest stomach in his entire team, and now he's reduced to being a jittery, nauseous, punk-ass bitch.

Fuck this.

What an idiot he was, agreeing to this job in the first place. But Ben knows it's too late to back out now, even if everything about the mission feels wrong. Just like everything in Syria was wrong.

He clenches his fists over the grass on the ground. Indi

whines, licking his knuckles and urging him to calm down.

"Yes, girl. I know." He sighs and loosens his grip, rising to his knees.

Above him, the thick blanket of stars has receded, giving way to dawn as the sky turns into a deep indigo. Ben stills as his eye catches movement in the dark line of trees some hundred yards away.

His breath lurches.

He squints but fails to discern shapes in the dim light. The rustling doesn't happen again.

As if sensing the same threat, Indi crouches low and growls.

Ben slowly backs into his tent and retrieves his Glock. His eyes stay on the tree line, but nothing happens. The air is completely still, and the hill remains silent. His hackles still up, he stays close to the ground, reaching over to slip open the zipper of Georgia's tent.

He utters her name as he tugs at her foot through her sleeping bag.

She wakes with a jolt, her voice slurred with sleep. "Ben?"

"Get up. We gotta go."

"What?"

"We need to leave. There's someone out there, watching us."

She sits upright, suddenly fully conscious. She begins to shove things into her bag.

"No, leave it. Let's go. *Now*."

Quietly she obeys him, grabbing her small day pack and following closely behind him as they steal across the few yards to the van. Indi leaps through the driver's door and straight into the back seat. As Ben starts the engine and drives away from the site, he still cannot shake the feeling that they're being watched.

"What happened?" Georgia's voice is quiet. "Was it the Russians?"

"No, I don't think so." He looks in the rearview mirror, even though he can see nothing.

"How do you know?"

"The Russians would've started shooting at us already. And we'd probably be dead." His grip tightens on the steering wheel. Whoever they are, they were extremely careful. Ben wonders how they managed to bypass his trip wires.

"Who, then?"

"I'm not sure," he answers truthfully.

As they drive on towards the brightening horizon, Ben begins to doubt his own instincts. Did he actually see anything? Or was it just some animal—a marmot, maybe? Has his PTSD-addled brain affected his judgement, making them abandon camp for nothing?

No. It was definitely something. And Indi's growl confirmed it. More than just a PTSD service dog, she's a damn good guard too, aptly protecting what little herd he has at home.

"We left Fujimoto's body behind," Georgia says.

He grunts. "I'll call Miller, tell him to alert the necessary people."

"Where do we go now?" Georgia asks in a whisper, holding her arms around herself. Ben doesn't miss the slight tremor in her shoulders. She seems really spooked.

That protective instinct rises in his chest again, and Ben chews on the inside of his cheeks. They are not in a good situation at all. Most of their supplies have been left behind. With the threat of the Russians and now another unknown party involved, they need somewhere safe to regroup and restock while they figure out their next steps. Out here in the harsh environment of the Mongolian wilderness, they won't last one night without the right provisions to keep them warm and fed. There is a long list of unknowns, and his training tells him he needs to eliminate as many as possible.

Ben knows precisely where he has to take them, but he's reluctant to do it. He loathes to retreat to the very last of his defences.

"Ben?" Georgia's eyes are fixed on him, glistening in the dim light.

Realising he doesn't have a choice, he snarls, "I know a place. We'll be safe there."

34

AT THE SOUND of the approaching horse, Gerel walks out of her *ger*, one hand shielding her eyes as she squints in the direction of the rising sun, seeing the unmistakable silhouette of Naran drawing nearer.

Her heart swells with affection. *Beautiful child.* Ever since the babe's mother died, Gerel has kept her near, instilling everything she knew in the girl, watching with pride as her charge grew into a strong, intelligent woman. Naran has been an exceptional student, in spite of her rebellious streak. That headstrong nature has its benefits and disadvantages, of course, but Gerel is starting to worry that it would affect the succession. She has no doubt that her grandniece is fully capable of taking over her role, and there is no question about her fierce loyalty to the clan, but the elderly woman cannot help but wonder if the ember of fury that burns within Naran would result in misguided efforts.

Efforts that could end in catastrophic consequences.

Gerel has thought there would still be plenty of opportunities for her to correct the course of her ward. But now that foreigners are on their lands interfering with Mongol affairs, she fears they may have run out of time.

On approach, Naran slows the bay mare with a tug of the reins. A frown mars her young, pretty face. Wearing a red *deel* and a matching fur hat, her hair is in strings of tiny braids hanging down her back. At seventeen years old, Naran holds herself with more confidence than most girls of her age. She has her father's almond-shaped eyes and fair skin, and her mother's small, rounded nose. The impertinent set of her lips, though, is all her.

She starts speaking before she dismounts the horse. "*Eej*," she says, addressing Gerel as her mother rather than great-aunt, as she has always done since she was a child. "They're on the move again. This time heading south. I watched them most of the night, and the man seemed to have caught my scent. He woke the professor and got out of there immediately, even left all their gear behind. He's sharp, that one."

Gerel considers this update. The events of the last few days have been surprising, and exceptionally well-timed. She can only attribute the miraculous synchronicity to the mysterious workings of the Eternal Blue Sky. Fate has brought the foreigners to Mongolia, and Gerel is certain that the heavens will bring them the outcome they require.

"My men are ready, *eej*," Naran continues, her hand tugging the bridle of her horse as if she's ready to jump back on.

"Yes," Gerel replies. "But we will wait."

"Wait for what?" The girl knits her brows together.

"We wait for a sign."

Naran lets out an agitated sigh, and Gerel expects the child to argue, to launch into the girlish whine that Gerel has grown accustomed to. But the young woman squares her shoulders and lifts her chin instead, asking, "What would our forefathers have done?"

Gerel smiles. "Our forefathers would have had the wisdom to act when necessary, but the patience to hold back and observe until it is the right time."

When Naran stares at her with a defiant expression, Gerel pats her reassuringly on the shoulder. "Patience, child. You forget, the Russians are still a problem for us."

Slowly, the girl's wilful pout melts away. She looks at her great-aunt with interest, an eyebrow raising with intrigue.

"Let them come," Gerel says with confidence. "Let them pit themselves against each other for the treasure. And we wait. We watch. We observe until it's our turn. You'll see."

35

GEORGIA SITS with her legs dangling outside the *furgon*, a pencil between her lips as she looks over everything she has on *The Secret History* so far. Notes are scribbled all over her copy of the Chinese transliterated version, and with Ben's help, she has managed to make some headway with the interpretation.

There are a few things bothering her about the text, and she's already found details in there which are in direct contradiction to other historical chronicles, errors which she can't imagine the original authors could have ever made.

She rubs her forehead. She doesn't know what it all means. Something is staring at her right in the face, and it is probably glaringly obvious. But for the life of her, she cannot see it.

She sighs and tosses the book to the side, deciding to take a break. The expansive steppes stretch endlessly in every direction around her, and as she takes in the scenery, she feels at once tiny and insignificant in the vast landscape. At the same time, it's also as if she is the only human being that is in existence at this moment, bearing witness to the majesty of the land. *Gers* like giant, girdled marshmallows are sparsely scattered across the flat, infinite terrain, some equipped with satellite dishes and solar panels. The grassy pasture is tinged with an atmospheric blue in the far distant horizon. Eagles coast through the sky high above her, and the staccato clicking of grasshoppers fills the air. She relishes the cool breeze sweeping over her loose-fitting slacks and long-sleeve top, kindly lent to her by Ben's aunt, Qara.

In the mad rush of abandoning their camp yesterday, Georgia had to leave most of her belongings behind. She only had time to grab her laptop and books before Ben pulled her into the van and drove them south to stay with his relatives. A nomad family of eight spanning three generations, they have generously packed every member into one *ger*, leaving the other for Ben and Georgia to share. As far as she knows, he has only introduced her as a friend visiting from the States, keeping from them the true reason of her stay.

She hops out of the van and follows the sound of excited chatter, spotting Ben some hundred metres away with a young girl. Georgia walks towards them, grasshoppers leaping into the air with every landing of her footfall. Ben appears to be teaching the teenager some archery skills. He winds a piece of red rope around her thin arm, which seems like a pale twig next to his enormous hands. Then, standing behind her and crouching down to her height, he guides her to pull the bow back. They pause in this position, Ben murmuring instructions at length in Mongolian, then they both release the string together, watching the arrow shoot high into the sky. It hits the target on the ground some distance away, and the girl spins around to look at Ben with a face-splitting grin, obviously pleased with the result.

The pair look up as Georgia approaches, Ben's dark eyes fixed on her as he watches her draw near. Georgia fidgets under his scrutiny, cradling her left arm to keep it immobile by her side, pretending that her non-existent injury is still healing.

"Hi." She smiles when she reaches them. "That was a great shot."

Ben places his large paw on the youngster's shoulder with pride. This is the first time Georgia has ever seen him smile, the rare expression transforming his usually stern, rugged features. The sight hits her square in the chest, and her breath lodges in her throat.

He says something in Mongolian to the teenager, at which the girl beams and stands taller. Switching to English, Ben says to Georgia: "This is Tuya, my niece. Qara's granddaughter."

"Hello, Tuya. I'm Georgia." She smiles, extending her hand.

Tuya grasps Georgia's hand lightly. She flashes a shy smile before saying something in Mongolian to Ben. He murmurs his approval, and Tuya sprints off in the direction of the target to retrieve her arrows.

"She's practising for next year's *Naadam* festival," Ben explains.

"'The three games of men,'" Georgia says, repeating what she read in the in-flight magazine on the way to Ulaanbaatar. Every summer, this Mongol-style mini Olympics stops the nation, with citizens travelling from every part of the country to participate in Mongolian wrestling, horse racing, and archery.

"It isn't just for men," Ben says. "Women and girls take

part in the archery too, and girls in the horse racing competitions."

Georgia is glad to hear that tradition is upheld. The mention of Mongol soldiers conjures up images of brutish men battle-ready on horses, but most people don't realise that there is a long history of women fighting alongside men in the Mongol campaigns, with many legendary stories of female warriors in the ranks. With their military tactics heavily reliant on horsemanship and archery, physical size was not as crucial as agility, accuracy with the arrow, and mastery of equines. In fact, for a long time women had vital political roles in the Mongol Empire, starting with the daughters of Chinggis Khan being sent out on diplomatic missions to coalesce the many tribes spread across the steppes as Chinggis began to build his empire.

"Sadly, Mongolian archery today is not what it once was," Ben says wistfully. "Mongol archers used to fire at enemies behind them while standing on the stirrups at a full gallop. Turning back and over the shoulder, like this." He demonstrates the action to her. "And composite bows aren't built the way they used to be. A cousin of mine is a bow maker, and he told me the kind of force from a traditional heavy bow was so astonishing, it would've had further range and more penetration power than some of the modern day bullets. You would need the strength of doing a one-armed chin up with only two fingers, just to pull the string of the bow."

Georgia smiles. Given his military background, she can understand his enthusiasm over the subject. But she's surprised at his chattiness today. In fact, there's been something very different about Ben ever since they arrived at his family's camp. He seems more relaxed. Calmer. Even

Indi, now nowhere to be seen, appears to have been off duty as soon as they got here.

She decides to ask him something that has been on her mind. "Ben, why does your family all call you *Buri*?" She has heard the word repeated over and over. It took a little while for her to realise that it is the name they use for him.

Falling quiet again, Ben's eyes stay fixed on Tuya as the girl returns with the arrows. "Buri's the name I was given at birth."

"What does it mean?"

"It means 'wolf.'"

"Wolf . . ." She smiles, liking how it matches her impression of him. A lone wolf. "I just realised I don't know your last name."

He hesitates. Then he says, "Well, my mother's last name was Myagmar."

"Buri Myagmar," she repeats the foreign sounds. "Can I call you that, too?"

He turns to stare at her quizzically. Then, seeing Tuya has returned, he says something to the girl in Mongolian. The teenager nods, out of breath from her short run, picking up her bow and returning to her practice.

His eyes are still on Tuya when he says barely audibly in English, "Sure. You can call me whatever you like."

At that moment, a boy bounces up to them, tugging on Buri's pants and saying something in Mongolian. Smiling down at him, Buri translates for Georgia: "Dinner is ready."

They all make their way to the *ger*, joining the family gathered around the table beside the central hearth. Qara and her daughter-in-law busy themselves over the stove, opening the lid of the large flat pan to release a blooming cloud of steam, revealing dozens of dumplings within.

Buri explains that they are called *buuz*, stuffed full with mutton and vegetables.

Dinner is not done graciously here. Rather, it is a mad frenzy with kids and adults all snatching up handfuls of *buuz* and shovelling them whole into their maws. Playful banter is exchanged around the table, with everyone speaking and laughing loudly around mouthfuls of food. Georgia cannot understand anything that is being said, but she catches enough from their body language and facial expressions. Every now and then, Buri translates a particularly funny joke for her so she could feel a part of the family festivities.

Then, almost as quickly as they started, the children get up and rush out of the *ger* to continue their ankle-bone dice games outside, their tiny hands still clutching onto a dumpling or two. Bowls of *airag*, the infamous fermented mare's milk, are passed around the table between the adults as Buri chats with his uncle, Och.

"Careful with that," Buri breaks off his conversation when Georgia has a second sip of the sour drink. "Takes your stomach some getting used to."

"Oh. Thanks." She smiles, appreciating the warning. She passes the bowl back to Qara. Seeing her opportunity, she asks Buri, "Hey, do you think you can ask Och what he knows about Chinggis Khan's death?"

Buri's smile is replaced by a scowl. "Why?"

"Locals usually have folklore knowledge that forms an important part of historical clues. There may be stories he has heard that could help us," she explains.

He considers this, obviously reluctant. It seems to take him a while to find the right words for the question. Och, who listens patiently to Buri, grunts with acknowledgement and responds at length in Mongolian. Buri translates simultaneously as Och speaks: "When Och was growing up, his grandmother would tell him that it is common knowledge among the Mongols that Chinggis Khan is not dead."

Georgia frowns.

"The story goes something like this: the Great Khan was stabbed by a princess-assassin," Buri continues to interpret for her, his eyes fixed on his uncle as the elderly man speaks, "and from this wound, he fell into a deep sleep from which he has never awakened. But Holy Chinggis is a shamanist—the most powerful warrior shaman this world has ever seen. He will heal himself, and once he is healed, he will rise and lead his people again."

Her interest piqued, she asks, "Does Och know where the Khan has been sleeping all this time?"

Och snorts and shakes his head when Buri has translated her question, and his answer is again relayed back to her in English, "Bad business, that. Foreigners are always so curious about the tomb. But Mongolians will never want it found."

"Why not?" she asks. "Don't they want a place to pay respects to the founding father of their nation?"

"We do pay respect," Buri interprets Och's response. "But the tomb is unimportant. Mongolians pay respect to his soul, not his body. The body should be left in peace. Besides, there's the curse."

This time, Buri is the one to ask questions. As Och replies, the younger man translates for Georgia, "It's a well-known prophecy. If The Holy Khan's tomb is ever disturbed, our nation will fall. The closer you get to the burial site, the more calamities will be unleashed. The sky will thunder and storm down on you. The earth will shake with rage. The rivers will boil."

Georgia says nothing, but her scepticism must be obvious, because Och adds something else, which again is passed onto her in English: "Surely you know the story of Tamerlane's tomb?"

"Tamerlane," Georgia repeats the name, looking at the old man. "Is Och talking about Timur Khan, the fourteenth-century Turkic-Persian conqueror who claimed to be a descendant of Chinggis?"

Och nods after Buri has translated for her. He continues, "I may not have been to school, but my son has, and they learn all sorts of wonderful things there. He used to come home on holidays and share with me everything he has learnt." Och's leathery face creases with a faint smile. "Tamerlane's body was exhumed by Stalin, who was obsessed with both Chinggis and Tamerlane. When the Soviet scientists opened Tamerlane's casket in 1941, they found an inscription inside. It said, 'Whosoever opens my tomb shall unleash an invader more terrible than I.' Three days later, Hitler invaded the Soviet Union, slaughtered countless people. It wasn't until Stalin ordered for Tamerlane to be reburied with full Islamic ritual more than a year later that the Red Army managed to gain advantage over the Germans in the war."

Buri looks impressed with his uncle's historical tidbit. But Georgia shakes her head. "Och is talking about Operation Barbarossa of the Second World War," she says.

"The largest military invasion in the history of warfare?" Buri's brows raise even higher. "The one where the War's biggest battles occurred, where some of the highest casualties happened, and where the Nazis captured and killed millions of Soviet soldiers?"

"Yeah," she confirms. "But Operation Barbarossa had

no actual link with what happened at the Mausoleum of Timur Khan. It was just a coincidence."

Buri looks unconvinced. His uncle speaks up again, followed by Buri's interpretation: "Compared to Chinggis Khan, Tamerlane was nothing as a warrior and as a shaman. Just imagine what the curse on Chinggis' tomb would be like. It would probably bring the end of the world as we know it. There's a reason the Darkhats have guarded the region with their lives for the last eight hundred years."

The question is out of Georgia's lips at the same time Buri asks his uncle in Mongolian. "What region?"

Och's answer does not require translation: "Ikh Khorig," he says.

36

GEORGIA TURNS over in the narrow single bed, checking her watch in the dark. It's just past two in the morning, and she has been awake for a while now, puzzling over things in her head. She needs such little rest these days—three, four hours a night, tops. That is, if she gets any at all. She wonders if Charlie was the same after he took the elixir.

She doesn't mind the additional waking hours. In fact, she welcomes it, as the extra time has been a blessing since she's been able to be more productive with the research needed for the mission. Besides, when sleep does come it is usually fraught with dreams about Ethan or Charlie or Wang Jian, all of which are plagued with staggering emotions of guilt, regret, or horror, leaving her teary and breathless when she awakens.

Deciding that it's time to get up and do some more work, she peels back the covers and swings her legs over the bed, placing her bare feet on the lino-covered floor. She looks over to Buri's side of the *ger* and sees that his bed is empty, the crumpled blankets left in a heap. Pulling on her shoes and jacket, she reaches for her laptop before walking out of the warm felt tent.

Outside, the spectacular Milky Way spreads across the black void above, a river of twinkling gems that seems close enough to touch. Ten metres away, a small campfire is burning. Buri is sitting before it with Indi dozing by his feet, the dancing flames casting a soft glow on the sharp angles of his face. He's staring at the fire as if mesmerised and doesn't even look up or acknowledge her presence when Georgia walks over to sit beside him.

This is not the first time she has caught him up so late, but she has remained in her tent on previous occasions, pretending to be asleep while reading academic papers in her torchlight under her sleeping bag. She wonders what keeps Buri awake at night, and what kinds of inner demons he may be battling.

They sit together in the quietude, each ruminating over unspoken things. After a long while, Buri finally clears his throat and says in a soft tone: "So, Ikh Khorig . . . The 'Great Taboo,'" he translates the Mongol term into English, referring to the place his uncle mentioned earlier.

Georgia nods quietly. After speaking with Och tonight, she has looked into the history of the region and discovered some very interesting facts.

"Do you think that's where the Russians are headed now?" Buri muses.

"It's likely." Georgia purses her lips, the mention of their adversary once again triggering a sense of urgency in her chest. "Fujimoto worked in Mongolia for many years. It's probable he would have had access to local insight regarding Ikh Khorig. He could have told Anya what he knew before he died."

Ever since their encounter with the Russian team at

Almsgivers Wall, Buri and Georgia have discussed several places Anya could have gone to, but the compelling information they've uncovered tonight could very well be the answer they've been searching for.

"It makes sense." Georgia continues, thinking about the articles she read before going to bed. "Ikh Khorig is right within the heart of the Mongol homeland where the ancestral Mongols first settled, and it's close to the places where Chinggis Khan was born and enthroned. It's also known as the Forbidden Zone. Access to the entire region has been restricted since the Middle Ages, first by the Darkhat warriors, then by the Soviets."

"The Soviets?" Buri cocks his head.

"During the Communist era, Mongolia was effectively a Soviet satellite state," Georgia explains. "Moscow viewed anything associated with Chinggis Khan to be potentially dangerous. They feared the worship of Mongolia's founding father would encourage nationalist ideals and notions of independence. So they sealed off the Mongol homeland and re-designated Ikh Khorig as the Highly Restricted Area."

She flips opens her laptop, and after it has booted up, she clicks into a file that was emailed to her by Sarah earlier. Turning the computer around to show Buri, she points to the old satellite image of Mongolia, showing extensive areas of dry, arid landscape, slashed by randomly criss-crossed trails. All of the tracks, however, stop at the edge of an extensive region of lush green wilderness, north-east of Ulaanbaatar.

"The Soviets built no roads to the Forbidden Zone," she explains, "so that no one could access it. This whole territory was literately untouched for almost eight hundred years, ever since Chinggis Khan died. It wasn't until after the fall of Communism that it was opened up again for the first time. Over the next few years, scientists and researchers came from all over the world, eager to explore the area that was considered one of the top potential sites for Chinggis' grave. But with all the unwanted international interest, the Mongolian government restricted foreign access to Ikh Khorig again."

"And the scientists found nothing when they came? How can that be?"

"Well, to be honest, many people still believe it's a decoy. What better way to keep grave hunters away from the actual tomb, than to draw their attention to a vast area of land for them to speculate over? Ikh Khorig spans twelve thousand square kilometres. It's virtually impossible to survey a place that big without narrowing it down first, especially without approval from the Mongolian authorities. The whole district is now designated an UNESCO World Heritage Site, called the Khan Khentii Strictly Protected Area. That means no excavation of any kind is allowed."

"Do you think we'll able to narrow it down?" Buri asks.

"Well, I believe so, yes." She brings up another file on her laptop and shows it to Buri. "My assistant, Sarah, dug this out of the university archives yesterday. It was written by the thirteenth-century Persian historian, Rashid al-Din. In this long passage, he described that during the division of the Mongol Empire, one of Chinggis' great-grandsons, Kamala, was given command of Chinggis' home estates, which included 'the great Khorig, and the place they call Burkhan Khaldun.'"

"Burkhan Khaldun . . . 'God Mountain,'" Buri translates. His eyes light up with recognition. "Och has told me he makes a pilgrimage there every lunar new year to pray for the year ahead."

"Really?" Georgia raises her eyebrows as she considers this, and an ember of excitement ignites within her. All of the information seems to converge towards one conclusion. She feels as if the answer is almost within their reach. "Rashid al-Din recorded that the great *ordos* of Chinggis Khan were here—the tents that contained his relics, which have since been moved to the Mausoleum of Genghis Khan in China. He also wrote that Kamala built a temple in Burkhan Khaldun, that the portraits of the Golden Family were kept there, and that the Mongol royals constantly burned perfumes and incense for worship."

"Portraits . . ." Buri muses. "Could the portrait of Chinggis Khan have been kept there, too? With his Spirit Banner?"

"At some point, probably," she speculates, smiling as that familiar thrill of a breakthrough surges up her spine. Judging by the expression on Buri's face, Georgia knows he feels it too. "That's not all. Going back over my notes, I noticed that *The Secret History* refers to Burkhan Khaldun many times. Chinggis Khan had a strong emotional and spiritual bond with this particular mountain. It was where he went to pray and seek guidance from the Eternal Blue Sky before every major campaign, and also where he returned after each victory to rest and recover. Burkhan Khaldun was the centre of his spiritual life, and he closed it off to all outsiders except for the Mongol royal family during his time."

Buri scratches his beard as he contemplates this.

"Problem is," Georgia points out, "everyone knows Burkhan Khaldun is one of the peaks within the Khentii Mountain Range. But no one knows exactly which. At least, not the outsiders. I was hoping you could talk to Och about that."

Buri's thick brows knit together. After a brief pause, he gives her a decisive nod. "I'll have a chat with him."

Georgia chews on her lower lip as she thinks everything over, then raises another issue. "But even if we knew which mountain it was, it's still an enormous area to search."

Buri grunts in agreement. He asks, "How are you progressing with *The Secret History*? Maybe that can help."

"Well, I've been going over our work so far, and compared to the existing translations of the text, we've pretty much uncovered nothing new. Nothing really stands out as a key to deciphering the information." She pauses. "So I started looking at the whole thing from another perspective. I asked myself, if I wanted to hide secrets within a document, but had to make sure that the right people got the correct message, how would I do it? The Golden Family were highly intelligent, strategic people, but they were taking a lot of risks with mistranslation by transliterating the information into Chinese. They should have anticipated this, though, and would have included details that could not be misunderstood or misinterpreted. There must be something in there, most likely something very simple, that leaves no room for error."

She brings up the file she's been working on over many sleepless nights since she got involved with this mission. With the aid of a special program on her computer, she has mapped out the entire Chinese text against interpretations from every known source, including Buri and her own work. Each significant detail is cross-referenced. There are texts and sections in different colours, highlighting information that could be useful.

"*The Secret History* is supposed to be a shamanic blueprint for world domination, so I thought the code could have something related to shamanism. To the Mongols, horses are creatures of mythical status, the most honoured and important animals in the world. And I noticed that there is an unusual amount of details on horses in the book. The authors hardly gave any descriptions of the locations or the people involved, but every horse mentioned in *The Secret History* has been treated with more attention than anything else in the entire document. It's very peculiar."

She points to the sections she is referring to, highlighted in red. She passes her laptop to Buri and watches as he looks it over.

After a long period of silence, he looks up at her and says, "It's not peculiar at all."

Her heart drops at his conclusion, and she waits for him to explain.

"It's a similar thing with the Eskimos, who have many dozens of words for snow to describe its texture, density, colour, freshness, and so on. For Mongolians, a horse isn't just a 'horse'. Last I counted, there are a hundred and sixty-nine terms to describe this single species, systematically identifying them by colour, character, physique, and even by the way they run."

Georgia creases her forehead, impressed by Buri's explanation. At the same time, she is disappointed. She really thought she was onto something. Now it's obvious she was just clutching at straws.

"Were there any other anomalies that stood out to you?" Buri asks.

"Well, that was all I came up with," she replies, feeling

defeated. "Aside from a few errors I picked up in the edited text."

"What kind of errors?"

"Let's see . . ." She scrolls down her screen, then points out a line she has highlighted in yellow. "Here, in chapter four, section forty-eight, it talks about Ong Khan having one son. In fact, he had at least two sons." She scrolls down further to another paragraph. "Here, in chapter ten, section one hundred and eight, it refers to Sacha and Taichu as the sons of Bartan-baatar, but actually they were the sons of Ökin-barqaq."

Buri grabs the pen and notebook next to her, writing down what she has just told him, but omitting the erroneous information and only noting the chapters and section numbers:

4, 48
10, 108

He says, "If I were to encode a text, making sure that my message is not mis-communicated because of translations, what is the one thing that is most easily transmitted and doesn't lie?"

Georgia's breath leaves her, suddenly understanding his train of thought. "Numbers."

Buri smiles. "Numbers."

The words on the portrait of Chinggis Khan flashes across her mind:

And only one who possesses the truth of our history
May find his eternal resting place . . .

A plan begins to formulate in her mind. She says with

excitement: "We need to find all the mistakes within *The Secret History* in order to *possess the truth*. I have to cross-check every detail in the book with other chronicles and historical sources to separate what's true and false in the text."

Buri nods. "In the meantime, I'll make the arrangements to travel to Ikh Khorig."

At this, Georgia recalls a crucial problem. "But the Forbidden Zone is marked off with a fifteen-kilometre fence, with Darkhats guarding the gate. And Burkhan Khaldun is strictly off-limits to foreigners like me."

"Then we'll have to go in as Mongols," Buri says, determination in his dark eyes.

37

PREPARING for the journey to Burkhan Khaldun takes a few days. Buri makes a trip to Ulaanbaatar to gather essential supplies, and Georgia uses the time to continue her work on *The Secret History*, liaising with Sarah in Sydney for information from the university archives.

According to Och, they will need to travel to Ikh Khorig on horseback. Thoroughfare for cars is almost non-existent within The Forbidden Zone, and the few that exist are in terrible condition. Vehicles that dare to attempt the journey often get stuck in mud or sand, and Georgia and Buri cannot afford to be bogged down in one of the most isolated regions in the world. The plan is to drive to the closest town, Mungunmorit, seventy kilometres away from Burkhan Khaldun. From there, they will hire the horses for the trek. The approach to the base of the mountain alone will take a couple of days.

The Darkhats guarding the gate will only allow Mongols access to pay respects to their ancestors, so Buri's aunt, Qara, is tasked with ensuring Georgia blends in as much as possible. The older woman brings out a traditional Mongolian *deel* in the large wooden chest at the centre of the family *ger*. Simple in design, the loose-fitting robe has a mandarin collar and an opening from the neck to the underarm, buttoned together by three Chinese knots. It is made from silk and is of a beautiful sapphire blue that makes Georgia think of the Mongolian sky. Qara ties a golden sash around Georgia's waist, then plaits her long hair into many strings of tiny braids. Finally, she is given a pair of black leather Mongolian boots that curl up at the toes, and a fur-lined hat.

Buri enters the *ger* in a flurry just as they finish, stopping abruptly when he sees Georgia. Brows raised, his dark eyes sweep over her, and she falters under the heat of his gaze.

"Hey . . . You're back," she says to break the silence. "How was Ulaanbaatar?"

"Fine. Got everything we need for the trip," Buri replies, his gaze still fixed on her.

She clears her throat, fidgeting with the sash around her. "Well, what do you think? How do I look?"

His voice is quiet. "You look like a Mongolian bride."

Qara is beaming as she examines Georgia, obviously happy with the result. She says something to Buri in Mongolian, and he translates it to English: "My aunt says that the last time she wore this was on her wedding day. Since she has no daughters, and Tuya is still many years from getting married, she wants you to have it."

Georgia flushes. She had no idea she was being dressed as a bride. "I couldn't possibly—"

"She insists."

Georgia frowns. "But I thought the whole point is for us to blend in? Why am I going in a *wedding* dress?"

Buri looks impatient. "The point is to go in as Mongolians. And *your* best chance of doing that is under the guise of my new wife. According to tradition, women aren't allowed to approach ancestral land unless they're dressed as daughters-in-law. Our story is that we're newlyweds, and we're paying respects at Burkhan Khaldun for an auspicious beginning to our marriage."

Georgia baulks at his answer. She doesn't know why it makes her so uncomfortable. After all, it's just a cover story for the mission. She watches as Qara rummages through the big chest again, producing another matching *deel* and handing it to Buri. He puts it on over his clothes and ties a sash around his midriff, and Georgia realises with shock that they are now dressed in a couple's outfit.

She stammers: "What does your family make of all this? Do they know the real reason we're going to Burkhan Khaldun?"

"No." Buri snorts. "The less they know, the better. Everyone just thinks that my girlfriend from the States and I are off to get our marriage registered at the nearest town. Then we're making the pilgrimage to Burkhan Khaldun. I told them we'll have a proper wedding celebration with the family when we return."

Her eyes bulge. "But . . . your family has been thinking that we're a couple all this time? And they think we're getting *married*?"

"Of course they do." Buri rolls his eyes. "Why do you reckon they let us share a *ger*?"

"But—"

"No more buts," Buri snaps as he marches out of the tent, making her scurry after him to keep up. "We're already behind schedule as it is. We gotta get moving to catch up to the Russians."

Striding over to the *furgon*, Buri emits a loud, sharp

whistle. Out of nowhere, Indi comes bounding across the field, reaching the van just as Buri opens the door. She leaps inside and settles herself in the hammock-style cot, her tongue sticking out of her open mouth.

The family gathers around the vehicle, all smiles as they shake Buri's and Georgia's hands to offer their congratulations to the betrothed couple. Georgia reluctantly climbs into the van as the big man starts the engine, craning her neck to look back at the waving children until they disappear into tiny dots in the distance. Her sadness at leaving surprises her. She realises that in the few days they have spent here, she has really enjoyed being with Buri's relatives. Despite the language barrier, the warmth of their personalities and the way they embrace everyone into one cohesive unit has shown her what a happy family can be like. Growing up, Georgia had rarely experienced that.

She sighs, finally turning to face the front and settling in for the journey. She smooths her hands over the silky fabric of the *deel*, quietly remarking, "You've got a beautiful family."

He throws her a glance, grunting his assent, then refocuses his attention on the road again.

"I feel bad about taking advantage of their hospitality," she continues, running her fingers over the golden sash around her waist. "They have been so kind and generous, even though they have so little."

"Daily life is hard out here. Agent Miller will make sure they're well compensated."

She nods, happy to hear that. They drive in silence for hours, both lost in their own thoughts. Buri's mood seems to decline with every kilometre they travel, and Georgia can distinctly sense the shift in the rigidity of his posture, the set of his jaws, and the growing intensity in his eyes. Wary of his taciturn state, she brings out her laptop again to bury herself in work, sifting through new information that Sarah has sent her over the past few days.

It is dark by the time they reach Mungunmorit, the township from which they will be leaving for Burkhan Khaldun on horseback. After camping overnight on the outskirts of town, they rise early in the morning to hire the horses they need for the expedition.

Georgia is looking at her mare hesitantly as Buri loads up their supplies on the team of five. Mongolian horses, Buri is telling her, may seem small but are deceptively tough. The reason the Mongol army was able to conquer so much land on horseback is in no small part due to the endurance of these beautiful beasts, unmatched in their speed and stamina.

Magnificent as they may be, Georgia is still reluctant to climb on. She watches Buri prepare the animals with admiration and envy, commenting, "You're really good at that."

"What?" His eyes stay fixed on the task at hand as he ties a rope around the bundle of supplies mounted on the gelding.

"Dealing with animals."

Buri's hands pause momentarily. Then, with a small smile, he caresses the neck of the chestnut horse with a long stroke. "It's a mutual affection. Truth is, I find them easier to be with than humans. I learned to ride a horse before I could walk. Many of the nomadic kids do."

Georgia smiles, reaching to pat her black mare tentatively, apprehensive about the long trek ahead. Horses have never liked her.

Buri studies her. "Have you ridden one before?"

"Of course." But she's never been able to get one to cooperate with her.

"Good." He says, holding onto the reins of Georgia's mare as he gives her directions. "Mongolian horses have to be treated differently, though. They roam free for half the year in winter and are only ridden during summer. So they're less tamed and scare easily. No sudden movements or noise, and always approach from their right side."

Great. She chews on her lip as she catalogues the instructions in her mind, but makes no move to get on.

"What's wrong?" Buri asks.

"Nothing."

"Need help?"

"No."

Georgia puts her booted foot in the stirrup. In one swift movement, she hoists herself up and swings her leg over the horse. Her actions are impeded by the long *deel*, but she manages somehow. The animal snorts with protest, thankfully staying motionless with Buri's sturdy hold on its bridle. She notices Buri staring at her intently from the corner of her eye, but ignores him. Exhaling the air in her lungs, she feels relieved now that she's sitting in the saddle.

That is, until she hears him ask with a low growl, "How's your arm?"

Georgia freezes at his question. In her nervousness over mounting the horse, she has forgotten to pretend that she's still injured.

She tries to feign nonchalance, babbling, "Fine. It's healing fine. The wound's not really hurting anymore. I'm fine."

Buri continues to stare at her, his expression unreadable.

Long seconds pass. Finally, he turns to his gelding and gets on the saddle with surprising grace for such a bulky man. He gives his horse a firm nudge with his heel, uttering, "*Che!*", and the animal lurches forward, leading the others with it.

They are a team made of a man, a woman, five horses, and a dog. Together they travel north, riding for the inner sanctum of Chinggis Khan's home, where the living conditions have always been harsher and the weather more volatile. Embarking on a course towards the unknown, Georgia wonders what they will uncover about the truth of Chinggis, and what ancient secrets the mountains will reveal.

38

SEVERAL HOURS INTO THE RIDE, Buri slows his horse to a trot, travelling alongside Georgia. He reaches into the hidden pockets of his *deel* and produces some dried curd, handing a large piece to her. "Here."

Georgia shakes her head, her stomach churning at the scent of food. But Buri insists, his hand steady as he holds the sheep-scented curd in front of her face.

"You need to eat," he demands.

Georgia scrunches up her nose and turns away. Her horse has been less than cooperative since they set off, first attempting to go in a completely different direction to the team, then, after reprimands from Georgia, Buri, and even Indi, the creature decided to stop altogether. Buri had to change the animals around, giving Georgia a more senior and docile mare. Now, after long hours of bouncing on the saddle, she is getting a serious case of motion sickness, as well as plenty of chaffing on her backside.

Buri studies her, narrowing his eyes. Then he halts his horse with a firm tug of the reins, and the entire pack stops with the leader. He dismounts and places a steadying hand on the bridle of Georgia's bay. Reaching into a bag on one of the spare horses, he retrieves a folded garment.

"Come down here."

Too sick to protest or to ask questions, Georgia obeys. She steadies herself with her feet back on solid ground, watching Buri unravel the bolt of red fabric roughly three metres long.

"Arms up."

She frowns.

"This will help. Trust me," he requests with a softer tone.

Georgia does as she's told, lifting her limbs in the air as he takes a step towards her, and she has to resist the instinct to retreat from him. Buri begins to wrap the cloth around her waist, his biceps flexing as he works. At this proximity, she is completely enveloped by the burly man towering over her. All of her senses are overwhelmed by his presence: the heat radiating off his body, the smell of his earthy, masculine scent, the sight of the broad expanse of his chest. When he finally finishes and steps away from her, she lets out a breath she didn't know she was holding onto, feeling at once light-headed and cold from his absence.

She gasps. "Does it have to be so tight? I can hardly breathe."

"This is an old Mongolian trick for distance riding. Helps to keep all the organs in place and prevents nausea," he explains as he helps her onto the horse, his hand lingering on the small of her back. The tiny, simple act makes her heart swell, a sentiment she pushes down as she flushes red. Shame fills her as thoughts of Ethan flood her mind.

What the hell is wrong with you? She chides herself.

They resume their journey, and the length of cotton tied around her midriff seems to do the trick. The team gradually gains speed, quickening into a full gallop. A sense of exhilaration surges through her as they race across the vast plains. The wind is in her face, and her thin braids are whipping wildly behind her. Unable to help herself, she breaks into a grin, her heart expanding as far as the limitless steppes, soaring high into the Eternal Blue Sky.

When they finally slow to a trot again to give the horses a break, she happily accepts the piece of curd from Buri. A ridge rises over the horizon ahead, a lone row of firs lining the top like the cropped mane of a horse. Buri checks his GPS and map.

"We're making good progress," he says, pointing to the scanty woodland at the base of the hill. "That's where we'll be camping tonight."

Georgia nods, munching on the curd and taking a drink from her water bottle. She's just starting to think that this whole horse riding thing isn't so bad after all, when the first of the arrows whistles past her head, skimming the top of her hat.

"Fuck! Get down!" Buri yells.

Everything erupts in a whirlwind of chaos as she ducks, pressing her body flush along the neck of her horse. More arrows rain down around them with short, high-pitched trills, and Buri bellows, smacking the rump of the horses to get them into a gallop. Indi is barking nearby as Georgia twists to see a dozen men on horseback, advancing towards them at an unbelievable pace.

Where the hell did they come from?

She kicks her horse with her heels, racing to keep up with Buri and Indi ahead. He draws his gun, firing a few earsplitting rounds at their assailants. When she glances behind her again, the plains are suddenly empty. The team is still running at full speed as she turns to scan the steppe.

Nothing.

What the—?

Then she spots one. A lone rider sitting tall on a stationary horse, at least half a mile away. At this distance and with the jarring motion of her own sprinting animal, she can barely discern his movements. It registers too late that the rider is drawing his bow and shooting into the sky. Less than a second later, there is a swift whistle and *oomph* from deep within her chest as she feels the stunning force of the arrow in her back.

"Georgia!" Up in front, Buri rears up his gelding. He's about to turn back for her.

"I'm okay!" she screams. "Go! Go! Don't stop!"

39

NARAN STARES after the man and woman as they race away, making a beeline for the foothills of the Khentii Mountain Range. They go quickly out of reach, and she stows her bow, nudging her gelding to a trot.

She stops and dismounts next to the injured mare left behind by the couple, the poor animal distressed and in pain from the arrow in its rump. She advances cautiously with her hands extended, and just as her men approach, she grabs hold of the bridle. Caressing the young creature, she coos soothingly in its ear as one of her soldiers yanks out the offending weapon. The chestnut horse whinnies and kicks out its hind legs, but Naran keeps her grip on the beast, calming it down with long strokes along its face.

From a hundred metres away, one of her archers comes back with another mare from the professor's team that fell behind. Naran eyes the supplies mounted on the two horses.

"Take them. Bring them back to the camp," she orders. "I want to see what's in those bags."

"*Beki.*" One of her officers rides up on his horse,

addressing Naran with her respected title. "Gerel *Khatun* wants to speak with you. She found out about the ambush and she's . . . not happy."

Naran scowls. She tips her chin and says, "Tell her I'm on my way."

She mounts her gelding again, staring at the distant Khentii. The professor and the half-bred Mongol are now nowhere to be seen, and Naran assumes that they've already reached the shelter of the Khentii Forest. Her gut clenches at the thought.

When she saw that the pair managed to make it this far, she decided to mount an attack, even though she was forbidden by Gerel from interfering. But, technically, she hasn't meddled. Not really. At least she's left them alive, merely shooting a few arrows in the air to scare them off track. But it seems the professor is still continuing on her course, and now the two are heading straight towards the gates of Ikh Khorig.

Naran doesn't like it. No one, especially foreigners, should ever be allowed into their sacred land.

Despite what Gerel has said, she cannot reconcile with her great-aunt's reasoning. After all, the elderly woman herself has proclaimed countless times that they are charged with the responsibilities of their ancestors, a tradition that has been passed down for eight hundred years. They protect the tomb. And they protect the Secret until the day of His reckoning.

She knows perfectly well that she's going to be in trouble when she gets home. Carrying out an unsanctioned ambush like this is almost treasonous. But she has only done what is right by her people. Since the fall of the Great Khans, the Mongols have struggled and suffered at the cruel hands and slanderous tongues of others. Even now, everywhere she looks, Mongolia is infiltrated by money-hungry foreigners, investors looking to make fat profits from the resource-rich Mongol lands, destroying natural habitats with the filth of their excessive mining operations.

And now they come to our ancestral home, to defile and disrespect what is sacred to us, searching to dig up the dead from where they should rest in peace?

No.

Naran flexes her fist, curling it around the reins. It's time her great-aunt realises that she is no longer a child, and that she's ready to take over the role that is rightfully hers. She will show the entire tribe that she is capable of stepping up as the leader she is born to be.

As she rides towards camp, she formulates the arguments for her defence in her head, countering each anticipated criticism from Gerel with a rationalisation of her own. The evening light wanes. When she finally approaches the familiar *gers* equipped with satellite dishes and solar panels, she sees the small yet commanding figure of her great-aunt, fists planted on either side of her waist, wearing a severe expression on her weathered features.

Behind her, a man exits the *ger*, tall and regal in stature. Dread ripples through Naran as she recognises his face, one she has not seen in the flesh since she was a child.

Her father.

That is when Naran realises the full extent of trouble that she is in.

"Damn," she swears under her breath.

40

HIS PULSE THUNDERING in his ears, his breath coming in short, stuttering bursts, Buri pulls his gelding to a screeching halt as soon as he breaks through the tree line of the forest. The horse rears up with a high-pitched neigh, but Buri is already off the saddle, mission-intent as he strides towards Georgia, who slows her mare to a stop several feet away.

"Let me see your back," he commands, unable to tone down the urgent harshness of his voice. She dismounts before he can reach her, and he winces at the sight of the arrow sticking out like a mast behind her.

"Careful," he hisses, rushing up to her.

"It's okay. I'm okay."

He's about to bark his retort, to demand that she let him help her this time, but she shoulders off her small day pack and swings it around to her front, taking the arrow with it. Air rushes out of Buri's lungs, and he blinks at the sight. Miraculously, the bag took all the impact from the weapon, stopping it before it pierced Georgia's back.

He tips his face to the sky, closing his eyes as relief quakes through him.

"It must have gone through my laptop," Georgia speculates.

Her delicate brows are knitted together as she opens her pack to survey the damage. The arrow has punctured through two thick volumes of books and penetrated the centre of the hard drive. Georgia's hands are quivering as she inspects the computer. She takes a few tremulous breaths, looking like she's trying her best not to lose her shit.

You and me both, baby.

"I'm guessing they weren't the Russians," she says, her voice tight, eyes still fixed on the laptop and books in her hands.

"No." Not with that kind of archery skill or horsemanship.

They must have been Mongols. And Mongols of a tribe he hasn't seen or heard of before.

Unease crawls over him, tightening the muscles in his back.

"Lucky they missed," Georgia murmurs, though she doesn't look convinced by her own words.

"I don't think it was luck." Buri shakes his head, recalling the matchless speed of the cavalry, the way the shots hit everywhere around but not *on* him, the way the whirlwind attack came out of nowhere only to disappear just as quickly. The archers must have been almost half a mile away, mounted on sprinting horses, and yet every shot they delivered was with pinpoint accuracy. Every arrow fell exactly where they intended it.

Just like the one that has destroyed Georgia's laptop, and all their research with it.

A chill radiates up his spine and neck, prickling through his scalp and all the way to the tips of his hair. He knows he is completely out of his depth now. The Russians, he can somehow handle. But this . . . these are Mongol warriors using battle skills that were lost long ago and have not been seen for hundreds of years. Warfare tactics which won Chinggis his empire, levelling everything in the path of his juggernaut of an army.

"Buri?" Georgia is studying him, and what she sees on his face seems to spook her even more.

"It's a warning." He tries to keep his voice casual. He's not sure he succeeds. "People don't want us here."

Georgia purses her lips. "Then it must mean we are getting close."

Indi canters over, leaning against his leg with a whine, as if seeking reassurance, too. He gives her an absent-minded pat on the head and looks around to survey their surroundings, realising that they are now two horses short. He curses, mentally taking stock of what they have lost. The missing mares had more than half of their food supply, one of the tents and other essential camping equipment, as well as extra rifles and ammunition.

He is now left with the Glock holstered to his thigh, two spare magazines, and the large hunting knife nestled in the folds of his *deel*.

"Fuck!" he cusses, balling up his fists. His fear rises, along with the urge to punch something.

Georgia's face blanches and she takes a step back, her dark brown eyes wide.

Dammit, Buri. Get a hold of yourself. You're scaring her.

With a deep inhale, he reins in some of his anger. Softening his voice, he says, "The sun's setting. I'm going to see what I can gather to start a fire. Set up the tent, will you?"

Georgia gasps as he turns to walk away. She stops him with a hand on his bicep.

"Buri." She gestures to his left shoulder blade. "You're hurt."

He cranes his neck to find his t-shirt soaked with blood, a long gaping hole torn through the fabric. He didn't even feel the scrape of the arrow in the mad rush of escaping their attackers.

"It's fine," he grunts. "Just a graze."

"But you're still bleeding," Georgia argues. "We have to clean the wound."

Ire rises. He's about to snap at her, to tell her that they have much bigger problems right now, to reveal that he's endured worse—much worse—injuries than this tiny little scratch. But the distress in her eyes stops him.

She's right. You need to get it cleaned.

With a nod, he mutters, "Later. The fire first. It'll be dark soon. We're higher and closer to Siberia here. It's gonna be cold tonight."

He walks off, venturing deeper into the darkening woods. He sifts through the ground covered by fir needles, his hunting knife in hand as he gathers an assortment of wood, kindling, and dried animal dung—whatever he can find to fuel the fire. He stashes the collection into the linen bag he retrieves from the pouch of his *deel*.

His mind still rattled, his nerves completely fried, he begins to wonder if they should even attempt to enter the gates of Ikh Khorig tomorrow. He's pretty certain that the archers were the same people who were hiding in the woods at Almsgivers Wall.

Have they been tracking him and Georgia since the beginning? How much do they know?

The incident today feels like a mere caution. It's unlikely they would be treated with the same courtesy next time. In fact, Buri's pretty certain they would not survive another encounter.

He considers calling Brandon for backup, but he knows what the DIA agent would say. This entire area, being deep in Mongol protected lands and so close to the Russian border, is a diplomatic minefield for the US government. The reason Buri has been brought in on this case is because there is no easy way for the DIA to send operatives in without causing an international uproar.

They're on their own.

As he finishes gathering what he needs and turns to head back towards camp, he finds himself questioning the ethics of his involvement in this mission, something which he hasn't thought to consider until now. He realises with startling discomfort that when it comes down to it, he is about to violate the sacred grounds of his own ancestors by searching for Chinggis Khan's grave.

For most of his life, especially throughout his rigorous training in the army, Buri has been loyal and committed to the country he has identified with since he was a child: the United States of America. It is where his father's side of the family has placed its roots in the early days of British colonisation, and where he has spent most of his childhood and adult life. He grew up in a military family: his father, step-mother, and brother all work in the same field, serving the interests of the American people. But Buri's years of service have left him disillusioned with the army, and with his government's political agenda. After the mess of the Iraq War, doubt began creeping into his mind until he just didn't know whose purpose he was fighting for anymore.

And in the years since he's returned to Mongolia—his mother's home and where he was also born—Buri has found a sense of belonging and kinship he's never experienced elsewhere.

Where, now, should his allegiances lie?

In the dark, he spots movement low on the ground, and his mind snaps back to the present moment. He freezes, his gaze zeroing in on the small animal scuttling away from him. Instinct takes over and he throws his blade with a sharp flick of his wrist, sending the knife hurtling through the air.

A soft squeal.

Then, silence.

He cannot believe his luck.

At least there'll be dinner tonight.

41

When Buri returns to camp, he sees that Georgia has already unpacked the one remaining supply horse. Their only tent is up, too, and she has spread a piece of tarpaulin on the ground to sit on. The damaged books rest in her lap, gaping holes yawning through them.

Her eyes bulge when she sees him draw near. "What's that?"

Buri grins as if he's just come back from his first hunt, holding up his catch with pride. "I'm making *boodog* for dinner," he explains, then translates: "Marmot barbecue."

She stares at the headless, bloody lump of fur and muscle in his hand. "But we've got freeze-dried meals—"

"We need to ration those. Most of our supplies are gone."

She blinks. Then, turning her gaze away, she says, "I'm not hungry."

The sting of her rejection surprises him. He curbs his annoyance just in time, startled by how he's so affected by the diminutive woman in front of him. Shuttering his expression and keeping his tone even, he says, "It's a

Mongolian delicacy. Indi needs to be fed. And you need to eat. We haven't had a proper meal all day."

At the mention of her name, the German Shepherd ambles over, sniffing at the game in Buri's hand with curiosity. Her mouth drops open as she looks up at him, flapping her tail with excitement.

At least someone appreciates it, Buri thinks, his dampened mood lifting somewhat as he watches the drool hang off Indi's lolling tongue.

He crouches down and gets the fire going, heating up stones he found from his scour through the forest. He already gutted and drained the blood from the large ground squirrel before returning to camp, knowing that the gory process would likely chase away Georgia's appetite. Once the rocks are red hot, Buri places them through the animal's neck cavity and sews up the hole, cooking the whole thing from the inside.

With his knife he splits the end of a stick, inserts a good amount of tinder, and sets it on fire. Using this makeshift torch he quickly burns the fur off the marmot, scraping charred layer off with his knife. The stench of burning hair makes him break out in a cold sweat, bringing back memories he has fought so hard to keep at bay. He scrunches his face up and holds his breath, soldiering through the roiling in his stomach.

With the rising temperature of the air inside, the stewing marmot inflates to the size of a watermelon, its four tiny legs sticking out at the ends. Buri has to brush off Indi's multiple attempts at getting too close to the meal as the fragrance of the cooking meat becomes more pleasant. Even Georgia throws an interested glance from where she is sitting cross-legged on the tarp.

Buri watches her as she carefully smooths out each torn

page of the books in her lap. Her laptop is on the ground beside her, and from the looks of the puncture through its centre, it is clear the thing cannot be salvaged.

"What are we going to do now that all the research is gone?" asks Buri. With everything that's been running through his mind, he is half tempted to call Miller and tell the agent that he's pulling the plug on the mission. Fuck the DIA and the Russians. If Georgia says the word, Buri will pack it all up and take them back to safer grounds.

"I don't know. But at least I've still got my notes and the books."

"Can you remember any of what was on your laptop?"

She shrugs. "Mostly. The material that I've worked through, anyway. The problem is that I can't receive any more emails from Sarah. Also, she sent me some satellite images of Ikh Khorig, and I haven't had a chance to go through all of them."

"Do we have enough to keep going?"

When she stares at him as if she's not sure what he's asking, Buri clarifies, "Do you want to turn back? Return to Ulaanbaatar?"

She jerks her head back as if she's shocked he even suggested it. Her answer is as resolute as the look on her face. "No."

Seeing her determination, Buri nods. "Okay."

Night falls and the temperature drops. Georgia pulls her sleeping bag over her legs to keep warm. Buri watches the marmot stewing slowly with hot rocks in its belly, guarding it from Indi's hungry advances. The sting of the wound in his back begins to really bother him. He realises that the cut may be deeper than he initially thought.

He sighs.

Well, let's get this over with.

Buri rises to his feet and walks over to Georgia. He grabs the neck of his t-shirt, yanking it over his head.

She staggers back, stammering up at him, "What—what are you doing?"

He stills, standing topless in front of her. The chill of the evening makes him break out in goosebumps. "You were going to help me clean the wound?"

"Oh," she whispers, her eyes travelling down his chest and continuing to his navel. She flushes, then clears her throat. "Oh, right." She snaps out of her shock and reaches for the first aid kit, fumbling with the contents.

Gritting his teeth, Buri turns and sits down, waiting for Georgia's horrified gasp when she sees the ungodly appearance of his body. The sound doesn't come, but her sudden silence is a heavy weight on his shoulders. He wonders what is going through her head as she takes in the myriad of scars all over his mutilated skin.

Is it horror? Is it disgust? Is it pity?

He knows the gash across his left scapular is nothing compared to the terrifying sight of the ugly, twisted flesh canvasing his entire back.

To her credit, Georgia doesn't utter a word. She attends to his injury with gentleness, the feel of her warm, tentative touch burning a direct path to his groin.

Too soon, she finishes her work, dressing the cut with waterproof plaster. Buri murmurs his thanks and reaches for a clean shirt, freezing when he feels her trembling fingers trace over his lower spine. It's one of the deepest gouges he has.

"Your scars . . ." she says hesitantly. "Is this why you got the Purple Heart?"

The muscles in his shoulders tense. He keeps his back to her, knowing that he won't be able to stand it if he sees pity in her eyes. "Yeah. It was from my last tour in Syria."

"What happened?"

He worries his fingers over the fabric of his shirt. Keeps his voice monotonous. Tries to make the story as succinct as possible. "We were sent in to gather intel. But it turned out to be a trap. The mission was a complete clusterfuck, doomed from the very beginning. When we arrived, we found the entire village dead—men, women, children, babies—massacred with chemical weapons. My team was ambushed. I was captured, interrogated for information until a rescue team got me out."

He finishes his story there, determined not to say any more, leaving out details he doesn't want to explore. Details like how he lost some of the people closest to him that day, brothers who trained and served with him, whom he trusted more than anyone else in the world. How he, as a medic, failed to do the single essential task of his job: to bring his teammates home alive. How he ended up being the only one who survived. And how it still surprises him that the shame and guilt of it all would burn him more than those fuckers ever did in Syria.

He expects Georgia to say something in sympathy, to express her regret for what he went through. He braces himself for that tone in her voice, the same voice everyone else uses when they find out, showing just how sorry they are for him. And if she does, Buri's probably going to stand up, walk off, and spend the night elsewhere in the forest.

To his amazement, she remains quiet. Curiosity takes over, and Buri steels himself before turning to look at her. What he finds in those big brown eyes is not pity, but rage.

"Those . . . *savages*." Her nostrils flare as she draws in a shuddering breath. "Is that why you got Indi?"

"Yeah," he admits.

Wary of getting too deep into the conversation, he pulls the shirt over his head, rising to check on dinner. He's relieved and also a little surprised when Georgia doesn't pursue the subject further.

Poking at the marmot and seeing that it's ready, Buri cuts into the flesh to release the hot air, then divides the steaming meal and dishes up portions for all three of them.

They eat in silence, chewing on rich, gamey meat. He watches Georgia as she consumes less than half of her plate, then gives the rest of it to Indi. He frowns. It has not escaped his notice that she scarcely eats enough, even for a tiny woman like her.

In fact, it's obvious that she is not taking care of herself at all. Buri has observed on many occasions that she barely sleeps a few hours a night. He wonders if the lack of rest and appetite are symptoms of grief from the death of her friends Ethan Sommers and Hiroshi Akiyama, or if the professor is hiding more personal troubles he doesn't know about.

He stares at Georgia as she resumes her task of smoothing out the torn pages of her books. The woman absolutely baffles him. He's never come across the likes of her, but he cannot pinpoint exactly *how* she is so different.

He puzzles over the strangely determined way she has thwarted all his attempts to treat her bullet wound. Perhaps Georgia is just fiercely independent and refuses to accept help from others, because he could tell she was lying when she made the excuse of being shy with her body. Come to think of it, she seems to have healed from the gunshot graze rather quickly.

Too quickly.

He also ponders on the peculiar way she moves. He's only observed it a couple of times, when she was engrossed in another task and seemed to unconsciously shift into a different sense of being: light, effortless, unhurried yet remarkably efficient. And fast. It's quite something to behold.

Indi finishes crunching through Georgia's food and now comes to him, begging for what's on his plate. He sets it on the ground for her and she works through the last of his meal, the bones and sinew disappearing in two gluttonous bites. With dinner done, Buri puts away everything so that scavengers don't come in the night. Then he stands, clears his throat and declares, "It's late. We should get some sleep."

She murmurs her agreement, then looks up at him when he stays there, waiting. She turns to stare at the lone tent a few paces away, then pulls her sleeping bag further up her torso.

"You take the tent," she says. "I'm sleeping out here."

What does she think, that I'm going to take advantage of her? He snorts. "You'll freeze."

"Indi will keep me warm."

"Indi is sleeping with me."

She glares up at him. "Fine."

"You realise there are bears out here?"

"Bears?" Her eyes widen.

He proffers his hand. "I promise I'll be a total gentleman. Besides, Indi will be right between us."

Georgia casts quick, darting glances around them, and

Buri knows she can see nothing but the pitch dark of the forest.

Somewhere in the distance, a wolf howls.

She starts at the sound. Scrambling up, she grabs his extended hand. He bites the inside of his cheek to suppress a smirk, the triumph of the moment giving him more satisfaction than he anticipated.

42

Anya guides her horse up the uneven slope of the Khentii range, leading her team south towards Burkhan Khaldun as the sun rises over the distant mountain. The locals call the peak Khan Khentii, or "King of the Khentii", and according to Dr. Fujimoto's information, Anya should be able to reach it later today.

Before he took his last breath, Fujimoto told Anya exactly where Chinggis Khan's tomb should be. The answer was so fitting, she knew straight away that it could be nothing else. Chinggis was a devout mountain worshipper. He attributed all of his successes to Burkhan Khaldun, and it has been said he once vowed to remember the sacred mountain in his prayers every morning, proclaiming that all of his descendants shall do the same.

The location is perfect. High up, tucked away from the rest of the world, impossible to get into, and even more difficult to get out of. Reaching over three-thousand metres above sea level, the Khentii is made up of some of the most ancient mountains on earth, smoothed by erosion over time. Surrounded by uninhabited dense forest, thick underbrush, and steep-sided ridges of scree, there are only deer paths through it all. Grounds are iced over in winter, wet and boggy in the summer. It is no mystery why excavation has never been done in this region. The entire operation would be such an undertaking that it'd be hard to keep it a secret. In fact, Fujimoto told Anya that when the Japanese came to Mongolia with their Three Rivers Project back in the 90s, some team members were threatened with death if they dared to investigate Burkhan Khaldun. And this is also the reason Fujimoto hadn't attempted to search this area himself.

She can already see the summit from here, jutting out above its surrounding forests and glistening in the sunlight. The sight seems like a remote and unattainable mirage, and she nudges her horse into a faster gait, eager to reach her destination. She swats away the swarm of small, black flies accumulating around her. To her rear, Lev and Alexey struggle to keep up on their own geldings, Lev's massive frame dwarfing the animal under him. It's obvious he's too heavy for it, but it was the best they could get given the situation.

Progress has been frustratingly slow, especially over the treacherous mountain terrain. It took her team a week just to drive back to Russia through the trackless wilderness, acquire the team of horses they needed, then cross the Siberian border again into the most difficult and inaccessible part of Mongolia. This was a much less convenient route, but one that was necessary. Approaching from the north meant they didn't need to go through the guarded gates of the Forbidden Zone, and their mission would escape the attention of the local officials.

She has already done her homework on the way here, assessing satellite images and working out a definitive plan with Alexey, going over the scientific imaging techniques they would employ. As soon as they get to the site that Fujimoto told them about, they will use their instruments to locate the exact spot and start digging.

Not long, now.

She smiles, thinking again of the secret Deda Dmitry whispered in her ear on his deathbed. All her life, all of her efforts have been for this purpose, and when she finally gets what she seeks, she will become the most powerful woman in the world.

It's not likely that they'll run into any resistance. This region is so remote, Anya doubts they'll encounter anyone else here. The locals make their annual pilgrimages over winter, no tourists are allowed in the Khentii National Park, and Fujimoto told her that Darkhat guards usually stick around the southern perimeters of the area, making sure that no one goes in and out without authorisation.

Her mind travels to the gorgeous Professor Georgia Lee, wondering where her esteemed colleague is now. Judging by her impressive track record, the woman is exceptionally skilled and resourceful. Anya has no doubt she will see the professor again soon enough.

43

GEORGIA HOVERS between the state of sleep and consciousness, struggling to pull her sluggish mind out of her dream. She is fighting so hard to get to the surface, clawing her way towards the light, but every time she gets close, she is sucked back down into the depths of oblivion again. Like this she drifts in and out, plagued with images and memories of Ethan, Wang Jian, and Charlie, her chest wrenching with fear, guilt, and shame.

When she finally wakes, she discovers that her cheeks are streaked with tears. The light of dawn filters through the trees, making shadows on the walls of the tent. She glances at her watch: ten minutes to five. She is surprised she's slept so late. But then again, she was awake for most of last night, too wary of Buri's presence to fall asleep.

Looking around, she finds herself alone in the nylon-fashioned shelter. She wipes the remaining traces of moisture from her face and unzips her sleeping bag to crawl out of the tent, seeing that Buri is already packing their belongings onto the horses. Indi is nearby, gnawing on a piece of bone from last night.

"Mornin'," Buri says, barely glancing over as he focuses on the chore. "Sleep okay?"

"No." She rises to her feet, stretching. "You?"

"No." He frowns. "Gotta get going though. The gate's not far from here. You hungry? Wanna eat something?"

"No. Thanks."

She disassembles the tent and helps Buri load everything onto their three remaining horses. Soon, they set off at a steady trot, staying under the cover of the forest this time. Buri seems even more alert than usual, his eyes darting everywhere, scanning the woods and the fields beyond. Georgia realises that he is expecting another ambush. The thought spikes her heart rate, and she urges her mare to pick up speed.

As they get closer to their destination, they see evidence of rituals and offerings dotted along the perimeter. Tepee-shaped *ovoos* of varying sizes have been erected: sacred mounds of log and piled stones decorated with blue scarves symbolic of the Eternal Blue Sky. The sight of them makes Georgia think of the eerie, paganistic constructions found deep in the woods in a horror movie. Empty bottles of vodka are scattered on the ground beside the *ovoos*, left over from recent acts of worship.

The team slows to a walk when they see a gate guarded by two Darkhat men.

"I'll do the talking," Buri says. "If they ask you anything, just act demure and blush like a new bride. Can you manage that?"

She wants to roll her eyes at this, but admits to herself it's the only thing she can do since she doesn't speak the language. They draw their horses to a stop at a respectable distance, and Buri dismounts and walks over to the guards. She nods her head at the men in greeting when they look over at her.

Unlike the Darkhats at the Mausoleum of Genghis Khan, these men are dressed casually in modern clothes. They are solemn in their demeanour and appear pretty ordinary and harmless, but Buri has warned her they are not to be underestimated. And it may seem like there are only two people patrolling the area, but reinforcements are always nearby.

When the trio begin to talk at length, she gets off her horse, watching from afar as the men continue their discussion. The Darkhats ask few questions and betray little emotion on their faces. She notices that both of them are wearing distinctive rings, bearing what she is guessing to be a *tamgha*, the identifying mark of their clan:

They throw occasional glances at her, shaking their heads. It doesn't seem to be going well. After a while, Buri sighs with resignation and walks back towards Georgia. One of the men brings out a satellite phone from his pocket to make a call.

"What's going on?" Georgia asks when Buri returns, keeping her voice low.

"They won't let us through," he replies as he places a hand on the rein of his horse, ready to get back on.

"Why? What did you tell them?"

"I said that my new, half-Mongolian bride and I have just returned to the country, and we are here to pay our respects to our ancestors. I told them we want to pray at Burkhan Khaldun for a baby as strong as our nation's father."

Her heart does an unexpected flip in her chest. "And?"

"And they said they understand our sincerity, but the journey isn't suitable for a woman."

"Why not?"

"Because the spirits that reside in the mountain are too powerful. Mongolians believe that if a woman climbs Burkhan Khaldun, the spirits will render her infertile."

The notion, as ridiculous as it sounds, actually makes her feel ill-at-ease. And it annoys her. She's normally the one who brushes off these types of superstitions.

"So that's it? We can't get through?"

"Not unless you want to go up against the Darkhats. And that's not something I recommend." He puts his boot in the stirrup. "Let's head back the way we came and see if we can find another access."

At that moment, the guard on the phone finishes his conversation and calls out to them. Walking closer, he stashes the device into his pocket and says something to Buri in Mongolian.

Buri turns to her, his eyes lighting up. "He says there's a way they can get you in."

44

GEORGIA RISES from the rock she has been sitting on for the past two hours as a black truck pulls up to the gate. She fidgets with the sash of her *deel*, feeling a flutter of nerves in her chest.

"I still don't understand why the Darkhats have asked for this," Georgia grumbles.

"I'm surprised, too. To be honest, I thought they'd tell us to go home." Buri turns to her. "Look, it's a simple shamanic ritual. They believe the only way to protect you is to make an offering to appease the spirits of Burkhan Khaldun."

Georgia scowls. Then she recomposes her expression as a young woman gets out of the vehicle. She's a pretty, dainty girl, looks to be about sixteen, and is wearing a violet *deel* with an orange sash. A matching fur hat sits snugly on her head, and her hair whips in the wind in long strings of tiny braids.

"*That's* the shaman?" Georgia asks Buri, surprised.

"No, that's the shaman's assistant."

They exchange nods and greetings, and Georgia stills when she senses hostility in the young woman's eyes. She blinks, thinking she must be mistaken, and offers a friendly smile, but the girl has already turned away, unloading various paraphernalia from the rear tray of the pickup. She sets up a trestle table in front of a nearby *ovoo*, carefully arranging instruments and items for worship.

Drums. Golden bowls full of curd and sweets. Ceremonial cups of vodka, milk, and *airag*. Oil lamps. Animal bones, hide, and horns. Strips of silk of blue, red, and yellow. Knives. And a living, kicking sheep.

Georgia widens her eyes at the ewe and turns to Buri, who looks apologetically back at her.

"That's uncommon these days," he admits, muttering under his breath.

Georgia stares at the poor creature, oblivious to its fate. Dread fills her, and she remembers as a child, her own superstitious mother would take her to all manner of astrologers and clairvoyants. These soothsayers would tell of Georgia's future, and more importantly, why she was such a wilful, ungrateful kid. They would also offer Georgia's mother enticing solutions: rites, potions, and talismans that promised a more docile and obedient daughter. These, of course, always involved exorbitant costs.

But none of those experiences ever included animal sacrifices.

Having set up the pagan shrine, the shaman's assistant walks back to them and speaks to Buri in Mongolian at length. He listens and nods, and when she is finished, Buri takes Georgia by the elbow and leads her to the altar.

There is a piece of deerskin spread over the soft grass, and Buri instructs Georgia to kneel down.

"When the shaman comes, he's going to perform a ceremony to invite the spirits of the ancestors into his body. Drumming, incantations, that sort of thing," Buri explains. "And once he is possessed, I won't be able to understand him since he'll be speaking in another tongue from a different time. His assistant will translate for me, and I for you."

"I don't like this," Georgia protests, unease creeping up her spine as she watches the young assistant make a fire from a pile of dried horse dung. From within her violet *deel*, the girl brings out a small pouch and sprinkles some brown powder into the flames. A sickly, pungent scent fills the air.

"It's okay," Buri reassures her. "I've gone through a few of these now. The ceremonies are pretty harmless. I promise."

The girl strides over to the passenger door of the truck. Opening it, she helps the shaman out of the car.

The hairs at the back of Georgia's neck stand on end as she watches the tall, dark figure stride towards the altar, stopping right in front of her so she has to crane her neck to look up at him. She takes in the long, ebony gown, the elaborate headdress wrapped in blue silk and topped with deer antlers, and the veil of black dreadlocks that extend to the shaman's chest, completely obscuring his face. Large eyes are painted on the front of the crown, above which is a golden coin with the symbol of the Garuda. Thick snakes of leather-clad cables hang down from the headdress, stretching the length of his robe, reaching all the way to his shins. There are several necklaces with large copper medallions dangling from his neck, and his shoulders are draped with strips of blue, red, and golden silk intertwined with strings of beads and bells that rattle with his every movement. Bulky rings of intricate symbols and designs adorn each finger of his hand. Tucked in his belt is a woven leather whip and a dagger.

Georgia swallows against the fear clawing at the back of her throat.

For a moment, the shaman just stands there, looming over her. Georgia cannot see his face, and she wonders if he is watching her from behind the screen of the dreads. His assistant hands him a large bowl of *airag*, and he parts the dreads to take long sips, revealing only his lips. He sprinkles the white liquid in the air and onto the ground, flicking droplets onto Georgia's head. He then passes the bowl to her.

"Drink," Buri instructs, kneeling down beside her.

She does as she is told, and the shaman repeats the same process with vodka, all the while muttering indecipherable words under his breath.

Then the shaman begins to sing. With a deep, resounding voice, he chants a repetitive chorus with the heavy beat of the drum in his hands. The combined sounds reverberate through Georgia's body. She is consumed by the intoxicating, suffocatingly sweet aroma of the incense, the buzz of the vodka in her veins, the ceaseless pounding that builds in rhythm and intensity until the atmosphere is absolutely electrified around her.

Beads of sweat trickle down her back. She lowers her gaze to the black leather boots on the shaman's feet. Her stomach roils as her head begins to spin.

All at once, the shaman drops the drum onto the ground.

Silence.

She lifts her face and sees the startling change in his

bearing, realising that this is the spirit possession Buri was talking about. The shaman towers above her, seeming to have become impossibly taller and broader in frame. He sways to the left and right, the beads and bells clinking along the length of his robe. His thumbs touch the tips of each finger in quick succession as if he is calculating something.

His movements suddenly still, and his voice is even deeper—a low, sonorous boom now—as he barks a quick command.

Beside him, his young assistant translates the message into Mongolian, and Buri says to Georgia, "What is your name?"

"Georgia Lee." Her voice comes out as a hoarse whisper.

Her answer is translated back to the shaman, who utters more words in the strange language. Again, the young woman passes on the message, and Buri translates for her. Like this, a series of questions and answers are transmitted between Georgia and the shaman:

"When were you born?"

"December seventh, 1982," she replies.

"Why are you here?"

"I . . . we—we want to pay our respects to the ancestors. To the Great Khan."

The shaman reaches for the whip in his belt and makes a sharp lash at the air. She flinches back in shock.

"Why are you really here?" he asks again. "What is your true intention?"

She darts a quick glance at Buri, who reassures her with his dark eyes. She drops her gaze to the ground, saying, "We . . . we want to pray for a baby."

The shaman pauses when her answer is relayed back to

him. He leans down to lift Georgia's chin. He watches her from behind those black dreads. Dropping his hand, he asks another question.

Buri says after the assistant translates: "Show him your hands."

She reluctantly complies, and the shaman holds onto her, examining the lines on her palms. He sways back and forth, more forcefully this time, the long strings of dreads and beads whipping about him. He is murmuring something that sounds like a chant, and Georgia wonders if he has once again slipped into the trance-like state. Then he stops moving and intones something with a low rumble, and even though she doesn't understand the words, a distinctive tremor travels down the length of her spine. When Buri says nothing after the young woman has given her translation, Georgia turns to look at him. She can't decipher the expression on his face.

He looks uncertain when he finally meets her eyes. "The shaman said you've already had your child," he tells her.

Jacqui. Her daughter.

Georgia's face drains of colour. Her chest hollows, and a deep, familiar ache radiates from the seat of her bowels, spreading to the tips of her toes and fingers, and all the way to the ends of her hair. She blinks at the sting in her eyes and tries to pull away, but the shaman holds her firmly in place, tightening his grip on her hands. At that moment his assistant steps up and slices Georgia's left palm open in one swift movement.

Georgia gasps and yanks her hands back, but not before the girl has smeared the blood onto a piece of animal bone. Buri surges to his feet, stepping in between them defensively as he growls something in Mongolian.

The girl ignores him and throws the scapular into the fire. Then there's a whole lot of commotion as the two speak over each other at the same time. Georgia scuttles away from the shaman, who just stands there, motionless. She reaches into her *deel* for her bandanna, wrapping her palm in a make-shift bandage.

Eventually, the shaman's assistant seems to pacify Buri. He turns back to her, glowering when he sees her hand clenched around the cloth. "You okay, Georgia?"

"Fine," she bites out, clutching her injury protectively to her chest. "What the hell was that for?"

"She said it was part of the ritual. They need to burn the bone and read the cracks to tell your fortune. I'm sorry. I've never seen that done before. Do you want to keep going?"

"No," she admits with an agitated sigh. "But let's just get this over with."

"You sure?"

She gives him a decisive nod.

He stares at her for a beat. Exhaling through his nose, he consoles: "We'll get this done and then I'll dress that wound for you, okay?"

She drops her eyes to the ground. Already, the sting in her palm has transformed into a numbness. There won't be a wound for Buri to dress before this is finished.

He helps her back onto the animal skin, kneeling once again in front of the shaman. The assistant brings over the sheep, and Georgia's heart sinks. Lifting the animal's front legs and pinning its wriggling body between her legs, the girl shows surprising strength as she holds the creature in place, exposing its white belly. The ewe thrashes and bleats, then stills as if knowing it is futile to resist.

That's when Georgia notices a large ring on the girl's

forefinger, not dissimilar to the ones on the Darkhats, but this one has a familiar symbol on it:

The drumming resumes, an intense battering that coincides with the throbbing in Georgia's skull. It seems to go on forever, and she wants to curl in on herself, to press her hands to her ears and to ask them to stop. As the shaman's singing reaches a crescendo, the young woman slits open the animal's throat with a violent tug of her dagger. Blood, thick and dark, pours forth from the gash, and the girl catches it with a golden bowl.

Georgia recoils and scrunches up her face, queasy from the sight.

When the last of the gore has drained into the crucible, the assistant lowers the lifeless body of the sheep to the ground and places the dish on the altar with the offerings of sweets and curd. She retrieves the burnt scapular from the fire with a pair of tongs, placing it on a platter and showing it to the shaman. He studies it for a long time.

His voice is soft when he finally speaks, and the message is relayed to Georgia: "Your past has damaged your heart and injured your connection with those you love and those who love you. You were sent here by your own soul so you can learn to heal yourself. It's your intention that matters. If your heart is genuine, you will find what you are looking for. The spirits have granted you their blessing to proceed to Burkhan Khaldun, where your true nature and destiny shall be revealed."

45

NARAN WATCHES as Georgia and Buri ride away with the dog trotting alongside them. Her father comes up to join her, having taken off his ceremonial robe and headdress.

"Did you really have to cut the woman?" he reprimands.

She shrugs. "I wanted to see how she would react."

He glares at her, but she ignores him and returns her gaze to the receding figures in the distance, now disappearing into the dense tree line.

As the *Teb Tengeri*, the nation's head shaman, Naran's father is one of the most respected men in Mongolia. The role comes from a tradition that dates all the way back to Chinggis Khan's time, where the revered *Teb Tengeri* would be consulted on all the pivotal decisions, on and off the battlefield. He would accompany the Khan on major campaigns, holding pre-battle ceremonies that called upon the spirits to ensure Mongol success.

At Gerel's request, he has travelled all the way here from the capital, something which he has not done for many, many years. But the tribe needs his counsel, and unusual circumstances calls for extraordinary measures.

"What did you see, father?" she asks.

"I saw enough."

She turns to him. "Tell me."

"I don't like your tone, Naran." His gaze is fixed on the distant mountains ahead, and Naran can tell that he is angry from the iciness of his voice.

She lowers her gaze and softens her voice. "Can you please tell me what you saw?"

His lips press into a thin, flat line. He lifts his chin, refusing to look at her. "That's for me to discuss with Gerel. Not you."

She quietly sucks in a breath, seething at his comment. It has been over a decade since they last met, and he still treats her like the child she once was.

But she knows better than to rebuff.

Besides being the *Teb Tengeri*, her father also holds one of the most important seats in the government, and it is for this reason that Naran was sent away as a child to be raised by Gerel. His high-profile political career brings far too much attention to himself, and it would have cast an unwanted spotlight on his daughter and the covert faction that she would eventually take over one day.

And Naran resents him for it.

"Naran." He finally turns to her, his stare boring a hole into her profile until she meets his eyes.

What she sees in there is the regard of a superior upon his subordinate, a man who only cares that his orders are carried out, and nothing else. Naran doesn't remember a time when he's ever gazed upon her with the warmth or affection of a father.

"I do *not* want you to interfere with the foreigners. The

woman is going to play a vital role in our prophecy, the prophecy that affects the fate of all of our people." He glowers at her. "So you stay out of this, you hear me?"

Her heart flutters at this morsel of information. She mutters under her breath, "Fine."

"*Excuse* me?"

She brings her gaze to her elder. Then, dropping her eyes to the ground, she says, "Yes, father."

46

BURI QUICKENS his gelding to catch up to Georgia. She was on her mare and cantering off as soon as the ceremony was over, putting as much distance between her and the shaman as possible. He has never seen anyone mount a horse with that kind of speed. And *levity*. The smooth, graceful manoeuvre was like something out of a Chinese martial arts movie.

He takes in his surroundings, feeling as if he's taken a step back in time. The remote, pristine landscape has been unchanged by the centuries, and he can see miles upon miles of uninterrupted forest, much of it impenetrable with thick vegetation and granite boulders. Indi wanders far up ahead of Georgia, sniffing for marmot burrows.

He thanks the stars that they did not come in a van. The national park is uninhabited, and there will be no one to seek help from if they get stuck.

Buri slows his horse as he comes up to Georgia, keeping pace with her. They ride abreast with each other for several silent minutes. He's trying to gauge her mood, to determine how to approach this. She ignores his presence altogether, her gaze steadfast on the trail ahead, her chest rising and falling with quick, trembling succession. He doesn't have to be a mind-reader to know that she's still rattled by what happened during the shamanic ritual.

The woman has racked up a few injuries on this mission, and Buri can't help but feel somewhat responsible. He certainly didn't expect the shaman's assistant to cut Georgia. The animal sacrifice was already bad enough, but to also shed human blood? He's never heard of such a practice in Mongolia.

In the three years of living here, Buri has come to admire and even take on some of the beliefs of shamanism, a form of animism imbued with a deep respect and reverence for the natural world. Shamanists worship the sun, the moon, the mountains, the trees, and above all, the Eternal Blue Sky that stretches over everything from horizon to horizon. The concept of God—of divinity—is so pervasive and immense, that He cannot possibly be contained within the four walls of a church or a temple. Every individual soul has a direct link to Heaven, under which all are born free and equal. And worship is a simple matter of immediate communication between oneself and nature, with no priests or monks necessary as intermediary.

Even though the philosophy resonates with Buri, he is still not a fan of the rituals, and what happened today seriously gives him pause. It wasn't anything he had ever observed before. To say that he is nonplussed by the experience is an understatement.

Staring at Georgia's hand clutched protectively over her chest, he says, "Let me have a look at the wound. We should clean it and dress it properly."

"It's fine," she responds, not meeting his eyes. "Just a small cut. The girl caught me by surprise, is all."

Bullshit. "Didn't seem like a small cut with the amount of blood that was involved."

She says nothing but clenches her left fist over the reddened handkerchief, showing no inclination to let him see it. Buri works his jaws, knowing that if he keeps pressing she's just going to shut down even more, and that is the last thing he wants. The haunted, ghastly look on her face when she heard the shaman's comment about children chilled him to the bone, and he wants to know what the hell that was about. Buri has read her file several times, the details of which are imprinted firmly in his mind. There was no mention in there about any dependents.

"You okay?" he asks.

She looks ahead, still not meeting his eyes. Her voice is soft when she says, "Yeah."

"Wanna talk about it?" The question is out of his mouth before he can stop himself. He smacks his lips together, wondering what the fuck he is thinking by asking her that. Talking has never been something he's good at. It's ironic that even with his linguistics major in college, words are far from his strongest skill. He prefers to do, to make, and he would much rather his actions speak for him.

Georgia peers over at him, looking equally surprised by the question. "I hate fortune tellers," she finally admits.

He gives her a wry smile. "I've gone through a fair few of these shamanic rituals since moving back here. They're not all bad. Some of the shamans can be . . . eerily accurate."

His smile fades as he sees Georgia's expression. He's

not sure if it is anger or sadness. Whatever she is feeling, he wants to make it go away.

"Did you tell him?" she asks, now looking like she wants to belt him.

His brows scrunch together with confusion. "Tell . . . who . . . what?"

"Was that in my file? I mean, I assume that the DIA has a file on me, right? Was Jacqui in my file?" she accuses again.

What? Dumbfounded, Buri reaches over for her reins. He gives a sharp tug, bringing both of their horses to a simultaneous stop. "Whoa. No. What are you talking about? Who's Jacqui?"

Her eyes suddenly well up, and his gut twists at the sight of the tear that escapes and rolls down her cheek. He balls up his fists, restraining himself from the urge to reach out and catch it with his finger. Georgia makes a quick swipe at her flushed face, looking at once embarrassed and annoyed.

"Jacqui, my daughter," she explains.

His frown deepens. "You have a daughter? No, that wasn't in your file," he answers truthfully, wondering why in the world Brandon Miller left that crucial detail out.

"I *had* a daughter," Georgia says. She drops her gaze. "She died six years ago. She was only two. How did the shaman . . . how did he . . . ?"

His chest constricts at the torment in her face. "I don't know. I'm sorry."

Georgia sniffles. She takes a deep breath. Finally, she straightens her posture, and when she lifts her eyes again Buri's surprised to see that they are no longer glistening with tears. Her expression at once resolute, she gives him a firm nod. She says, "It's fine. He probably just made it up. People like him usually do. It was a lucky guess."

She gives her horse a kick and moves on. Buri rushes to keep pace, scrambling for something to say, to comfort her. He comes up short.

Before he can stop, he hears himself ask, "Tell me about Ethan."

Her movements falter at his question. For a brief moment, her beautiful face contorts with despair. And something else.

Guilt, maybe?

"What about him?"

"Was he . . . the father of your child?" Buri asks, troubled at the twinge in his chest.

Last night while sharing her tent, he heard Georgia whisper Ethan's name over and over again as she tossed and turned in her sleep. He had to get out of there before it drove him mad.

"No," she says. "Lucas was the father. We got divorced recently."

"Ethan was your boyfriend, then?"

"Ethan . . ." She falters. "He was my best friend, the oldest friend I had. And he was . . . he was—" She sighs. Finally, she says, "It was complicated between us."

Buri nods as if he understands her meaning. He bites on the inside of his cheek so hard, he tastes blood. Something gnaws at him in his gut, and he doesn't want to acknowledge what it is.

"How are you dealing with what happened?" he asks, knowing perfectly well the pain she must be experiencing right now.

"I'm not." Her eyes harden as she says, "I'm just trying to do what I can to make sure that the Russians don't get what they want. It's the least I can do, for Ethan and our friend Hiroshi. And I want Anya to pay for what she did."

He studies her. He marvels at the concealed strength that is within the delicate appearance of this quiet, tiny woman. He wonders how—after all she has been through, the death of her child, the failure of her marriage, the murder of her friends—she is still able to hold herself together and be here, travelling to the ends of the earth with him and solving century-old riddles. Lord knows he dealt with his loss with much less grace than she seems to be. Her determination inspires him.

"Okay," Buri says. He decides then that he is going to do everything in his power to help Georgia achieve what she desires.

They ride on into the woods, making slow progress through the thirty-kilometres of marshland that naturally protects Burkhan Khaldun. The midday sun is harsh as the temperature soars. They stick to a mud track, made by infrequent pilgrims to the area.

It has been a particularly wet summer in the Khentii, and that means much of the ground is boggy and knee-deep with sludge, and thick swarms of small black flies hover like dense black clouds. Speaking becomes impossible without swallowing mouthfuls of insects. The horses wag their heads up and down, whipping their tails in the air, snorting loudly to dispel the pestilent midges. Pools of water are covered with an oily film from peat. Mud flicks up as the horses trudge heavily, sloshing through the gurgling puddles, spotting everyone's faces and bodies as they traverse through the swamp. Indi is much quicker and more nimble on her paws, hopping between patches of vegetation as she makes her way further ahead.

When they finally make it out of the bog, they ascend a

low grassy ridge. Buri checks the map and his GPS, identifying the place as the Threshold, the point past which it is taboo for women to travel. Wild flowers in all shades of pastel disperse through the grass. An impressive *ovoo* made with long pieces of pine has been erected here, covered by tattered lengths of blue silk flapping about in the breeze.

Everything is as his uncle Och has described.

Ahead, the ground falls away, the muddy, rutted trail steeply descending some seven hundred feet into the valley. Far beyond and rising high above the forests, is Burkhan Khaldun, the Khan of the Khentiis.

47

BURI AND GEORGIA travel another twenty kilometres through mud and water before finally reaching the base of Burkhan Khaldun. By the time he decides that they should stop and camp for the day, the sky is already darkening, and the temperature is dropping rapidly. He puts on more layers of clothing to keep warm, instructing Georgia to do the same before venturing into the woods to search for kindling and fuel.

Dark clouds hang low over the mountain, and an occasional distant rumble travels down to the valley. Buri keeps looking up, hoping that a storm doesn't break out on them tonight. In this land of marked extremes, the weather can be fierce and abrupt. It's not unusual to experience all four seasons in a day, and one has to be on the constant lookout for shelter in case a squall hits, especially one that blows in from Siberia.

With most of their food gone and no game in sight, he makes a light dinner out of the freeze-dried meals, careful to conserve what they have. Georgia doesn't seem interested in eating at all and is sitting on the tarp with her notebook in her lap. She stares at the same page with a pencil between her lips for the longest time, and Buri looks over to see what she is studying:

1, 4

2, 40

3, 45

4, 48

10, 108

"Are these the mistakes you found in *The Secret History*?" he asks.

"Yeah," she replies, tapping the end of her pencil on the page. "I've written down the locations that the mistakes appear in. The numbers on the left denote the chapters, and those on the right are the sections."

"So you've finished?"

"I believe so," she says. "But I have no idea what it means. Maths has never been my thing."

"What about chapters five to nine? No mistakes in those?"

She shakes her head. "I couldn't find any. It's odd, right? There was an error in every chapter until five. And then oddly another pops up again in chapter ten."

Buri studies the progression of numbers, spotting no immediate patterns. "May I?"

"Sure." She passes the pencil and notes to him.

Unlike Georgia, Buri has always had an affinity for numbers. Mathematics was his second best subject in school, and as a kid he enjoyed solving puzzles. But what he is seeing now is unlike any ciphers or games he's ever come across. He tries a few different ways of writing the information down, searching for commonalities and logical progressions. When that doesn't shed any more light, he examines the two columns of numbers together, and then separately.

"Maybe it's not about the chapters. Maybe it's got more to do with the section numbers," he hypothesises.

Georgia is quiet as she considers his theory.

He plays around with the numbers in the right column, jotting them down in a random order:

40

108

45

48

4

He lets his eyes move across the page, the digits drifting in and out of focus until he feels a sense of familiarity. He has an uncanny feeling that he's seen some of these before. But that makes no sense at all. Why would he have seen them? And where?

Then he realises that his eyes keep coming back to the figures on the right: 48 and 108.

He closes his eyes, picturing them in his mind.

48, 108 . . . 48, 108 . . . 48, 108 . . . Where the hell . . .

A bolt of realisation hits him, and his eyes shoot wide open.

No way.

The Golden Khan

He reaches for his GPS and checks their current location, realising that he has been staring at these precise numbers for the last three days. With the pencil he copies down their exact location right now:

48.7467, 108.6714

He quickly converts the coordinates from the decimal system to the sexagesimal one:

48° 44′ 48″ N
108° 40′ 17″ E

Georgia peers over his scribbling hand. She gasps. "You think they're *coordinates*?"

"Sure as hell looks like it," he mutters as he works to rearrange the section numbers from *The Secret History*, shaking his head with disbelief as the figures align into place:

48, 45, __
108, 40, __

↓

48° 45′ __″ N
108° 40′ __″ E

"But . . ." Georgia says, incredulous, ". . . that makes *no* sense whatsoever."

"Why?"

"*The Secret History* we've been working with is the only

293

surviving version, it's the Chinese edition that was transliterated in the fourteenth century." She points to the coordinates on the page. "This longitude, latitude system didn't exist back then, because most countries only adopted Greenwich as the zero-reference line in the nineteenth century."

Buri scratches his beard. "I don't know how to explain that, but it can't be a coincidence." Comparing the locations, he adds, "The coordinates from *The Secret History* would place the location within a few kilometres of where we are now, somewhere just north of here."

"Where does the four go?" Georgia asks, referring to the digit Buri doesn't know where to place.

"No idea. It could be on either line. And we seem to be missing another number, too. We need a total of six to give us a complete set of coordinates."

Georgia is flipping through her books. "I could only find five mistakes in the text. I've gone through the whole thing over and over again, cross-referencing everything I know with all the historical accounts and chronicles Sarah has sent me over the past week. I can't think of what else there could be."

"Let's go back to the clues," Buri suggests.

She turns the pages of her dog-eared notepad, showing him the verses in her handwriting:

> *When the spirit and the seat of the Golden Khan are*
> *together again,*
> *Then shall the truth be revealed,*
>
> *And only one who possesses the truth of our history*
> *May find his eternal resting place . . .*

"So we need the *spirit*, the *seat*, and the *History* to find the tomb," he summarises. "We've got the *History* and you've examined the *seat*—the portrait of Chinggis Khan at the National Palace Museum."

"Pretty thoroughly, yeah. I'm sure I didn't miss anything on that painting."

"Then that leaves the *spirit*, the *sulde* where you took the first verse from, which is in Anya's hands right now. And you mentioned that you could have missed something when you inspected it."

"That's right," she confirms. "I only had a very short amount of time before the Russians took it back. It's very possible that there are more clues on the *sulde* that I've missed."

"Then we need to get it back."

They fall into silence as Buri contemplates the enormity of this task. From Miller's warnings and the information in the dossiers, it is clear Lev Ivanov would not be easy to take down. Part of the *Spetsnaz*, the Russian special forces, Ivanov has the kind of weapons and combat training that would make Buri's old team look like cadet boys. He's more than a decade younger, and probably a hell of a lot faster, too. And now that Buri is left with very little firepower after being attacked by the Mongol archers, he needs to somehow gain as much advantage as possible.

He needs an element of surprise.

"Where do you think Anya is now?" he asks Georgia. "If you were her, where is the first place you would search on Burkhan Khaldun?"

Georgia falls quiet, her face a picture of concentration as she contemplates this. She speaks softly, almost to herself: "I've only had a quick look at the satellite images of Burkhan Khaldun that Sarah sent me. She highlighted some geological anomalies, places she thought were worth investigating . . ."

She pauses. Then, her eyes light up and she lifts them to meet his gaze. "I think I may have an idea," she says.

48

FROM THE REMOTE sensing analysis Anya conducted of Burkhan Khaldun, it was already pretty clear to her before she left Moscow that there could only be three places in the mountain where the tomb could be. But among these candidates, one stood out above all else. And when Dr. Fujimoto confirmed her suspicions, she could not help but give a mental fist pump at his affirmation.

The location makes perfect sense according to Mongolian culture, too. Judging by the staggering number of *ovoos* that have been set up all over the place, it's clear that the locals have established a cult around the national park. But none of those cairns compares with the gigantic pile of stones right on top of Burkhan Khaldun. Indeed, it is the closest one can be to the Eternal Blue Sky.

The summit.

The sun is rising just as Anya marches up to her destination. She slows to a stop, taking in the impressive sight. It has cost them much more time than it should have to get here. The climb from the east would have required any fit person a mere two, three hours, and ever since arriving at

Burkhan Khaldun yesterday they have made several attempts to get to the top. But every time they did so, a fog descended upon them, making it impossible to see their way. Then the wind would pick up and clouds gather, threatening to storm down on them. They've had to leave their horses tethered in the shelter of their camp midway down the mountain, since the damn animals keep getting spooked by the crack of thunder and lightning. Even Lev and Alexey started whispering between themselves about the rumoured curse of Chinggis Khan until Anya ordered them to quit their superstitious whining and shut the hell up.

By some unexpected luck this morning, they managed to ascend to the plateau at the peak without much drama. It is a beautiful place, full of purple wildflowers dotting the grass. Just up ahead, a mammoth mound of roughly two hundred and fifty metres in length looms over the plain.

A definite geological anomaly, indeed.

Anya breaks into a smile, her entire body shivering with the thrill of discovery. This has got to be it. There is no way the huge heap of stones can possibly be a natural phenomenon, and that's why it showed up on the satellite images like a blazing red flag.

It *must* be a tumulus.

She looks around the plateau, half hoping to find Georgia Lee here. She feels a stab of disappointment when she finds no one else present except for her team. So much for keeping the Asian woman alive to see how far she can get in the race for the tomb.

The professor has piqued Anya's curiosity, and that is not something that happens often enough. She finds the woman extraordinary: smart, talented, resourceful, breathtakingly beautiful. And there is something . . . ethereal and other-worldly about her, so much so that when Anya first set eyes on Georgia she almost thought she'd conjured the woman from her own imagination.

Ever since she was a little girl, Anya has known she is different. Deda Dmitry and her mother repeatedly told her so. Her mother would walk her to school, and some days she would nod at the neighbourhood kids and murmur to Anya, "Look at those kids in the playground. You see their dirty faces, their dull eyes? You can sense how dumb they are just from standing here. That is what most people in the world are like, Anya. But not us. And especially not you. You are the smartest girl in school and you're even more intelligent than most of the adults we know. That's because you're special. You are better than all of them. And you are going to do something great one day. You are going to make your mama proud."

Then, gripping Anya by arm, Mama would say, "Don't go near those kids, Anya, because stupidity is contagious. Don't ever let them taint you."

Anya would look at her peers and know that what her mother said was true. But sometimes, when she saw the boys and girls laughing without a care in the world, she wanted to join them and play, too. No matter how dull-witted they all were. Some days, she didn't want to be special at all.

All her life, Anya has sought a kindred spirit. She has dreamed of what their conversations would be like, what they would discuss and debate with each other. She has fantasised about what they could accomplish together, two powerful minds focused on one purpose. When she met Georgia, she hoped she finally found someone of her kind.

With all the legendary tales of Georgia's accomplishments floating around the academic circles, Anya wanted to witness first-hand just how good the woman really was. And she was craving a challenge, a healthy little contest. Just for once, it would have been nice to have a worthy adversary to compete with.

Regretfully, though, Georgia hasn't lived up to her reputation at all. Maybe Anya should have let Lev finish the professor and her driver off back at Almsgivers Wall.

Anya casts the image of Georgia from her mind, refocusing on the prize before her. She says in Russian, "Alexey. Get the drone in the sky. I want to see this baby clearly, from all angles."

Alexey lumbers up with a heavy pack full of imaging equipment. He crouches down and begins to set everything up. Within minutes, the drone is in the air, mapping the terrain of the area. Later, he will upload the data onto his laptop to create a digital topographic model accurate to a few centimetres. From this, Anya will be able to detect any flat areas or peculiarities that are worth excavating.

"I want thermal imaging of the entire thing too," she says. Turning to Lev, she orders, "Make yourself useful. You can help Alexey with the Ground Penetrating Radar."

While the two men get busy, Anya takes the opportunity to walk around the entire circumference of the enormous tumulus. She notes the uniform sizes of the stones that make up the cairn, another confirmation of the fact that it is an artificial construction. There is a large *ovoo* at the southern base of the hillock, and one more at the top, both adorned with blue silk, flags, and an assortment of Spirit Banners. It appears that the cult is strong, and that the Mongols have continued to worship at this place.

When she finally returns to where the men are working, she sees that Alexey has set up the laptop on one of the equipment cases and is loading up aerial footage from the drone. The bird's-eye view gives Anya a clearer understanding of the barrow, and what's more, she can now make out a distinctively man-made, linear boundary between the plateau and the burial mound. As she noted during her walk, there is an *ovoo* just outside of the marked border, and the other is right at the centre of the majestic tomb. The entire dome is of a perfect geometry, and it is something she has seen before.

It has a startling similarity to the Han imperial tombs in China.

Anya can hardly contain her excitement.

All I need now is a way in.

49

GEORGIA AND BURI make their ascent from the south, following deer-paths up the slopes of Burkhan Khaldun. They have reluctantly left their horses tied to a tree by the river, with Buri reasoning that the skittish animals would make things complicated when they come upon the Russians. Approaching undetected on foot instead would give them the stealth they need.

As they walk, Georgia explains why she believes the Russians are on the summit of Burkhan Khaldun: "The Mongols don't like to talk about death, so they refer to it by saying things like 'go up to the heights.' To them, the mountaintop is among the most sacred places for one to pray at, because it is closest to the Eternal Blue Sky. Also, when I looked at some of the satellite images that Sarah sent me, I saw something . . . unusual at the peak of Burkhan Khaldun."

"It *would* be the most obvious place to bury a conqueror like Chinggis Khan. Right on top of the world," says Buri.

"Yes. And if Anya has used remote sensing technologies, she would have spotted the geological anomaly there. It's so remarkable it would be impossible to ignore."

Georgia brings out her phone. "There's something else," she adds, scrolling through her photographs. "When we were searching for Dr. Fujimoto in Avarga, I had a good look at the museum displays at the Archaeological Centre. I found something interesting."

She locates what she's looking for and hands the device to Buri. It's a picture of a poster, showing the snow-covered, plateaued summit of Burkhan Khaldun. There is a strange hillock jutting out atop the highland plain, and a ghostly image of Chinggis Khan's face has been superimposed directly above the colossal mound.

At the bottom of the poster, there are three lines of texts in Mongolian.

Buri looks at the picture and translates the words into English. "This is a quote from Chinggis Khan . . . 'All of my seeds and their seeds shall pray to Burkhan Khaldun morning and night.'"

"Meaning that his descendants should always worship this mountain," Georgia says. "Looking back through my photos, I realised that there were actually quite a few photos of Burkhan Khaldun placed all over the museum."

"You think Fujimoto had put them up, and maybe he told Anya about the place before he died?"

"Precisely. And this image would also suggest that Chinggis Khan's tomb is on the summit, with his spirit hovering over the site."

They push their way through the dense fir forest clogged with fallen trees, loose boulders, and thick under-brush. Quite a few times they hear the grunts of wild boars nearby, and they are careful to make sure they avoid an encounter. Boars can get aggressive, especially when defending their young. Their bulky weight and sharp tusks mean that attacks can often be fatal, if one is unfortunate enough to come face to face with such a beast.

Georgia is mindful to maintain a slow pace, pretending to be winded by the climb as they get higher up the mountain. She makes sure she is always some distance behind Buri, giving him the impression that she is struggling to keep up with him. In actual fact, along with the other changes to her body from the elixir, she doesn't find these activities to be physically taxing anymore. She can easily walk faster than him if she wants to. Indi trots happily up ahead, exploring the forest at her own free will, but after being reprimanded by Buri, she slows down to stay close to Georgia.

As they hike towards higher grounds, the earth turns to scree, the woods become thin, and the trees begin to shrink. Georgia notices sizeable patches of stony circles and ovals dotted along their path. These rocky mounds are covered with moss, and some of them are the exact size of graves.

She pauses, taking pictures with her phone and contemplating what they could be.

After three hours of climbing, the sparsely scattered trees now give way into open plains, and Georgia finally sees the summit and the distinctively bald, rounded ridge. The sight makes her pick up the pace.

A few short minutes later, the hill ahead becomes completely obscured by mist.

Buri stops in his tracks.

"What is it?" Georgia asks.

He turns and hurries back to her, then pulls her along with him. "Storm's coming. We gotta go."

She tugs her hand from his grasp. "It's just a fog. I'm sure—"

"No. You don't fuck around with the weather up here. We need to get out of here, *now*."

She looks up to the mountain top, and sure enough, a darkening cloud bank is now rolling towards them, building in density and speed. She scurries after Buri, who emits a sharp whistle as he quickens his stride. Indi bounds over and trots at his heels as the three of them make their way back into the forest.

The shrill of the wind escalates as the fog catches up to them. Soon, it becomes impossible to see more than a few metres ahead.

"Fuck," Buri swears, stopping next to a couple of larger trees which partially shelters them from the gust. "This'll have to do. Help me with the tent."

They fight with the flapping canvas as the gale howls through the forest. Indi barks wildly, then whines with fright as the first of the thunder cracks open the sky. A deluge of rain is dumped upon them as they struggle to get under the shelter. Indi leaps in, shaking all the water off her coat in a flurry. Another bolt of lightning splits the darkened heavens, chased by a roaring boom, and the German Shepherd burrows herself into Buri's lap with a yelp.

He strokes the dog and says something soothing to her, his voice drowned out by the pelting rain.

"What do we do now?" Georgia yells through the frightening din.

She has to read his lips for his reply. "Now, we wait."

50

BACK IN THE dry comfort of her tent, Anya opens her laptop to study the infrared images Alexey collected before the squall hit. Outside, the storm rages on, a spectacle of thunder, lightning, and torrential rain. After two days of thwarted attempts at ascending the summit, Anya is accustomed to this melodrama by now—practically *bored* by it. But Lev and Alexey seem increasingly petrified by the inclement weather, judging from the way they sprinted off the plateau as soon as the clouds came in.

She rolls her eyes with disgust. *Men.* On the outside they may pretend to be tough, but deep down, they're all just fearful, weak boys who were not loved enough by their daddies and still yearn for their mummies. It's one of the long list of reasons she's always felt repugnance towards them.

Flicking through the many images on her computer, Anya pauses when she comes across something peculiar. She squints at the hyper-colour picture of the tumulus, making sure that her eyes are not playing tricks on her. The infrared filter depicts the sky in black and the ground in spectral colours ranging from orange to purple. She can make out the faint outline of a perfect circle on the slope of the dome.

Is that—?

She zooms in on the motif that is too deteriorated to be discerned by the naked eye. Mongols have a habit of making geoglyphs like this as part of their worship. The one that is showing up in the infrared imaging must have been made in the recent past, since it's not possible that it has remained intact for the last eight hundred years.

Noting its shape, Anya then goes through the rest of the photographs, counting six other designs, all dispersed over the southern slope of the burial mound. Some she recognises, others she has never seen in her life.

The highly secretive Golden Family kept all of their written records and the great seals of the Mongol dynasties secure in guarded vaults and away from public knowledge. These *tamghas*, the identifying mark of clans, were initially utilised as signs of ownership. The nomadic Mongols branded them on their herds, then later used them as the imperial seals. Some of the *tamgha* symbols appeared on coins, but the one for Chinggis Khan has never been found.

Anya can only think of one reason so many *tamghas* unknown to scholars have been placed over the tumulus.

Here must lie the Mongol dynastic necropolis, the secret tombs of the Great Khans.

She quickly copies down each symbol, recognising one of them as that of Ogodei Khan, son and successor to Chinggis Khan. Out of the six *tamghas*, one in particular stands out to her:

She reaches for the black case to her left. Clicking open the top, she grabs the *sulde* and examines the carving deep in the bottom end of the rod.

The designs are identical.

It would appear that she has just uncovered the lost seal of Chinggis Khan.

And the way into his tomb.

51

WHEN THE WEATHER finally calms down two hours later, Buri ventures from the tent, almost tripping over Indi who is just as eager to get outside.

He peers through the foliage above to see that the dark clouds have all but disappeared, and what remains is a startling clear blue sky. It's as if the downpour never happened.

"How bizarre," Georgia comments from behind him, echoing his sentiment.

Unease fills Buri as he remembers what his uncle said. "The curse . . . Och mentioned that things get worse as you go closer to the tomb."

Georgia brushes off his theory. "We're high up here. Of course the weather would be more unpredictable."

The whole thing nags at him, but he says nothing further. Georgia turns and starts to disassemble the light-weight tent. He stops her.

"Maybe we should leave that here," Buri says. "We'll be quicker on our feet if you don't bring your backpack either."

All throughout their climb earlier, Georgia seemed to struggle with the steep hike and lagged behind him by several yards. He had to keep looking back to check on her. The air is thinner up here, and even Buri has to push himself hard at times to maintain a steady speed. With the heavy weight on her back, it would hamper their progress even more.

She murmurs her agreement. They reorganise the contents of their bags, leaving unnecessary things behind in the tent and only bringing the water and bare essentials in his pack. They make a quick snack out of some energy bars, wary of how little food they have left.

The rucksack once more on his back, he looks at his watch and says, "It's just past two o'clock. Let's get up there."

They resume the climb, making good progress for the first half hour, but then Georgia falls behind again, and every once in a while Buri has to check that she is still keeping up. Twice, he catches her taking photographs of the ground.

Halfway up the hill, puffing from exertion and lack of oxygen, he turns to find her crouched down by a circle of stones, removing some rocks and examining what's underneath. He shakes his head at her fascination with the pile of scree, then continues his pace on the deer trail. He's hungry and on edge, eager to get to the top before the Russians beat them to the tumulus. Georgia can run and catch up if she wants to take so many breaks.

What if they are already digging up there? What if they found a way in several days ago and have looted the tomb?

The thought pesters him and he turns again to ask Georgia to keep moving, only to stagger back when he suddenly finds her right at his heels.

What the fuck.

"How'd you catch up so fast?" he asks.

She falters in her steps. "Wh—what do you mean?"

"You were studying the rocks back there. How'd you cover that distance so quickly?"

Something fleeting crosses her face. Before Buri can decipher what it is, her breath quickens. "I ran up," she says, looking all at once winded. "It wasn't far."

He's sure she was at least a hundred feet away when he last looked.

"I found something," she continues, getting the words out in between the heavy inhales. "I . . . ran up to tell you I —I found something under those rocks. It might explain what's on the summit."

He frowns. He must be losing his mind.

"Anyway, let's keep going," she says. "We don't have the time to stand around like this."

She brushes past him and resumes the hike with renewed vigour, and Indi canters up to her. Buri scratches his head, wondering if he's getting light-headed and confused from the lack of food.

He rushes up to join them.

52

BACK ON THE summit at last, Anya watches as Alexey and Lev remove stones from the tumulus. She fidgets with her imaging equipment as the two men labour at an infuriatingly slow rate, grunting and moaning as they heave each piece by hand.

Enough time has been wasted already. She needs to get in there before another squall hits. After the last one cleared, it took them an hour to hike back to the top, all the while tripping over rocks and fallen branches. Then it was another thirty minutes before Anya was able to pinpoint the exact location they needed to dig with the infrared camera.

Impatient with the men's progress, she flies the drone into the sky again to observe the process through the VR headset. With the sizable mask over her face, she can see the entire site with an elevated view, and switching to the infrared filter, she makes out the outline of the *tamghas* dotted over the slope of the dome, with the bright-red figures of Alexey and Lev standing over the *tamgha* of Chinggis Khan.

She suspects that each symbol marks a separate tomb for a Great Khan. But Anya has no interest in the others, and she really isn't motivated by the vast amount of treasure that must be buried beneath her feet, either. She's here with one purpose only, and that is to get her hands on the original copy of *The Secret History* and unravel the greatest mystery of all time.

With the controls in her palm, she flies the drone over to the other side of the dome, investigating the northern slope. This truly is a magnificent tumulus, and Anya has no doubt it took no small number of Mongol warriors to construct it. Flying the remote-controlled aircraft higher, she swears when the visibility is suddenly hampered.

She pulls down the mask and looks up. *Shit*. Weather is coming in. With the headset over her face, she didn't even notice the sky darkening.

Looking over to Alexey and Lev, she sees that they're still busy hauling chunks of rock out of the hole, which is even now only one metre deep. They seem oblivious to anything else other than the task at hand. She tips her head upwards again to find the cloud bank accumulate in mass with haste.

No.

She's so close, she can almost feel that book within her hands. She can't possibly stop now.

Putting on the VR mask once more, she sees nothing but darkness. She checks the controls, then realises that she's lost connection with the drone.

A few drops of rain land on her head.

"Fuck," Lev says, lifting himself out of the cavity, finally aware of the drizzle. "We gotta go."

"No," Anya says. "It'll clear. Let's keep going."

"We gotta go back to camp." Lev ignores her. "We have to get out of this weather."

Lev and Alexey scramble around, packing up the equipment with panic-stricken eyes. They're working much faster now than when they were digging for the tomb.

Frustration rises, spilling into wrath. "Get back in there and keep working." Anya barks her command at Lev. "Finish what we've started. That is an order."

A flash of lightning brightens their surroundings, followed immediately by the deafening clap of thunder. Something falls from the sky and crashes to the ground a few metres away. Anya stares at the blackened, steaming lump, and it takes her several seconds to realise that it is her drone.

Or what's left of it.

The men mutter expletives at the sight of the destroyed instrument, their faces contorting with fright. Alexey's keening whine breaks into a hysterical pitch as he picks up the piece of fried plastic hardware with trembling hands.

"It's the curse!" he wails, dropping the shapeless chunk when it scalds his skin. Turning to Lev, his voice escalates. "I *told* you we shouldn't be digging up here!"

Oh, for fuck's sake.

Before she can berate them to regain some common sense, the two men hightail it off the dome and onto the plateau, racing east towards their camp down the hill.

Cowards.

She briefly considers continuing their work herself, but water is pouring out of the sky now, quickly pooling in the pit. She also doubts she could carry all those stones out herself.

Shit.

Another spark of lightning illuminates the heavens. Cursing, she runs in the direction the men have disappeared. Fog descends, and soon there is only a blanket of white everywhere. Anya can make out what's within two, three metres of her, nothing more. She keeps running towards what she thinks to be east, but after tripping over a rock, she can no longer tell where the camp is. Stumbling down the slope, she finally breaks into the woods, unable to keep her eyes open in the stinging, pelting rain. A powerful gust almost blows her off course, but she rights herself, only to lose her balance on the slippery peat, careening forward and smashing her side against a stone protruding from the ground. She screams as pain explodes in her left arm and chest from the impact.

The sky lights up, and a split second later, she feels the fierce might of thunder reverberate through her body and eardrums. Her breath whooshes out of her lungs from the violent force, and it takes her several moments to remember where she is. Her ears ringing, she turns to push herself up from the ground, looking up just in time to see the massive tree plummet towards her.

53

BURI CROUCHES low at the edge of the plateau, watching through his binoculars as the Russians begin their excavation on the mini hill several hundred feet away. From this position, it definitely looks like a burial mound, one that is large enough to contain all the Great Khans of the Mongol Empire.

"Do you see the *sulde*?" Georgia asks, squatting beside him. Indi lies on her front next to Georgia, huffing with her tongue hanging out.

"No." He has his eyes trained on Lev, sizing up the brawny man and the smaller guy working alongside him. Buri's mind is going over different ways of how to take both men out before dealing with the Russian woman. "Forget the *sulde*. If that's really the tomb, we need to get in there now before the Russians have what they came for."

"I don't think that's the tomb," Georgia says.

He lowers his binoculars and tips his head in the direction of the mammoth cairn of stones. "That sure as hell looks like it to me."

"What does your GPS say?"

He brings the palm-sized device out of his pocket, checking the screen:

48° 45′ 16.0″ N
108° 39′ 49.8″ E

"We're a minute off the longitudinal coordinates from *The Secret History*," he says with disbelief.

"And at this latitude, that would make the location . . .?"

He does a quick calculation in his head. ". . . over half a mile from here." Puzzled, he asks, "How did you know that?"

"That's what I figured out while we were climbing up here," she explains. "I saw this dome on the satellite images, and it bothered me because at first glance, an archaeologist would instinctively think of the shape as a tumulus. But Mongols don't make mounds over graves. And why would they do so, especially when all this time they've been trying to keep it a secret? Then, as we were hiking, I saw those stony circles on the hill and I realised that I've seen these kinds of formations before. I believe they're a natural phenomenon."

Buri stares at the immense pile of rocks. It looks too perfect to not be man-made. *That* thing was created by nature?"

"It's a geological process known as frost cracking," she explains. "It happens when huge boulders under the ground get broken up by repeated freezing and thawing from the changes of temperature throughout the year.

Then in winter, when the water in the earth turns to ice, it takes up more space and forces the fragments of stone up to the surface, scattering them according to size."

Buri pushes his brows together. "I have no idea what you just said."

"It's one of the things that geocryologists study. I only know that because my ex-husband is one," she says. Nodding in the direction of the hillock, she adds, "That would be the same thing, but on a much bigger scale."

He doesn't know which he wants to learn about more, the frost cracking process or her ex-husband. The idea makes his skin prickle with jealousy. But at that moment, their surroundings begin to darken, and he tilts his head up to see clouds gathering above them.

"Shit," Buri says. "That didn't last long."

On the stony slope, the Russians seem to be getting into an argument. Buri wastes no time, pushing away from the boulder and dragging Georgia with him to make a run for the forest below. He glances back to see the two Russian men running in the opposite direction, abandoning Anya on the plateau.

Halfway down the hill, Georgia yelps behind him. Turning to see that she has tripped, he runs back to pick her up. When they sprint down the plains again, he stays to her rear, keeping his sights on her. Indi is bounding so far ahead, she's already disappearing into the tree line of the woods. He releases a sharp whistle to slow her down, but his dog doesn't seem to hear him.

Lightning strikes, swiftly succeeded by the roar of thunder. Georgia jolts with terror at the explosion of sound, and she suddenly ramps up her speed, bolting after Indi so quickly he loses sight of her within seconds.

What the—?

He's never seen her run so fast. Hell, he hasn't ever witnessed *anyone* move at that velocity. By the time he makes it into the forest, the rain is blasting so hard in his face he has to squint to keep the water out of his eyes. He slows as he weaves through the fir trees, looking around frantically. Georgia and Indi are nowhere in sight.

Fuck.

Lightning continues to rip from the sky, accompanied by earsplitting booms. Buri notices that the time between the two seems to be getting shorter and shorter, which means they are striking closer and closer to him.

"Georgia! Indi!" He whistles and shouts, but his voice is swallowed up by the howling wind.

Far off to his right, a bolt of lightning strikes a tree, creating a brilliant spark in the gloom. The hairs on his arms stand on end as the air becomes charged around him. He turns and sprints away, by now having no idea which direction he is headed. He trips over something and lands hard on the forest bed.

"Buri!" Finally, he hears Georgia's muffled voice over the cacophony of the gale.

He scrambles to his knees just as she reaches him and pulls him to his feet with surprising strength. With her hand still clamped over his arm, she leads them towards a large rock formation. There is a sizable indentation on the side of the enormous boulder, not deep enough to be a cave, but it offers some protection from the weather.

They squeeze into the shallow cavity, and Buri squats down to avoid headbutting the low ceiling. His gaze darts across the darkened forest. "Where's Indi?"

Her eyes are wide with concern. "I don't know. By the time I got into the woods, I couldn't see her. And then I couldn't find you, so I had to turn back."

Lightning and thunder continue, some hitting so close to them he can again feel the air charged with electricity. The temperature drops rapidly. Drenched, Georgia sits on the ground, hugging her legs to her chest. She's shivering.

He looks all over, finding nothing he can make a fire with. Everything in the forest is soaked. And they've left all their dry clothes back at camp, where they took shelter from the last storm. Opening his pack, he rummages and produces two thermal blankets. He wraps one over her and another around himself. The large square of silver mylar completely envelops Georgia but barely covers his bulk, reaching only to his mid-thigh.

"You need to take your wet clothes off," he says.

Her teeth chatter as she stands, turning away from him. Averting his eyes, Buri rises to his knees and turns too, shrugging out of his dripping clothing beneath the thermal blanket. Then, sitting down with their backs pressed to the rock, they huddle together for warmth as the storm continues.

The crash of trees resounds through the woods, and his worry for Indi churns his stomach. She's never been good with storms, and when she panics, she charges off without discerning where she's going.

What if she gets hit by lightning? Or a falling tree?

Just like that, gruesome images of what could happen to his dog burst into his mind.

His breath quickens.

He breaks out in a cold sweat.

Fear grips his chest to the point of pain, blocking off his airway.

He claws at his throat.

"Buri? You okay?"

He surges to his feet. He doesn't feel a thing when he bangs his head against the low ceiling.

"What are you doing?!" Georgia grabs him by the arm just as he's about to charge out into the storm.

"I need to find Indi." His heart thrashes in his chest like a violent beast, compounding his anxiety.

He must be going into cardiac arrest.

Georgia stands, keeping one firm hand on his arm and the other clinching the thermal blanket to her chest.

He realises he has dropped his own covering.

"You can't go out there," she says.

As if agreeing with her, the heavens rip open with another flash of lightning. The force of thunder that follows reverberates all around, shuddering the ground beneath them.

"Breathe, Buri." Georgia places her hand on his back, coaxing him to sit down on the forest floor.

He struggles to draw air into his lungs.

"Indi will be okay," Georgia says. "She's quick on her feet. She's probably found somewhere to burrow into by now. We'll find her in the morning."

She puts the mylar blanket over him, stroking him on the back as she urges him: "Breathe."

He squeezes his eyes shut and focuses on his respiration:

Four seconds in, four seconds out.
Four seconds in, four seconds out.
Four seconds in, four seconds out.

54

GEORGIA STIRS, drifting from the depths of slumber. Dreams of Wang Jian and Charlie linger, swirling all around her. Her mind groggy, her eyes still closed, one of the first few things she becomes aware of is the pain in her face from the lumpy surface she seems to have fallen asleep on. Her entire body aches from the hard, uneven ground. And there is an arm, heavy and warm, draped over her middle.

She tenses. Her eyes snap open, and the strong limb tightens its hold on her. Buri's familiar, earthy scent fills her head. His slow, steady breathing indicates that he's still asleep, even though he's unconsciously moved in reaction to her alarm. She realises that she is wrapped in his embrace, his chest flush against her back. Looking down, relief floods her when she discovers that she's covered by her thermal blanket, since she's wearing nothing underneath. His backpack is serving as a pillow under her head.

Slowly, her heart pumping, she shifts gingerly under Buri's thick arm, trying to escape his grasp. She freezes when the blanket falls away from the motion and her naked skin brushes against his.

Shocked, embarrassed, acting out of instinct, she skitters aside. Buri bolts up, reaching straight for his gun under the rucksack.

"Georgia?" His voice laced with sleep, he blinks rapidly. He grips his pistol with his right hand, his eyes now alert and scanning their surroundings. "You okay?"

"Yeah. Sorry," she says, averting her gaze when his thermal blanket drops from his movement. "I tried to not wake you."

Buri clears his throat and straightens, lowering his weapon and readjusting his covering. "The storm's stopped," he remarks.

She looks out to see dawn approaching, and events of last night come to her mind. The storm lasted for hours on end, with both of them trying to stay as warm as possible. It was impossible to keep dry, as the wind kept blowing the rain into their shallow shelter. She was exhausted from everything that had happened and worried sick about Indi. And about Buri, too. She doesn't even know when she fell asleep.

"Indi," she says as she gets up, bumping her head on the rock. Wincing and ducking lower, she reaches for her damp clothes.

She wrings out the excess water and dresses under the covering of the thin silver blanket. From the rustling sounds behind her, she knows Buri is doing the same. They walk back towards their camp from yesterday, warming up from exertion as they climb over boulders and the mess of debris from last night's catastrophic storm. Her legs scratched up from the branches, her cheeks wet with tears, Georgia shouts out for Indi until her voice cracks and her throat is raw. There are fallen trees everywhere, some split open down the middle by lightning. The sight of the devastation spikes her anxiety even more. Buri emits high-pitched whistles for the German Shepherd, but she's nowhere to be found.

"Where can she be?" Georgia sobs.

Beside her, Buri is quiet, looking more and more upset as time goes on. When they arrive at their camp, they find it utterly destroyed. The tent has collapsed under the weight of fallen branches, its canvas torn in several places. Luckily, her backpack, being waterproof, is still okay. Famished, they eat what's left of the food.

"What do we do now?" she asks.

He shrugs, looking lost and distraught. She worries that he may have another panic attack like last night.

"Let's keep moving." She needs to keep him busy, take his mind off things. "Maybe we'll find Indi on the way."

He nods.

"What do you think happened to the Russians?" she asks.

"There's only one way to find out."

They take all they can salvage from the camp and ascend the summit again. They find the hole that the Russians excavated on the mound of stones, water draining from all sides of the dome and flowing down the slope. There is no one in sight.

They walk in the direction that Buri saw the men run off in, down a steep hill and into the forest. All around, there are firs toppled over with their roots exposed.

Georgia gasps when she stumbles over a body among the wreckage. The man lies on his front, equipment sticking out of his large pack like a giant lightning rod. His clothing is in tatters, and his skin is mottled with burns wrapped around his torso.

"One of the Russians?" Georgia grimaces at the sight. Lev is a much bigger guy, so she suspects this must be the other man they saw on the plateau.

Buri kneels by the body and touches the neck, checking for a pulse. He leans down to look at the man's face.

"Yep. He's dead. Looks like he was struck by lightning."

They push on. Halfway down the mountain, they find the Russians' camp at a clearing. Three collapsed tents are crushed under fallen branches and trunks. Anya and Lev don't seem to be around. Georgia clears the fragments from one of the tents and looks under the canvas. She finds bags and supplies in there.

"Doesn't look like they made it back," she says. "Do you think they survived?"

"If they didn't get hit by a tree or lightning, they probably froze to death overnight." He speculates. Then he adds, "But Lev Ivanov is Russian Special Forces, which means he'd have enough skills to keep them alive." Buri's going through the bags, removing the food and putting them into this backpack. He finds a rifle, boxes of bullets, and a machete, taking them with him as well.

Georgia moves on and searches the other tents. In the third one, she uncovers the familiar long, black case, the hard plastic cracked under the weight of a heavy log. She calls for Buri, and together, they push the thick piece of timber away.

Sitting on her haunches and opening the receptacle, her breath leaves her when she sees the *sulde*. Luckily, with the protective foam lining the inside of the case, the Spirit Banner is unharmed. She sits down on a tattered piece of tarp and carefully lifts it out, her eyes travelling down its length. Anya has completely stripped the wood of the black paint, leaving all the etchings undisguised. Brushing away the horse tail hair, Georgia looks at the first verse she previously discovered. At the lower end of the pole, there is another line she did not pick up when she first examined the artefact.

She traces a finger over the inscription, then sweeps her hand over the bottom of the pole. Feeling bumps and grooves, she tilts her head and finds a symbol carved deep into the surface.

Is that—?

She reaches for her phone and scrolls through the photos.

"What is it?" Buri asks beside her.

"I've seen this design before," she says, finding what she is looking for. She shows Buri the petroglyph from the rock formation known as Chinggis Khan's Saddle. "At Almsgivers Wall."

"Looks like a *tamgha*," Buri says.

"The lost *tamgha* of Chinggis Khan." Her eyes widen as she makes the connection.

Passing the *sulde* to him, she points at the inscription at the lower end of the rod. "Can you read this?"

She grabs her notepad and pencil from her rucksack

and hands it to him. Buri sits down, copying the text onto the paper. It takes him several minutes of scribbling, and when he's done, he shows her the result:

A place designated by his father's name, where the sun always shines,
And from which the Golden Throne shall rise again.

55

BURI STARES at the cryptic words. They make no sense to him at all.

"What does it mean?" He turns to Georgia, who's staring at the passage with her bottom lip caught between her teeth.

She takes over the notepad and pencil and jots down the message in its entirety:

> *When the spirit and the seat of the Golden Khan are*
> *together again,*
> *Then shall the truth be revealed,*
>
> *And only one who possesses the truth of our history*
> *May find his eternal resting place,*
>
> *A place designated by his father's name, where the sun*
> *always shines,*
> *And from which the Golden Throne shall rise again.*

For the longest time, she doesn't speak. Buri watches

her gaze trace over the lines back and forth many times. He's about to get up and leave her to ponder on the puzzle when her face lights up with recognition.

"Of course," she whispers.

He looks at her expectantly.

"Chinggis Khan believed in numerology," she explains. "And to him, nine was an especially lucky number, because being in the centre of eight directions meant that one would never become lost. He called his eight main generals the 'Four Hounds' and the 'Four Warhorses', and he organised his army into eight units, with his personal guards being the ninth. With the administration of his government, he divided responsibilities among four of his sons and four of his daughters. He always placed himself in the middle as the ninth, in the most important and auspicious position."

"But what does this all have to do with the verse?"

"Chinggis' father's name was Yesugei," she says, looking at him pointedly.

"Yesugei . . ." Buri repeats, then translates its literal meaning: "'Like nine'. *A place designated by his father's name* . . . Nine is the number we were missing in the coordinates."

"Yes."

Her brilliant smile takes his breath away. His heart does an unexpected flip in his chest, and he blinks.

He clears his throat. Pointing to the verse again, he asks, "And what about this bit . . . *Where the sun always shines*?"

"It means south." Her smile broadens. "I should have known."

"Ah. Right." The significance finally dawns on him. South is the preferred direction for the Mongols. They always face the door of the *ger* south, away from the cold northern winds and towards the light and warmth of the southern sun. "The tomb must be somewhere on the southern slope."

Not for the first time, he is in awe of this woman's intellect. He watches as she checks the position of the southern slope on the map, then completes the sequence of numbers, putting the four and the nine in place:

$$48° 45' 4'' N$$
$$108° 40' 9'' E$$

Locating the place and marking it on the map, Buri does a quick mental calculation. "At this latitude, the precision of these coordinates means that the tomb could be anywhere within quite a large area. We have some searching to do."

She nods. "Let's get there first and see what we find."

"What about the last bit though? *And from which the Golden Throne shall rise again*?" Buri reads the ominous words out loud. "It sounds like some kind of prophecy."

"I don't know. Maybe it's another clue to narrow down the location." Georgia gets to her feet, looking like she's itching to get moving. She says again, "Let's go to the place and see for ourselves."

They take what they need from the Russians' camp, bringing the *sulde* with them. Together they hike back up to the summit and down the southern slope, with Buri checking his GPS and map throughout their trek.

Along the way, he scans the forest for Indi, but sees no signs of her. With Lev and Anya still at large, he doesn't want to draw attention to themselves by calling out for his dog.

A profound sense of grief overcomes him. He knows very well that the chances of Indi surviving the night are not good. Thoughts of the six-year-old German Shepherd fill his mind, of the day they met and of all the precious moments they've shared. Indi saved him, dragged him back to shore when he was drowning in his own depressed mind. Without her, he would have never made the kind of recovery he has. Buri is a completely different person now compared to the shell-shocked, broken man who couldn't even go to the grocery store without having a panic attack.

When his doctor at the army declared him fit for duty again, he was supposed to give Indi back. The Service Dog Foundation was short on trained canine companions at the time, and they were hoping Indi's success streak would continue with other PTSD sufferers. But Buri just couldn't let her go. After months of back and forth, he had to use his father's influence to sway the decision, a trump card he loathed to employ. But he was desperate to keep Indi. And for once, his father's reputation actually worked in his favour.

He remembers the episode he had last night with a mixture of shame and exasperation. He can't believe he lost his shit in front of Georgia. He didn't want her to see him like that, ever. He's meant to have recovered from his condition, for Christ's sake, and he should have been the stronger one to pull them through the devastating storm, not the other way around.

To his relief, Georgia made no mention of it this morning, and hasn't brought it up since.

They finally reach the location of the coordinates. The area they need to search in is roughly the size of a small village. There are no visible deer tracks here, so Buri leads the way, using the machete he found in the Russians' bags to cut through the dense underbrush. Soon, they find themselves on a plateau bordering a cliff. There's a clearing, and at its edge among the tall trees stands a big ovoo of fir-trunks, strewn with tattered blue silk and flags. It's a small wonder that the sacred construction is still standing after last night's storm. Next to the ovoo are two large cauldrons with dark pools at the bottom of the vessels, looking suspiciously like blood. Evidence of recent rituals is scattered across a stone altar. Cups, bowls, pieces of sweets and curds, all sodden or filled with rainwater. The air feels . . . electrified.

The back of his neck tingles. Gooseflesh breaks out over his arms. The eerie atmosphere of the place unnerves him, and he keeps a hand on the Glock holstered to his hip.

The effects of the storm are also evident here, with trees that have been upended with their roots attached. Strangely, the clearing has only a thin layer of creepers covering the soil and no other shrubbery. It is as if the entire area has been kept empty intentionally.

A few paces away, Georgia halts in her steps and crouches, picking something up from the ground.

"What'd you find?" he asks, walking over to her as he hears a crunch under his feet. He bends and lifts the object he stepped on, realising it is a broken piece of red tile.

Georgia is studying another one in her palm, astonishment written all over her features. Looking around, she walks to a fallen tree at the edge of the open area, its roots exposed as if it was plucked out of the ground. She reaches her hand into the soil clumped at the base and retrieves something.

"These . . . are building fragments," she stammers,

staring at the object she is holding. "My God. It's Kamala's temple, it must be. The one built by Chinggis' grandson, to worship the spirits of the Golden Family. We are standing right on top of it. They must have built it on the cliff and over time the vegetation grew on top."

"There must be a way in around here." Buri strides over to the edge of the plateau. If the temple is under them, maybe there's an entrance down the hill somewhere. He looks over and discovers a thirty-foot sheer drop to the next ledge of the mountain. Surveying the surroundings, he sees no obvious access. He squats and reaches into the backpack, producing a coiled length of rope.

Understanding his intention, Georgia points to the tree overhanging the ledge. "There," she says.

He ties the rope to the trunk, pulling on it a few times to test the knot. Satisfied, he wraps a length around his thigh and torso to act as an old-school belay, then positions his feet against the sheer slope to rappel down to the narrow shelf below. Once on the ledge, he releases the rope and looks around, finding nothing but rocks and dense shrubbery hugging the cliff side.

"What do you see?" Georgia calls out from above.

"Not much," he answers.

She pulls the rope up and he gives her instructions on what to do for the belay. He watches as she climbs down, once again struck by the graceful, weightless efficiency of her movements. He also notices that she's gripping the rope with both hands, even though her left palm—now bandaged—was sliced open by the shaman's assistant only two days ago. But there is no evidence of pain in her expression as she quickly descends the slope.

He frowns.

Landing nimbly on her feet, Georgia scans the shelf

and points to the thick vegetation over the cliff face. "It's got to be behind all those vines," she speculates.

Buri pulls the machete out of his pack and begins to hack away at the creepers. Fifteen minutes later, he encounters a large doorway made of stone nestled within the cliff face.

Shocked at the finding, he exchanges a glance with Georgia. His scalp prickles with anticipation as he moves forward to examine the door, running his hands over the cold, smooth surface. It's fashioned out of sandstone. There is no handle, no visible keyhole, not even a crack in the flawless, polished finish. He gives it a hard push, but it doesn't budge.

"Let me see," Georgia says, squeezing in next to him.

He steps aside to give her access, the heel of his shoe kicking into something behind him. Looking down, he uses his boot to uncover the vine over the rock he's stepped on. Puzzled, he crouches down and examines the perfectly round protrusion on the ground.

"Georgia," he says as he peels away the last of the vegetation. "What's this?"

She kneels beside him to study his finding, running her hand over the smooth stone. There's a circular hole at its centre.

Her voice laced with excitement, she asks, "Got a torch?"

From the pocket of his cargo pants he draws out his penlight and passes it to her. "What do you see?"

"There's too much dirt in there. I need something to dig it out."

From her own pockets Georgia produces a rolled-up leather pouch, unravelling and spreading it on the ground. Lined up in the numerous slots are a set of archaeological tools, complete with different brushes, mini trowels, and carving tools of various shapes and sizes. Georgia picks one that looks like a cross between a spoon and a scythe and pokes it into the hole, removing the earth scoop after tiny scoop.

Between checking her work with the penlight and taking out more debris, it's another twenty minutes before she stops and gives a sharp blow into the orifice. Muck sprouts out from the cavity and straight into her face, and she coughs and sneezes. When she points the light into the hole again, her entire body stills.

"Find something?"

She lifts her head and grins guilelessly, her face covered with splatters of dirt. "Yeah."

Intrigued, he takes the penlight and shines it into the aperture. At first, all he sees is black. Tilting the beam of light left and right, he finally makes out the pattern carved into the bottom:

Perplexed, he looks back up at Georgia. He doesn't have to ask his question, because she's already blurting out with enthusiasm, "It's a keyhole."

"And the key . . .?"

". . . is the *sulde*," she replies, her eyes bright as she bounces on her haunches. She jumps up. "I left it up there, I'll go get it."

"I'll do that," he offers. He motions to rise to his feet, only to be tugged back down again.

"Wait." Georgia says, her delicate brows drawn together.

"What is it?"

She chews on her lower lip.

"What's wrong, Georgia?"

"I'm not so sure about going in there, after all."

"Why?"

"The Russians are gone. They could be dead, for all we know. But they certainly don't have the *sulde* anymore, which means they'll never be able to get into this place. Isn't that what we came here to do? To prevent Anya from getting what she wanted?"

Buri pauses, thinking about what Brandon Miller said.

Whatever you find, make sure it doesn't fall into Russian hands. Destroy it if you have to. That's the primary objective. But if you can, bring it back to us.

"I'm worried that . . ." Georgia continues, "If the speculations are true, and there is a powerful weapon in there that could destroy countless lives . . . isn't it better if we leave it be?"

"What, and just walk away after coming all this way?"

She shrugs. "Yeah."

"Aren't you curious about what's in the temple? You're the archaeologist here."

"Of course I'm curious," Georgia says. She wrings her hands. She opens her mouth to say more, but stops herself.

Buri can read what she isn't saying from the look in her eyes. She doesn't want *anyone* to have access to a potential weapon of mass destruction.

That includes the Americans.

And he cannot fault her for it.

With a nod he says, "Let's take the *sulde* and get out of here."

Georgia smiles.

Rising and walking over to the dangling rope, Buri grips it and climbs up the cliff face. When he reaches the ledge above, he freezes, finding himself staring down the barrel of a semi-automatic pistol.

"I will take it from here," the man says with a low voice.

56

Buri stares at the Russian crouched over him. Up close, the soldier is bigger than he appeared from afar. Looking to be at least six foot eight, the blond, brawny man is pressing the muzzle against Buri's forehead with enough force to leave an indentation.

Lev Ivanov.

Ivanov's face is muddied and cut, and his clothes are dirty and torn at the sleeves and the knees. He's obviously had a rough night from the storm. Buri remains quiet and motionless, keeping his gaze trained on the *Spetsnaz* operative.

"Buri?" Georgia calls from the shelf below.

Ivanov shakes his head at Buri, bringing a finger to his lips as a silent warning. "Come up slow," he instructs with a heavy Russian accent. "No sudden movements. Hands where I see them. Or I give the professor a *special treatment* after."

That threat makes Buri want to launch himself at the man. His nostrils flaring, his breath coming in short bursts, Buri grits his teeth as his knuckles turn white around the rope. He cautiously climbs up, taking the rope with him and out of Georgia's reach.

When both of Buri's feet are on the landing, Ivanov moves in with astonishing speed, striking him on the temple with the grip of the gun. Pain explodes in Buri's skull and he stumbles to his knees. Another blow to the back of his neck makes him drop face-first to the ground.

His ears ringing, his head screaming in agony, he squeezes his eyes shut and opens them again, fighting to stay conscious. He's seeing double images of everything. Blood flows freely from his scalp, getting into his right eye. He keeps the left one open, blinking again and again to dispel the blurriness of his vision.

Don't black out. Don't black out.

Ivanov pats him down, removing the Glock holstered to his thigh and the knife sheathed at his ankle.

"Buri? You okay?" Georgia calls out again. "Throw the rope down for me."

Fuck.

"Buri?"

The Russian keeps the gun trained on him, walking over to kick the rope down the cliff.

Don't come up. Don't come up.

Ivanov returns to Buri's side, crouches down and presses the muzzle to his cheek.

As his vision finally begins to clear, he sees the rope around the tree go taut. Within seconds, Georgia's face appears over the ledge and she pales when she realises what's going on. Scrambling up the rope with remarkable speed, she looks like she's about to run towards them when Ivanov warns, "Careful, professor."

She stays near the tree, her chest rising and falling

rapidly as her eyes flick from Ivanov to Buri and back again.

"Let him go," she demands.

"Run, Georgia." His voice hoarse and cracked, Buri finally voices the words that he's been shouting in his mind.

"Uh-uh." Ivanov tuts, pressing the pistol harder against Buri's face. Addressing Georgia, he says, "You get me into the tomb. Or your boyfriend dies."

"Where's Anya?" she asks.

Buri meets her gaze, seeing the desperation in them. He can tell she's trying to buy them time by engaging Ivanov with conversation. His breath coming in short and shallow, he keeps his eyes on her, all the while working his mind furiously over how they're going to escape this.

"Dead. Crushed by a tree," Ivanov answers, spite evident in his rough voice. "Is what she deserved. Fucking cocktease." He jabs the gun at Buri's face and leans in, spittle flying as he asks, "What about the professor? Is she . . . cocktease, no?"

Buri jerks, fighting to push off the ground, but Ivanov sees that coming and drops his knee onto Buri's back. The air is forced out of his lungs as he stays pinned to the soil. Then Ivanov shifts and presses his weight on Buri's neck, cutting off his airway with a carotid choke.

"How—hey!" Georgia yells to get Ivanov's attention. "How'd you find us?"

"I saw you raid our camp. I followed you."

"But why would you do that?" Georgia asks. "Anya is dead. You're only here because you were following orders. You can go home now if you wish, put in a report to tell your bosses that the mission failed."

Buri slows his breathing. Forces his muscles to relax. He goes completely still, fluttering his eyes closed.

The big man seems to fall for it. He eases his weight off with a snort. "Nice try, professor. But my bosses don't like failures. You are right. I do not give a shit about the tomb or the book. Or whatever Anya was obsessed about. I am here for the gold."

"So that's it, you're after an early retirement? Take the treasure and disappear so you won't be punished for Anya's death?"

Ivanov pauses for the briefest moment. "You are smart. For an Asian," he remarks with disdain. His weight disappears from Buri as he moves to his feet. "Now, get me into the tomb."

Buri's eyes snap open. Acting on instinct, he reaches for Ivanov's ankles and yanks hard. The bulky man loses his balance and his pistol goes off, narrowly missing Buri's head. He hits the ground with a grunt but is quick to recover, sending a savage kick to Buri's shoulder. Ignoring the burst of pain from the impact, Buri scrambles over his opponent to grab his gun, wrestling for it against Ivanov's death grip. But he's in the wrong position, too low to gain an advantage. The Russian man throws a left hook at the side of Buri's head, blurring his vision, but he doesn't let go. Then his arm hits something solid at Ivanov's waist and he suddenly remembers the knife that was confiscated from him.

Elbowing Ivanov in the ribs, Buri grabs the knife and goes in for the kill as the deafening boom of the gun rings out.

57

Searing pain erupts in Lev's left leg as he pulls the trigger. Incensed, he lets out a roar, pushing his opponent off his lower torso. The man groans at the movement, flopping onto his back with little resistance, a blossoming of red staining his shirt.

Lev looks down and sees that he is also covered in gore, then realises that most of it is not his. There is, however, a hunting knife sticking out of his top thigh and the sight of it makes his blood boil. He lifts his arm and slams his elbow across his adversary's face, knocking him flat out.

Cursing and growling, he yanks out the blade and tosses it aside, satisfied to see that it has missed all of his major arteries. He rises to his feet. The gun still in his hand, Lev aims it between the eyes of the unconscious man.

That's when he feels the sharp blow to the back of his skull.

The professor.

He spins around and staggers to the side, shocked at

the force she has managed to exert with the rock in her hands. His head spinning, he blinks and loses balance, falling to one knee and dropping his pistol. The professor lifts the stone to strike again, but Lev reacts just in time, ducking and grabbing her by the leg. He yanks hard.

The tiny woman weighs nothing and goes down easily with her arms flailing. Lev crawls over her until they're face to face, ignoring the kicks and punches as she thrashes wildly beneath him. He grabs her wrists and pins her down with his weight, his cock hardening when she doesn't stop struggling against him.

"You will pay for that," he growls. His head throbs in agony. Something warm trickles down his neck. Realising it is blood, his rage flares.

"Screw you," she retorts.

He slaps her across the face, unleashing all of his fury into that single strike. Her head snaps to the side. She coughs, spitting blood from her bruised lips, her cheek instantly red. Lev's mouth twitches with satisfaction when she finally goes still, and warmth rushes once more to his crotch. He's trying to decide if he should fuck the professor before or after she opens the tomb for him. There's an ache in his groin he needs to relieve, and she's the only woman around within a hundred kilometre radius.

But experience tells him that women like her do not cooperate easily, and his only leverage is on a ticking clock. Opting to tend to his needs later, he says, "You will take me to the tomb."

The professor turns her icy glare back to him. "Go to hell."

Fingers twitching, Lev balls his fists to restrain himself from hitting her again. She would be useless to him unconscious. So he plays the card he knows is going to give him what he wants. "Your boyfriend is bleeding out," he states as a matter of fact. "If you want to save him, you will do what I say. He does not have much time left."

The hatred in her face is instantly replaced with concern. Her brown eyes flit to the body next to them and she pleads, "Let me stop the bleeding first."

"No." Out of patience, sick and tired of being told what to do by a woman, Lev rises to his feet and pulls her along with him. She struggles ferociously, kicking him in the shin and breaking out of his grasp. She makes a run for the boyfriend lying on the ground.

"Buri—"

Lev grabs her by the hair and wrenches her back. She screams.

"Sooner we get in there, sooner you can help him. Tick-tock, professor." He drags her to the ledge.

Obviously realising she has no other choice, she yanks her arm away and reaches for the rope tied around the tree. Gripping it with both hands, she rappels down the cliff to the next shelf with startling strength and speed. From there she calls out to him, "Give me the Spirit Banner."

He lowers the black case to her. Wrapping the rope around his torso, he keeps one hand on the cord, the other on his gun, and his watchful eye on the Asian woman, then descends the steep slope with rapid, successive hops.

The professor opens the case and lifts out the Spirit Banner. Walking over to the stone door built into the cliff, she places the end of the pole into a protrusion out of the ground. She adjusts the angle and something aligns within the cavity, allowing the Spirit Banner to drop further into the hole. Gripping the pole with both hands, she twists to the left.

Nothing happens.

She rotates it to the right, and still the door does not budge.

She frowns, sucking her lower lip into her mouth.

The professor pushes down on the pole, and this time, something gives. When nothing else happens, she tries swivelling again. A soft click sounds, and the stone door slides open, making a slow sweep into the darkness beyond.

Lev looks into the inky abyss, and his pulse escalates. Now that he's at the tomb, he's hesitant about going in. Alexey's warnings of a curse plague his mind, and he wonders how much of it is true.

He tilts his head up. Clear skies. No storms this time.

All he needs is ten minutes. In. Grab the gold. Out.

But what if there are . . . booby traps inside?

"Well?" The Asian woman demands. "I opened it. Go in. I'm going to help Buri." She heads for the rope, but Lev grabs her by the arm and pulls her to him, the front of his body flush with her back. She yelps in surprise.

He presses his lips to her ear. "After you, professor."

She looks like she's about to argue, but realising that she's wasting valuable time, she stops struggling and pulls out a penlight from her pocket. Shining it down what appears to be a long, narrow passage, she walks over the threshold.

Taking a few tentative steps first, she quickly gets swallowed up by the pitch black void.

58

WARY AND VIGILANT, Georgia treads slowly through the sandstone tunnel. There's an earthy smell to the air, but it is not musty or stale, which would suggest that there is airflow through the temple. And that probably means there is more than one way to get in.

Or that someone has been here recently.

The passage curves to the left and then right, and soon the light from the doorway disappears behind her. Hearing nothing but the thud of her own pulse, she sees only the circle of light emitting from her torch, beyond which is a murky pool of gloom.

She presses forward, fear and worry for Buri at the forefront of her tumultuous mind. She can sense Lev to her rear, hear the sound of his breathing. She keeps going, and about fifteen metres in, the walls fall away and expand into a cavernous chamber.

The first thing she notices is the scent. It's something strangely familiar, and she searches her memory for where and when she has encountered it before. Then recognition dawns on her, and a chill travels up her spine.

It's the same incense from the shamanic ritual.

She's about to turn and warn Lev when she hears a faint, hollow hiss. Behind her, the Russian man lets out a low guttural sound. She whirls around with her torchlight, finding him glowering accusingly at her with a hand to his neck, his mouth open as he tries to formulate a word. He takes a step toward her with his other hand raised, but before he can follow through with the movement his eyes roll to the back of his head and he crumples to the floor with a thump, his heavy arm falling on hers and knocking the torch away.

The flashlight hits the ground and scatters across the surface, quickly blinking out.

59

SHIT.

Georgia stays frozen, shocked at the turn of events. Unable to see, she crouches down and crawls in the direction where she last saw the torch, her hand sweeping over the cold, smooth floor as she searches for it. She encounters Lev's immobile body, which blocks the entire width of the passage. Her hands feel something protruding from the side of his neck.

Poison dart.

Panic rising to her throat, she clambers over him, seeking the exit.

The sound of a match striking resonates in the space, and a dull glow appears. Turning her head, she sees a silhouetted figure.

A woman. She is facing away from Georgia, igniting candles on a tall table as the light progressively becomes brighter.

"Who are you?" Georgia demands.

She doesn't get a response. The woman shifts to the left and strikes another match, dropping it into a large cauldron. A hiss, a burst of flames, and the room is suddenly illuminated. The altar is the first thing Georgia sees. Tendrils of smoke rise from an ornate silver censer, filling the space with a sweet scent. There are cups, bowls, and plates of food placed in front of the shrine, where a brocaded golden scroll hangs against the wall, the painting hidden behind a protective silk cover.

The chamber appears to be of a perfect circle, with eight doorways spread evenly around. Above each is a unique *tamgha* carved into the stone surface. Georgia doesn't know them all, but she recognises two as those belonging to the sons of Chinggis Khan, and she realises the significance of this place.

The royal tomb of the Golden Family.

The eight entrances must each lead to the crypts of his four sons and four daughters. And that only means one thing. This central ninth room is where the Golden Khan lies.

But there is no sarcophagus here. The only object that rests on a stone plinth in the middle of the space is a small gold chest, its polished surface glistening in the firelight of the cauldron.

Another woman appears out of one of the darkened entrances. Dressed in a cerulean silk *deel*, the Mongolian elder looks about as old as Georgia's grandmother. Short and hunched over, her round, leathery face is marked by deep creases and her gaze is bright as she meets Georgia's eyes. The most remarkable thing about her is the elaborate headdress of felt and feathers rising high above her head. Strings of lustrous pearls dangle down both sides of her face and over her forehead, clanging against each other every time she moves.

Georgia has only seen this type of headpiece worn by a very specific group of people.

Mongol queens.

The woman at the altar finally turns, and Georgia sucks in a sharp breath as she recognises her face. It's the shaman's assistant, the one who cut Georgia's palm at the ceremony.

Her hand throbs at the memory, even though the injury healed long ago. But she still wears a bandage around it to conceal that fact from Buri.

"Buri," Georgia murmurs as she suddenly comes to her senses. She rushes to her feet.

"He will be fine," the shaman's assistant says in accented, perfect English. It's clear she did not need Buri to translate for her at all during the shamanic ceremony. "I have sent someone to tend to him."

"But—"

"He has lost some blood. But I am confident he'll survive."

Unconvinced, Georgia turns to head back through the tunnel.

The older woman speaks up. Communicating in Mongolian, her voice is authoritative but kind. Her younger companion translates for her simultaneously into English: "Professor Lee. I give you my word that your friend is being cared for by our best medical professionals. There is nothing else you can do for him right now. Please. Speak to us. We have a lot to discuss and we need some privacy for this."

"Who are you people?" Georgia stares at the women with suspicion. "What is going on?"

The shaman's assistant replies, "This is my great-aunt, Gerel *Khatun*, and I am Naran *Beki*."

Georgia lifts her brows, recognising the Mongolian titles. *Queen* Gerel and *Princess* Naran. She eyes the identical, chunky gold rings on each of the women's forefingers, both bearing the *tamgha* of Chinggis Khan.

"We are daughters of the Borijin clan, descendants of the Golden Khan, guardians of his tomb and his *Secret History*," Naran continues, confirming Georgia's theory.

The Mongolian elder, Queen Gerel, speaks up. Again, Naran interprets her words so Georgia can understand: "I see you survived the storm. The Eternal Blue Sky must favour you."

Before Georgia can reply, Naran steps forward and grabs her bandaged hand, ripping off the gauze.

"Hey!" Georgia tries to pull back, but the girl has a surprisingly powerful grip.

Naran holds Georgia's unmarred, open palm in plain view. There's not even a scar from the cut that Naran administered only two days ago. The Mongolian women gasp at the sight.

"Just as Gerel suspected." Naran drops Georgia's hand and takes a step back. "You are the same."

"The same? The same as what?"

Without replying, Naran walks over to the shrine. Stepping onto a small stool fashioned out of stone, she slowly rolls up the protective covering over the scroll to expose the picture underneath.

Georgia stares at the image being unveiled in front of her from bottom to top, recognising how it is identical to the one she examined at the National Palace Museum in Taipei. This piece, though, is much bigger, and she remembers how her friend Ling Ling suspected that the painting in the museum was actually a first draft shown to the emperor for approval before the larger commissioned work was made. What Georgia is seeing must be the actual portrait used for worship in the imperial shrines.

But as Naran reveals the face of Chinggis Khan, Georgia's eyes widen with astonishment.

Her mouth drops open. In a chill of realisation, she suddenly understands why the painting that Ling Ling showed her has sketch-like marks in the strokes. The picture at the museum has been altered, and what she is seeing on the wall is the real image of the Golden Khan himself. It is now clear to her that there was a very practical reason for Chinggis to forbid any images of him to be created during his lifetime.

It was to conceal his true identity.

A cold sweat breaks out over her body, and she is gripped by sudden nausea. In spite of herself, she feels drawn to the image hanging on the wall, her legs moving of their own accord. As she walks closer, she notes the changes that had been made on the smaller sketch at the National Palace Museum. They are only minor variations, and she marvels at the anonymous artist's obvious mastery of his craft. With a few simple lines, the face on the smaller painting had been transformed into an elderly sage. In the version she is seeing now, the Khan is still wearing the same hat and clothes, but here, he is depicted as a young man. And his head is cleanly shaven.

Round face.

Well-trimmed goatee.

Broad chest.

Dark, beady eyes which don't quite portray the brutish glimmer that Georgia will never forget.

But what gives her the most astonishing sense of déjà vu is the long, deep scar down the side of his right cheek.

The resemblance is so uncanny, the details so precise, it cannot possibly be mistaken for anyone else.

Wang Jian.

60

A<small>IR RUSHES</small> out from Georgia's body as if she's been kicked in the gut. She staggers back.

The words of Buri's uncle repeat in her mind, retelling the folklore of Chinggis Khan:

. . . it is common knowledge among the Mongols that Chinggis Khan is not dead. Holy Chinggis is the most powerful warrior shaman this world has ever seen. He will heal himself, and once he is healed, he will rise and lead his people again.

Now that his actual identity has been revealed, Georgia knows that those words have more truth in them than one would suspect. Chinggis Khan could not die.

Because before he became Chinggis, he was Wang Jian. The general sent by Emperor Qin over two millennia ago to track down Hsu Fu, the imperial alchemist, who never returned with the elixir of life.

An immortal, just like Charlie.

And as Naran has said, Georgia is the same as him.

Her mind reeling, she whirls around to look at the women, stammering, "Th-that's . . ."

"You've met him before," Naran says, watching her closely as if seeking confirmation of her statement.

"But—" Feeling lightheaded, Georgia cannot articulate her words. She leans against the wall for support, fearing her legs may give out under her.

She remembers the last time she saw Wang Jian in the caves on the east coast of Taiwan. She recalls with gruesome detail the way he stuck a knife through Mark Lambert's throat, and how he laughed with chilling cruelty when he confronted her and Charlie. She can still picture the rage and torment in his eyes as he described how Charlie had taken from him his only son.

"How . . . can this *be*?" Her gaze flicks between Naran and Gerel, seeking answers.

Naran says something in Mongolian to her great-aunt, and the old woman sighs, weariness suddenly apparent in her features. Moving closer to Georgia, she eases herself down onto the squat stool beside the altar and pats another near her. Already wobbling on her feet, Georgia gladly takes a seat next to Gerel. The Mongol elder speaks as Naran translates for her simultaneously.

"You and the Russians have come looking for Chinggis Khan's tomb, but as you now know, there is no coffin here. His sons and daughters are within this temple, yes, but not himself." Gerel gestures to the box in the centre of the room. "All that we have left of him is contained in that chest."

"Is that . . . *The Secret History*?" Georgia asks.

Gerel nods once Naran has interpreted Georgia's question. "Yes," Gerel replies, her words being relayed through Naran. "But it is not what you think. Contrary to the rumours, it contains no magical powers and holds no secrets to world domination. It is merely a detailed and truthful account of our Khan and his life."

"His life." Georgia ponders this. "You mean . . . his *entire* life?"

"From the time he was born in Mongolia, to when he was known as Wang Jian—"

"Wait. Wang Jian was *Mongolian*?"

Naran gives her a patronising smile. "Of course. Our Khan only took on his Chinese name after being recruited into Emperor Qin's army. You are completely missing the point. Please allow me to finish."

Chastened, Georgia presses her lips together and waits for Naran to go on.

"As I was saying," Naran continues, "the book describes his life from childhood, to how he became one of the greatest generals of the Qin state, to his transformation into an immortal in Japan. *The Secret History* also tells of how he came back to Mongolia to unite its people and follows the events right up until he left us again. All in all, it spans almost fifteen centuries of his life."

Stunned into silence, Georgia reflects on how, despite what Gerel said, *The Secret History* does hold a powerful knowledge that would bring any foe to his knees. And it is also a weapon that Agent Miller would kill for. After all, what is more formidable than an enemy who cannot die?

Gerel continues to speak as Naran translates for her. "You see, as Emperor Qin's general, Wang Jian believed in the vision of the man he served. Qin wanted to bring all of his known world under one rule. He thought this was the only way people may benefit from peace and prosperity: under one global order founded on a universal law and with one writing system."

"But Emperor Qin . . ." Georgia interrupts, considering

the similarities between the two men. "Most saw him as a tyrant, a ruthless ruler who killed too many people to achieve his goal."

"Yes," Gerel agrees. "And so was also said of our Khan. But in the minds of Qin and Wang Jian, peace came at a price, and they felt that the cost was ultimately worth it. They believed in bringing order to the world through strength and power. As controversial as this may be, you have to remember that China went through two centuries of war and turmoil between the Seven Warring States before Emperor Qin finally ended the conflict. It was the same with Mongolia. Before our Khan, the steppes were occupied by rival tribes who fought incessantly against each other."

Not knowing how to respond to this because she, too, has argued for the numerous contributions made by both men, Georgia remains quiet as she waits for Gerel to continue.

"Our Khan identified with this vision," Gerel says again, "and he saw the potential in his own people. He recognised in us and in the geostrategic positioning of Mongolia a means to finally accomplish what he set out to do a thousand years before."

Folding her weathered hands in her lap, Gerel goes on: "Chinggis Khan won wars not because of his shamanic powers. He battled and conquered without defeat because he was driven by a single-minded focus on his goal, and more importantly, because he had the advantage of many centuries of experience in warfare. As the mighty power of the Mongols increased, and as our trade routes opened up connecting the east to the west, people of Eurasia benefited not only from the free flow of goods but also from the exchange of knowledge and technology. But there was another thing that travelled along the Silk Road that was far more valuable to our Khan than anything else."

Georgia pales, knowing what it is. "Information."

"Precisely. As the empire expanded, our Khan's focus changed. He became less interested in ruling the lands he had conquered, and more intent on gaining intelligence that he previously did not have access to. He wanted his influence to reach as far as the ends of the earth, and he wanted to develop one avenue of communication that led straight to him."

Georgia's gut sinks. "He was looking for Charlie."

"Charlie?"

"Hsu Fu, the alchemist that Qin sent to find the elixir. I know him as Charlie."

Gerel listens as Naran relays this to her. The Mongolian elder's eyes glisten in the dim light, shining with something Georgia cannot pinpoint. Is it sorrow? Is it remorse?

"Yes," Gerel confirms what Georgia has suspected. "Hsu Fu killed Wang Jian's son. And even though our Khan had many children later, he still could not forget the wrong that was done to him. His firstborn was his favourite, the one who fought alongside him as soon as the boy was old enough. Everyone else who came after paled in comparison. As Chinggis, he felt that the sons he left his empire to were an utter disappointment."

Gerel gestures at the chamber around her, empty but for the gold chest, the cauldron, and the shrine. "Most grave hunters come looking for his tomb thinking there would be mountains of treasures to loot from. But as you can see, all of that was gone long ago, spent on the excessive decadence of Chinggis' extravagant, heavy-drinking sons. There are no more riches to be found here."

After a brief pause, she continues to explain, "The

larger our empire grew, the more restless our Khan became. The Wang Jian part of him was mad for his search for Hsu Fu. That is why he sent men all the way to Europe for battle but never did anything with the lands they conquered. He was secretively looking for leads. Then, on the brink of defeating northern China, he finally received word of where Hsu Fu could be. Against the advice and the pleas of his closest confidants and family members, he decided that he had to pursue this for himself. He left behind all of his loyal followers and everything he had built, to track down the one man he could not forgive or forget."

Georgia nods. "Because after harbouring his hatred over a thousand years, he was finally going to exact his revenge."

"Yes. But there were also other reasons. His enduring youth was starting to raise suspicions, no matter how powerful a shaman everyone believed him to be. And to our Khan, his condition was an aberration of nature. He hated it. He saw it as a curse, carrying around centuries of pain and loneliness with no reprieve. He had no intention of allowing anyone else to attain immortality, and he was going to hunt down the only other man who was the very reason he became that way."

Georgia rubs her forehead, feeling confounded and utterly lost. She has a sudden yearning for her deceased and wise friend, Charlie. She remembers vividly her conversations with him when they were looking for the cave in Taiwan. Oddly enough, they did speak about Chinggis Khan once. When she asked him if he had ever met the conqueror, Charlie replied no, telling her he was in Europe at the time.

Gerel continues, "Before our Khan left, he ordered for

the conditions around his faked death to be kept strictly confidential. He gave instructions to his sons and daughters, strategies to continue his work in uniting the world. These, together with the truth of his life, were recorded in *The Secret History*."

Aided by Naran, Gerel slowly rises. She walks over to the gold chest across the room. "This is the only remaining copy."

Georgia joins the women as Gerel opens the casket. Lined with dark velvet, a thick volume lays within. The intricately decorated cover is forged from gold, studded with gems of blue, green, and red that glint in the warm light of the fire. A vertical line of Mongolian text is carved down the centre. Spell-bound by its beauty, Georgia is aching to touch it.

Looking to Gerel, she asks, "So there were other copies?"

"There were only two ever made," the older woman answers through Naran. "One was entrusted to Ogodei Khan, Chinggis Khan's successor. The other—the one you see here—was given to Alaqai Beki."

"Princess Alaqai. Chinggis' daughter," Georgia says, recognising the name. "The one who ruled over the Onggud people."

"That is right." For the first time, Gerel smiles. "This surprises most people, but the Mongol Empire was built by the women as much as the men. Our women have fought side by side with men for centuries. They have even led Mongol armies to battle. And while the warriors left the homeland for long periods of time to conquer foreign nations, it was women who stayed behind and managed the empire. There was a time when our queens and princesses controlled and administered the largest empire in the world."

"But the role of women was erased from your history," Georgia points out.

"I know what you are thinking. You believe that it was because of chauvinism and the persecution of female rulers. No." Gerel shakes her head, the strings of pearls dangling down from her headdress clanking against each other. "The role of Mongol queens in the empire was erased deliberately to protect us."

At Georgia's surprised look, Gerel explains: "The sons of Chinggis Khan were charged with the responsibility of expanding the empire. It was the daughters' job to maintain the home affairs, and more importantly, to guard the secret truth of our Golden Khan. The book was kept under restricted access so that only our very select circle would know the truth of our origins. The Darkhats were then put in place to protect us and to seal off our homeland from outsiders. Like this, we passed the torch from generation to generation, awaiting the day when our true Khan returns."

Georgia's heart pumps faster at the latest revelation. "So he was meant to come back?"

Wang Jian is never coming back. He died in that cave, along with Charlie.

"Yes. He promised to, once he accomplished his goal. But we never saw him again, and something went very wrong with many of the Mongol leaders that came after him. Factions developed within the Golden Family. They fought amongst each other, assassinated their own kin to attain more power. As the empire crumpled, we lost our unity, our direction, and most importantly, the knowledge of our history. Alaqai Beki's copy of *The Secret History* was kept safe by our small group. Ogodei's copy was destroyed in a fire when the Mongol Yuan Dynasty in China was overthrown. Mongolia descended back into a chaotic array of feuding tribes for centuries, and we've had constant foreign threats from China and Russia since. These outsiders . . . they did unspeakable things to our country, persecuted so many of us for our faith and culture. For a long time, we were not allowed to speak of our Khan."

Gerel looks fatigued from the conversation, but she continues, "When things got desperate, we released the transliterated version of *The Secret History*. Of course, we omitted the information about his immortality. This redacted, edited adaptation of the Mongolian original was to serve two purposes. We wanted our people to remember who we truly are, to rejoice in our Khan. After all the foreign slander shaping the Mongols into mindless barbarians we never were, it was time to recall our real identity, the power we once wielded, and what our empire actually built for the world. For the Mongols, this newly rediscovered text was like a divine message from the Golden Khan, bringing them hope and inspiration."

"And the second reason for releasing the book?"

"It was a cry for help. We needed Chinggis Khan to come back to us again."

All at once, the clues and discoveries that have led her to this place finally make sense. Georgia now understands why the verses were composed with the lyrical tone of the Mongol army's ancient system for transmitting important messages. It was what someone from that time would have recognised straightaway as a communique.

"You embedded clues in the *sulde* and *The Secret History*, planted the coordinates in here . . . so that Wang

Jian would find this place," Georgia says, her eyes widening at the realisation.

"Yes. War was coming. Wedged in between Russia and China, we were dealing with threats from both directions. This temple is the last sanctum of our Khan's legacy, and we wanted him to lead us again from here."

"*And from which the Golden Throne shall rise again*," Georgia repeats the last verse of the clues, realising what it means.

"It is an old Mongolian prophecy," Gerel reveals. "Our shamans have foretold that it is from here the true spirit of our leader will be resurrected from the ashes, and hope and strength will once more be restored to our people."

Georgia shifts uncomfortably. She sees the gleam in the women's eyes as they speak of their sovereign from long ago, a demigod who would somehow bring their salvation. But she knows him only as Wang Jian, and the thought of him brings terror to her very core. He was a merciless monster who had tortured and hunted Charlie, who went to extraordinary lengths to trap Georgia in his scheme for retribution, who drugged and kidnapped Sarah, and brutally murdered Mark.

After a period of silence, Naran finally speaks of her own accord. "Which brings us to why you are here, Professor Lee."

Georgia swallows thickly. The back of her neck prickles with trepidation. It alarms her that these women know more about her than they should. "How . . . how did you know I'm a professor?"

"Because we saw you on the news when you were being rescued from the landslide in Taiwan," Naran replies. "And we saw the picture of our Khan in the report. We realised that you were with him in Taiwan."

The Mongolian women exchange a few words, then Naran turns to Georgia. "We realise he must have passed his powers to you. What we do not understand is why. What happened to him? What happened in Taiwan? And how did you end up in Mongolia?"

61

ANYA JOLTS AWAKE, crying out as pain sears through her body. She is wedged in the most uncomfortable way at the bottom of a crevice, squinting up at the sunlight glaring through the foliage of the trees above. Her head is thudding with such intensity it makes her stomach heave, threatening to purge its contents.

She struggles to a seated position, crying out again from the agony of the movement. Her right arm rests uselessly in her lap, and her heart stops at the mangled sight of it.

What the hell happened?

Then, bit by bit, memories of last night come back.

The storm almost killed her. By the time she saw the tree toppling down, it was too late to scramble out of the way. The huge trunk landed on her arm with a sickening crunch, and the excruciating pain was so overwhelming it must have knocked her out.

When she came to, rain was coming down so hard she was spluttering and gasping for air. She was trapped with her limb still crushed under the tree, and her teeth chattered violently from the cold. She searched all over and finally found a stone to dig away at the surrounding mushy peat to get free, a task that took forever as she fought to stay conscious.

Once she liberated her arm she staggered to her feet, utterly lost and stumbling around the dark, chaotic forest. By then she was delirious, hallucinating from the horrific pain in her shattered limb and the howling cacophony of the raging tempest. She was convinced she'd arrived in the depths of hell and terror overtook her as she half ran, half tumbled down the mountain. At some point she lost her footing and slipped, smashing her head against the hard ground.

That must have been when she fell into the crevice she now finds herself in. Ironically, it was probably what saved her, as it provided shelter from the rest of the squall.

Dizziness and nausea grip Anya as she drags herself to a standing position, and she wonders if she may have a concussion. The back of her skull screams with pain when she touches it, and there is blood caked all down her neck. She winces when she puts weight on her left foot and looks down to find her ankle purple and swollen.

Fucking great.

At least the fissure isn't too deep. The ground is at her chest level, but that doesn't mean getting out of the hole with one working arm and a severely twisted ankle is going to be easy. She grunts and curses through the entire feat, and when she at last claws her way out she gingerly flips onto her back, taking an age to catch her breath again.

Hungry, her throat parched, wondering what happened to her team, Anya eventually musters the energy to rise. She follows the downward slope, limping towards what she hopes to be where her camp is. The forest is completely unrecognisable from the damage of the storm, the detritus on the ground making it even more difficult for her to walk.

After what seems like an hour, she comes across Alexey's dead body.

She pauses and takes in the sight, noting the damaged equipment still strapped to his back.

Then she pushes on.

When she finally makes it to the camp she finds it utterly destroyed. Not only that, someone has raided the supplies, taken all the food, weapons, and—what is most infuriating—her *sulde*. She had left it in her tent with the plan to return for it once they uncovered the tomb, knowing it could take a few trips to fully excavate the site.

Lev.

Anger burns up her torso, the bitter taste of betrayal sharp on her tongue. The image of him running off like a coward is still strong in her mind, and she fumes over the fact that he hasn't even come to search for her in case she survived. Instead, he took the *sulde*. And he's probably on the summit now, digging for the tomb to claim the glory of the find.

Fucking traitor.

Picking through the wreckage, she exhales with relief when she finds the first aid kit. She fashions a sling for her ruined arm, patches up the worst cuts to her body, secures her ankle with a tightly wound bandage, and pops a few pills for the pain.

Then she rummages through her rucksack and digs out the Nagan M1895 Revolver that belonged to her grandfather.

The thing is pretty much an antique, but Anya has taken good care of it since Deda Dmitry died. There is no doubt it'll function perfectly. Deda's favourite choice of firearm is the only item of sentimental value she has brought on this trip. Carrying it in her pack has been like having him beside her every step of the journey.

She loads the pistol, stuffs a few essential items into a small backpack, and with simmering fury spurring her to action, she gets up to go after what belongs to her.

The Spirit Banner is the key. As she hobbles her way up to the summit, Deda Dmitry's gruff voice comes back to her. He had said those words to her countless times before he died. But Anya never realised that the *sulde* is the *literal* key to the tomb until Dr. Fujimoto confessed the information at Almsgivers Wall.

And without the key, there's no way of getting in.

She grips the small gun in her hand, ignores the complaints of her battered body, and walks faster towards the peak. By the time she reaches the top she is so winded she has to crouch down and take a break.

A gentle breeze ruffles the grassy plains, and the sky is a startling blue completely devoid of clouds. The overhead sun beams down, mocking her. She sneers, realising this is the first time she's experienced such clear weather up here.

She looks around for Lev, but the plateau is deserted, making her scowl in confusion.

Where the hell could he be, if not here?

Then it occurs to her that he may not have been the one who took the *sulde* after all. But if the person who stole it isn't here . . . then that would mean he or she believes the tomb to be elsewhere.

Georgia.

The startling realisation leaves Anya breathless, but she knows it to be true because there's no way that meathead Ivanov could have figured otherwise about the location of the burial site. Professor Lee has obviously caught up in the race.

Starving, thirsty, and utterly exhausted, Anya doesn't know whether to be impressed or enraged. She eases herself down on a nearby rock, still wheezing from the exertion of the climb, and that's when she remembers that all is not lost.

It seems long ago now, but when she got the *sulde* back from Georgia in Sydney, Anya installed a tracking device in the case. She had no intention of losing it again, but the artefact is so valuable she didn't want to take any chances.

She taps the smartwatch on her left wrist, flinching at the movement. A small red dot appears, blinking brightly on the screen.

For the first time today, she smiles.

"See you soon, Professor."

Anya pushes off the rock and marches towards her destiny.

62

GEORGIA'S THROAT is suddenly dry. She doesn't know how to tell the Mongolian women that the beacon of their hope is gone, and that she had something to do with it.

Despite the solemn way in which Gerel speaks, the Mongolian elder has a gentleness and a sense of wisdom about her that reminds Georgia of her own grandmother. The young princess, though, seems to have a serious chip on her shoulder. She is unlikely to take the news well.

Should Georgia lie? Spin a tale to let them hold on to the faith of their Khan's return?

When she doesn't respond for the longest time, Gerel nods knowingly with sadness in her eyes.

"Look, Georgia," she says. "There is nothing to be afraid of here. We simply want the truth. For far too long, our people have been told lies, and not just about our identity and our origin. So much of our own account has been lost or destroyed, only to be rewritten by those who hated us. It's one of the reasons we released the transliterated version of *The Secret History*, to remind the Mongolian people of our authentic story."

"I . . . He . . ."

The tiny old lady steps forward and grasps Georgia's hand with both of her own, staring up at her earnestly. "It's okay," she says. "Start from the beginning."

Georgia swallows thickly, staring at her hand trapped between the old woman's leathery, calloused palms. Her breath escapes her when she gazes into Gerel's eyes.

For the past few weeks, she has devoted her every waking moment to interpreting *The Secret History*, and throughout the process she has been keenly reminded of the fact that history is an entirely subjective, fluid concept. Too often, the human story has been written by those who controlled the information, shaping facts and reality as they pleased.

Thankfully, though, truth always endures no matter what. It is there, hidden under cleverly constructed words which obscure the light of something that may have been forgotten, but never eradicated. And it is the job of people like her to separate fact from fiction, to *re*-present the findings to the world. Isn't that her purpose? The constant and relentless pursuit of verity, uncovering all that has been lost or intentionally concealed, and piecing together our collective narrative as human beings?

She cannot possibly deceive these women, when their people have been denied honesty for too long.

She drops her head, taking a long moment to steel herself. Then she begins to tell the Mongolian women her story. Starting from the day she met Mark Lambert, she describes how she was prompted to search for Hsu Fu—or Charlie—and how she came to meet him. She talks about the original source of the elixir of life, and about Charlie's friend Naaya, the woman who first discovered it by accident. Charlie wanted to find the place where it all began, so that he could study the extraordinary healing properties of the water. She recounts the fateful events that brought her, Charlie, Mark Lambert, and Wang Jian to the cave in Taiwan, and finally, the horrific deaths of the three men. She also speaks about how she ingested the elixir without intending to, a fact she realised weeks after the event, and something she has been struggling with ever since.

Then she goes into the most recent events that brought her to Mongolia: Anya and her team seeking the tomb, the DIA and their military interests, the death of her friends Hiroshi and Ethan, and all the clues she has followed to bring her to the temple.

When Georgia finishes her tale, a long silence echoes through the chamber. Gerel takes a stuttering breath, looking all at once weary and aged beyond her years, grief shining in her glistening eyes. The old woman sways on her feet, and Georgia barely manages to catch her from falling. She guides the Mongolian elder to the stone stool by the altar, her chest aching with remorse for being the bearer of bad news.

Naran is pacing up and down the chamber, her distress fiercely evident. The young woman says something to Gerel in Mongolian, but her great-aunt only shakes her head in response.

Frustrated, Naran switches to English, addressing Georgia: "But you did not see Wang Jian die. All you saw was that rock falling on him. Maybe he is still trapped in there."

Georgia frowns. She can still picture the whole event in her mind: the collapse of the cave and a giant boulder crashing down on Wang Jian, the rock so massive that his entire body was crushed under its weight, and only his grotesquely twisted feet were visible from underneath. She knows exactly what she witnessed, and she is also certain there is no way he could have survived something like that, immortal or not.

"I'm pretty sure he couldn't have healed from what happened," she says, then explains how the elixir works.

"That is not possible." Naran's voice escalates. "The prophecy said—"

Gerel calls out to her grandniece, saying a few words to pacify her. Naran retorts vehemently, and the two women engage in an extended, heated dialogue. Georgia cannot understand what is being discussed, and it takes a while before Gerel has a final word in the argument. The younger woman huffs with indignation, but comes to sit by the foot of her elder.

When Gerel speaks again, her voice swells with unspoken emotions. She stutters and pauses many times, struggling to find the words in her grief-stricken state. "Thank you for being so candid with us . . . I am sorry for what you have been through. We dearly loved our Khan, but we also understand that he was just a man, and he undoubtedly had his shortcomings . . . Sadly, it seems the Wang Jian part of him won, and he was driven mad by his obsession for revenge. I wish you had the chance to know Chinggis Khan as our people had."

"I'm sorry. I feel somewhat responsible," says Georgia, surprised that the Mongolian elder holds no hostility for her the way Wang Jian did.

"No." Gerel's voice is firmer now. "Wang Jian did this to himself. This is what I am trying to explain to Naran. He refused to let go of his hatred, and even though he had a new family who loved him and was devoted to him, he left it to pursue revenge for a son he could never bring back. He could have let go of his past and started anew. He could have chosen forgiveness. He did not see that he was given a second chance, and he never realised that he was giving up so much more for something he could never regain. Unfortunately, life does not give many second chances."

At those words, Georgia is reminded of Charlie and his daughter, Hsu Jen, and of how he regretted not cherishing his time with her while she was alive. Then, Ethan's face resurfaces in her mind and she winces at the pang in her heart. Was he her second chance, like what Sarah claimed in their office weeks ago? Has she blown that too, just as she did with her daughter and ex-husband?

Minutes pass before Gerel places a hand on Naran's shoulder, speaking to her in Mongolian. When the old woman falls silent again, Naran chews on her lips, mulling over what was said for a long time. She raises her gaze to Georgia and appraises her with open scepticism.

"Gerel says the prophecy does not exactly say that Chinggis Khan would be returning to us. It only proclaims that *the Golden Throne shall rise again*, which can be interpreted in a number of ways. And perhaps it is time we stopped waiting for our past to return, and move on into our future instead. Learning from the mistake of our Khan, we need to stop looking to what was before, and make the best of what we have at hand." Naran pauses, having difficulty with what she's about to say next. With a deep frown she reveals: "Gerel believes the prophecy means that whoever finds this place will bring back the true spirit of our nation, something which rightfully belongs to us."

Georgia widens her eyes, realising that Naran is referring to her as the one who located the temple. "I'm not sure how I can possibly do that."

"I'm not either." Naran looks at Georgia with undisguised doubt. Then she turns to dutifully translate for Gerel. Her elder gives her another drawn-out response, and Naran says in English: "Well, there *is* one thing we'd like your help with."

"What is it?"

Georgia listens quietly as Naran describes their request. She smiles. "Yes. Of course." Then, curiosity overcoming her, her gaze moves to the gold chest. She asks, "Is it okay for me to take a look at the book?"

Giving Georgia a satisfied nod, Gerel rises to her feet, returning to the box in the centre of the room as she motions for Georgia to join her. She reaches into the chest and lifts the book out, leaning it against the underside of the open lid. She opens it to the first page, showing Georgia a replica of Wang Jian's portrait, then proceeds to leaf through the pages. It is an illuminated, hand-written manuscript, filled with lines upon vertical lines of traditional Mongolian script.

"Against all odds, you managed to decode the clues," Naran says, translating for Gerel as the older woman speaks. "You survived the storms and overcame your enemies too. This is the Eternal Blue Sky's heavenly sign to us. Our Khan had no interest in allowing others to become immortal, nor to spread knowledge of it. It was a secret he charged us to guard with our lives. Now that he is gone, you are the remaining carrier of his legacy. His secret is now yours to keep."

Georgia regards the thick volume in Gerel's hands as the elderly woman carefully turns the pages, reflecting on how it represents everything she has been battling with for the past few weeks. Wang Jian's story is one full of hatred and torment, but he was also blessed with people who were whole heartedly devoted to him. The way he chose to spend a lifetime of eternal youth, however, determined the unfortunate outcome of his fate. Unable to forgive Charlie for what he had done, Wang Jian harboured his wrath until it drove him out of his mind, committing all his efforts to the single purpose of retribution. In so doing, he brought not only suffering to himself but also afflicted it upon other people.

The repercussions are like a ripple effect, and Georgia shivers to think of everyone who has been affected by his actions.

With a chill of realisation, Georgia also sees how her own desire for vengeance could drive her down a similar path. She has started her life of immortality in the same way Wang Jian once had, embarking on this mission with the DIA to hunt down the very people responsible for the death of someone she loved. And throughout her journey she has increasingly identified with Wang Jian's thirst for retribution, consumed by a kind of vile rage she has never experienced before.

Is this how she wants to live, imprisoned by her own past, ignoring what she has at hand, and never moving on into her future?

Once again, the weight of responsibility comes crushing down on her shoulders. However she chooses to spend the long life that is ahead of her, whatever she does from now on, will have lasting effects not only on herself, but on those around her.

Ever since she found out about her new condition, she has struggled and debated inwardly over what to do with the powerful knowledge. She has experienced guilt when she's had to lie about it, especially to those who care deeply about her. She has even felt shame over her ability to heal when others could not. The fear of Miller and Buri finding out has her on constant guard. And there has been one question that has ceaselessly plagued her mind.

Is humanity ready? Should she share her secret with the world?

She thinks about her daughter Jacqui, about all the children who have suffered illnesses and premature deaths, and the pain that their parents have gone through. Her thoughts move to Ethan, and she wonders yet again if there was something she could have done to save him. Then she remembers Naaya, the woman who first found the elixir, and how the gift of immortality had driven her people mad until they ultimately destroyed themselves.

Were Wang Jian and Charlie right in their belief that the elixir should never be allowed to be disclosed, that life in perpetuity is an aberration of nature, that the impermanence of being is actually a blessing in disguise?

Gerel's dark gaze seems to penetrate her, and the old woman nods as if privy to Georgia's thoughts. "I can see you are struggling with this, as our Khan once did. I cannot imagine what it is like, or presume to know what you are battling with."

Georgia's face drops. She admits, "I'm not sure what to do with this. This knowledge could be a great gift to humanity. Or it could bring destruction to us all."

Gerel sighs. "I cannot tell you what to do, but this is what I know. The Eternal Blue Sky has chosen you, and it is you alone who has to decide what to do with the power you now have. Let our Khan's lessons be your own. You have a long life ahead of you. Ask yourself: what kind of existence do you wish it to be?"

Georgia searches her heart and mind. Before she can come up with an answer, however, the loud bang of a gunshot resounds through the dark hall.

63

IGNORING the scratches to her limbs, fighting her way through the dense thicket, Anya eventually makes it to a clearing on the southern slope of Burkhan Khaldun. She walks tentatively into the empty plateau and looks around, seeing a looming *ovoo* and ceremonial cauldrons among the nearby trees. She jumps when her boots crunch over something. Lifting her foot, she frowns down at the fragment of roof tile she has stepped on.

Odd.

Too focused on her goal to contemplate what it all means, she moves on, keeping an eye on the glowing dot flashing on her watch. She limps with effort towards the edge of the plateau, coming across a patch of dark liquid that has soaked into the ground.

Blood.

She scans the area, not seeing a body or a trail of red that might tell her where the person went. She wonders

378

who has been injured, and if Lev came for the tomb after all. Her grip on the pistol tightens.

When she reaches the verge, she looks down the sheer drop and the first thing she sees is the *sulde* standing erect, its bottom end inserted into a small circular mound on the ground. Beside it is an open doorway carved into the mountain.

The tomb.

Anya's pulse quickens as she contemplates the tile she discovered only moments before. She realises she must be standing right over the grave site. How Georgia managed to locate this godforsaken place boggles her mind. Anya was so certain, so absolutely convinced, that Chinggis Khan was buried on the peak of the mountain. And throughout this race to find the location, she had all the advantages on her side, getting to every spot and every clue long before Georgia did. Yet in the end, she was still completely off the mark.

The professor has won. Spectacularly.

Anya shakes her head, feeling both humiliated and astounded by the fact.

Eager to get to the lower shelf, she searches for a way down. Her heart sinks when she sees the rope tied around the base of the tree. There is no other access from where she is standing. With her ruined arm in a sling, making it to the bottom safely is going to be a serious challenge.

Fuck it. She shoves the pistol into her belt, then encircles her waist with the rope. Bent over with one end of the nylon cable in her good hand and the rest of it between her thighs, she begins to fasten it around her. After many, many failed attempts and too much time lost, she finally manages to get a half-decent knot. By then, she's drenched in sweat with the effort. She further winds the cord over her torso—just in case—and swathes her left palm in a spare shirt from her backpack. Then, slowly and gingerly, with the cord burning trails in her skin and her muscles screaming with exertion, she walks down the cliff with her legs perpendicular to the stone wall, her single functioning hand gripping the rope and releasing it one agonising inch at a time.

The only thing that keeps her going is Deda Dmitry's words, repeating over and over again in her mind. She chants it under her breath like a mantra: *"The Spirit Banner is the key to the tomb, and the tomb holds the secrets to immortality."*

And as soon as she finds what she is after—she reassures herself—all of these physical afflictions will be as good as gone.

When Anya was seeking funding for the expedition more than a year ago, it was firstly the lure of undiscovered treasure that convinced the interested parties. And the possibility of a military weapon of unfathomable might was something they could not walk away from, either.

But unlike her investors, Anya has never been interested in either of those fantasies.

No, what she's after is something far more powerful, something Deda Dmitry had learnt of when he opened the tomb of Timur Khan decades ago in Uzbekistan. Carved all over the inside of the sarcophagus were inscriptions, words that had chilled him to the bone.

When I rise from the dead, the world shall tremble.

Whosoever opens my tomb shall unleash an invader more terrible than I.

These well-known verses have been linked to Operation Barbarossa in the Second World War, causing superstitious idiots like Lev and Alexey to also believe in the curse of Chinggis Khan. But what people don't know is that Colonel Dmitry Petrov had uncovered more than just two lines inside the casket, and it was the other words that had prompted his dogged fixation to find Chinggis' grave. It is the same reason that has made Anya search ceaselessly for it, too.

Countless times Anya has studied the writings scrawled in the blood-stained notebook of Captain Boris Baretski, a man who died on the very night of the discovery. He was the one who translated the etchings inside Timur Khan's coffin, and the only other person who knew about the information that was extracted. Colonel Dmitry Petrov never shared the finding with anyone else except his granddaughter.

Not even Stalin, who had sent him on the mission in the first place.

As a scientist, Anya has often questioned what was revealed in those writings, wondering if they were fairy tales dreamed up by Timur Khan himself, who had also searched for the elusive text that holds the key to immortality. He claimed to be a descendant of Chinggis even though he was not born of the same clan and he attempted to restore the Mongol Empire, hoping that by doing so he would be privy to the location of the dead Khan's tomb. The two famous lines carved on his coffin were not a curse. They were the wishful thinking of a man who sought eternal life himself.

Historians have studied, theorised, contemplated at length over what it was that made Chinggis Khan completely unrivalled on the battlefield. These scholars have compiled a long list of factors, each one as mundane as the next: the mobility of his great nomad army, their diet, his willingness to choose officers based on merit rather than social ranking, et cetera, et cetera. The Mongols attribute his success to the belief that he was the most powerful warrior shaman to have ever walked the Earth. But is it conceivable that the mysterious weapon wielded by one of the greatest conquerors was just as extraordinary as the man himself? Is it possible that Chinggis never lost because he was immune to death itself?

The inscriptions in Timur Khan's sarcophagus revealed something tantalising. They described Chinggis' legendary healing powers, yes, but more importantly they promised that *The Secret History* would reveal how one could become the same as him.

Over the years Anya has argued with herself over these extraordinary claims, but the chaos of her inner debate has always been silenced by a single question.

What if? What if everything is true?

The concept is so captivating she couldn't possibly ignore it. Just think, if she were to live forever, frozen in a state of perpetual youth, never to experience age or death —how blessedly wonderful a life that would be! At times she would catch herself fantasising over the immeasurable potential immortality could bring, and the daydreams would be enough to push her to the point of obsession.

Absolute power. That single idea alone makes it all worth it.

And now, after so many years of searching, Anya finally has the answer at her fingertips. And as soon as she has the book in her hands, she is going to disappear with it, for such potent knowledge is not something to be shared.

So close. She is so close.

Those are the thoughts that keep her going as she lowers herself at a snail's pace down to the bottom shelf, biting the insides of her cheeks to keep from crying out. She almost sobs with relief when her feet finally touch the ground. Taking a long moment to steady herself, she wipes the moisture off her face and reaches for her gun once more. With a shaky hand rubbed completely raw, she cocks the hammer as she hobbles over to the entrance.

She peers into the dark passage. Muffled sounds echo through the tunnel. Her heartbeat escalates and she ventures over the threshold, leaning against the cool wall for support while trying to keep as quiet as possible. The light of day disappears behind her, but a warm glow ahead draws her forward. As her surroundings brighten again, the voices become clearer.

She holds her breath, straining to hear. There are three women speaking, but their muted sounds bounce off the hard surfaces and make it difficult to discern what is being said. One voice is familiar, however.

Georgia.

But who are the other two?

Her eyes adjust to the dim light as she moves closer, and the tunnel opens up into a room several metres ahead. There's a shrine against the wall on the right-hand side, and three silhouetted forms are standing by a fire burning brightly in a large vessel.

Anya's gaze zeroes in on the smallest figure. The woman is holding something in her hands. It glimmers in the light like a yellow diamond.

A book.

The Secret History.

Her breath lurches to her throat. Drawn by the vision, Anya's legs move forward of their own accord. Her foot bumps into something and she almost cries out with shock. In the darkness, she makes out the shape of a man lying on the ground. The figure stirs from her disturbance and lashes out a long arm to grasp at her ankle. This time she does yelp, instinctively pointing the revolver at his head and pulling the trigger.

The deafening boom reverberates through the space, making her ears ring. Blood and tissue splatter on her and she grimaces with dismay.

Shit.

She acts quickly.

Stepping over the body, she glances down and recognises Lev. The back of his skull has a hole through it, spurting with blood. She successfully avoids the gathering pool despite her awkward movements. Training her weapon on the women with her good hand, she moves into the light.

The trio by the fire stare at her, frozen with shock. Georgia's clothes are as dishevelled as Anya feels, her long black hair in tiny braids behind her back, looking right at home with the two traditionally dressed Mongolian women standing beside her. The older of the pair is wearing an elaborate headdress reaching high above her head.

Something that only Mongol queens wear.

Anya frowns in confusion, unable to understand what she is seeing. She keeps her gun pointed at the elderly woman, eyes fixed on the book in her hands.

In all of Anya's imaginings of what it would look like, the reality far surpasses them all. With covers forged in what can only be gold, *The Secret History* is decorated with gems of all colours conceivable, glittering alluringly in the firelight.

Momentarily enchanted by the magical sight, she almost doesn't react fast enough when the youngest of the three makes a move towards her. Taking a quick step back, Anya thrusts the gun in the direction of the Mongol girl.

"Stay where you are!" she commands. "Or you'll end up like the man on the floor."

The young woman stops in her tracks, glowering at Anya.

"Anya—" Georgia breaks off when Anya swerves her aim to the professor.

Her gaze meets Georgia's dark brown eyes, and she wants to ask her colleague how she managed to beat her to the tomb. Anya wants to pick that brilliant brain of hers and play out all the engaging, titillating conversations she has fantasised about ever since meeting the professor. She has so many questions crawling up her throat, all of them demanding immediate answers, but she swallows them down, focusing on the most important matter at hand.

Sweat beads on her skin. She can feel moisture trickling down her back. Anya takes a tremulous breath to stop her hand from shaking. The painkillers are starting to wear off.

She turns once again to the old woman in the regal headdress, ordering, "Give me the book."

The girl to her right hisses. "She doesn't speak English," she says as if Anya is a moron for thinking any differently.

Impatient, Anya snaps, "Then translate for her."

The girl mutters something in Mongolian, but the elderly woman remains motionless, her eyes focused on

Anya. Completely unfazed, she is strangely calm for someone who has a gun pointed at her face.

"I won't ask again," Anya grinds out impatiently, her hand starting to tremble.

She needs to get the book now, get the hell out of there, and pop a few more of those pills to stave off the pain. She doesn't have much time if she wants to ever use her damaged arm again.

Something fleeting passes across the old woman's face, and her jaws set with a look of determination. She utters Mongolian words which the girl translates: "You want it? Come get it yourself."

Shit. Seeing what's coming just as the elder begins to move, Anya pulls the trigger.

Nothing happens.

She swears as she realises that she's forgotten to cock the hammer after shooting at Lev.

Too late.

Everything seems to move in slow motion all of a sudden. By the time she readies the pistol and fires again, the Mongol has already dropped the book into the blazing cauldron and Georgia has lurched forward to push the woman away from the line of fire.

The professor catches the bullet directly in her stomach.

An anguished cry escapes Anya's lips.

No.

Georgia drops to the ground, clutching at her wound with an agonised moan. Blood pours out of her gut through her clenched fingers. Shocked, Anya doesn't allow herself time to regret her actions. She charges towards the fire, catching movement to her right. The Mongol girl is coming at her with fists drawn, and Anya cocks the gun and pulls the trigger, but with her shaky hand she only manages to hit the girl in the leg. She aims higher for the head and shoots again, missing her mark completely as the girl falls to the floor. Swivelling, Anya points the weapon towards the Mongol elder, but in the last moment decides to keep her alive just in case she needs answers.

The harmless, tiny old lady raises her hands in a placating manner, saying something she doesn't understand.

Frantic, Anya ignores her and stashes the revolver into her sling, reaching her hand straight into the flames. She grabs the heavy volume and hurls it out of the vessel, screaming as the heat scorches through her flesh. She drops the book on the floor, the charred gold covers clanging open on the ground, its contents still burning earnestly.

Smoke and ashes spew up as Anya tramples on the fire with her booted feet. *No.* Coughing, swatting at the polluted air, she sinks to her knees to examine the damage.

No no no no no . . .

Over half of the pages are gone, the rest blackened beyond repair. The devastation hits Anya squarely in the gut, constricting her throat and clawing at her chest. Her bosom rises and falls in rapid succession, and she opens her mouth to release her outrage with an ear-splitting howl.

She grabs the pistol and surges to her feet, closing in on the object of her fury. "Why the *hell* did you do that, you bitch?!"

But the Mongol elder isn't even looking at her. Her gaze is focused on something behind Anya instead, an indecipherable expression on her face.

Anya whirls around and finds herself face to face with

Georgia. Her eyes drop to the professor's middle, seeing the bloody mess of her clothes.

To her surprise, Anya's first reaction is relief.

The professor is still alive.

Georgia strikes her with an astounding right hook before she can speak or react. She staggers and drops, passing out before she hits the ground.

64

BLOOD ROARS in Georgia's ears as rage consumes her. Anya falls to the floor with a heavy thump, her eyes rolling to the back of her head.

But one punch was not enough. Not by a long shot. The haze of wrath overcomes Georgia, and she straddles the Russian woman and hits her across the face again.

And again.

And again.

Anya's head snaps from side to side, her limp body jerking with the movement. Blind with anger and with all of her fury, pain, and guilt over Ethan's death thrumming through her veins, Georgia grabs Anya's head to smash it against the cold stone floor.

"Georgia!" Gerel's voice stops her.

She blinks, snapping out of her momentary outburst. She looks down at Anya's face, taking in the damage she has done. The woman's nose is broken. Her left eye is swelling rapidly, and blood is trickling out of her nose and lips. Her jaw is set in a funny way, most probably fractured. Those are not Anya's worst injuries, though. She clearly ran into trouble during the storm last night, judging by all the horrific afflictions visible on her body.

What the hell *are you doing, Georgia?*

With shaky hands she releases the Russian woman's head, her shame compounding at the thud of Anya's skull against the floor. She scrambles to her feet and spins around to find Gerel crouched beside Naran.

Gerel has her hand pressed to Naran's thigh. Blood is oozing through the gaps of her wrinkled fingers. The old woman motions for Georgia to take over, then retrieves a satellite phone from the pocket of her *deel*. She dashes outside to make a call.

Gerel's frantic voice travels down the tunnel as Georgia looks down at Naran. "You're going to be okay," she tries to reassure the girl.

Pain is clear in the young woman's features, but she is stoic, not even moaning a complaint. With a tight smile and sincerity in her eyes, she says, "Thank you."

Georgia is surprised at the sudden transformation in the girl's demeanour towards her. "For what?"

"For taking that bullet. For saving Gerel."

Unsure of how to respond, she gives the young woman a nod.

"Did it hurt?" Naran asks.

Georgia laughs. "Hell, yeah. Being immortal doesn't mean you're immune to the pain. I think the bullet went straight through, though." With her free hand she feels the large exit hole in the back of her shirt. The fabric is sticky with gore.

Naran's expression shifts, regarding Georgia with a mix of wonder and fascination.

Gerel comes back into the chamber, speaking to her

grandniece in Mongolian. "Help is coming," Naran translates.

Five minutes pass before two men enter the room from one of the eight doorways. Georgia recognises them as the Darkhat guards at the Ikh Khorig gate. She realises that her initial suspicions must be correct: there is more than one way to get inside this temple. She wonders just how many there are, and if the place is like a rabbit warren full of tunnels all leading in different directions.

One of the men rushes to Naran's aid with a medical kit in hand and starts attending to her wound. The other speaks in Mongolian to the women.

Naran says to Georgia, "This is Altan. He will take you to your friend."

"What about you?"

Naran chuckles. "I'll be fine. Your friend needs you though. They've managed to stop the bleeding, but he is going to need surgery. We have horses ready to take you down to the gates, then a truck will drive you to the hospital in the nearest town."

"Thank you." Then, remembering a crucial point, she says, "Buri works with the American government. He has the coordinates to this place."

Naran snorts. "Grave hunters have been trying to search these lands for eight hundred years. I'd like to see the Americans try, if they dare. My men will deal with them. Don't worry. Besides, now that *The Secret History* is destroyed, all they will ever find are the remains of the Golden Family."

"I still can't believe Gerel burnt the book." Georgia shakes her head.

Naran looks to her great-aunt and translates this to her, and Gerel responds with the help of her grandniece, "As far as we are concerned, the secrets of our Khan died with him. The book was only something we held onto as we awaited his return, so that each generation would have a group at the ready to serve him once again. Now that he is gone, the book is of little use to us. As I have said, we need to stop looking to our past and plan for the future. Our Khan's secret is now your responsibility."

Georgia nods slowly. Her gaze travels to Anya's motionless form on the ground, noticing for the first time that there is a blinking red dot on the woman's smartwatch. Moving closer for a better look, she realises it's a tracker.

The sulde. She makes a mental note to remove the tracking device as soon as possible.

Turning to Naran, she points to the Russian woman and asks, "What about her?"

"My father will deal with her," Naran replies. "He'll make sure she is handed over to the appropriate authorities."

Then, as if reading Georgia's thoughts, Naran adds, "Don't worry, Anya will be justly punished for her crimes. For excavating illegally on our sacred lands, and for the murders of your friends and Dr. Fujimoto."

Satisfied, Georgia rises to her feet. She is about to bid them farewell when Naran says, "One more thing. Your dog . . ."

Her heart skips a beat. Hope surges through her. "Indi?" she gasps, her voice too loud in the chamber.

At Georgia's overtly eager reaction, Naran's face breaks into a lopsided smile. "We found her wandering the woods this morning. Altan will take you to her now, too. Good luck, Georgia."

65

WHEN BURI FINALLY COMES TO, the first thing that hits him is the all-encompassing pain. Groaning, fighting to not let it overwhelm him, he isolates the sensations as he's learnt to do in the military. The top left of his chest throbs rhythmically with the beat of his pulse and it hurts every time he takes a breath. His head also feels like someone has driven a tank over it.

Memories come flooding back, and he opens his eyes to bolt upright, only to yell out at the shock of the movement and the influx of bright daylight.

"Hey hey," a woman reprimands. "Stay down. You're going to ruin the stitches."

"Georgia?" Speaking comes with effort. Buri can barely recognise his own voice. He looks to his left, relief surging through him as he sees her sitting beside him.

He does a quick scan of her to check for injuries, the tension in him easing when he finds none visible. She's had a change of clothes and cleaned up, too. He doesn't even see a graze on her body.

"You're in a hospital in Ulaanbaatar," Georgia explains

quickly. "We went to Mungunmorit first but they couldn't treat you properly there so they had to call for a helicopter medical evacuation. The bullet just barely scraped your lung, and you needed surgery. You were very lucky."

Buri finally takes a moment to look around, seeing that he is in a large ward with several other patients. A nurse comes by to check on him, asking how he is feeling as she takes his pulse and blood pressure. She offers him something for the pain, which he gratefully accepts.

When the nurse is about to leave, Georgia lightly touches her on the arm. The two women exchange a wordless smile, and the nurse heads out of the room again.

"What was that about?" Buri asks.

"You'll see." Her smile widens into a grin, and she grasps his hand with both of hers. "I'm so glad you're okay."

Baffled by her cryptic smile, he asks the question that's been pressing on his mind. "What happened? The last thing I remember was Lev shooting me . . . Did he . . .?" He trails off, all manner of horrific scenarios playing out in his head. He won't be able to forgive himself if the Russian man hurt Georgia in any way.

"I'm fine. Everything is okay," she reassures him, squeezing his hand.

"How—"

"I had a little help," she says, her smile broadening. She looks expectantly in the direction of the door just as the nurse comes back with a lead in her hand.

Buri's spirits soar as the woman enters the room with a dog trotting at her heels.

"Indi!" His voice cracks, choking on the emotions ballooning in his chest. The German Shepherd lopes up to the bed with her mouth agape and her tongue lolling. She plonks her two front paws beside him and reaches straight for his face, panting hot doggy breath and slathering him with drool. She licks him all over as if greeting an old friend after years of separation. Her thick hairy tail thumps behind her, the frenzied motion waggling her butt.

"Where the hell did you go?" He ruffles Indi's fluffy coat, laughing at her exuberant affection, then winces at the movement. Turning to Georgia, he asks, "Where did you find her?"

"I didn't. *She* found me."

With one hand still stroking Indi, Buri listens as Georgia tells the incredible tale of what happened after he was knocked out by Lev. While the Russian man was distracted with Buri, Georgia hit him in the back of the head with a rock, making him lose balance and drop the gun. There was an angry tussle between them, but Georgia was of course no match for him. Just when all seemed to be at a loss, Anya showed up at the site.

"Wait. I thought she was dead."

"That's what Lev had said, but she obviously wasn't. She was looking really banged up though, cut up everywhere and limping badly. She and Lev got into a huge argument. There must be some sort of history between them. Anyway, Anya pointed her gun at his face and shot him."

"Fuck."

"Yeah," Georgia says. "Then she turned the gun on me, and that's when Indi came out of nowhere." She smiles, scratching the dog on her neck. Indi leans into her hand, her wandering tongue reaching for Georgia's palm.

"I've never seen Indi like that before. The way she went at Anya . . ." Georgia says with a solemn look on her face. "She's one a hell of a guard dog."

"That she is," Buri pats the dog with burgeoning pride.

"I managed to knock Anya out while she was preoccupied with Indi. The next thing I knew, those Darkhat guards showed up."

"They must have been following us." He frowns. The Darkhats have known their intention all along. It was not a coincidence that the men turned up just in time.

"I think so. And anyone would have heard those gunshots from miles away. In any case, the Darkhats were able to get us help so we could bring you to the hospital."

"And the temple?"

"Never got to go in there." She pauses, then says, "Uncovering what's inside the tomb was never so important to me. I just wanted to make sure that Anya didn't get what she wanted, especially after what she did to Ethan and Hiroshi. Whatever is in there belongs to *your* people, Buri. A foreigner like me should never access it without permission."

He nods, his respect for Georgia growing by the minute. "Where's Anya now?"

"I left her with the Darkhats. I assume they'll be handing her over to the authorities."

Buri wonders what consequences await the Russian woman. Excavating at the summit of a World Heritage Site without sanction and desecrating the most sacred, protected land of Mongolia ought to end her career as an archaeologist for good. He wonders how he and Georgia managed to get off so lightly, even though they were also found at the site of the temple.

He voices that exact question, to which she responds, "I explained everything to the Darkhats, told them how we were trying to stop Anya from getting to the tomb. And they . . . well, they've asked me to do something for them."

She quickly describes their request.

"They spoke English?" Buri cocks his head.

"One of them did, yes."

So the Darkhats were pretending the whole time. "And they believed what you told them?"

Georgia's forehead crease as if she's offended that he would think otherwise. "I guess they did. After all, I told them the truth."

"Did they say anything else?"

"No."

They lapse into silence, and Buri works his mind over the entire scenario. Something doesn't quite add up. He has always known that the Darkhats are not to be taken lightly, but there seems to be more at play than he can comprehend. Why let him and Georgia through the gates in the first place? Why keep them alive at all? Not knowing the Darkhats' true intentions really disturbs him, and it will continue to do so until he understands what's going on.

"What are you going to tell Agent Miller?" Georgia asks.

Buri shrugs. "I can only tell him what I know."

Something flits across her features. "Will you tell him about the coordinates?"

Buri considers this. The DIA's chief concern was the immediate threat of the Russians. They did not want Anya to find a potentially dangerous weapon that could give her government an advantage over the United States. The primary objective was to ensure *The Secret History* did not fall into the wrong hands. As far as Buri's concerned, his mission is now accomplished.

But he knows that even with the Russians out of the

picture, the covert unit that Brandon Miller works for is counting on getting access to whatever is in that tomb.

And deep down, he doesn't believe they should have it.

Like Georgia said, if what lies in there is something so powerful it could rob countless innocent people of their lives, maybe it should stay buried.

"I'm not sure," Buri finally answers Georgia's question.

She stares at him for a beat with her dark brown eyes. Then she smiles and gives a gentle shake of her head as if none of it is important anymore.

She squeezes his hand once more, repeating, "I'm just so glad you're okay."

66

Two weeks later, somewhere on the Mongolian steppes

"AND THEN THEY just took you to the hospital . . . and let you go as if nothing had happened?" Brandon Miller asks as he stares at Buri incredulously.

"Yep," Buri replies, pouring himself another bowl of *airag*. He offers to do the same for Brandon, but the blond man refuses, grimacing at the sight of the white-coloured drink. "It's all in my report. Didn't you read it?"

They are in Buri's *ger*, sitting once again at the low table where this whole mission started for him weeks before. Having sent the report to Washington a few days ago, he was not surprised when Brandon showed up at his place today seeking answers.

Buri was under observation for several days before being released from the hospital. After ensuring he was okay to manage on his own, Georgia had to leave and return to Sydney. She has asked him to stay in touch, and even hinted that she'd like to work together again, if he is ever interested in consulting in the field of linguistics.

"Sure I did," Brandon replies, "but it still makes no sense to me." He taps one of his fingers repeatedly on the surface of the coffee table as he thinks aloud. "If they knew what you and Georgia were planning to do, why did they let y'all in the gates? Why the charade, the hocus pocus bullshit with the shaman? And then they kick you out just as you're getting into that temple? Why let you find the place at all?"

"No idea," Buri says. The whole thing still troubles him. "It's not sitting right with me, either. Got me jumping at shadows everywhere I look. Keep thinking they'll get me when I least expect it."

The frown between Brandon's brows deepens. He cocks his head as he speculates, "Well, there's gotta be something we're missing . . . And I've a feeling it has something to do with the professor."

Buri bristles at the mention of Georgia. He tries to divert the DIA agent's attention. "Why don't you send another team in, see what's actually inside the temple? I've sent you the coordinates."

Over the week, Buri has battled with what to tell the DIA. What Georgia said to him at the hospital kept repeating in his mind.

Whatever is in there belongs to your *people, Buri.*

He just couldn't go through with assisting the US government in violating Mongolian sacred grounds. Buri felt compelled by the moral obligation of protecting the heritage of the Mongols from any threat, be it Russian or American. But he didn't want to exactly lie to the DIA, either. In the end he kept all of his accounts truthful, except for the coordinates. With Georgia's help, he went through the transliteration of *The Secret History* again, picking out a few other spots where the information could be regarded as erroneous, and changed the sequence of numbers. If the DIA ever tries to access the location, they will not be finding the temple there.

He knows it will most likely come back to bite him in the ass, but he is banking on the likelihood that the DIA won't be able to access Burkhan Khaldun with the Dark-hats on guard.

"Oh, I want to, believe me," Brandon says. "But after everything that's happened, the whole area has been clamped down. There's no way we can poke around without stirring up a shit storm. Best to wait a little, let the dust settle. But who knows if it'll all still be there by then?"

"How about just leave it the hell alone," Buri counters. "The Russians didn't get to it, and that's what you asked me to do. Mission accomplished. Besides, some things should probably remain buried."

"Maybe," Brandon mutters, but doesn't look convinced.

Remembering something else, Buri asks, "Any word on the whereabouts of Anya Mihailovich?"

"Nope. It's like she's disappeared off the face of Earth. My informants tell me that even the Russians don't know where she is. They assume she's dead."

"Whatever happened to her, the Darkhats won't let her off lightly for digging a hole on the summit of Burkhan Khaldun. They're not people you wanna fuck with."

Brandon nods slowly, looking puzzled and discontented all at once. He says almost to himself, "It's *gotta* have something to do with her."

"Who, Anya?"

"No, the professor."

Irritation rises again but Buri keeps it contained. "Have you spoken to her?"

"Sure. Saw her in Ulaanbaatar yesterday before she flew back to Australia."

"And?"

"She told me the exact same thing you did."

"Well, then she told you the truth."

Brandon's gaze is far away as he thinks on it. "No." He rubs the stubble on his chin, repeating, "No, something ain't right. I had this feeling ever since meeting her, like she's hiding something the whole time. You ever get that feeling?"

"No." Buri lies. "Georgia told you everything she knows."

Brandon fixes him with a stare. "All due respect, Doc, you weren't even conscious when all that shit went down. There's no telling what she ain't given us."

Buri can't argue against this, because the thought of Georgia concealing information has also crossed his mind. But why would she? As one of the most renowned archaeologists in the world, finding anything extraordinary in the tomb would just add to the long list of accolades associated with her name. In the end Buri decided he doesn't actually give a damn if she isn't sharing everything she knows. All he really cares about—and is grateful for—is that they managed to walk away unscathed. Georgia could have been killed by the Russians. Buri almost lost his dog. The bullet could have strayed a tenth of an inch down and punctured his lung. And if it did, he would not be having this conversation with Brandon today.

He came all the way to Mongolia to get away from all that shit, not to bring it along with him.

But Buri knows Brandon through and through, and he is well aware that the man will dig and dig until he gets to the bottom of it. And Buri doesn't want Georgia harassed.

She doesn't deserve that after everything she's been through.

Against his better judgement he says with more bite than he intends, "Leave Georgia alone. I'll vouch for her."

Brandon's eyes snap to Buri, studying him intently.

"What?" Buri demands.

Brandon cracks a crooked smile. "You got a soft spot for her, don't ya? Don't worry, bro. We'll just keep an eye on her. She won't even know."

Fuck. He needs to warn Georgia that she's on the DIA's radar now. Buri struggles to keep a straight face. "You're wasting your time. Actually, you're also wasting mine. I got shit to do today, families to visit."

Brandon leans back, his smile broadening into a knowing grin. "Holy shit, you really *do* like her." He holds up his palms when he sees Buri's expression. "Hey, I'm sorry. Just covering all my bases. It's my job. I got a boss to report to, you know."

Fighting the urge to punch the man in the nose, Buri changes the subject. "What did Susan say about it all?" He can't imagine ever working for Susan. The Deputy Director of DIA is a ferocious woman with a fearsome reputation. More importantly, Buri happens to know that she hates his guts.

"Well, she's glad the Russians didn't get what they wanted. But she's also curious about what's in that temple."

"I'm surprised she even took me on board for the mission," Buri says.

Brandon expression shifts. "Hey, I get it. You and Mama don't get along. But can you blame her when Dad showed up with you all those years ago, a boy he had out of wedlock? But believe me when I tell you this: she has confidence in you and your skills. Hell, she probably has more faith in you to get shit done than she does in me."

"Honestly, I have no idea why you would ever want to work for your own mother." Buri rolls his eyes and shivers with horror. He asks the question that's been on his tongue since Brandon got here. "How's Dad?"

"Fine. Misses you, of course, but he'll never admit it. He still can't understand why you'd want to move out here. He was gonna visit after hearing that you got injured, but having a United States general show up in a place like this will raise flags, especially after everything that's happened." Brandon then lowers his voice to mimic the tone of their father. *"You tell Benjamin Miller that his family is waiting for him to come home."*

Buri smiles. He can't imagine returning to the States, though. Mongolia is his home now. He gives his brother a once-over, again struck by how different the two Miller boys are from one another.

Benjamin and Brandon Miller.

Their physical dissimilarities work in their favour as they don't like to advertise their family ties, particularly when on mission. Experience shows it tends to complicate matters, especially in enemy territory.

Despite sharing the same father as Brandon, Buri definitely resembles his mother's side more. Most people wouldn't even know that he's half-American by looking at him.

And Brandon is the American golden boy with the blond hair, blue eyes, and orthodontically perfected smile. The mama's boy. The one who was consistently favoured in their childhood home and who always got the girls at school.

But he and Brandon are brothers at heart, and their

bond was sealed as soon as they met each other. Growing up, Brandon was the annoying younger sibling who tugged at his shirt and nagged for his attention. Much to his annoyance and often at great inconvenience to himself, Buri has never been able to deny his little brother anything. It's the primary reason he took on this job. Because Brandon had begged him to.

"Anyway, I got shit to do, too. Better get going." Brandon rises from the table and heads for the door.

Buri follows him outside with Indi tagging along. He shakes his brother's hand after the man opens the door to the black truck.

"You know," Brandon says, pausing before getting into the vehicle, "I've been looking into the side jobs Georgia took on over the years. Fascinating stuff. The girl's got some notches on her belt. Might be handy if we ever need her for future missions. Her most recent one was commissioned by Mark Lambert, the English billionaire. You heard of the guy?"

Buri shakes his head.

"Anyway, the man got it in his crazy-ass head that there's an elixir of life out there somewhere in the middle of the jungle in Taiwan. He paid Georgia a hefty sum for the expedition. Their search turned up nothing, though, and the trail ended up collapsing on them in an earthquake. They never found Lambert or his assistant's body, and Georgia was spotted unconscious down the river days later . . ."

Brandon's voice trails off into the background as something shifts in Buri's brain, clicking into place like intricate cogs in a well-oiled mechanical device.

The machine of his mind whirls into overdrive, projecting images of Georgia in quick succession, and he fights to keep his expression blank despite the chaotic beating of his heart.

The peculiar way in which she moves, as if she weighs nothing and is made of air.

Her astonishing speed and agility.

Her unusual physical strength.

How little she eats and sleeps.

The fact that he has never, ever witnessed any of her wounds or seen even a cut on her body, despite everything they've been through together.

He frowns.

No. It can't possibly be.

Buri is silent as his brother finally finishes speaking, climbs into the vehicle and drives away. He watches the trail of dust over the infinite plains, knowing full well that the DIA is going to be watching Georgia's every move from now on.

Fuck.

67

Three weeks later, Sydney University, Australia

At the mention of Professor Georgia Lee's name, applause and cheers erupt through the auditorium. Sarah Wu watches from offstage as her boss rises from her seat and walks towards the podium.

The poor girl has been inundated with work since she got back to Sydney three weeks ago, which also means that, as her assistant, Sarah has had to carry her fair share of the load too. They've barely had the chance to speak, apart from the briefest rundown of what happened in Mongolia and addressing the most urgent matters at hand to prepare for the presentation today. With their quarrel still unresolved from almost two months ago, Sarah has resigned herself to never being able to talk to Georgia about what transpired between them, or to address the growing gap in their relationship.

Sarah was disappointed, but not really surprised. She understands Georgia like she's her own daughter, and she knows that the girl will always avoid emotional encounters at all costs. Georgia's heart is shut as tightly as a dead clam, and Sarah may just have to finally accept that she—or anyone else for that matter—will never be able to prise it open.

But, to her shock, this morning her boss took her aside and asked her to stay after the presentation. Georgia said she wanted to talk about what happened, that she would have done so earlier but hadn't found the right moment, given the mad rush of arrangements they had to make for the press conference today.

Pride surges through Sarah now as she watches Georgia walk across the stage and ponders the implications this discovery will have on her boss' career. Flashes of light burst from all directions as pictures are being taken. Georgia shakes hands with the chancellor, who smiles and steps aside to give her access to the microphone.

Sarah blinks. Something about Georgia's movements makes her narrow her eyes.

Her breath lodges in her throat.

At that precise moment, she finally realises what has been bothering her all these weeks, and why Georgia has been more cagey than ever.

Sarah has known that something has been off ever since Georgia returned from Taiwan. The girl has been different somehow, and for the life of her, Sarah hasn't been able to pinpoint exactly what it is. She has worried about Georgia's dramatically diminished appetite—something which has never happened before, no matter how stressed she was. And all this time Sarah just assumed it was emotional factors at play, attributing it to the trauma of almost dying in that earthquake and her relationship issues with Ethan.

But she never considered that the difference she picked up is something *physical*.

She observes the light, fluid way in which Georgia moves, a vast change from the awkward and occasionally clumsy woman Sarah knows. She remembers Georgia describing Charlie in exactly the same way: a sense of *weightlessness*, his actions *unhurried* yet *efficient*.

Her eyes scan Georgia from head to toe, and she realises that the woman doesn't have a single scratch on her despite what she has been through in the most remote region of Mongolia.

Casting her mind back, she thinks of when Georgia was in hospital after being found unconscious in Taiwan. Yes, the woman burned a delirious, high fever all week, but she came away from the harrowing events without so much as a bruise or mark on her.

Sarah's mouth falls open. Her eyes widen with sudden comprehension. Then, as if sensing her tremendous shock from metres away, Georgia looks over at that moment and meets her eyes.

What Sarah sees there confirms her worst fears.

Oh, fuck.

Georgia freezes momentarily on stage, her heart leaping to her throat at Sarah's expression. Eyes wide, face pale, Sarah has her mouth hanging open as if she's been punched in the gut.

She knows. She's figured it out.

This is the worst possible timing.

Silence echoes through the lecture hall. Dignitaries and

distinguished guests stare up at Georgia from under the stage. Anticipation is palpable in the air.

The overhead spotlights are harsh, but she can still recognise many of the faces in the crowd. Eminent professors, authors, and researchers are present, having travelled here from all around the globe. Members of the press are seated to the side, their expressions rapt as they scribble notes. The entire venue is filled without an empty seat in sight. In all her years of teaching at the university, Georgia has never seen this auditorium so packed. It is abundantly clear that the press conference has attracted the attention of both scholars and the general public from far and wide.

Her pulse thuds heavily at her temple. Sweat trickles down her spine. She swallows thickly, trying to ignore the flutter of nerves in her stomach.

Throwing Sarah a desperate look and begging silently for her assistant to wait for an explanation, Georgia steps up to the lectern and moves closer to the microphone.

Clearing her throat, she stammers her greetings to the audience. Then she looks down at the notes in front of her.

C'mon Georgia. Get through this.

"We have all gathered here today to remember an extraordinary man with a phenomenal story." Her voice reverberates through the hall. "Temüjin was his name, though most know him by another. Born in the twelfth century, he emerged from his mother's womb with a clot of blood in his hand . . ."

As Georgia eases into the speech, she regains her usual confidence from years of lecturing at the university. She gives a lengthy account of Chinggis Khan's life, the version that has been hidden and distorted by his enemies and time.

". . . And in the thirty years of his reign, not a single

one of his generals betrayed him—something practically unheard of for any leader in the entire course of human history. He was brutal, but also just. He hunted his opponents to the ends of the world, yet treated his followers with respect and loyalty. The dual qualities of this man are so puzzling that eight centuries after his death, scholars are still struggling to understand who he really was . . ."

Over the past few weeks, as Georgia composed this speech, she has been conflicted about what to say. She remembers him as Wang Jian, the image of whom still evokes fear in her. To the Mongolian people, however, Chinggis was a genius of incredible vision who inspired their tribes to unite and to become something more than what they were individually. Georgia still cannot resolve the disparity between the two—the blood-thirsty general versus the founder of a mighty empire. In the end, she has conceded to the fact that perhaps the man was both, that as a paradoxical, flawed human being he was full of astonishing attributes and perilous flaws. In Wang Jian, she recognises that there exists in the hearts of people a duality, a capacity for greatness as well as the potential to bring ruinous destruction to all that surrounds them.

And isn't that also true of humanity in general?

As she makes her way through the speech, she brings up the Stalinist Great Repression in Mongolia in the 1930s, describing the persecutions that destroyed an entire generation of intellectuals and scholars, and how Chinggis Khan's *sulde* was stolen from the Shankh Monastery in Mongolia.

". . . The disappearance of the *sulde* was, in effect, the symbolic loss of the spirit of a nation. For almost a century it has not been seen, and is presumed to have been destroyed by the Communist authorities . . ."

When Georgia was with Naran and Gerel in the temple at Burkhan Khaldun, she was given specific instructions with regard to their request. They wanted a formal and public unveiling of that which was taken from them. And they wanted the whole world to learn a different story about their leader.

Georgia realises that, in a way, Gerel's interpretation of the prophecy has come to fruition.

. . . whoever finds this temple shall bring back the true spirit of our nation, something which rightfully belongs to us.

And in keeping her promise to the Mongolian women, this is exactly what she is doing now.

". . . Well," she continues, "I'm very pleased to announce that the *sulde* has now been rediscovered."

She signals to two of her PhD students, who move into view, pushing a tall glass display case on rollers to the centre of the stage. The *sulde* is standing erect within the receptacle, and as the spotlight is focused onto the artefact, gasps and murmurs fill the lecture hall. The air is buzzing with excitement as once again cameras flash in the audience.

As the noise of the crowd dies down, Georgia delivers the conclusion of her speech: "The story of the *sulde* is a bloody one. From the time it led men and women into battle and inspired monks to die protecting it, until very recently, when two of my friends lost their lives after its rediscovery. It is my hope, and the hope of all of us at our university, that the violence will stop, that the *sulde* will now inspire the world to recognise a history that was erased, and to learn of the foundation that Chinggis Khan and the Mongol Empire laid for our modern society. The world has only been told of what he destroyed, but we will now also remember what he created."

She gestures for the Chancellor and the man beside him to rise from their seats on stage. "Without further ado," she continues, "it is my privilege to return the *sulde* of Chinggis Khan to its rightful owners. Please welcome our distinguished guest of honour, the foreign minister from the Mongolian government, Mr. Bayarsaikhan!"

A thundering ovation echoes through the auditorium, and Georgia moves offstage as the Chancellor and Mr. Bayarsaikhan proceed with the ceremonial exchange of the *sulde*. She walks straight up to Sarah, who is still gaping at her.

"I'm sorry—" Georgia begins, raising her voice over the excitement both on and off stage.

"Jesus fuck, Georgia, why didn't you tell me sooner?"

"I tried . . . I didn't know how to—"

"When did you realise?"

"The day I went to see Ethan in Melbourne. I cut my finger while trying to make him dinner, and . . . well, the wound healed itself within seconds."

"Holy shit." Sarah blanches. "That's why you didn't end up telling him what happened in Taiwan?"

Regret piercing through her, Georgia nods grimly.

Sarah is pacing now, and Georgia gulps nervously at the expression on her assistant's face. She has never seen Sarah so panicked before.

"And to think you were off in Mongolia with those DIA dickheads. My God, what if they found out? You realise they would lock you up and experiment on you—"

"I know. I had some close calls."

"Fuck. Shit. *Fuck*." She grips Georgia by the arm. "You can't tell anyone about this. You can't let anyone else know."

Georgia nods, blinking back unexpected tears. "I

should have told you earlier," she says. Then, all of the words she has been rehearsing in her mind come tumbling out: "I'm sorry for what I said about Ethan being my only friend. It's not true at all. I've taken you and everything you do for granted, and that's not right. And I'm sorry I've pushed you away. I just couldn't figure out how to deal with this . . . hell, I'm still trying to wrap my head around it—"

Sarah's expression softens, and she places a hand on Georgia's shoulder. Reading the younger woman's mind yet again, she says, "This must have been a real burden on you."

The staggering sense of relief from Sarah's words breaks down Georgia's final defences. She bursts into tears, her usual restraint gone. Everything that has transpired over the past two months comes crashing down on her.

Wang Jian. Charlie. Ethan. Lev. Anya.

The only positive thing that has come out of it all is her friendship with Buri, but even so, she will never be able to let him learn the truth of who—or what—she is.

She realises with a pang in her chest that she can no longer allow anyone close enough to know.

In all of her life, she has never felt so completely and utterly alone.

Sarah's arms envelop her, squeezing her in a tight embrace. When Georgia's sobs cease, Sarah pulls back and looks at her earnestly.

"You listen to me, Georgia," her assistant says. "You don't have to figure this out straightaway. And you don't have to do it on your own, you understand? We will navigate this together. While I've still got a breath in my body, you will never have to face this alone."

Georgia sniffles. She wipes at her damp cheeks and says, "Thank you. For everything."

Sarah squeezes her hands. "What are friends for, right?"

Georgia smiles. She jumps with surprise when she feels something warm and wet licking her calf.

She looks down. A German Shepherd is staring up at her, huffing with an open-mouthed grin.

"Indi? What are you doing here?"

Looking around, her eyes fall on the man standing by the door at the rear of the auditorium.

Georgia's heart does a somersault in her chest.

EPILOGUE

National Palace Museum (NPM), Taiwan

LING LING HSIA walks through the tunnels deep within the cave vaults of the National Palace Museum. She has just returned some of the precious items from the latest exhibition of Ming Dynasty ceramics.

Earlier this morning, she watched the live broadcast of Professor Georgia Lee presenting her latest findings at Sydney University. Ling Ling is so proud of her friend, who has uncovered the lost *sulde* of Chinggis Khan. What's even more admirable is that she has returned the relic to the Mongolian people. Georgia could have held onto the item, keeping it at the university for further study, or given it to a museum in Australia. But the professor clearly recognises and appreciates the deep emotional meaning of the *sulde* to the Mongols.

One only needs to look at the exhibits of most notable museums around the world to know that this is not a usual practice. Indeed, too many of the pieces on display are stolen articles and spoils of war.

Ling Ling stops when she reaches the section containing the museum's Mongolian artefacts. Large crates line the wide corridor, stacked neatly in place. Most are items passed down from dynasty to dynasty, imperial treasures of Chinese sovereigns throughout the centuries. But there is one particular box of unknown origin, part of the "uncatalogued" collection. The history of how it was found is not clear—at least, not to Ling Ling, who lacks the necessary security clearance. She has only seen the contents of the crate once, but it was a sight she will never forget.

Bound in covers forged with solid gold, it is a book covered in gems of all colours known to man. And in the centre, a single etched line of Mongolian text.

Ling Ling still feels guilty about lying to Georgia during her recent visit. Her friend asked if there were any other copies of *The Secret History* within the museum's treasury. Ling Ling replied no at the time, but the truth is, there *is* one other copy, and it is in the box right in front of her.

The original Mongolian version that has not been seen since the end of the Mongol Empire. The copy that was thought to have been destroyed in a fire.

According to the rumours, it is one of only two copies ever made, the other having been entombed with Chinggis Khan himself, and the primary reason for many of the archaeological searches in Mongolia.

As far as Ling Ling knows, the museum's volume has never been taken out of its crate. Only the director and a select few of the conservation department know about it. It is one of the very closely guarded secrets of the museum.

She places a hand on the crate, imagining the book safely nestled within the confines of the box.

Perhaps one day it will be shown to the world. And maybe then it can be returned to the Mongolian people, just like the *sulde*.

Ling Ling sighs. She turns, walks down the long passage, and shuts the heavy vault doors behind her.

ACKNOWLEDGMENTS

Writing may be a solitary pursuit, but it takes an entire team to make a book come to life. I would like to thank the following people for their tremendous help:

To the crew at Eternal Landscape, who looked after us so well during our research trip to Mongolia. Big thanks to Jess, who designed the trip and made sure everything ran smoothly, and also continued to be of help whenever I had questions after returning home. Mishka and Zaya, for being such fantastic guides and looking after all our daily needs. Ganbaatar and Sodoo, our drivers with big, beautiful smiles—I still can't get over your amazing navigation and van-fixing skills. Together we travelled over 1300 km across Mongolia, visiting every location I had in mind for the book, traversing some of the most awe-inspiring landscapes I've ever come across. It was an adventure I will never forget.

To Gordon, Emma, and Toby, for helping me with research and answering all of my (often repetitive) questions.

To my beta readers, for your invaluable feedback: Jenny, Ness, Claire, Anthea, Katrina, Tara, Ryan, and Shannon.

To my editors, Mark Will and Pat Woods—I have learnt so much from you both.

And to my husband, for being there every step of the way.

ABOUT THE AUTHOR

A. H. Wang is a contemporary visual artist and author with a fascination for history and a passion for adventure. Born in Taiwan and raised in Australia, her travels have taken her across five continents and dozens of countries. Throughout her journey, she has developed a sincere appreciation for local cultures and the lore of ancient civilisations.

As well as making art and writing, you will find her deeply involved with her meditation practice. In a previous life, she was also a scientist, an engineer, a holistic counsellor, and a Reiki Master. She now lives in Taipei, Taiwan, with her husband.

www.AHWangAuthor.com

facebook.com/ahwangauthor
instagram.com/ahwangauthor
goodreads.com/ahwangauthor
bookbub.com/authors/a-h-wang

The next instalment of Georgia's story is coming soon! Join A. H. Wang's Readers' Group to be notified of new releases, giveaways, and pre-release specials:

www.AHWangAuthor.com/contact-me

Printed in Great Britain
by Amazon